Kragan

by

Dennis K. Hausker

Published by
Melange Books, LLC
White Bear Lake, MN 55110
www.melange-books.com

ISBN: 978-1-61235-890-1 Print

Published in the United States of America.
Cover Art by Stephanie Flint

Kragan
Dennis K. Hausker

Prince Damon competed with his younger brother Prince Tabor to be crown prince, but Tabor bested him in the final contest. Thereafter, Damon feels his life has no meaning until stunning Beth rides into his life fleeing the great trauma of her life. Fate is not done with Damon who is forced to overcome self-pity to become the person he was meant to be. Their world is threatened with destruction as the vast barbarian horde, the Argore, suddenly invade the lowlands from their mountain realm. Damon, shackled with doubts, strives to become that better man, trying to win the love of Beth, but her disdain and personal focus on revenge thwart him time after time. Is it him she rejects? Does her heart belong to another?

Chapter One

Prince Damon pivoted to parry the thrust from his brother's attack, Prince Tabor. He was starting to fatigue in the lengthy contest and that meant he was worried if he could win this fight. It wasn't as if this battle was insignificant. The ascension to their father's throne was determined by who won the match.

He looked into his brother's eyes and saw confidence. Tabor was the younger of the two, but he was the stronger physically and more aggressive in his tactics. They'd sparred for all of their lives and Damon won very few of those fights. It was part of the reason he wasn't confident in his fighting or in his chances to win the throne. Tabor had always been driven in his practices while Damon had not. To an extent, constant losses for many years led to his defeatist attitude against his talented brother. Damon never mustered an answer to that talent and that was true in more than just the sparring pits. All their lives, Damon's best efforts had never been enough and it seemed nothing had changed for the better in this critical test.

Tabor made a feint and then swung decisively driving Damon back against the wall, unable to escape. At this point, there could only be one outcome. Damon glanced at his father who was eyeing the match closely. He felt ashamed to fail before him, again. His mother was seated beside her husband. Her eyes were filled with sympathy for her older son.

Time seemed to stand still in Damon's mind as he watched the final stroke approaching him, knowing he couldn't stop it. The strong blow knocked his sword out of his hand leaving him defenseless and defeated. Tabor cried out in triumph and thrust a fist into the air. He turned to face his father who smiled with pride. Damon stood aside ashamed, too embarrassed to move. He looked down at his sword, useless to him on the ground, like it was a symbol of his life of futility.

The king stood up and turned to the assembled throng. "The decision is made. Tabor will follow me to the throne of Kragan."

The large crowd of people cheered loudly and hurried from their seats to surround the victor. It wasn't a surprising outcome for the contest nor was the effusive response from the crowd. Tabor was a popular figure at court. His outgoing personality lent to his air of command and competence. He was a dashing figure, well-muscled, with thick dark hair, and highly sought socially. His easy confident manner charmed the ladies and intimidated his rivals. He was a sharp contrast to his brother, Damon, who wasn't a bold young man in any substantive way, and to this point, Damon had been unlucky in love in spite of being a prince of the realm. Receding away from the limelight was Damon's learned habit though to an extent it was one forced on him. His romantic choice of aiming selectively at stunning women was wrong for him and added an element of needless self-destruction with their inevitable rejections. Damon wasn't one to indulge in palace intrigues or games in pursuing women.

Damon watched his brother basking in the adoration of the masses. Not a single person came over to offer condolences, nor did they even notice him, as if he'd dropped off the planet. Shame flamed his cheeks to a deep red and he lowered his eyes, again, to stare at the floor. Picking up his sword to put back in the sheath, he slunk around the crowd and made his way toward the door out of the training pits. Before he could get out the door he heard his mother's voice.

"Damon, wait a moment please."

She glided across the floor, ever the regal beauty, a fitting queen for his father, the king.

"I'm so sorry, son. Don't let this ruin you. There's so much you can accomplish in your life. You're a wonderful young man with a great deal of potential."

"We just saw who has the real potential in this family, Mother. I appreciate your attempts to console me, but I've always known how this would end. He's been the pride of the king all of our lives, and I must admit he deserves it. I couldn't measure up to Tabor before in any meaningful way and I can't measure up now. He should be the next king when the time comes. I don't dispute it."

"Damon, please don't say belittling things. I know it's difficult, but please stay and support your brother. It would be a noble thing to do that would make a great statement to the people about your fine character."

"I wish I was noble, Mother. In truth, handling the shame is too great a burden for me. Maybe that's another of my many weaknesses. I need to be alone right now, I'm sorry. I love you, but I've just experienced the greatest failure of my life. It's beyond what I can endure. I really wish the best to Tabor, but I've got to go."

The queen suddenly grasped her son and embraced him tightly. He closed his eyes as his turbulent emotions roiled explosively within him. After a brief time, he pulled out of her hold, kissed her on the forehead and hurried out the door. No one else noticed him leave, or cared.

He went to his rooms to bathe and change his clothes. Though he was a prince, Damon chose to dress relatively modestly, unlike his brother who tended toward ostentatious garb. Drawing attention was not something Damon ever sought. He glanced in the mirror at his reflection with sadness. His hair was thick like his brother's, but brown in color like his mother rather than the black of his brother and his father.

"You did it this time, Damon," he muttered pensively. "This time there are consequences you can't avoid."

For a stranger to the city, if they saw Damon walking about the palace, they would have assumed he was a servant rather than a royal prince and Damon was fine with that.

Damon waited for a time, calming his nerves before he left the privacy and relative security of his rooms. Ironically, the first person he saw was the last person he wanted to see. Selena was the main object of his affections, at least from his vantage point. She was the consummate maiden, a stunning beauty, and the heart throb of nearly every young man in the city with her long dark hair and angelic face. She broke hearts merely by passing by, her aura was so enthralling. Adding in her charm, and her fine mind, it made her the perfect mate for the next king. She'd always acted coy with Damon, but he'd believed her heart belonged to Tabor. He wasn't wrong in that assessment.

As usual, she was in the midst of her entourage, those 'hangers on' that sought self-validation by associating with persons of import. Every face turned to Damon. He saw universal disdain and contempt as he neared them. It took a great deal of courage to approach the intimidating assemblage without revealing his extreme distress. Only Selena's face was not reproachful. She had a look almost of confusion, like she was unsure how to act toward him.

Damon couldn't gather his wits to speak to her. He nodded as he passed. She returned his gesture. He heard them whisper and snicker as he walked away toward the main palace entrance. Damon took a deep breath as he fought the rise of his emotions which were transforming from self-pity into anger. He scowled at the glance from the guards as he went outside into a light rain, making no attempt to cover himself, or to hurry. Getting wet had no impact on him in his current mood. Rather, it was fortuitous because it meant fewer people were moving about for him to face.

Damon went straight to the stables to get his horse and rode steadily out of the city headed for the nearby forest. He never looked back at the city of his birth. The painful issues there were too powerful to face. Solitude was the only thing he sought. His emotions were heavy burdens dragging at his spirit. It was hard to feel any optimism as his future life seemed pointless after his defeat.

Wallowing in self-pity wasn't his intention when he left the city, but it occurred nonetheless as he sunk into self-castigation and remorse reliving the individual failures in his life in his thoughts. It was a necessary process of catharsis he needed in order to cope with the traumatic event. Seeking out a secluded spot where he could be sure to have no visitors Damon sat down, hidden inside a thatch of brambles, on his riding blanket to heal his emotional wounds. Rather than finding peace, his mind punished him further with visions of ridicule behind his back amongst the courtesans. It compounded his angst with imaginations rather than facts. Damon wasn't particularly hungry but he ate a brief meal of slices of fruit, chunks of meat, and cubes of cheese. He washed it down with cold water from his drinking gourd. It stilled the rumbles in his stomach enough he could close his eyes to doze off briefly. The rain tapered off and ended so he felt no urgency to return to the city.

Instead of a brief nap, he awoke the next morning at sunrise sitting up with a start at the sound of the crack of a dead branch lying on the ground being broken. He looked cautiously out from his retreat and saw a large elk stopped only a few feet away. It turned its head in every direction and sniffed the air. It happened Damon was down wind so it didn't catch his scent. Suddenly there was a blur of motion as a cat sprang from the underbrush. The stag tried to flee, but the cat was too close and leaped onto its back. The stag bellowed in fear and tried to shake the cat off, but it was too late as the predator closed its powerful jaws on the neck of its prey. The stag struggled to survive, but it was a hopeless fight for a dying creature. A snap of its neck in powerful jaws ended its life and the big cat dragged it away into the brush to feed.

Damon was stunned by the fight so close to him. Even though he routinely hunted elk, the plight of this unfortunate creature touched him deeply resonating with the anguish he already felt. The cycle of life was displayed before him in all its most brutal forms. In this world there were only predators and prey.

"Damon, what's wrong with you. Animals die in the forest all the time. You're lucky the cat didn't come after you. Sitting out here alone probably isn't the best idea."

He gathered his things and got back on his horse to return to his father's city, Kragan. There was safety in the city, but Damon always felt more at home in the woods. It was one of the few places where he was better than his brother, being the better hunter and tracker. Damon really didn't mind his own company. In the woods there were no smirking faces to deal with.

On the way back he shot another elk, carried it through the city gates where he made a detour to the poor section of town. He saw a young mother with her brood of scrawny children and stopped at her door.

"Here is meat for your table, madam," he uttered shyly. "You must feed your family."

He saw tears form in her eyes.

"Thank you, my lord. My husband was taken by illness. It's been so difficult without him."

Her misery resonated with Damon. He got off his horse and carried the heavy animal around behind her house. He stayed long enough to help her dress the kill and extract the meat. She had no children old enough to help her, a woman poor in wealth but she had something Damon didn't see in the palace women, she was courageous, determined, and self-reliant. She wasn't going to let the tragedy in her life destroy her. It heartened him to reconsider his own poor approach to adversity.

"My Lord, I have no way to repay your kindness."

"Madam, I require nothing from you. It's my honor to be of service, especially to a mother in distress. Think nothing more about it."

He saw something in her eyes he wasn't accustomed to, adoration. That was normally reserved for Tabor. She curtsied to him and he returned a bow before he continued his ride back home. His 'good deed' managed to ease his emotional distress and replace it with a feeling of warmth at helping the young widow.

When he walked back into the palace he actually smiled as he thought about the look in her eyes. Damon had little occur in his life that allowed him to feel validation. It gave him hope that perhaps he could find useful purposes for whatever remained of his life.

His pleasant mood was short lived though.

"Damon," he heard from behind him. "Wait for me."

His brother jogged down the long hallway to join him before he could get to his room, even though Damon never stopped walking.

"Where did you go? I thought you would be at my celebration party last night."

"I went to the woods to hunt, brother."

"Why? It was a great bash. You should have come to my party."

"I didn't think it was important that I be there."

"Are you jealous because I won?"

Damon felt frustrated he couldn't avoid this unwanted conversation. Keeping an even tone in his voice was a test.

"Tabor, I don't care about it. I really don't. You're welcome to the throne and all of the headaches that go with it. You know I haven't been a social person. I'm comfortable in the woods. That's no change for me from the past."

"I would have gone hunting with you."

"I needed to be alone for a time. I'm here now, did you need something?"

"Not really. I wish you'd told me. I think some people noticed your absence."

"Tabor, don't waste your time worrying about what other people think, I don't."

"So, there's not going to be trouble between us?"

"Not from me. The book is closed on the whole 'ascension to the throne' thing and I'm glad that it is, finally."

"Good."

Damon forced a smile on his face, though he really didn't feel like smiling. He wanted to part from his brother and get to his room. As if on cue, Selena came down the hallway from the opposite direction. She could never go anywhere without a large group of courtesans following her.

"Hello, Majesties," she said in a dainty voice.

Tabor blazed a smile and took her arm. "Hello, darling, you give me a reason to get up out of bed every day."

She smiled demurely and glanced at Damon.

"Hello," he whispered, turning his glance away quickly. "Excuse me, but the queen asked that I call on her."

"What does she want?" asked Tabor. "Does she want both of us to attend her?"

"I believe she had some minor matter to discuss with me. I think she saves the important things for you, brother."

"Oh, I see. We'll go hunting later, Damon."

Damon bowed briefly. "Selena," he whispered and worked his way through her entourage to escape the uncomfortable moment. Her followers seemed determined to obstruct his quick exit to extend his misery. Again he was confronted with the smirking pretty faces he so despised. It generated his usual emotional feelings of anger.

"He can have her," he muttered as he broke out of the pack and walked away, as if saying it made it true. Of course it wasn't the case at all. He would have feelings for Selena until the day he died. He understood with his head Selena would never be his bride, but his heart never seemed to get the message. She was Damon's first love, but it was one sided. She didn't share his affection and there was nothing Damon could do to change it.

On this trip away from social distress, he ran into people he was happy to see, Berne and Amal, his two closest friends. They had been his cohorts since his earliest childhood memories. Though they were all older than Tabor, they'd all been relegated to lesser places in the social hierarchy to Tabor and his popular crowd. Over time, that galling development simply became their lives and they'd come to accept the order of things carving their own niche, away from the notice of the socially relevant.

"Here cometh his highest highness, the regal prince of princes himself, we salute you, Sire" Amal joked with a mock salute.

"Shut up before I administer a royal beating. I'm in no mood after, well you know why."

"At least it's over with, Damon. We all knew this day was coming. Now we can move on. We have an entire world out there waiting for us."

"To do what?" Damon huffed, unable to excise his ire.

"To do whatever," Berne replied with a smile.

"You two are so pitiful. You're as bad as I am."

"Isn't it great," Amal answered, and they all laughed.

"I've got to see my mother about something of hers. We can get together later and get out of here."

"I heard you skipped the celebration party for Tabor. Is that why he was talking to you?"

"I don't care if it ruffled some feathers amongst that crowd. They're rid of me now. Why would they care what I do or what I think?"

"Disgruntled princes do spawn discord."

"Not me, I don't want the throne. In truth, I don't think I ever did. As a little kid I guess I thought about it briefly, but when Tabor started whipping me regularly, I let it go as a goal. The new king should be the champion."

"Competence has never been a requirement for being a king. There are plenty of examples of that fact in the other cities around us. Blind ambition and ruthlessness seems to be the usual ingredients in anointing a king. We've been lucky to get one of the few good kings with your father. Life is pretty difficult in many of the other cities," Berne related.

"Berne, you should be a scribe and write down all these great thoughts."

"Maybe I will someday, if I can ever get rid of my first job of protecting your back. You're so careless it takes all of my time keeping you from ending up in the belly of a predator in the woods."

"I can take care of myself," Damon huffed.

Amal and Berne laughed heartily. "Sure you can, Your Magnificence."

Damon scowled at them, but then smiled. "I'll see you later, buffoons."

He walked swiftly to the royal chambers, pausing at the door and listening for voices. Damon preferred to avoid his father, a fact which wasn't lost on the king. It added to their difficult relationship. The king never consciously intended to slight his eldest son, but Tabor was easy to like and he succeeded where Damon failed so many times. Both Damon and the king eventually gave up trying to work out their differences. Damon simply made himself absent as often as he could. He wasn't publicly disrespectful of his father, or brother for that matter, just keeping them away at arm's length, seldom advising either of them of his plans. Keeping his whereabouts private suited Prince Damon. Only his very small circle of trusted companions was granted that knowledge and usually they were with him.

His life revolved around what time he could spend with his mother, the queen. She was the balm in his otherwise discouraging life and she provided what little validation he'd ever felt. She was imminently patient with Damon, but never accepted his life choice of a second class status and sometimes chastised him for doing so. As much as she tried, it didn't change his approach. He merely waited until she finished her tirade and nodded his head blithely.

"I might as well be talking to the wall," she would say in frustration. "You're not going to change a thing, are you?"

"Do you want me to say I will?" he asked mischievously. "You taught me not to lie."

She shook her head. "You can be very frustrating, Damon. Go back to your friends. You're going to do it anyway, no matter what I say."

"I'll see you later, Mother." He always hugged her tightly before leaving.

"Be careful, Damon. Those woods are dangerous."

"The woods I can handle. It's the palace that's beyond me."

On this occasion when he heard no sounds inside her room he tapped on the door. It took a few moments before he heard movement. His mother opened the door and peered out looking strangely at him.

"Mother, is something wrong?"

"Damon, I'm sorry. I forgot you were coming. Excuse my confusion. I was involved in some engrossing studies. Please come in."

Damon was surprised to see her table was filled with great tomes from the royal library. The tomes were open there with several library scholars sitting about immersed in reading. The royal historian was present also.

"Am I interrupting something, Mother? I can leave."

"No Son, I want you here."

"My Prince," said Boleran, the chief scribe.

"Hello, sir, it's nice to see you again. What are you doing, if I'm not being too nosey?"

Boleran glanced at the queen for her to respond to the question.

"Son, we're researching a perplexing possibility with the hope it won't become a problem."

Damon was instantly intrigued.

"Please sit down," said his mother nodding to an open chair.

Damon sat down beside his mother and looked at the nearest open book.

"There are troubling rumors we're hearing coming from the far north. You know our geography. Our land is a collection of loosely organized independent city states across the lowlands. We've never had occasion to question our political organization. Actually we've created enough trouble amongst ourselves in the cities with petty rivalries and small scale banditry. What news has recently come to us is the great wild region in the mountains, a vast area of land, is the home of a savage race that has chosen to ignore us in the past. Apparently that has changed as raiding parties have crossed the borders in numerous places and attacked farms and small villages. The stories of those depredations are truly appalling. They've shown no pity for the helpless victims of the attacks. In fact, they seem to delight in the mayhem. If those actions continue, we fear it may lead to a wider outbreak and actual hostilities with their armed forces. As you know, we only have local militaries for each city. There is no combined army we can muster if there is an invasion. Boleran and I are both extremely concerned about this development."

"What does the king say?"

"I'm afraid he doesn't share our sense of the urgency of the threat. The border is a great distance away from Kragan. I'm afraid he thinks more highly of our fighting forces than is warranted."

"I understand, Mother. What do you propose we do?"

"We don't have a plan at this point, Damon. That's part of the problem. In spite of what happened with your brother, I think it's critical you take a hand with helping us in this. I'd like for you to join me and these scholars in developing a real plan I can take to your father. It may be we have less time than we might think before our world changes. Deluding ourselves into thinking we're safe here behind our walls, Kragan leadership believes us immune from outside disaster. Nothing could be farther from the truth, in my opinion."

"I can't disagree with you, Mother. I'm not sure if I can provide much help, but if it's your desire, I'll certainly try."

Both the queen and the master scribe smiled warmly at his acquiescence to their request.

"Thank you, My Prince. You'll be far more of an asset than you could imagine," said Boleran. "This is excellent, My Queen. I'd hope for his cooperation."

"Thank you, My Son."

Damon was perplexed at their reactions, unsure why they'd think his assistance would cause any good effect. Nothing he'd done in his past would seem to support any optimism he could accomplish anything of merit. He shrugged his shoulders which they took as his dismissing the matter.

"I was going out hunting with Amal and Berne, Mother."

Annoyed, she looked at him liked he'd reverted back to his infancy.

"Those two louts are lazy brainless rascals, Damon. I wish you wouldn't waste your time in idleness."

"We donate the meat to the poor, Mother." He responded defensively, unaccustomed to this kind of disapproval from the queen. Her expression softened. The loving look returned to her eyes.

"I know that, I'm sorry to complain, Damon. I'm concerned about this invasion matter and it's affected my mood. You're a good person to help the less fortunate, but please don't be gone for weeks like you usually do. I want you close at hand to assist us."

"Yes, Mother. We'll be back soon." He nodded to Boleran and then embraced his mother.

Damon left the room, emotions astir. The revelation of border troubles surprised him as he'd assumed his mother was only going to continue trying to console him about the throne and his brother. The appearance of this new threat intrigued him. He couldn't get it out of his mind pondering the matter as he walked. He didn't notice the clump of people ahead and ran into Selena and her clingy crowd.

"Damon, what are you thinking about with this severe expression on your face?" she asked.

"It's nothing to concern you, Selena." Her 'people' stood by eavesdropping as they always did, like dim witted sheep.

"I can decide what concerns me, Damon. I wanted to talk to you. I'm sorry about what happened to you. I'll always be your friend. I hope you know that. You're important to me. With Tabor and I, well, it's complicated."

"Selena, it's not necessary to apologize to me. His getting the crown, it really isn't a factor for me. I went through the motions of seeking the throne because I was required as first born of the king. Very frankly, I'm glad it's over. I know he's your love. I admit I care for you, but it was never meant to be between us. Don't think any further about it. I'll cope."

He was surprised she looked upset, like it wasn't the response she wanted to hear from him, that she still wanted him to endlessly pine away for her.

She started to speak, but Damon cut her off.

"I'm sorry, but I've got to go. We're scheduled to go hunting and I have people waiting."

"You mean Amal and Berne," she snapped. Her entourage chuckled at the mention of their names.

"You know that already, Selena. Is there something I'm missing here? I don't understand why it would make you angry."

"Just go," she hissed. "You could never understand anyway. Go to your stupid friends."

He looked at her in confusion before nodding and walking away.

"Women make no sense," he muttered as he walked away.

Three horses were tied to the hitching post outside the palace entrance. Amal and Berne were standing idly by talking when he came out to join them.

"It took you long enough," Berne complained.

"I had things to see about. Selena gave me a sweet sendoff."

"Right," his friends sneered, laughing heartily. Damon laughed with them.

"Get your royal butt in the saddle, we're burning daylight," said Amal.

They mounted up and trotted toward the main city gate. The sun was hanging low on the horizon already.

"Let's go, we need to find a campsite before it gets dark," said Damon. "The last thing we need is to stumble onto a predator in the gloom."

They rode away at a trot following the road toward the large forest. The rainstorm had passed on but the ground was still wet and the road muddy. The sight of the tree line ahead beckoned to Damon and brightened his mood.

Prince Damon was in the lead but not by his choice. His friends just fell in behind him by habit. Damon didn't like it, but they wouldn't change and he'd given up arguing with them.

They found a campsite quickly just inside the tree line as it was dark by the time they got to the woods.

"This is much better," said Damon looking about with a smile.

"Yeah, there are no scary pretty maidens here to assail us," Berne joked.

Damon glowered at his two friends who were highly amused by Berne's comment.

Chapter Two

The three friends spent the night camped in the forest and got up with the sun to begin their day of hunting. Animals usually moved about at dawn in the dim light to feed and seek water, both the herbivores and the carnivores. It was a gray day with clouds covering the entire sky. There was a cold bite in the air as the fall season was fading toward winter. It wasn't raining, but the smell of moisture was heavy in the air as fast moving weather fronts came up frequently at this time of year. As a precaution, the men wore warm clothing against the possibility of sudden inclement weather.

All three were excellent with bows and seldom missed their marks. It was a level of expertise they'd acquired over time, skill they took for granted with each other. None of them bragged back in the city about their prowess. They were practical men concerned about their goals which, at that point, focused on feeding the poor. Disinterested in fame, they sought anonymity. There were plenty of others seeking fame.

"Do you want to hunt together, Damon?" asked Amal.

"While it's gloomy, I'd say yes. If there are cats on the prowl, I'd rather have us together."

"Here kitty, kitty," Berne joked.

"Keep calling them, moron, you might get your wish," Damon commented shaking his head and smirking in derision.

"I'm not afraid of them," Berne replied, striking an attack pose and trying to look fierce. Instead he looked comical, a gangly young man still growing into his body, physically immature. Amal tended toward the stocky side. He dismissed his excess girth describing himself as 'fleshy' by nature, as if his excessive eating habits had no part in his size.

"Which proves you're a complete dolt. You wouldn't last a minute in a close quarter fight with a big cat. You'd just be a snack in their den for the cubs."

"Bring 'em on. We'll see who ends up the snack."

They snickered with each other with more senseless boasts before setting out to follow the animal trail deeper into the forest. It was a broader path than usual deep in the thick woods as traffic was heavier here both of prey and the predators hunting them. The men knew this trail well having been on it many times. Traveling for several hours before reaching the large lake which served as a watering hole for the animals, they carefully surveyed the scene checking for danger. It was also a place they fished frequently. On this day there was a slight morning mist hanging over the water so the far shore was obscured from view. Herds of elk and deer came here in large numbers, but they were very cautious as the predator cats hunted here as well.

"This should do," said Damon, looking at a blind they'd built long ago.

"That thing is going to fall down one of these days," Amal remarked.

"Possibly, but not today," Damon replied.

They crawled into the feeble wood framed structure. It was covered by branches and brush. They hung scented bait just outside to lure their prey. One of them would stand watch while the other two rested. It wasn't long before a group of deer ambled in their direction, particularly skittish looking all about, sniffing the air, ready to bolt in an instant. The reason quickly became clear as wolves broke out from the brush to attack the herd. They weren't close enough to make a kill as the frightened deer fled in a blur of motion speeding off eluding death in predator jaws. The three young men watched quietly. One of the wolves at the back of the pack stopped and turned its head in their direction and sniffed the scented lures, pausing to stare with baleful eyes. It was chilling to see the animal ferocity in its eyes, a quick death for the unwary. Damon notched an arrow as the wolf continued to stare and took one tentative step toward them. They heard the yelps of the pack in the distance and the wolf turned and raced away to join the chase.

Within moments a huge cat walked down to the lake to drink quickly lapping the water to quench its thirst. It looked around, but not out of fear. It was the supreme hunter of the forest and had few worries of any sort of attack. It looked in the direction the wolves had gone for a moment before trotting along the shore going in the other direction. Damon admired the sleek powerful animal for its great prowess, the master of any situation it faced. It was a level of competence he had no belief he could ever achieve. The cat was an animal but it had an aura which terrified, and that made Damon was jealous.

He glanced at Berne. "Here kitty, kitty," he chided.

They chuckled softly and resumed their vigilance.

It was over an hour of waiting before another group of deer wandered up. This time Amal fired out of the blind and downed an animal. Damon and Berne raced outside firing at the fleeing herd and each bagged a deer also. Hauling the kills inside the blind to harvest the meat, they packed large pouches full.Taking the carcasses back outside to leave them to the scavengers, the great predatory hunting birds and also the four legged types, they went to the lake to cleanse their hands in the cold water.

Once the meat was loaded onto the pack horse the men headed back toward Kragan. It took the balance of the day to ride through the forest and cover the ground back to arrive in the city and distribute the meat to the poor, so they went to their own rooms late to sleep the night. Getting up early the next morning at daybreak they returned to the hunt. There were too many hungry mouths of the unfortunate to be able to feed them all but they never gave up trying.

On his way out of the palace, Damon made a detour and went through the royal kitchen where the cooks were just starting breakfast. The fat master chef saw him coming eyeing Damon with a stern look. He still saw Damon as the little prankster he'd been as a child rather than a grown prince of the realm.

"You can wait your turn just like everyone else, Damon. The kitchen is no place for eaters. We prepare the finest cuisine in the realm here and to do so we can't allow interruptions from louts and delinquents. Don't think to steal away any food." He scowled and pointed his finger in Damon's face.

"Chef Mathias, I can't wait for those 'lay-abouts' to fall out of bed. I have pressing business."

"Pressing business? You're going to join those two derelict friends of yours to go off into the woods to play. I know you very well, Damon."

"We're consummate hunters, for your information, Mathias."

"Hah, you're consummate at thieving my desserts and nothing more."

"Speaking of desserts, I smell the cinnamon pastries. Are they out of the ovens?"

"No," he replied, stepping sideways to block the aisle way. Damon leaned to peer around him so Mathias moved again.

"Oh, I forgot to tell you my mother asked for you to attend her. Apparently there is some matter of what you're feeding them which requires her intervention."

"What!" Mathias shouted. "What matter?"

When he turned to instruct his staff, Damon slipped around him and hustled to the cooling pantry.

"Stop," shouted Mathias lumbering after him.

"Thank you, Mathias, I'm in your debt," Damon yelled as he quickly wrapped up and stuffed pastries into his pouch and raced away.

"Curse you, Damon," shouted Mathias in irritation. "The king shall hear about this."

Damon laughed and jumped on his horse just outside the door. He rode away to meet his friends, pleased with his 'food coup'. He licked his fingers from the sweet delicious glaze on the pastries as he rode.

Amal and Berne smiled as he rode up.

"One of these days, Mathias is going to have a meat cleaver handy. He'll lop off your hand for your troubles," said Amal, shaking his head skeptically.

"It's worth the risk. I got cinnamon pastries fresh out of the oven."

"It's worth the risk if you're the one taking that risk," Berne retorted.

They rode steadily back to the forest and headed for the lake again in good moods.

Though they trotted steadily they were in no real hurry, chatting idly about various pretty young women of the castle and their lame romantic plans about them.

"I'm going to talk to her," said Berne.

"You're such a coward. Sure you'll talk to her, while she's on the opposite side of the palace in a different room," Amal chided. "If you ever got her attention, she'd run for the door, or you would."

"Look who's talking. Who's your sweetheart? The only female that pays attention to you is your horse and if you don't feed her she'll drop you like a hot potato."

Damon and Berne laughed.

"Hah, hah, hah, very funny," Amal responded in a huff.

Damon smiled and glanced at his friends. "We truly are a sorry lot. Can you imagine if I'd actually won against Tabor? Kragan wouldn't be the same with me in charge, I can tell you that."

"What would you do, Your Majesty?" asked Berne.

"Maybe I would make a law saying pretty women must talk to us."

"Instead of snicker at us?" asked Amal. "I'd like that law."

"They pay attention to you, Damon."

"Only because I'm a prince, not because I'm interesting. They pay attention to Tabor."

"What else would you decree?" asked Berne.

"Let me think, possibly we should double the production of pastries in the royal kitchen."

They all laughed at the silly propositions Damon concocted.

"Now that's a law everybody can support," Amal yelled. "I don't know how Mathias would like it though."

Their banter distracted their attention from the task at hand so when they came upon a lone stranger, riding into his camp, the friends were startled and unprepared. He was tall, powerfully built, and he wore a green leather hood which obscured his face from their view. He had a great longbow and quiver slung over his back along with a broadsword. The colors of his clothes blended perfectly in the forest.

They stopped and stared at each other. The man slowly extracted his sword and assumed a defensive stance.

"We mean you no harm, stranger," said Damon quickly. "We're out in the forest to hunt. This trail leads to our hunting grounds."

"Is that so," the stranger replied, keeping his weapon at the ready.

Damon glanced at his friends. Even combined, the three of them were poor challenges for any competent fighter.

"Can we have peace between us? I don't think we're much of a threat to you."

The stranger chuckled.

"That's not much of an attitude for you to take. Are you from that city over there?"

"Yes, sir."

"It happens I'm in need of meat to replenish my supplies. Perhaps I'll join you on your hunt, if you're agreeable."

"That would be great," said Berne, enthusiastically.

"Berne, shut up," Amal snapped. "He'll think we're incompetent."

"We are incompetent," Berne replied.

The stranger shook his head mirthfully.

"May we know your name?" asked Damon.

"You may call me Argon. It's a name that suits me at the moment."

"You have other names?" asked Berne, senselessly.

The stranger chuckled. "Obviously. I have my reasons for what I do. Don't concern yourself about it. Are you the leader?"

Damon shrugged. "Possibly, but in reality it's better to think of us as leaderless. None of us are capable of leading. We just go about together."

Argon pulled back his hood. He had a close cropped beard and mustache. He was handsome but his skin was weathered from a rugged life outdoors. He looked to be the age of Damon's father and mother. He had thick brown hair.

"I'm picking up a theme here amongst the three of you. I'm not sure what's happened in your lives to take away your self-confidence. It's something you all need to recover, and the sooner the better. This world can be cruel and weaknesses can be fatal flaws. It's none of my business what you do. It's just friendly advice. Stumbling into the camp of a stranger requires utmost caution and alertness. You could have died if I was a different sort of man to act first and ask questions later. Do you hear me?"

"Yes, sir," they replied in unison, like delinquent schoolboys.

"Take me to your hunting grounds. We have work to do while the daylight holds."

Quickly packing his things, he mounted his horse and followed them along the path to the lake.

The three rode in silence. They weren't sure what might upset this dangerous stranger so they took no chances. He was very vigilant looking all around constantly, like he expected an ambush. It worried the three friends.

When they got to the site of their blind and dismounted the stranger glanced around quickly, expertly assessing the place. He smiled at the feeble structure.

"You use that thing to hunt?"

"Yes, Master," said Berne.

Argon looked at him severely. "I'm not your master, Son."

"What are you?" Berne continued, like a simple child.

"I'm merely a fellow hunter at this moment. We happen to be in the same place at the same time. There's nothing more to it than that."

They stood waiting for his further thoughts and comments, cowed and unsure of themselves.

"This is a good spot. I see why you come here. I'm surprised the predators allow you in their hunting grounds."

"We try to be cautious," Damon replied. "We've had a few close calls but so far we've survived."

They set up camp and entered the blind.

The three gave Argon first choice as sentry. He declined.

"There's something about you which is different," he said, looking at Damon. "Tell me your story."

"There's not much to tell. I'm the first born son of the king, but a lesser man to my younger brother. He's everything the king seeks in an heir. I'm an average man who happened to be born into royalty. It was just blind circumstance, I was never worthy of the title and it didn't take long in my life before it became obvious to everyone around me. My brother exceeded me from the start. I and my friends learned to live away from their notice. It's all right, we're accustomed to it."

"It's all right?" Argon questioned skeptically. "I seriously doubt that. Every man has the need for self-worth, Prince. I don't need to see your brother as I look at you. Perhaps he has skills and attributes, but that isn't what defeated you. You are your own worst enemy. It's true of your friends too. When those self-righteous egotists put this mantle of inferiority upon you, there was a need to fight back. There is no man who can't be conquered. I suspect you allowed him to work to his areas of strength and you lapsed to your areas of weakness. That was a huge mistake."

"What could I have done differently? Tabor exceeded me in all ways."

Argon shook his head. "You defeated yourself before you ever began any contests with him. The outcome was never in doubt because of your attitude, not for any lack of skills on your part."

"Sir, I think you're mistaken. These are fine words you say, but it's clear to us you're a man of great accomplishment. You could never understand people like us. We don't know success but it isn't because we never wanted it. We tried, but came up short time after time. Failure erodes your spirit after a long enough time."

Argon looked very angry for a moment.

"You have no idea the type of man I am. Don't make assumptions about me, or anybody else for that matter."

"I believe you, sir," said Berne weakly.

Argon ignored him, lost in some troubling thoughts of his own past.

"Would you teach us?" Berne whispered.

That got Argon's attention snapping him out of his ruminations.

"Teach you?" as if it was a ludicrous question. "I don't teach. I live alone and it suits me nicely. Besides the fact, you've already chosen your paths living as shadows to those willing to face the challenges of life."

"I'm sorry we offend you," Damon added. "Berne meant no insult, and perhaps you're right, we're beyond help. From our perspective, I say we're willing to consider your harsh assessment of us, but if you think there was another way, that we had possibilities, then why say it if you aren't willing to prove that point. None of us are happy living as shadows, as you say, but we have no way out of it now from our own efforts. What else would you be doing? Can life alone be so fulfilling? I doubt that."

Argon stared at him darkly.

"What do you think would be enticing for me about tutoring you three? I fully expect it would be a waste of my time."

"Does that mean you'd consider it?" asked Amal.

"Can any of you follow instructions?"

"Yes," they replied in unison.

"I would be a severe taskmaster. I brook no weakness, sniveling, complaining, or incompetence. If you're to be my first apprentices, you represent me and I'm very protective of my reputation."

"Reputation, with whom, sir, you said you live alone," Damon uttered, speaking before thinking.

Argon glared. "Lesson number one, I also don't like back talk. Are you willing to do everything I say and follow my teachings to the letter without question?"

"Yes, sir," they replied, again in unison.

"Those swords, do you know how to use them?"

"We aren't the most skilled, sir, but we've had training," Damon ventured.

"We'll see about that," said Argon. "What we're about is deadly and serious business. You must understand that if nothing else. The world won't care about your age, your relative incompetence, or your timid spirits. If an opponent looks to take your life you must not allow him. It's you or him. This isn't your safe city out here. Death awaits you just around the corner for all of us. You must take control, or else you won't be with us among the living."

They eyed him soberly and nodded.

"From this point forward, if you agree to follow my instructions, your old selves must be cast aside completely. No longer will I tolerate this appalling self-deprecation and inferiority complex. You must evolve into different persons, men of significance. If you're unwilling to do this, speak now because it's your last chance to avoid the severe rigors you'll face under my tutelage. If you persist in your old ways, I want nothing to do with you. Do you agree?"

"Yes," they answered.

As the three friends stood waiting, Argon stepped in front of each of them, one at a time and stared directly into their eyes looking for the needed determination in each of them against his daunting stare. They realized this so none of them averted their eyes. That in itself was significant, behavior uncharacteristic and previously missing in the young men.

"So be it," he said solemnly. "Let it begin."

They nodded and glanced at each other. Argon ignored their excitement.

"We'll hunt first to build up our supplies and then begin the exercises later."

"Sir, may I explain the reason we come here to hunt is we provide free meat for the poor in our city. There are so many of them in distress, people with infirmities, elderly, widows, and so forth."

"Are you saying we donate all of our kills?"

Damon grimaced. "I didn't mean that. We would still like to help the poor. Will you allow us our charitable practices? Those people have so few options. Starvation is always close at their doors for them and their children."

"I'm not one to get involved in the lives of others. Already I'm regretting this partnership. I should just ride away, but I've given my word, so I'll accommodate your request, but understand I don't prefer spending any time in cities."

"Thank you, Argon. Is it your desire we live here in the woods rather than back in the palace working in the training pits?"

"The soft life you have back there works counter to what we need to do, so yes we should live in the woods. You need to discipline yourselves in your lives and that screams out at me. There are too many lures back to your old ways in your city. Do you understand? If you commit to changing, the pathway lies out here in the open. You can't harden your minds and bodies back there."

"I need to explain this to my mother, the queen. There's another thing about that. She's asked that I assist her in preparing a contingency defense plan to take to my father about the troubles in the north."

"What troubles in the north?" Argon was suddenly very interested.

"Would you come with us to meet her? She and the scholars can explain it to you. I don't know enough about it to explain it properly."

Argon seemed to struggle with the suggestion like it was a threat to him. He scowled and stared away in the distance looking in the direction of Kragan, deep in thought.

"I'll think about it. My prior dealings with city dwellers haven't been positive."

"You'll be in our company, Argon. My mother will not be a problem for you. She's truly a wonderful person."

"That remains to be seen if she'd be a problem for me. I don't like my whereabouts being known to the public. It's not a small matter for me. As I told you, I have reasons for everything I do."

"We're not trying to pry. If you choose to share your tale, we'd love to hear it. If not, we'll work with you under any arrangement you're comfortable with."

"Enough of this talking for now, let's go and hunt."

They killed for the meat for several hours, dressed the kills and loaded up full their carrying pouches. When they could load no more meat Damon turned to Argon to reiterate his request.

"Will you ride with us to Kragan? We must feed the poor but I'd like to have you meet my mother. I think it's important you hear what she has to say about the threat to the city."

Argon scowled again. "You're more trouble than you're worth. I know I'm going to regret this, but I'll follow you there."

Argon rode at the end of the procession behind the pack horses. The gate guards eyed him curiously as the prince passed into the city bringing along a stranger. With as much meat as they had, they were able to distribute food to more families than usual. Damon made a point of seeking out the young widow. She smiled warmly when he knocked on her door and she greeted him.

"Thank you so much, My Prince. Your generosity humbles me."

"Madam, your courage humbles me. We will not forget you in your distress. Your little ones need food."

"Prince Damon, the people will never forget you," she replied with a serious demeanor.

He was taken aback, and he was pleased.

"I don't seek anything."

"Who you are as a person makes you a champion to us. We're your people, regardless of who sits on the throne."

She glanced up at Argon who looked like a raptor ready to strike. He smiled at her.

"It's the truth," she said to Argon, almost like she was challenging him to argue with her.

He nodded in respect. "Madam, I'm new to your city. Please don't look at me as an enemy for I'm not."

"As with all people, sir, we common folk judge people by their deeds not their words. We've heard enough of empty promises from the privileged. Their arrogance doesn't solve our problems."

He chuckled. "I can understand and I accept your statement completely. I pledge this to you. As the prince promises to sustain you and yours, I add my pledge also. You will not starve. If you think I'm of the privileged, you're wrong."

"Then I'm in your debt, sir." She did a curtsy before closing her door.

They continued their ride ending at the palace. Unlike the guards at the city gates, the palace guards eyed Argon closely as armed, he walked into the seat of power in Kragan with the three young friends. Outwardly, he ignored the guards completely, though Damon noticed Argon kept his hand on his sword hilt. Equally, the King's guards watched Argon the entire way and sent men to follow the four.

They went first to Damon's rooms to refresh and wash their hands and faces from the grit of the trail. After having some cold water to drink, they made their way to the royal suite.

As always, Damon listened at the door before he knocked. His mother's handmaiden opened the door.

"My Prince," she said in a sweet voice and bowed to him.

"Is my mother available?"

"She's momentarily occupied. Let me speak to her."

They waited patiently in the hallway. More guards arrived peering at Argon who acted oblivious. In the pursuit of Argon's requirement to act differently and be different people, it was hard for Damon to dismiss his old feelings standing here. Feeling vulnerable he listened closely for his father or brother to approach. Finally, he muttered softly.

"Stop this, Damon. You're a new man."

The maiden returned. "The queen will see you. Please come in."

They took seats at her table. The scholars were busy reading and nodded to Damon. The queen came in from another room.

"Damon, my son, I'm happy to see you."

She spoke to him, but her eyes were fixed on Argon who smiled at her beauty appreciatively. The gesture seemed to unnerve her. Damon had never seen his mother flustered.

"Who is this?" she asked a little stiffly.

"Mother, this is our friend, Argon. He was traveling through the land when we made his acquaintance. He's a skilled warrior and he's agreed to accept us as apprentices in learning the war arts. I felt it important he meet you and that he be apprised of the situation in the north."

She stood a little uncomfortably and she didn't make eye contact with Argon. This puzzled Damon. His mother was always composed and in control of every situation. What was different here, he couldn't discern.

"I'm pleased to make your acquaintance, majesty," Argon said, and executed an elaborate bow. "You're as impressive a person as I've ever met. Actually, I would say you have no peer."

She blushed and Damon noted a slight smile.

"You're too kind, sir. I'm simply a woman, no different than any other."

"We both know that's not true, Your Majesty."

It evoked puzzled feelings in Damon. He wasn't sure what it meant this exchange between them and he wasn't sure if he should be offended. Argon was acting correctly enough though edging close to acceptable boundaries, but there was some other level of this exchange escaping Damon. It was clear it wasn't escaping his mother.

She turned her head toward Argon who winked at her. Again she fought against her smile, but lost.

"Your son informs me you have information I should know about. Please proceed with your explanation, Your Majesty. I have some knowledge of the north. What's happening there is of keen interest to me."

She blinked her eyes to regain her composure and focus on the issue at hand.

"Of course, please have some berry wine, Argon, while I call for the royal scribe."

Damon glanced at Argon who seemed like a visiting king instead of an itinerant soldier of fortune. There was nothing here of royal presence that intimidated him in any way. Seemingly, it was the other way around.

Damon glanced at his two friends. They looked to be dumbfounded and a little uncomfortable.

The chief scribe arrived after a short time. The queen brought him into the room. The scribe was cordial and businesslike in his greeting, and a little curious. The queen, cleared her throat, blinked her eyes and quickly averted her glance from Argon. He was supremely confident, noting it all. "Argon, this is our great mind of the palace, Boleran. He is my intellectual inspiration and mentor."

"Her Majesty has been most gracious in greeting a stranger and allowing me into the royal suite," Argon stated. "I'm happy to meet you, Boleran.

Perhaps we can share our knowledge regarding the events in the north."

"Thank you, sir, I'm pleased to meet you. Have you been to that region? We can only make our assessment on hearsay from others. I'm sure you understand how difficult that makes it to create a proper response to any potential threat."

"It does, indeed, for many reasons. Yes, I've been to the land of the barbarians. Frankly, I'm surprised to hear they're venturing south. It hasn't been their nature to invade other places. Normally they create havoc enough with their own infighting. What's causing them to move is the important thing to know. Their incentive is the biggest answer to why they're here and how far they'll go. Understand too they're not like you, their belief system is totally different, their morals and ethics are completely foreign to yours. I would say, they present the greatest risk to your network of city states of any you could imagine. With your lack of cohesiveness, cooperation, and forethought, you're the ideal prey for them. They fight relentlessly and mercilessly. You won't find pity from them even for the innocent and helpless. You need more than a contingency plan, you need a miracle."

The room was shocked by his frank and alarming revelation.

"My husband believes our army the equal of any challenge," said the queen, her face a mask of concern.

"Your husband is sadly mistaken, Majesty. Your little city is barely a bump in their road of conquest for the enemy. Do you understand me?"

"How did you survive amongst such ferocity as you describe?" asked Boleran.

"I fought often and I barely escaped. It was a visit I questioned why I did it when it was too late. At the point I realized what a mistake I'd made, I could only concentrate on surviving. It took all of my skills to accomplish it. They couldn't be reasoned with. If you're not one of them, you're an enemy in their viewpoint. Even in their society, life is cheap. They value strength and ferocity. The weak amongst them don't survive for long. Again, we must learn what has caused them to leave their homeland to come here. It's the answer to whether any of us can live through this challenge to your way of life. I fear your cities will realize too late what's coming for them. Living in self-created delusions of grandeur, their arrogance will be their undoing. The Argore hordes will overwhelm any who try to stand against them. You don't even want to think about what unspeakable things happen after their victories. Suffice to say, you must find a way to prevail, as impossible as is that task."

The color went out of the chief scribe's face. He sat down in consternation. The queen looked on the verge of tears. Damon and his friends were frightened.

"Does your king understand any of this, Your Majesty?"

"No," she whispered.

"There is your task. I'm not one to dwell in cities for any amount of time, but I'll help you as I can. I intend to teach your son, as I promised. Does this meet with your approval?"

"Thank you, Argon," she answered, looking deeply into his eyes for the first time.

"I'm sorry to be the bearer of such dark tidings, but it is better you know the truth to make your plans while you still can."

"I appreciate your honesty. If it be agreeable, I'd like for you to attend our supper meal to meet the king and my other son, Tabor. I have hopes you can persuade his majesty of the gravity of the threat. As I said, he doesn't understand our point of view here in this room and he believes our army can…well, I guess it doesn't matter."

"I'll speak to him if he'll hear me, but it sounds as if he has his mind made up."

"We need this miracle you speak of, Argon."

"I'm not an answer, Your Majesty, simply a messenger."

No one in the room could utter a word at that point. The scholars looked at their texts realizing what a waste of time it was. There was nothing written there that would be helpful, or would save them from destruction.

"Mother, I will fight in our defense to my last drop of blood," said Damon impulsively. It broke the dire mood in the room.

"As will I," Amal added.

"And I also," Berne said.

It was merely false bravado from the trio, but it was sincere and the perfect tonic for the situation. Argon smiled at them. The queen suddenly hugged her son.

"Mother, we'll protect you, don't worry."

She smiled warmly, but glanced at Argon for affirmation. Argon merely looked back at her.

The queen turned to Boleran.

"It seems senseless to continue our studies at this point. We'll think about what we've learned. Perhaps an idea will come to one of us. If we can convince the king, I think that's the best outcome we can hope for any pending further developments."

Chapter Three

Supper with the king worried Damon for many reasons and not just his prior ongoing and unresolved personal issues. With the threat of invasion on the horizon, the presence of Argon and the strange chemistry he evoked in the queen, the king's closed mindedness, and his brother's pompous attitude, the potential for disaster seemed too great to take the risk. Damon would gladly have gotten on his horse and ridden away from the evening but it wasn't an option for him.

Rather than don the princely military dress uniform customary for such occasions, Damon decided to take his first step down the path of independence which Argon required of him. He would ignore the disdain and disapproval from the royal courtesans and dress plainly in forest garb to match Argon's rugged appearance. If it was going to be a new day and a new Damon, this seemed an easy enough first step, but when he got to the door to the royal dining chamber he felt panic. He nearly turned and left but Argon arrived at that moment.

Argon eyed him mirthfully. "I think there might be better forms of rebellion against the royal ceremonies but it's your choice to make, Prince."

Argon opened the door and the royal herald announced their entry.

"Damon, a prince of the realm, and Argon, a traveler."

Argon started to chuckle at his modest introduction.

Damon felt every eye was on him as he walked to his place at the table. He kept his face straight forward looking at no one at all. When they came before the king they knelt.

"Please rise," said his father. "Damon, apparently all of your clothes were in the laundry?"

Rather than quake in shame, Damon bristled. "No, My King, I've decided to forgo the fineries of the palace in favor of functional clothing. As you have no doubt heard, Master Argon has agreed to take on me, Amal, and Berne as apprentices to learn the war arts. We intend to devote our utmost effort to achieve that goal. Since we'll be training in the forest, I'll have little use for decorative wear."

It was the closest he'd ever come to defying his father and everyone in attendance was shocked.

"I see," his father replied acidly. "Master Argon, is it? Am I seeing an example of your tutoring with this impertinence in my son? I must say it does not please me."

Argon was nonplussed. He seemed to have no fear, even of royalty.

"I can't say this is my tutoring, Sire, but I do like to see him expressing himself. He's a man now, after all. It's time for him to make his way in the world. Does that distress you? I'd understood it's your other son who is named crown prince and heir to your throne."

The king simmered noticeably.

"You're correct, sir, with the order of succession. That doesn't mean my eldest son has no relevance here in the city or that I no longer care for him. I care a great deal about what he does and with whom. I think you're in a poor position to judge the condition of things in my city and in my palace."

"Your Majesty, I didn't come here to judge anything, or anybody. I was invited in. I live a solitary life and seldom have occasion to deal with city dwellers. I'm happy to leave your city at the earliest possible time and never return."

"Husband," said the queen quickly as the situation continued to deteriorate. "Please forestall your judgment. There is a vital matter which we need to discuss with you. Argon is well traveled and he has unique information and perspective on matters directly affecting this city. Will you allow us to dine in peace and then have that necessary conversation?"

"I think this charlatan needs to apologize to us for his offense," said Tabor petulantly. "He seems to have no concept of proper behavior before royal persons."

"Such as yourself?" asked Argon scornfully.

Tabor arose angrily, his fists balled up.

"Perhaps we should continue this discussion in the training pits," he snapped in rage.

Argon merely smiled.

"Tabor, take your seat," his mother bellowed. "This is no time for your childish temper."

Tabor glared at Argon and at Damon.

"This matter is not over. I will have satisfaction for your insolence."

Argon shrugged, dismissing the threat contemptuously. He looked at the king who was still shaking.

"Sit down, sir," the king said. His terse facial expression was clear to see. The corresponding emotions behind that look weren't hard to surmise.

Damon quickly led Argon to his mother's side of the table to the empty seats assigned for them. Argon smiled pleasantly at all of the faces staring at him, appalled. He nodded as if no tensions existed in the hall. Damon was worried regardless of his new master's confidence.

The confrontation cast a pall over the meal. Conversation was hushed. Damon happened to notice Selena sitting beside Tabor. She was staring at him and Argon with fascination. Their conduct intrigued her. Argon ignored her and spoke with the queen. That didn't please the king at all.

The meal was consumed rapidly and most of the courtesans were sent away. The king remained along with the crown prince, the queen, Boleran, and some other dignitaries and high ranking officers from the army.

"We've given you your free meal," said the king. "What is this important matter my wife insists I hear from you."

Argon eyed the king before standing up.

"I think perhaps you don't like me. You should know I don't care if you do or do not. As I said, I avoid cities and the petty people that live in them."

"How dare you," Tabor shouted, jumping up and drawing his sword.

The amused look on Argon's face changed in an instant to deadly intent.

"You're young, so I'll let this pass one time, boy," he hissed. "If you ever draw a sword on me again, it will be your last day to draw breath. I'm not some weak villager and you're not my liege, neither of you. My patience is quickly fading for this charade of stuffed shirts. Now put away that toy and sit down while you still can. I won't ask you twice."

Tabor teetered on the precipice of foolish action.

"Sit down, son," said the king icily. "I will deal with this man."

Tabor stared daggers at Argon, but obeyed his father.

"Let me say this, Argon. You may be a dangerous man alone in the woods. I don't know you, but understand, we will not tolerate such temerity in our royal chambers. You were brought here as a guest. It will be your final time to come here. If my eldest son is in your thrall and is determined to follow your path, it will also be his final visit here. Do I make myself clear?"

"Perfectly," Argon replied. "I'd be happy to leave you to your fate, but I've seen the poor innocents that live in your city and I've been moved by the good hearts of your wife and eldest son enough to extend this warning to you. The Argore are coming for you. Their hordes are more numerous than the stars in the sky, they live for battle and little else, they have no pity for their enemies and they are absolutely ruthless. When they come to your gates, and they will, there will be only one outcome to that fight. I can see you're full of smug arrogance, deluding your people into believing your pitiful little army can withstand that flood. You'll be swept away as if you never existed in this land. If any survive, they will be under the boot of barbarians in a life that's worse than death. Those who are slaughtered in the invasion will be the lucky ones. I've been to their land and seen what they do. I have nightmares to this day about it. I have no wish to face them ever again, so I'll train your son and his friends, as I promised, but I will not remain here to share your deadly fate. Am I clear, Your Majesty? Please feel free to sit on your little throne and wile away what little remains of your life. You're all doomed. I feel sorry for your women because when you're all dead it will be your women who will live on to face Argore hell."

The hostility in the room drained away during Argon's dire speech. No one challenged him. They had no doubt he was serious and knowledgeable about the matter.

"What would you have me do?" asked the king, suddenly absent of his rage. "I do care for my people. If what you say is true, what options do we have?"

"The first best choice is to flee, but I can't guarantee you could escape them even if you ran. Without knowing why they've broken their traditions and left their land we can't know how far they'll go. If they track you, they never give up until you're captured or dead. Those Argore who tracked me I killed, or else I'd be dead. If it were possible to organize all of the city states, the best you could do would be to make a valiant ending in a pitched battle. The Argore peoples have never been conquered. They are fearsome foes who have no military peer in this world. For you, they are the coming of the end of days."

The king and his advisors sat ashen faced. There was nothing anyone could say. Their arrogance and hostility was completely gone replaced by worry.

"How can this be?" the king asked finally. "How can this tragedy come over us?"

"I'm truly sorry to tell you this. I have no love for city people, but no person should face such a fate. You should get your affairs in order. There are rumors Argore raiders are racing south at this very moment. Your time is shorter than you realize. Perhaps you can send word to your neighbors and that may slow the invasion slightly. The unavoidable fact is the Argore will appear at your gates, it's just a matter of when."

"I ask you again, what can we do?"

"As I said, I don't know if fleeing is a realistic option. It would probably only postpone your deaths. The miracle would be if the Argore turn away before they get here for their reasons. I don't know how you could discover their goals and therefore how far they're willing to go. In a military sense, the farther they stray from their mountains the more vulnerability they will exhibit.

They will be looking to live off the land. Denying them supply sources would be an effective step, if it were possible. They are not the type of army to have long established supply lines to fuel the march. The problem is they won't stand still to allow you time to implement any plans to deter them. Do you see?"

"Are you willing to consider cooperating in our defense?"

"No, what I will do is what I promised. I'll train your son and his friends for whatever time we have, but I plan to stay ahead of the Argore horde as long as I can."

He turned his head directly to the queen.

"I'm sorry, madam. You're a good person and you deserve a better fate than this."

He bowed to the queen.

She sat motionless, aghast at the future he painted and cognizant of the possibility of her impending death, or worse. The distress mirrored on her face was sobering for everyone in the room. None of them had ever felt vulnerable before.

"Majesties, I'm afraid I have nothing more to offer you, so I'll take my leave. If your son will follow me, or remain behind to stand with you in battle, that is his choice."

The king looked at Damon who was moved like he had never been before. All thoughts of his personal shame were gone. He was now truly thinking and acting as a changed person. Damon looked up at his father.

"Your Majesty, I choose to follow Argon not for any rejection of my home or my family but because I'm a lesser person as a fighter. I cannot abide to be this way any longer. I will allow the master to reform me into iron so I can be a force in this approaching war. Brother, I repeat I have no desire for the throne. That will never change, so please don't think I have some ulterior motive in play. Our childhood rivalries are over. I must become the best man I can be and I know I can't do that here living in my old life. I hope you will all understand why I'm making this choice. Please leave us to our work. When we're ready, we'll return to join you."

"So be it, son," the king replied. "I have no issue with your choice and I wish you all speed in becoming the man you're capable of being. I look forward to meeting that man. Argon, let there be peace between us. This unfortunate evening is unimportant to the survival of the city. I let the offense pass and I hope you can do likewise."

Argon nodded and turned. "Call forth your friends, Prince Damon, we must be going now. Time is not on our side."

"Yes, Master," Damon replied. "Goodbye, Father and Mother."

* * * *

She rode at a gallop looking behind her frequently. The enemy had finally spotted her again after frightening ‘near misses’ too numerous to count, and they were relentless in the chase. She was exhausted after months of flight, hiding and scavenging for food in the ruins of abandoned and destroyed farm houses and burned out small villages. The enemy always left the dead lying about unburied. The vanguard of Argore raiders were still ahead of her, but the second tier of their forces was close behind.

Each day she rode too late into the evening darkness trying to avoid their snare, but the risk of doing so meant she could stumble into hazards she couldn’t see. She had too little to eat, she got too little sleep, and she couldn’t escape the fear that had become her daily companion. It would have been easy to simply give up and accept her fate, but something inside her kept her moving, refusing to surrender. She ached for her family and for revenge. It was a traumatic memory seared into her brain she would never forget, that fateful night when the savage Argore marauders came to her family farm.

She came to a halt in the dark out of sheer fatigue and nearly fell off her horse. There wasn’t a good place to camp here in the open, but she’d reached the end of her strength that day. She tied the reins to her arm and fell deep asleep in utter exhaustion on the ground beside the horse in an instant. Her sleep was racked with nightmare memories punctuated by her feelings of guilt that she alone had survived while her family had not. The events replayed in her mind constantly as she lamented allowing her father to hide her alone under the floor boards.

She awoke with a start just as the sun was peeking over the horizon. She sat up and scanned the area in all directions for signs of her pursuers. She had no food or water in spite of being famished. What worried her more was having nothing to feed her horse. It was the difference between life and death for her if her horse faltered. Ahead she saw a large forest. It gave her a destination in an area she didn’t know where she might find concealing cover, food and water. Rather than ride, she decided to walk. It was slow progress, but it saved on fatigue for her horse.

The forest appeared to be closer than it really was. She walked all morning without seeming to get any closer. Her legs were already feeling rubbery from her hunger and exhaustion.

She came upon a small stream of gently flowing water and drank thirstily along with her horse. It helped both of them a great deal, but it awakened the hunger pangs in her stomach with cramps. She decided to stop long enough to allow her horse to graze on a small patch of grass. She watched all around protectively, patting the horse gently and possessively, her only living friend at this point.

Afterwards, she resumed her trek toward the forest, still walking the horse. There was still a distance to go, but she finally felt she was getting closer. She daydreamed as she walked for a time, thinking back of better days on her farm, and her happy life there. Her father had been a strong man as well as her older brother. They were demanding in their personal lives, but it took that to eke out a living from an unforgiving land. She had her chores to do, but she didn't mind, liking the chance of contributing her part to the family. Her mother was the balm in her life understanding how a young woman feels and she seemed to know when to do little things for her daughter to ease her moods and to show her love. It wasn't a perfect life, but it was fulfilling enough and she'd been content. None of them had any inkling what was coming for them that morning when they got up that fateful day.

She heard a cry and looked behind her in terror. The Argore raiders were racing toward her, whooping with war cries. She jumped on her horse and galloped toward the forest. Whether that was a mistake, she had no way to know. Her heart was thumping in her chest like it would explode. Her feelings were gone wild with fright. She heard soft sobbing and realized it was she.

She broke through the edge of the tree line and took to a trail going into the interior of that forest. She had no thought in her head other than to flee for her life and escape the deadly hunters.

* * * *

Months of arduous training had, in fact, changed Damon and his two friends. The first thing Argon had done was institute various muscle building exercises. They picked up heavy logs to carry and to run great distances alone and in concert. They ran for untold miles and then ran again. They climbed trees as rapidly as possible, crawled on their bellies, practiced traveling soundlessly, and performed a myriad of other arduous tasks Argon demanded. The initial week had been hell, but gradually, their muscles acclimated to the demand and grew, the pain and soreness subsided, and they started to make rapid progress. When they fought and acquired those weapons skills, it was until they could barely move their arms and legs from exhaustion.

They never made a trip back to the city, so none of their acquaintances there would have recognized them in their new bodies.

The eventual acquisition of martial skills caused an increase in their self-confidence almost to the point of swagger.

"Don't be so taken with yourselves," Argon would caution. He would follow up with personally fighting each of them, or in concert with his immense skills. Initially he humbled them, but with time the gap lessened substantially.

At last they reached a point where they could rightly state they were on a similar level with Argon. He was the clear master, but any of them could at least test him. Their former humbled selves long since discarded to be replaced by better versions. They were warriors now and legitimately so.

It was during a practice session where the three were sprinting along the trail with a huge log on their shoulders that a horse suddenly appeared in their path racing straight at them. It occurred so fast they couldn't immediately see who or what was before them and if there was a threat.

They dropped the log and went to their swords. The horse whinnied and reared up as they blocked its way. The rider fell off the horse with a thud as she hit the ground.

Argon appeared quickly and calmed down the horse and grasped the reins. Damon eased over toward the rider along with his friends. They were shocked to see it was a young woman with long blond hair, a very pretty one. She stared at them in shock like her mind and body wouldn't function properly. Finally she shook her head to clear away the cobwebs, snapped to alertness, and arose warily.

She pulled out a sword to brandish at them. It was very clear she had no idea what to do with it.

"I will not go quietly. Test me if you dare," she challenged.

It made Damon smile and then chuckle. That riled the woman.

"Maiden, we offer no threat to you," said Argon, stepping forward. "Put down your weapon and be at peace with us. I'd say you could use a hot meal and drink."

She looked at him and suddenly her total countenance changed. It was like her false bravado drained away and her youth replaced it. Her face contorted with sorrow and tears formed at the edges of her eyes.

They heard movement approaching down the trail.

"The raiders," she cried in despair. "They have me now."

The Argore war party broke into view and raced toward them with war whoops and swords waving.

"Form a line," Argon ordered. "Get behind us, child."

They were outnumbered two to one, but even against opponents as fierce as the Argore, it wasn't an even fight. Argon scythed through the attackers like he was harvesting wheat. For Damon and his friends, suddenly they were in a fight for their lives. None of them had ever killed a man before. Doing so was a shock, but it happened so fast it was over before they could think about it. It was truly a situation of kill or be killed.

Afterwards they looked around in confusion and dismay. They were frightened, staring at the forest for any new threats.

"Come," said Argon quietly. "The scavengers will clean up the dead. We must be away from here if they have mates following them."

The young woman followed them unquestioningly. Damon glanced at her again. She looked up with challenge in her eyes.

They made their way to the base camp. Berne and Amal started a fire to cook food. Argon turned to the woman.

"I'm Argon, and these are my apprentices, Damon, Berne, and Amal."

"Beth," she answered softly.

"Are you injured or in any distress, Beth?"

"I'm not injured, but I'm in great distress. I don't know where I am, or who you are."

"I'd like for you to tell us your tale, but I think first we should allow you to bathe, to have a meal, and perhaps get some sleep. We'll take care of your horse. You're safe here."

Again Damon saw her become teary eyed.

"Thank you, sir," she replied softly. "It's been so long I've lived in fear. Death has been just a step behind me. I've forgotten what it feels like to be safe. Are you sure we're safe. Those raiders are deadly and they never stop."

"I know of them well, Beth. Please trust us to protect you."

"Thank you, sir."

"Please call us by our names for we stand on no formality here."

"Yes, sir," she replied. Damon chuckled generating a scowl from Argon.

Beth bathed her body savoring a steaming bath, washed her dress but instead of putting it back on she donned a leather forest outfit she borrowed from Berne. He was the slightest of the three boys, but it was still too big on her.

"It feels good to be clean. It's been a long time between baths. I think I prefer to dress as one of you if that's acceptable," she explained to Argon.

"Perhaps we can get you clothes from the city. It's probably best we take you there to start a new life."

"Argon, I lived as a woman on our farm and saw the ending of such a life. I no longer wish to be weak and unarmed. I carry my father's sword but I have no skill with it. I carry his bow but I've had no training. I ask that you transform me as you have done with your apprentices."

Argon looked at her with shock.

"Is the idea of a female apprentice so daunting," she snapped. "Is this a task beyond your abilities?"

Argon chuckled.

"You have no idea what you're asking of me. I don't spend time with young women. How do you expect we would accommodate your, well…?"

"I can take care of myself, and as far as those personal things, you need not concern yourself. It won't be a problem. What's your answer?"

Argon looked at the three young men, all of whom were greatly amused.

"Is this a task beyond you, Master?" Damon chided.

Argon scowled at him.

"If I do this, can the three of you abide her exceeding you with her skills, because that's what will happen? She has in her heart the one thing you three lack. She has that fire which consumes the soul. She can be a living weapon with the rage that burns within her."

Beth smiled darkly.

"So be it, maiden. You shall join our little venture."

"Welcome," said Damon.

She looked at him angrily. "You don't think I can do it. I can see it in how you look at me."

"What? What are you talking about? I don't look at you with judgment. I look at you because you're beautiful."

She looked stunned and confused at his assertion. It wasn't what she expected to hear.

"Damon is a prince in the city, Beth," said Berne.

"Berne, shut up," Damon replied quickly. "Beth, please don't treat me differently. I'm a prince by birth, but that's as far as it goes. My younger brother is the crown prince."

Beth looked astonished. "What a strange turn of events in my life. I'm the daughter of a farmer. We were simple people, so I know nothing about high people. I can only act toward you as I would anyway because I know no different."

"Good, thank you, Beth."

"You think I'm beautiful?" she questioned. "I don't think of myself that way."

Damon started to reply, astonished at her viewpoint, but Argon spoke first. He was sympathetic and gentle with her.

"Beth, I'd like to hear what happened in your life if you're up to it. Sometimes when we carry an inner burden it's useful to share it with others. It can lighten that load."

She looked back at him sadly.

"I don't like to think about it but it haunts me daily. I don't know that I'll ever cope with it. My father owned a farm not far from the northern border. We knew there was danger in the mountains, but those demons living there had never come down upon us. I guess we were complacent about danger so nearby us. We had a tough existence tilling the land, but we were happy. My older brother teased me a great deal, but I knew he loved me down deep. That terrible night they came in the dark. We heard screams from a neighbor's farm and we saw the flames. Father forced me under the floor boards to hide but my mother refused to come down there with me. I feel ashamed that I hid in terror and let my family die."

"Would your dying have changed anything?" asked Argon. "Don't do this to yourself, child. Your father cherished you and wanted you to live on behalf of the family he knew he couldn't save. It was his bravery you must remember. Realizing there was no escape for your whole family, he did the only other thing he could. He saved you."

She was silent a moment before she resumed.

"I know my father and brother fought them, there were enemy dead lying about when I came out, but they couldn't win in that fight. The raiders slew them and then came for my mother. It was terrible beyond description. It was a long time before they finally took her life. I blame myself most for that, lying there like the coward I am while my mother endured such abuse to spare me."

"Child, there was no other way, don't you see? You can't build your new life on this wreckage. Let it motivate you to achieve the most for yourself, but honor your family with the life you live from this point forward. We've killed those Argore who were close on your heels so you can see they're not invincible. We can extract some measure of retribution on your behalf. You can be a mighty instrument against them, but first you must deal with this unfair guilt you feel. If you don't, it will destroy you and possibly us along with you."

"I've never known such hate in my life," she continued. "When you killed them, I rejoiced in it. What kind of person I am to feel such dark things?"

"You're a real person like the rest of us. There's no perfection in the real world. Any of us can be moved by the darkness we encounter in life. You shouldn't dwell on that aspect. I'd say it's better to see what we're doing to counter their evils acts. In this world, I'm sorry to say violence can't be avoided though we would wish otherwise."

She sat solemnly for a time and then looked up at Argon.

"I want to thank you for giving me a chance with you. I won't forget it. You didn't have to show me compassion and generosity but you did instead of taking advantage of me. I was vulnerable in your hands but you protected me. It speaks volumes to me about your character and that is a critical factor for me in choosing a mentor. It's a nice bonus that you also have some martial skills."

Everybody chuckled.

"We'll let you decide later if I have skills," Argon responded mirthfully. "I like you, Beth, but don't misinterpret that to mean I'll go easy on you. You say you want to become our equal. For that goal, it will be an incredibly difficult road for you. I'm sorry but there is no other way. You will always have an alternative life available in the city as a maiden, at least until the Argore come here."

"I've made my choice in that regard. I wish to become a warrior maiden. All that remains for me to reach that status is I have considerable work to do about it."

"As you wish, Beth. Rest to recover your strength. Eat your fill because you'll need strength and vitality. This lengthy time of hunger cannot be reversed in a single meal."

Damon smiled at her. She looked back at him but then turned her face away. It wasn't what Damon wanted, but the rejection of females was something he wasn't unfamiliar with. It was his assumption interpreting her mood as rejection, but it was based on his personal experiences and resulting skewed views rather than actually asking her what she felt. The possibility it might not be a rejection but in fact other things she was dealing with never crossed his mind.

Damon had been crafted into a daunting warrior at that point, but none of his tutoring dealt with the other prior problems in his life.

"Incidentally, Argon, I look forward to the day when you stop calling me, child," Beth added, eyeing him ruefully.

"As do I, child," he responded. "As do I."

"I would say we should head for Kragan tomorrow morning, early," said Amal.

"That's your stomach talking," Berne chided. "You've lost all of this weight here and gotten into fighting shape and you can't wait to get fat again."

"Berne, I will twist you like a pretzel if you don't shut up," Amal retorted. He glanced at Beth to see her reaction. Damon watched and realized his friends viewed Beth as a romantic interest. It vaguely annoyed him.

Beth smiled at their silly exchange. She felt Damon's eyes on her, turned her head and looked at him. What she was thinking with her pensive expression was unreadable for him, but her feminine allure was something he couldn't ignore.

"I heard Chef Mathias has a bounty out on us," Berne continued.

"You're such a dolt," Damon replied, chuckling, breaking his stare at Beth to look at his friends.

"It's true," Berne continued, but he started laughing at his lame joke.

"This is another test for you, Beth," Argon added, "listening to these infants on a daily basis. That's probably your biggest challenge avoiding the insanity they can cause with their idiocy. After a time you want to knock their heads together."

"I can see that," she replied, smirking at Berne and Amal.

"Hey, I object," Berne huffed.

"Me too," Amal added.

They shared a supper of thick meat stew, thick sliced bread to dunk in the stew, cubes of cheese, and slices of fruit. Beth ate hungrily. Her body was still recovering from her extended privation. They downed some berry wine from Kragan with their food. Drinking wine reddened her cheeks with a flush. Not previously being a drinker, she acted less resistant for an evening putting her trust in her new companions.

When it was time to sleep, Damon waited for Beth to pick her spot before he tried to casually ease his bedding near to hers. She looked at him edgily, like he was a threat.

He swallowed his pride and whispered, "Good night, Beth, I'm glad you're with us. I'll see you in the morning."

"Night," she replied and rolled over in her blanket facing the other way.

"That went well," he muttered as he lay back to stare up at the star filled sky. There were no clouds, so it was a beautiful sight the panoply of twinkling lights displayed from horizon to horizon.

In the morning she was already up when Damon opened his eyes. It was dawn and the light was still dim. The air was crisp and they could see their breath in the chill of the morning air.

"Good morning, Beth," he said.

"Morning," she replied. She was facing the lake trying to braid her long hair.

"Would you let me help you?" he asked.

She stopped her efforts.

"Why? Why do you want to help me, Prince? What do you want from me?"

"Trust, for one thing," he answered. "I'm not sure what I've done to make you cautious about me. Is it possible I just want to be helpful?"

She turned her head and eyed him skeptically. "My father taught me people in the world always want something. I believe him."

"I'd like to be your friend, but that seems to be a problem for you."

"I'm in strange territory. No offense, but I don't know you. I'm a cautious person in anything I do. Is that hard for you to understand?"

"Not at all, but I hope you'll make the effort to give us a chance. Is that so difficult a task?"

She smiled. "No, it's a fair request. All right, if you're intent on braiding my hair, get over here and we'll see if you can do it properly. If I'm going to your city, I don't want to look like a…"

"You won't, Beth. I don't think you see yourself the way other people see you."

“Perhaps, but I suspect that’s true for everyone. It’s obviously true for you, Prince Damon.”

“I’m not sure what you mean by that, but I’ll make you look fetching with my awesome braiding skills.”

They both laughed sharing the rare moment of rapport. Getting any connection with Beth gave Damon great satisfaction. Being optimistic about his future with her, however, was far more difficult.

Chapter Four

As they rode toward the city, Damon watched Beth's countenance change from determination to concern. Facing the people of a city seemed to intimidate her which puzzled him.

"Beth, there's nothing for you to worry about," he offered. "They're just people."

"I've never been to a city before. I'm sorry but it's unnerving for me having all of these people gathered around me close together like this."

"We'll be right here with you. It's no big thing."

Hearing them talk, Argon glanced back but said nothing. He smiled wryly at Beth. She scowled at him in return, like he saw her as weak. It added to her angst and her poor mood.

Damon looked at his city as Beth would look at it. The thick massive walls were built from huge thick wood timbers soaked with a flame retardant on the outer course and also the inside wall. They were layered over a course of stone in the center of the wall to add solidity. It would be impossible to smash through that wall, or burn it down. Soldiers could be stationed on the walkway inside near the top to fire at enemies and repel soldiers trying to climb over the wall. The great gate was also made of wood, but so massive it required levers to pivot the huge weight. Breaking through that gate would be another virtually impossible task.

Kragan was relatively more prosperous than their neighboring cities. They were populated with numerous shops offering wares for vanity in addition to those items required to sustain life. The best craftsmen and artisans in the region migrated to Kragan because the king chose to patronize their work and allow them complete creative freedom. Consequently, the inner city was brightly decorated and colorful far more so than any other city. The art collections were the finest anywhere. The standard of the king flapped in the breeze prominently all over the city mirroring the people's love and appreciation for him. His policies benefitted all and supported the positive lives the people enjoyed. He was a rare king in being tolerant in most aspects of life leaving people to make their own choices and to prosper as they could from their labors. Kragan had taxes, been they weren't debilitating to the people like in the other cities.

As he considered these truths, Damon realized the legacy of his father and felt personal pride at what the king accomplished with his reign. He'd never really stopped to look at his home through outsider eyes. He liked what he saw from that perspective. The people were well cared for and content. Equally the royal family, his family, was well thought of, a rarity in the land.

Though it was a crisp day, it was a cloudless sky, clear and invigorating. It lifted Damon's mood, though Beth didn't seem to share in his euphoria.

Many people stared as they rode by. The three former rascals were so changed physically they seemed to be strangers to the masses. Acting self-confident was a major improvement they'd managed from their efforts in the forest and it had an effect on the people viewing them. They had the look of men of great stature.

Beth, too, was an object of considerable attention. A beautiful stranger dressed in a man's oversized clothes. She glanced to the side only to look at children. The look of grim determination returned to her face, like she hoped to slay somebody at some point along the way. It amused Damon. He was happy she was riding beside him. He knew the people would assume she was his romantic mate and it added to his confidence. She was extremely pleasing to the eye.

Their lengthy route to the palace took an hour. Damon wasn't surprised the announcement of their arrival had been forwarded to the palace. Servants waited to take the horses to the stables to water and feed them.

"My Prince," said a young maid, but she stared at Beth. "The king asked you meet him in the throne room."

Damon nodded and followed her. The hallways were packed with curious courtesans gaping at the 'five-some' like they were exhibits in a museum.

The frequent questions they heard were, "Who is she? Why does she dress as a man? Her clothes don't even fit her."

Beth girded her composure to walk this nattering gauntlet of superficial critics.

"Ignore them," Damon whispered. "Think of them as a flock of sheep, sheep without their wool."

Beth smiled and chuckled. "Thank you," she whispered.

Entering the throne room they faced another large gathering. Again the king included generals from the army, high ranking nobles, city dignitaries, and of course the family.

They were seated with solemn looks on their faces, all except the queen. She smiled warmly at her son, returned from his training after so long a time.

He smiled back at her.

Tabor looked grim, unwilling to forget his grievances.

The five stopped before the king and dropped to a knee. Beth followed their example having no experience with royal protocol.

"Rise," said the king. "I'm happy you've returned, my son. Have you achieved your goals?"

"I would say I'm much changed, Your Majesty, but achieving expertise, that's not so easily accomplished, however. I will say we're far better men than we were when we left. We continue to strive for improvement. Master Argon has been an excellent guide helping us down that difficult path."

"Good, but are you saying you'll be returning to the forest?"

"This is true. There's plenty of room for more improvement. The reason we've come is we've made the acquaintance of this young woman, Beth. She was fleeing feral pursuit when she came upon us. She has asked to dwell with us to share the master's tutoring. She had no clothing for this task, so we've come to rectify that problem here in the city. I'm sure the tailors can craft suitable forest garb to meet her needs."

"Granted," said the king.

"If it's your will, we'd like to visit with the queen, if she can spare some time."

He looked directly at Argon and then looked at his wife. Her eyes were down staring at the floor.

"If this is her wish, I won't interfere. Is there anything you need from me?"

"No, Your Majesty, your time is too valuable. We have nothing to offer which would be important enough for you to hear."

No one in the room missed the real reason for the king's request. Did his eldest son wish to spend time with his father? Damon's response did nothing to heal their rift, and the fact he never looked at or acknowledged his brother, Crown Prince Tabor, was a glaring move many perceived as a slight.

"My queen, we'll await your convenience to meet with you. Please send word to us when you're ready."

"Of course," she answered.

They turned to walk out.

"Welcome back, brother," said Tabor, in sharp punctuated words.

"Thank you," he answered evenly, but he never looked back and he never stopped walking away. Beth looked at him though before following the men out the door of the royal chamber.

They went to Damon's palace rooms. He closed the door on the royal guards watching Argon and they finally felt they could relax.

"Do you want us to go to our homes?" asked Berne.

"If you want to see your families, but I have no problem with keeping us all together here. I think Argon's perpetual vigilance and distrust of every other living person has rubbed off on me. Do you have a problem sleeping here in my suite, Beth? It will be viewed at court as scandalous."

"I have no thought about such things. I wouldn't choose to be separated from the others of you for the reasons you named."

"Good, feel free to avail yourself of all of the facilities here. You can enjoy soaking in a nice steaming bath."

There was a tap on the door. Damon went to open it. Servants carried in trays of food and delicacies, sweet desserts and excellent berry wine.

"I think we should eat first before we go visiting," said Amal.

"You're a pig, Amal," Berne chided.

"The name for you I can't use in front of a lady, Berne."

They dined on the feast until they were stuffed to the point of feeling uncomfortable. Beth went to the bathing room and closed the door after Damon gave her instructions to operate the plumbing. Berne and Amal slipped out of the suite.

"We'll return soon, Damon," said Berne. "We're a team now and we'll stay that way."

"Say hello for me to your families."

"We will."

While Damon waited for her, Beth stayed in her relaxing bath for over an hour before she came out including washing her hair twice.

"I never knew people live this way," she reflected in awe. "We were always hungry on the farm. To have this excess of food is astounding to me. Somehow it doesn't seem right."

"I understand you," Damon replied. "I was raised in wealth, but early on I understood about the poor and how lucky I had it. I've spent many nights hunting to feed them. It wasn't much, but at least I was doing something to balance the inequity."

"Truly, you hunted to feed the poor? You're a royal prince."

"It was a choice I made to be able to live with myself. I had the same impression as you, that it wasn't right how things were."

"Is there a problem you have with your brother? I noticed hostility in that meeting, Damon."

Damon paused a moment staring away out the window before he answered her question. "He thinks I want to replace him to take the throne. I don't want it, but he won't believe me because he could never feel the way I do. He can only see things through his eyes of coveting the throne and power."

"That's a great shame. I loved my brother."

"I love him, but there are issues between us I can't overcome by myself."

"Your father seemed to wish you would ask to spend time with him."

"There is a chasm between us we've never managed to broach. It's easiest to simply go about our lives separately. It's how he wants it. He has his favored heir in line for his throne. That's enough for him."

"Are you sure about that, Damon? That's not what I saw and I'm a stranger here. You have only one father. I have none. He was taken from me."

Damon grimaced at her pain. "I'm sorry, Beth. Perhaps we can be your family now if you will allow it."

Argon sat silently watching the exchange. Damon looked for judgment in his eyes but he saw contemplation instead. He was pondering some issue of his own life. Guiding his students in personal matters didn't seem to be something he wanted to do.

Now it was Beth lost in her emotions staring vacantly out the window.

They heard a tap on the door. Guards opened the door and the queen entered the room.

"Is this a bad time, Damon?" She was looking at the distress on Beth's face.

"I'm sorry, Your Majesty," Beth whispered. "I'm not doing well controlling my feelings today."

"Child, it isn't a problem. I'd like to spend a little time with all of you if it is agreeable."

"Of course, Mother. We're glad to have you here," Damon replied.

The queen came over to the bed and sat down beside Beth eyeing her with compassion before she spoke.

"What is it? I'd like to help you if I can."

"There's nothing you can do, Your Majesty. I can't escape the loss of my family. I was so close to my mother but she's gone forever. My father hid me from the Argore raiders, but my mother refused. She didn't want to live without her husband. I'll never forget those sounds of her suffering. I was a coward to lie there trembling. I should not have survived that night. I don't deserve to be here now."

Thick tears rolled down her cheeks and she began to sob. The face of the queen was stricken with pain at the story. She grabbed Beth on impulse and hugged her tightly. She kissed the top of her head gently.

"No one should experience such horror, or feel such misplaced guilt. You had no fault for that terrible night, Beth. Guilt lies elsewhere."

Beth could only sob wretchedly in despair.

"I'm alone now," she whispered. "They're all gone, my whole family."

"You'll never be alone again, Beth," the queen answered soulfully. "Will you allow me to be your friend? I never had a daughter. Would you let me become close to you?"

Beth sobbed but nodded her head. She sat up. "I'm sorry to be so weak. I never got a chance to grieve. I had to run for my life after that night."

"Let me comb your beautiful hair. I always wanted to do that. I've envied watching mothers with their daughters."

"It isn't necessary, ma'am. You're a queen. I'm just a farm girl."

"It would be my pleasure. Please say yes, Beth."

She pulled her own comb out of her pocket and gently stroked Beth's silky smooth hair. Beth closed her eyes and smiled with contentment.

"You remind me of her, my mother. She would comb my hair for hours while we talked. It was a great comfort for me. She made me feel safe. I had her exclusively all to myself at those times, she was so patient. I learned so much because she had experiences. She was city born so she told me about cities and city dwellers. I was curious to see a city, but not that curious. I was happy to be safe on our farm if that makes sense."

"It makes perfect sense, Beth. I really do hope you'll allow me to become close with you. I'd like that very much."

Beth shrugged her shoulders, but smiled at the queen. "I would like that too."

"I must ask you, are you sure this is the path you want to follow, becoming a warrior? It's your choice, but I can guarantee you a good life here living with us in Kragan."

"Thank you, ma'am, but I have my reasons. Never again will I be helpless before any man. I couldn't ignore what was done to my family. I must make an answer to their savagery. It's not something I can get past otherwise. Perhaps you can't understand, but it's an open wound that burns in my soul. I'm filled with hatred and it dominates me."

"I'm sorry, Beth. I hope that doesn't define the rest of your life."

"It's all I can manage right now, I'm sorry."

"I must go for now as I have some royal duties, but possibly we can meet again?"

"Certainly, Your Majesty, I look forward to it."

The queen arose and turned to embrace her son. "Damon, I wish you could stay longer."

"I have much more work to do, Mother. I'm sorry too. For me there's no way around it. I've made great progress but I'm not where I need to be."

They queen nodded and left them.

After she left, Damon looked at Beth as she sat silently staring out the window deep in her painful memories and choked with difficult emotions of loss and shame at what she still felt was her failing in not trying to help her mother. She was beyond the touch of logic that she would have died horribly had she made such a foolish attempt. Thick tears rolled down her face still and splashed on her top leaving large wet spots. It evoked sadness in him too.

Damon pondered trying to comfort Beth, as his mother had just done, but he didn't feel qualified for the task. His turbulent emotional history factored in to his viewpoint in virtually every facet of his life.

The other person in the room, Argon, also seemed to be daunted by the moment as he looked on like an unintended eavesdropper. He looked at Beth reflectively, still dealing with issues of his own she seemed to evoke in him.

Their joint though separate contemplations were broken by another rap on the door. The outer guards opened the door to admit Selena with a group of her female acquaintances. They were dressed elegantly in expensive dresses, bright colored with tight laced bodices, but what Damon noticed was the looks on their faces, smugness and to an extent, contempt. They looked at Beth disdainfully. Even amongst her gorgeous friends, Selena stood out like a rose between the thorns. Her full bodied long brown hair flowed over her shoulders, chest and back. Her hair was her pride, the envy of other women, and a lure for men. With her angelic face with delicate facial features, she was the center of attention in every room she entered. A lifetime of such attention crafted her into a confident self-assured young woman. Her friends, though also beautiful, were lesser lights in her shadow.

In contrast to Selena, her two close friends, Katherine and Elle had straight blond locks. The several other women with her had hair of various colors. Uniformly they were pretty but they weren't a group Damon would have chosen to spend any time with.

They moved to circle Beth where she sat. Beth still stared out the window, but finally she glanced at them when one of the women made a snide comment.

"Nice clothes."

The women were like a pack of vultures waiting for their prey to die. They chuckled at the rude comment.

"Ladies," said Selena reproachfully. "I'm sure she has a reason for wearing these mannish clothes. We were hoping you would join us at a party we've arranged for tonight. It will be a grand time. If this is your preferred clothing choice, you may dress as you like."

Damon cringed at the affront and for the first time, Beth came out of her funk. She recognized what she was facing here with the mean attitude of these 'city women'. She also recognized their trap, their desire to humiliate her though she wasn't sure why. She had no prior experience with 'catty' girls.

"I'm sorry, My Lady," she replied evenly. "I'm the daughter of a farmer. I have no experience with refined folk such as you. If my appearance offends you, I apologize. It wasn't my intention. Perhaps you haven't heard I'm going into martial training with Master Argon and his charges."

"Why would you do that?" asked Selena in true curiosity. "You're a woman."

"I have difficult goals which a cruel life has put upon me."

"I don't understand," Selena replied, glancing at Damon in confusion.

"It isn't a matter I discuss with strangers. I will only say my life has been trying. I have unfinished business on behalf of my family."

Damon felt a helpless spectator observing the unexpected female contest. He too couldn't grasp Selena's purpose since she was his brother's girl. It was another situation where he wanted to intervene to protect Beth, but this wasn't his arena. This was a battle Beth had to fight on her own.

Beth's comments didn't blunt the assault. Selena simply looked calculating, glancing again at Damon.

"I gather you claim friendship with the prince, Beth. We've known each other since childhood. I don't know Master Argon as a tutor, but I can tell you Damon is the most skilled hunter in the city. There is much he can teach you about wood lore and hunting skills. I think he has no peer amongst us."

Damon was surprised and a little embarrassed. He'd never heard Selena speak so favorably about him before. Actually, he'd never thought she paid much attention to him at all. He had no idea how he should react. He looked at Beth to gauge her reaction.

Selena smiled at Damon, walked over and put a hand on his powerful shoulder. Damon frowned. He would have given anything for this attention from Selena before, but now he was stricken with competing emotions. It was gratifying to have her rare positive words, but Beth had come to be important to him. Seeing Beth's face, like he'd proven to be a faulty companion, it bothered him a great deal.

"Beth, do I assume you have romantic plans for our prince?" asked Selena pointedly.

Beth frowned. "Selena, it seems you and your friends misunderstand me. I'm not here to pursue romance with your prince, or any other man for that matter. My focus now is, and always has been on hardening my body and gaining war skills. Nothing else matters to me. I thank you for your invitation to your social event. Please don't take offense that I decline. I'm not a person of any importance for you to waste your time about. I'll be out of your city at the soonest possible time. I wish you and your friends the best with your event and with your lives."

Beth turned her face back to stare out the window, effectively dismissing Selena and her friends. Some of the women huffed indignantly. However, Selena nodded.

"Beth, I also wish you well in your daunting endeavor. You've chosen a path few women would ever consider. I don't know you, but I think perhaps you have the fortitude to prevail where most others would fail."

She turned her head and looked at Damon.

"My Prince."

Damon nodded to her.

"Come ladies, we've taken enough of their valuable time."

Damon watched them file out the door in radically different moods then when they'd entered. Their intended victim wasn't the easy mark they'd expected.

After the door was closed he walked over to Beth.

"What did you mean when you said you don't want any man? Are you saying you don't intend to be a wife, ever?"

Beth sat silently for a moment before she replied. "Being a wife isn't one of my goals. I have other concerns of far greater importance to me."

She turned her face toward him. "Is that so foreign a concept, Prince?"

"I, eh…"

"Why is it a concern for you what I choose? I'm still just a simple farm girl. I'm not from your city. You have no responsibility for me."

"Beth, I'm not a man who has great skill with words. I don't know how you see me as a man, but know that you matter to me, though it would seem that you don't wish for my regard. I'm sure my errors and my many flaws are off putting for you. I can only apologize I'm not a better person."

She got a confused look.

"You're a royal prince, Damon. What possible interest could you have in a common woman, not even from your city?"

"Do you truly not understand?"

The concept of his intent seemed to dawn on her for the first time. She glanced at Argon who'd remained silent through the exchange.

"I can only tell you I must focus totally on my task, Damon. I'm too simple a person to grasp the complexities of city lives and considerations."

The doors opened and Berne and Amal returned to the room. They looked at the two curiously.

"Are we interrupting something?" asked Berne.

"No," said Beth, eyeing them warmly. "Welcome back, did you enjoy seeing your families?"

"Yes, Beth," Amal replied. "It was strange to be treated as men. We've been such embarrassments before. I think they now have hopes we'll no longer shame them."

Beth smiled. "You've never been a shame for me."

Amal and Berne smiled broadly at her compliment.

"You've never been an embarrassment for us either," said Berne, foolishly.

Beth chuckled. "That's good news for me, kind sirs."

Both of them stared at her, agog. That they were hopelessly taken with her was glaringly obvious. Again, it irked Damon they could have aspirations about Beth too.

"We'll leave for the forest at dawn," said Argon. "We have plenty of work ahead and time is short to reach your goals. Beth, I hope you understand I can't coddle you if you truly wish to become competent. Whatever the men are doing, you will do also. You're a woman, but you must develop your strength. Fighting against men intent on killing you isn't a situation where you can expect forbearance and latitude. You must be better than them every time. One weak moment and your life could be over. Do you understand?"

"I understand perfectly, Master. It's exactly as I would have it. When I meet those demons who took my family from me, I'll have an answer to their vileness. They can't do such horror and expect to face no consequences. I pray I can be the equal of the task."

"Sleep well tonight. It will be your last easy night. I take no pleasure in the pain I must impose on you. If there was another way, I wouldn't subject you to it, believe me."

"I agreed to the training, Master. You do what you must, and I accept that pain gladly."

"You will sleep in the bed, Beth. We'll all sleep on the floor."

"That isn't necessary, Master."

"Don't ever refuse my instructions, Beth. Here in this moment, I'm granting you an amenity. Unfortunately there will be few of them ahead. Simply accept what I offer. I have good reasons for everything I do. I won't take away from valuable time to explain them.

"Yes, Master. I'm your obedient servant from this point forward. I'll do whatever you require of me without question."

"Good, Beth. After we dine this evening we'll bed down early. Damon, would you leave instructions that we be served an early breakfast tomorrow morning?"

"I'll see to it now, Master."

"I'll ask you one more time to be sure you completely understand and accept the path you've chosen, Beth," Argon continued. "You will face every test as your male companions. You'll be living with us so expecting accommodation for your female matters will be impossible. We'll do what we can to respect your modesty, but even there you must exercise good judgment."

"If you're talking about my monthly bleeding, I'll tell you I'm not a moody woman as some others are. I won't allow it to affect our training."

They all looked at her skeptically.

She scowled. "Don't judge me by the other women you've known. I can control myself."

Damon smiled weakly. Selena was notorious for her abrupt personality changes from that issue being often foul tempered and irritable. Even his mother the queen experienced changes for that week each month.

"So be it," said Argon.

Damon went out the door to go to the kitchens. He smiled to see the sudden scowl on the face of the master chef at seeing him approaching.

"I don't know what you want, Prince Damon, but the answer is no."

Damon chuckled, walked up and patted the chef on the shoulder.

"Can we not put aside our differences? I admit I was a poor citizen as a child but I've turned over a new leaf, so to speak. Actually, I was sent by Master Argon, our mentor. He wishes to advise you that we must leave early tomorrow with the rising of the sun. He asks for an early breakfast to assist our prompt return to the forest."

"So, you think I should lose my sleep catering to your whims, Prince? Do you never have consideration for others? I'm not a young man. I need my sleep to be able to face the daily tests of running the royal kitchen."

"It isn't necessary that you personally make the meal. Perhaps you could delegate the task to your underlings?"

"What? You know I'm responsible for every morsel of food that leaves this kitchen. Do you honestly think I'd allow you the chance to besmirch my reputation if another failed in the preparations? Do you think me a complete fool? I'll personally prepare this extorted meal you demand. I understand you have a lady amongst your troop so, on her behalf, I'll prepare Eggs Benedict. For you I should cook beans drowned in bacon fat, but to show you I'm the greater person here, I'll grant you fine cuisine also. What do you say to that, Brat Prince?"

Damon laughed. "I say thank you, Master Chef. Will you allow me to repay your kindness? Perhaps I could obtain some certain chocolate you favor?"

"Chocolate, from the south?" asked the chef, his eyes suddenly aglow at the thought. "For this kindness, I'll include those cinnamon pastries you like so much."

"It's done then. We'll be leaving tomorrow, but I'll leave instructions to have the chocolate delivered to you when it arrives."

"Thank you, My Prince," he cooed. "That chocolate is a weakness of mine. I'll accept your offer gladly."

"Good day to you. I must return to our room. Thank you again. We'll see you in the morning, Chef Mathias."

Damon smiled as he left the kitchen. It was one of the first times he wasn't being chased away by the master chef. Times had indeed changed.

He went back to the suite. The door guards saluted as he approached and opened the doors. Beth had apparently bathed again in the interim, enjoying a luxurious bath for the final time before the grueling training started. She was sitting on the bed combing out her long hair. Amal and Berne were sitting entranced like two puppies, talking at her as much as with her. Argon was studying some maps.

Beth looked up at him. He nodded.

"Beth is telling us about life on a farm," said Berne.

"Oh? What have you learned, Berne?"

His face suddenly clouded. Questions had never been his friend going back to his school days as an underperforming student.

"I, eh…" he stammered.

"Damon," said Beth reproachfully.

"I was just curious what I missed," Damon replied defensively.

"Right," said a skeptical Amal.

"What of the morning meal?" Argon interrupted.

"Everything is arranged, Master. We should be on the road promptly, as you requested."

"Good, Damon, thank you."

Beth went back to toweling her hair and continued combing it. She ignored the male attention. When she finished the task she went to sit at the table with Argon.

"May I join you, Master?"

"Of course, Beth."

"What are you studying?"

"These are local maps of this region. I want to be sure I'm familiar with the territory. Sometimes unexpected events happen which require a hasty exit. I always want to have a place to go, if need be."

"I understand. When I fled from my home, I wish I'd had an idea of what was around me and the best place to go. It was pure luck I happened upon you and saved my life in the process."

"That's an excellent example. Being prepared at every moment can be the difference between life and death. Often it isn't the most worthy who survive, it's the people who live on an edge. Being salty is a good way to be, I think so anyway."

"I agree, Master."

"You look very nice, Beth. You have lovely hair."

"Thank you, Master. I have my mother's hair. My father often combed it for her. He took great delight in those close moments they could share. Sometimes she allowed him to wash her hair too. How they acted together at those times, I felt like I was an unwelcome intruder on their private time. Now I look back and would give anything to have them back."

Argon seemed about to share something of his past, but he frowned and looked away.

"We all have things in our lives we would change if we could."

"Argon, before we start this training, I want to thank you again," Beth added. "Not many men would give a woman such a chance. I'm in your debt and I will find a way to repay you."

"You owe me nothing. I think after a week you may not feel so anxious to reward me. I think probably you'll be dreaming of a million ways to torture me."

Beth laughed.

There was another knock on their door. The guards opened the door to admit Prince Tabor. He looked around at all of the faces in an awkward moment.

"Am I not welcome here?" he asked pointedly.

"Of course, you're welcome, brother. This is your city and your palace. We're simply guests at your disposal."

"Selena advised me she invited you to her social event and you declined. Why is that, Brother?"

"We have an early departure tomorrow morning at dawn followed by an arduous day of training. We needed our rest before we begin the ordeal."

Tabor walked over to Beth.

"I'm sorry I haven't had the chance to spend time getting to know you, My Lady."

He bowed to her.

"I'm not a social person, Crown Prince, and I'm a commoner so it isn't necessary to refer to me with My Lady," she replied. "As I explained to your women friends, I'm not here to do social things."

"I find that to be a great disappointment. I'd love to show you the wonders of my city."

Damon bristled and grimaced as Beth stared at the incredibly handsome Tabor and gave him a small smile. Damon looked away but Tabor had already seen his reaction and smiled.

"I appreciate your generous offer, Crown Prince, but perhaps another time?"

"I'll look forward to it." He took her hand and kissed it.

The possibility Tabor could impress Beth where Damon seemingly couldn't, it burned in his gut. The fact she'd used 'Crown Prince' in addressing him said to Damon it made a difference to her, like she was thoughtful about his failure to prevail against his brother.

"Goodbye, Brother," said Tabor, smiling like he'd scored another triumph.

Damon grimaced, but simply nodded. Both brothers clearly understood the nature of the exchange and who was perceived as the victor in the moment.

Chapter Five

Damon wrestled with his emotional issues and it took a long while before he could fall asleep that night. The others were quick to doze off, but Damon struggled with yet another bout of feeling inadequate, something he'd thought was behind him. All of the confidence he'd gained working for Argon seemed to have drained away in one moment. Once again, he felt to be the poor shadow to his brother's radiance. There were too many memories of failures for him to simply dismiss from his mind. He questioned if he could ever understand women and reach a point of achieving any competence around them. Self-castigation was too easy to revisit. Lying on the hard floor while Beth occupied his soft bed didn't help. Every time she moved the squeak of the bed springs echoed in his head, tantalizingly close and untouchable. Amal's snoring didn't help either.

He awoke the next morning poorly rested and a little groggy. When they went to the dining hall they were greatly surprised when Master Chef Mathias personally served the breakfast because the queen also rose early to join them. Damon quickly downed a cup of strong coffee to gather his wits and clear away the cobwebs.

"I hope I'm not intruding," the queen remarked rhetorically.

"Of course not, Mother," Damon replied warmly smiling gratefully for her surprise visit. "I cherish every moment I can have in your presence. I'm sorry you had to lose sleep though with rising so early."

She chuckled and hugged her son.

"You may think the life of a queen is very busy with important tasks. In truth, often I'm required to do mundane things in the company of people I don't prefer to spend time with. I don't mind getting up early to be with all of you. Beth, did you sleep well? I hope you've had a chance to think about my offer of a close friendship. It's important to me."

"I'm flattered, Your Majesty," she answered. "Of course I accept your companionship. I felt close to you from the first moment we met. You're a good person. I thank you for your courtesy with a stranger and a lowly commoner. To answer your question, I did sleep well. The men were kind enough to cede the royal bed to me. They would not take no for my answer."

The queen laughed again. "You have an appealing way, Beth. I wish more women were like you. I want to say I respect your determination in the face of such a difficult life choice. It's another trait for others to learn from your example. If everyone had your grit, I think we'd have a much better world. If I was young, I might choose to stand at your side in the training. Women in this world lack for enough adventure."

"Thank you, ma'am, I don't see what I'm doing as special but I accede to your kind words. I'll do my best."

"Your Majesty," said Mathias as he placed before her the first breakfast serving for her approval before serving the others.

"Thank you," she answered with a kindly smile. "I'm sure it will be delicious as always, Mathias."

They ate the food in no great hurry as Damon enjoyed the time with his mother. Beth chatted amicably with the queen pleased by the interest from royalty and a mother figure. When they finished the meal and collected their things, she hugged her tightly.

The queen then turned back to her son, Damon.

"Be careful, My Son. Every time you go out into that dangerous forest, I worry."

"I'll be fine, Mother. I'm no longer a little boy. I can take care of myself, and I'll be surrounded by skilled companions. Tell my father and brother farewell and I hope the best for them. I've come to realize the wonder of my father's reign. His city is a marvel and he deserves the credit for it. I never wanted to be his embarrassment as a son, and now I'm finally capable of appreciating his considerable accomplishments, though I'm sure he doesn't believe me."

"Your father loves you, Damon. He regrets the state of your relationship and wishes it otherwise. He would change things, but I think you're both too stubborn and set in your ways. It's a matter you should resolve. Things should never have been allowed to get to this point."

"You're probably right, Mother. Whenever I'm brought before him, I feel all of those old tensions, like I should be ashamed to be alive. I don't blame him any longer and I'm working on not blaming me."

"I've long hoped you'd reach a point you could see yourself as others see you, Damon. You're much beloved in the city for your generosity, selflessness, and empathy. Those aren't traits you can mimic, they're born into you."

"I got those traits from you, Mother."

"I don't know about that, Son. I appreciate your compliment. I've always been proud of you."

"At any rate, we must be going, goodbye, Mother."

They went outside where their horses were tethered.

"Are you ready for this, Beth?" asked Damon.

"I am," she answered, tightening her new forest garb against the cold wind. "Actually, I'm anxious to get started."

They rode away into the frosty morning in the dim light of dawn. They could see their breath billowing from their mouths and from their horses mouths too. Damon pulled his jacket closed buttoning the top slots against the chilly breeze. He glanced at Beth. Her cheeks were already reddened from the wind and the temperature. Her long hair flapped in the brisk wind.

They traveled steadily to the forest and followed the familiar trail leading to their forest camp. As always, it required great vigilance at this early hour as herd animals were on the move which meant the predators were also about and on the prowl. Lone travelers would have been in greater peril then a fast moving group of riders on the trail.

Damon looked up into the sky and saw dark clouds of a weather front rolling their way.

"Great," he muttered as they rode along. "A major storm is a great way to resume the training, as if it's not difficult enough without weather issues added in."

"What?" Beth yelled. "Did you say something to me?"

"No, I was just talking to myself."

He smiled at her pretty face. She frowned and turned her head away.

It took a long time to complete the journey before they came to a halt in the camp and dismounted. A wolf came out of the woods and growled at them, but it quickly left on the run. They carried their supplies into the cabin they'd built and put the horses in the small barn safe from predators.

Beth looked at the beds in the cabin. "Which one is mine?"

"The three of them will be over there," Argon explained. "I'm sorry we can't give you seclusion. I'll be here and you'll be on the other side of me."

"That's fine, Master," she answered. "I'll manage just fine."

Damon was disappointed at his lack of progress with her and did his best not to show it. His feelings for Beth were growing on a daily basis and the fact she didn't show him any romantic interest in return didn't stop his evolving feelings. He also recognized a similar reaction in his friends. They too shared his fascination with Beth. It irked Damon she seemed to act more favorably to Amal and Berne than to him.

Again, he was his own worst enemy. Viewing romantic situations impartially and accurately were beyond him in his current state. His skewed versions of reality tended to cloud his judgments into wrong directions. The residual of his old self haunted him still.

His answer was to turn again to anger, his old standby. Though he thought of it as the righteous indignation of a wronged man, it was actually petulance and misguided transference of accumulated rage without a valid reason.

Argon eyed Damon, like he could read his mind. He said nothing, but Damon felt another familiar emotion, he was ashamed of his flaws.

Beth acted oblivious to Damon's turmoil. She laid out her things and turned to Argon with a ready smile.

"I'm ready to start, Master."

Argon smiled back at her and shrugged.

"Come, my children, duty calls."

They filed out of the cabin into an increasing wind that cut through their warm clothes.

"Beth, I regret to say the first thing we must start is to develop your muscles. They've been doing this for months so they're hardened to the task. You will join them to carry that heavy log for a run. Do the best you can, but realize you can't close the gap with them in one day. Don't get discouraged."

"I understand, Master."

They picked up the log. Beth stationed herself between Amal and Berne, irritating Damon further. The task was no easier with her added to the team. The heavy log tested them all. She lasted much longer than Damon would have thought before she was forced to drop out to the side, bending over at the waist and panting heavily. She massaged her neck and shoulder muscles.

"Take whatever rest you need," said Argon eyeing her clinically to assess her fitness level.

Instead of resting she gritted her teeth, and then she jogged over to rejoin the men in the arduous task. They finished the trek and moved on to the next assignment. Beth showed a certain amount of natural aptitude when they put a sword in her hand. She only lacked strength and practice, but even on her first day, she surprised them with some of her lightning moves and with her ferocity. Argon took her aside to practice standard moves and countermoves, as well as beginning to teach her some moves he'd never taught to the men. It was incredible she could still function physically on her first day with her sore muscles.

She was a quick study and she was diligent. When they came back to the cabin at dusk, she was drained completely, but she doggedly kept her eyes open as Argon explained many things of war to her.

When she lay her head down on her pillow she fell deep into sleep immediately.

Beth endured the initial week of tormented muscles and daunting assignments in silence unwilling to fail and give up her goals no matter how painful the tests.

"How are you faring, Beth?" Argon asked her frequently. "Do you still feel the fire within you?"

"Yes, Master. I knew it would be supremely difficult, but this is my desire. I'll endure this, somehow."

"Beth, you can do it. After this first week, it will get better for you. I'm seeing improvement in your strength already. Have faith, child."

"I know, Master."

Argon devised some different kinds of strengthening exercises exclusively for Beth, in addition to what she did in concert with the men. His prediction came true that she did feel noticeably better starting with the second week, her body no longer in perpetual torment.

Within a month, her body was markedly transformed, taut and fit. As beautiful as she'd been before, the physical work reformed her body to near perfection of appearance. Her curves were extenuated and her legs were taut, and her hips idyllic. That development did nothing to douse the adoration of the three young men. They had to fight daily to keep from ogling at her and from making silly statements to draw her notice. In that fight they were only partially successful. She was just too alluring and it brought out foolish acts in all the young men. Argon said nothing to their gaffs as long as no problems developed leaving it to Beth to fend them off.

Beth wasn't unaware of their clumsy interest. She simply chose to ignore it to concentrate on her physical goals. Nothing mattered more to her than becoming lethal as fast as possible. Responding to their awkward overtures would have wasted time and distracted her concentration from her goals, so she developed her own ways to cope. She gave none of them any hopes at all. Her emotions were locked within her, separate and private, just like her life. She revealed only select facets.

As they sparred in joint practice over time, the men shared the mutual feeling Argon favored Beth, his new favorite and prized pupil.

Damon tried to learn from afar the moves Argon was teaching her separately, watching their private sessions closely. In her second month she began to do more than react to the attacks of her male counterparts, she started to take the offensive and it wasn't something rudimentary. She was quick and decisive in her swordplay and gradually she was transforming her skill to a higher level. None of the three men could easily handle the fights with her any longer. They stopped holding back as she reached their measure of skill and began to exceed them. Her aggressive lightning moves were a danger even in supposedly controlled fights. Beth was always driven and never relented like the practice in sparring were real fights.

Berne was the first one to experience the humiliation of having his sword knocked from his hand by Beth. How he handled it was much better than Damon could have.

“Beth, that was incredible. I bow to your superiority.”

She smiled warmly and rewarded him with a firm hug and a kiss on the cheek.

“Thank you, Berne. I feared you would despise me if I bested you.”

“That could never happen, Beth. I rejoice at your prowess. If we were ever forced into battle, I’m glad you could answer that call and I wouldn’t need to worry about you.”

“You’re a rare and a wonderful man, Berne. There aren’t many men who’d be so magnanimous. You occupy a special place in my heart.”

She never looked at Damon, who felt devastated. Instead, she turned to Argon who smiled.

“Don’t be so taken with your success, Beth,” he reflected. “This is an important step, but we have far to go.”

“Of course, I’m sorry, Master. You’re right I should control my feelings. It’s just that it’s been so hard to get to this point. I allowed myself to savor it too much. I apologize.”

“That’s not what I meant, Beth,” he responded. “War is an unforgiving art. As good as we see ourselves, as skillful as we become, it’s no guarantee against a lucky sword stroke, a stray arrow, or a surprise attack by overwhelming forces. Don’t get me wrong, I rejoice with your accomplishment, but never lose your edge and your vigilance.”

“Yes, Master.”

He walked over to embrace her.

She chuckled and hugged him tightly.

“I’m proud of you, Beth. You already know that.”

Watching the development while standing aside, Damon stood a moment in a daze, feeling as if he’d again been rendered irrelevant. Amal walked over to Beth.

“Congratulations, Beth. I’m also happy that you’ve made it to this esteemed state. I would be proud to have you at my side in any battle.”

“Thank you, Amal,” she replied, hugging him also.

It prompted Damon into motion. He walked up to her seeing her eyes aglow, but when she looked at him, her expression changed slightly. She couldn’t look him in the eyes.

“I want to add my congratulations, Beth. That was a great fight and a remarkable ending. We all knew you could do it. We’re all proud of you.”

“You’re proud of me?” she questioned.

“Of course, why wouldn’t we be?”

She didn't answer him, but she did look into his eyes.

He felt his emotions gather as they stared. Beth reacted breaking the moment by turning her face away.

"Thank you, Prince," she said quietly.

"Come inside, everyone, this is a good time for a meal," said Argon, after an awkward moment.

* * * *

Another month of training added further skill and strengthening to Beth. Although the men worked diligently, her progress out shadowed theirs just as Argon had predicted. She worked on Argon's moves, but she started to try to develop moves of her own. Her cat like reflexes set her apart from the men who, though they were all daunting fighters, none of them were swordsmen without peer like Beth was becoming. Argon fought with Beth increasingly and from what Damon could see, she was a test even for him.

By this time, she'd grown in more than just her physical appearance. She was supremely confident and showed command presence that kings and queens would have envied. To say she was breathtaking to the eye was a colossal understatement, but it meant nothing to her. The only person she seemed to care about impressing was Argon. He was her standard of behavior and guide to improvement. His efforts to keep her humble were increasingly difficult. She merely looked at him with mirth and in fact it seemed it was she who humbled him.

Beth was friendly with Amal and Berne, and civil with Damon, but she never allowed him the closeness he craved. Seldom talking about her past, her feelings, and her perceptions, when she did so, it was in low tones with Argon, her trusted mentor.

That was another ongoing irritant for the prince feeling on the outside looking in, helpless to change it. Gradually, he couldn't help his mood souring with his endless feelings of rejection from her and that was a change which she noticed. Afterwards for the first time, she seemed to pay attention to him and what he was doing. She even spoke to him initiating conversation which hadn't been her habit before but he was too far gone at that point.

Finally, she asked him one day after the evening meal.

"Prince Damon, is there a problem between us? I've felt a shift in your opinion of me lately. Have I done something to earn your ire?"

"What?" he asked in surprise at her spin on their rocky relationship. "I could ask you the same thing, Beth. I thought us friends at the very least, but I always seem to be the least of your companions. You say I've treated you differently. Has that not been the case with you all this time we've been together? What did I do to earn your scorn? I realize I have many flaws, but I have no recollection of causing you any offense. If I have I don't remember it. Please feel free to enlighten me."

She looked shocked. "Prince, I'm taken aback by your accusation. I meant no harm to you. If you've read some motive into my behavior, you're wrong. I too see you as a friend. I'm a commoner. I didn't think it proper I act with unwarranted familiarity with a royal person. It isn't my place. I'm not of your status in society. You're above me in every way. I didn't know you misread my actions. I sincerely apologize for the misunderstanding."

"Beth," he said, mellowing his anger and frowning in disappointment, "I'm a man who's made mistakes the norm in my life. As I've told you before, I'm the least skilled to speak my mind, and my heart, to any woman. I'm the one needing to apologize to you. Just because I'm a prince, it doesn't make me a worthy person. I know that from a long and painful life. I can't know what's in your heart, but I feel moved to share with you what's in mine. Will you hear me?"

Beth looked daunted and frightened, like she could tell what was coming and couldn't deal with it.

"From the first time I saw you, I, eh…"

He looked in her eyes, suddenly hesitant to go further and put himself out there with the chance to be rejected and humiliated, again, by a woman. She had a neutral expression on her face.

"What, Prince?" she asked.

"Perhaps I'm a fool to admit this, but I desired you then and the feeling has never left me since."

"Why, I'm not a special person. What makes me different? You have a city full of beautiful women who would kill for the chance to be your companion. I've told you my purpose in life. You know the burden I carry and the cost of it."

"Beth, there's nobody you could find who would agree with you that you're not a special person. Surely you know I'm hopelessly in love with you, and so are Amal and Berne, for that matter. You are a special person. It's an undeniable fact."

She shook her head in denial.

"What do you want from me, Prince? If you have a thought for me to warm your bed, I must tell you that isn't my way. I don't mean you any offense, but I've chosen a different path to follow. I don't see a time when I could carry a child to term. Do you understand? There are plenty of other women willing to fulfill that role for you."

"Beth, no, I certainly didn't mean anything seamy. I'm trying to speak the truth in my heart. Do you not hear what I'm saying? I care about you deeply.

I've never had such feelings for any other woman."

"I don't know what to say. I can only reiterate I'm not at a point to seek such a relationship. I cherish your friendship. Were I of a different mindset, I would be honored by your interest. Can you accept what I've said because my mind is set on the path I've chosen? It won't change."

Damon was distraught. He'd finally spoken to her openly about his feelings, but the happy ending he wanted eluded him, again.

"I have no choice but to accept your decision," he answered solemnly and quietly looking away.

"Prince Damon, I have no wish to cause you pain. I hope we can get past this. I'm sorry I can't give you what you want. I tried to tell you this. I'm your friend."

He nodded and turned to walk away. He felt shame again and he was greatly in need of solitude. Damon went into the forest, in spite of the deadly dangers and spent the night alone. He went to the lake and into the old blind to sleep there. He wasn't safe, but at that point a quick death to predators seemed a good option in his tormented mind.

He lay awake thinking about Beth late into the night before he could fall asleep. The pervasive feeling of anxiety punished him painfully. He felt a personal failure on the scale of his loss to his brother.

When Beth returned to the cabin alone, no one needed to ask her why she was upset. The fact Damon didn't come also was testament to what transpired. They knew Damon was besotted with her and it was only a matter of time before this would happen.

Argon stood up and took her into his arms while she sobbed silently.

"I'm sorry," she said over and over again. "I've hurt him terribly."

"Be at peace, child," said Argon. "Everything will work itself out."

They started their work the following morning, minus Damon who remained in the blind, too ashamed to face his friends at that point.

It was another day before he ventured out half of a mind to go away and seek a new life in a new place. He was punished by distressing thoughts.

Back at the camp, they worked efficiently, but with a pall cast over the crew. They all worried about Damon. Beth battled in the fights that day with dangerous intent evoked by the incident with the prince. Argon took the place of Amal after she battered him down to the ground. Argon fought Beth for the rest of the day to spare the young men any injuries.

Damon walked through the woods in a dark mood. If he'd met a predator it wouldn't have bothered him. As it was, he happened to avoid them and returned to the camp in the late afternoon.

They were just finishing an exercise when they saw him. They stopped and looked while he went into the cabin ignoring them.

"We can end our work for the day," said Argon.

They went to the cabin to see Damon. He was sitting on his bunk cleaning his dagger.

Amal went over and patted him on the shoulder, as did Berne. Beth pondered doing something also, but he turned his back to her, so she dropped the idea.

Argon acted as if nothing was amiss.

"Tomorrow, we'll go to the lake for practice fighting in the water, swimming exercises, and for boating lore. Not every fight is on dry land."

"Yes, Master," they all replied, except Damon who said nothing.

Damon stayed silent in his bunk that night. It was another test to fall asleep with Beth so nearby. She was imminently alluring, yet the instrument of his great humiliation. He blamed himself for the situation and consequently wrestled with dark thoughts lost again in self-castigation.

He rejoined the team for the following day of very difficult training. Argon worked them to the point of near exhaustion in the frigid waters of the lake. Trying to control their muscles in the icy waters was a severe challenge as well as the grueling pain of the ice cold lake water. Later when the wind picked up, it was too dangerous to stay in the weather, so Argon called a halt to their day early. They shivered as they hurried back to the cabin.

Beth tried to object, but the men insisted she be first to soak in a hot bath protected from view by blankets hung to hide her. They built a roaring fire in the fireplace to warm the cabin while they waited their turns. Damon went last to bathe, by choice. Amal and Berne knew him well enough not to protest.

The stress on their bodies from exposure to the coldness left them fatigued and feeling a little ill.

"I'm sorry to cause you such discomfort, but you must be able to handle any situation you meet. If you faced a battle in the winter and were driven away to try to survive off the land you would need to overcome these very types of problems. I know this from experience. When I was younger, I faced such a circumstance in that I was on the run for over a month subsisting on the meanest of supplies. I often questioned if I could conquer the challenge and survive. You must have great inner fortitude in addition to the war skills you've learned, do you understand? We'll rest tomorrow. We don't need for any of you to become sick."

"Thank you, Master," said Berne. "I think I've reached my limit for cold water, except to drink it."

Amal and Beth chuckled. Damon simply sat unresponsive, like he was no longer a part of the group but merely a co-inhabitant of the cabin.

* * * *

The following day Damon went outside the cabin after they'd eaten breakfast ostensibly to stretch his legs, but actually he just wanted separation as he continued to react poorly to his perceived failure. He had yet to speak to or even acknowledge Beth since he'd returned to the group.

He jogged through the chilly early morning air following an animal trail. It was a great risk at this time of day with the predators in the area but he didn't care in his sour mood.

Damon stopped suddenly when he heard a metallic clink. He turned and hurried back toward the cabin in time to see his brother arrive at the head of a column of royal troops. They were bedecked in bright ceremonial uniforms rather than the field uniforms that they'd normally have worn to go afield.

Tabor went to the cabin door and entered. Damon decided to hang back in the woods and watch. He had no desire to meet his brother, ever. Especially now that he was living in self-imposed shame, he especially kept away. He was hardening in his destructive feelings and poor choices.

Crown Prince Tabor stayed in the cabin for quite some time before he came back out along with Beth, Amal and Berne. Beth had a warm smile on her face as Tabor chatted with her. She chuckled at whatever he said along with the two men.

Although Damon was curious about the reason for Tabor's visit, he didn't go over to find out. Instead, he scowled at Beth's warm demeanor for his brother and stayed hidden from view. He had no need to risk another rebuff at her hands if she favored his brother. His own mental self-flagellation was punishment enough.

Prince Tabor rode away with a flourish of thundering hooves at the head of his personal guard unit, their pennants flapping sharply in the breeze.

Damon waited for a time before he pretended to be finishing a jog in returning to the cabin. Beth, Amal, and Berne remained outside talking. They all looked at Damon as he approached. Damon said nothing, he merely nodded at them.

"Your brother was just here, Damon," said Berne.

"Oh," he replied with outward disinterest.

"He passed on his regards to you and regretted he didn't see you."

Damon shrugged and went in the cabin.

The others followed him in.

"We're all invited to the palace for a ball hosted by the queen. We accepted on your behalf since you weren't here, Damon. It will be tomorrow night."

Damon looked at Argon.

"You can go. There's no time limit to when we get to the various training steps."

"Are you going, Master?" asked Damon.

"I don't normally attend such things. It's not what interests me, and I'm not a particularly social person."

"I understand what you mean when you say that," Damon replied. "I feel exactly the same way. I never did like the social responsibilities I had to endure as a royal prince. I'm happy to stay here with you. The others can go to enjoy Tabor's hospitality."

"No, Damon, you're going because it's your mother's wish. I may choose to go with you as I have great respect for the queen. She's a person of great character and that interests me."

He looked at Beth.

"We'll go back to the city today to spend the night at an inn. We'll obtain a proper dress for you for such an august occasion. You aren't going to forego your status as a woman, Beth. Though you wish to concentrate on martial skills, you can't ignore such an important part of your life."

She started to object, but he held up his hand.

"The matter is closed. Gather your things, we're leaving immediately."

They rode away from camp half an hour later, Damon the last of the riders creating separation like he was no longer a part of the group. When they arrived at the city gates the guards saluted them eyeing Damon curiously for riding apart, and then they went to an inn on the outskirts away from the prominent locales. It wasn't an establishment which was ostentatious in any way, but it was neat and clean. After eating a quick meal Argon took them to a dress maker, minus Damon who stayed behind. The owner of the inn fell all over himself trying to impress Prince Damon. Damon was polite but mostly non responsive during the stay.

Meanwhile Argon sought out a particular shop to fulfill their needs.

"You're well thought of for your work," he said to the older woman proprietor. "I've spoken with your neighbors enough to realize this."

"Thank you, my lord. How can I be of service?"

"We need your best dress for this young lady, but the ball is at the palace tomorrow. Will that be a problem?"

"No, my lord. As I look at her form I think she's perfect for a dress I've held back for a special person. I suspect I'll need to make no alterations. I think she's a perfect fit for it."

Beth looked a little embarrassed at the frank appraisal of her physique and the compliment.

The lady led her into a back room and closed the door. The men waited while she tried on the garb. They heard the women talking and they heard the seamstress exclaim in happiness.

Beth wouldn't reveal the dress to them, changing back into her forest clothes before she came back out, but she was clearly pleased.

"I knew she was the one," said the seamstress effusively.

"Name your price," said Argon.

"This dress is her. I can't charge for it."

"I insist," Argon replied. "This is your masterpiece. You won't go uncompensated for such mastery."

He paid her in ample gold coins.

"Thank you," said Beth to the woman. "I've never seen such a wonderful dress. I wish my mother could see it."

"You're more than welcome, child. You've made me a happy woman. I always felt there was a good reason I made it. I think you will look the part for a royal soiree."

"Master, you must allow me to reimburse you for this considerable expense."

"No, Beth. I have more money than I need. This is a gift I want to give to you. If I had a daughter…"

He paused as a look of distress crossed his face.

"What is it, Master?" she asked.

"Nothing to concern you, Beth, the past is gone."

"Thank you, madam," said Argon as they left the shop. Beth carried the package with the dress showing an interest in a feminine article for the first time her companions had ever seen.

"It's nice to see you happy, Beth," said Berne.

"Thank you, my friends, and thank you again, My Lord."

Argon nodded to her and smiled.

They returned to the inn. Argon normally housed them in the same room, but on this occasion he opted for separate rooms for all of them. Damon quickly took advantage of the opportunity thinking and speaking quickly.

"Master, with your permission, I'd like to return to the palace to my own room. My clothes are there and I'd like to see my mother tonight. I can see all of you tomorrow at Tabor's party."

Argon eyed him suspiciously, but nodded. Damon turned and left abruptly, again ignoring Beth and his friends.

He went into the palace and straight to his rooms. He changed into casual garb to go to the royal suite. As always, he listened at the door before tapping on it. A servant girl opened the door.

"My mother?" he asked.

"Greetings, Prince Damon," she answered in a dainty voice. "The queen is in the city. She didn't know you would come calling today."

"Please send word to me when she returns."

"My Prince, are you attending the ball tomorrow?"

"Yes, I am, though it's not my favorite thing to do."

She chuckled. She was pretty and a petite young lady.

"Perhaps I will see you there. The queen told me I could attend as a part of her retinue. It will be my first royal event."

"I'm happy for you. What's your name?" He smiled at her youthful exuberance.

"Madelein, sire."

"I'm happy to meet you, Madelein."

"It's my honor, My Prince. You're a legend in the city and I've hoped to meet you. I'm recently arrived to Kragan and added to the queen's staff. I grew up in a far less prosperous city. My parents thought this would be an excellent opportunity for me to expand my horizons, as my father said."

"What sort of legend would that be?" he asked with a chuckle.

"My lord, surely you're jesting with me."

She amused Damon with her bubbly personality and her sweetness. He smiled warmly. "I'll see you later, mistress."

Chapter Six

Damon wrestled with the hurdle of the royal ball which was another chance at distress in his brother's shadow. He'd been to more of them than he cared to remember and this one could be the most trying of all. He had no desire to attend with Beth seemingly in Tabor's sway. Adding in the usual social issues of his misperception of a poor personal status in the minds of attractive women, another competition with his brother in an arena of his strength and Damon's weakness, it was the last thing he wanted to do. Looking his best was no guarantee of success against Tabor. It had never worked in the past.

Seeing Beth's smile looking at Tabor at the cabin had been worse than the cut of a knife for Damon. His years of seeing his brother capture the hearts of every woman he came upon didn't prepare him for this. Beth was a woman Damon truly cared about. In her case, it mattered to Damon what she thought and what she felt. Viewing her through the faulty filter of his own skewed opinions left him virtually unable to reach a correct conclusion about reality.

The only reason he didn't immediately flee back to the forest was the fact his mentor, Argon, would be there at the ball, and as a sidelight seeing delightful Madelein again was mildly intriguing. Argon had been right that the queen organized this event so Damon had to attend.

Dressing in his finest Kragan military uniform was the logical choice, but Damon was stubborn and to an extent rebellious in his compromised emotional state. He wanted to make a personal statement against the unfairness in his life, so instead he picked a plain outfit. He dressed and smiled in perverse satisfaction staring at the mirror and the person reflected there. He looked like a glorified servant, perfect for his contentious mood.

Damon didn't leave his room until it was time for the ball. He waited until after the event started before he made his way through back hallways to the rear servant entrance to the kitchens.

The workers looked at the prince in surprise when he appeared abruptly in their midst. They bowed to him in true deference. He was a hero to them and though they wondered at his inappropriate garb no one asked him about it.

"Good evening," he said, passing through them slowly, nodding and smiling.

"My Lord," they replied.

To Damon, these simple folk were his people, not the stuffed shirts on the other side of the door in the ballroom. Those haughty folk out there were in a different universe with their arrogance, one which Damon would have loved to forgo. Staying in the friendly confines of the kitchen briefly crossed his mind.

Damon paused to take a deep breath and steel himself before he went through the kitchen door into the ballroom. The instant he opened the door, he was beset with an overload of sounds, scents, and color. The room was decorated with the battle pennants of the various units of the royal Kragan army in addition to the entire spectrum of colors of the rainbow of tapestries, streamers, and ladies adorned in expensive dresses. They were dancing, twirling, bowing and stepping in concert to the lively music.

Instantly, Damon regretted his clothing choice but it was too late. His intended challenge to his social affronts seemed senseless and weak standing here exposed in public to the judgment and scorn of the aristocracy. He'd accomplished nothing but making himself an unfortunate spectacle.

The king was dancing with Beth, the queen with Argon, and Selena with Tabor. Damon grimaced at the amused looks as people noticed him. He locked his stare straight ahead and awkwardly made his way toward the royal table. His place was untouched being located beside his mother's seat. Where everyone else would sit, he couldn't tell, and at that point he didn't care.

Selena's friends Katherine and Elle made a beeline toward him like predators closing in for the kill.

"My Prince," said Katherine, with amusement.

He nodded stiffly, avoiding looking straight in their eyes. He tried to keep his embarrassment from showing on his face.

"Did you have another task prior to this celebration?" asked Elle.

"I did, actually," he replied, wishing they would simply go away and leave him in peace.

"It seems you had no time to return to your suite to dress for the dance," Katherine commented.

"So it would seem," Damon replied in a terse tone. His emotions were beginning to transform with the continued conversation from two women who wouldn't take the hint to leave him in peace.

The music ended abruptly, so Damon's reply came out too loud and drew the notice of the throng. He saw surprise on his mother's face, and disappointment. Beth looked confused. She didn't look to be amused at his antics. She was like a blazing sun in the room in her unique dress, stunning and outshining any other woman.

Argon accompanied the queen to the table.

"Damon, what are you doing?" she asked like a reproach.

"I'm sorry if I shame you, Mother. It seems to be in my nature."

He looked at Argon who eyed him ruefully.

"Prince Damon, I've told you before, there are times and places for everything. I believe I understand your motives, but I think you can see it was a poor choice for tonight."

"I'd be happy to leave," he retorted brusquely.

"It's too late to run away. You've made a choice and now you must deal with the consequences."

His father came over with Beth. He didn't say anything. He didn't need to. The look on his face of anger was unmistakable. The king knew exactly what Damon was saying with his actions, the insult he intended. Unfortunately the king took it as a personal attack on him, and the crown prince, rather than the generalized statement Damon intended.

Tabor had a smirk on his face and Selena looked appalled at Damon.

"Greetings, Prince Damon, my brother, I hope this social event isn't keeping you from your other important tasks."

Damon glowered in embarrassment. There was nothing he could say at this point.

The music started again. Argon took Beth, the king took his wife, and Tabor took Selena, again.

"Would you care to dance, My Prince?" asked Katherine.

"I would not," he responded.

They bristled at his ire, turned in a huff and left him.

Damon sat down and drained a full glass of wine in a lengthy gulp. He felt the burn tingle throughout his body, but it didn't alleviate his troubles.

"My Prince," he heard and turned his head to see Madelein. "I told you I would be attending with the queen."

"Yes, you did," Damon replied, smiling warmly at her.

"I'm happy you came, though I'm surprised you dressed like a stableman."

Damon laughed. "My attempt at humor has failed, as you can see."

Madelein laughed. "I'm sorry, Prince. I'm not sophisticated to understand the doings of royal persons. I'm too ignorant to grasp your higher reasoning."

"You're not ignorant, Madelein. My choice was ignorant. Would you care to dance?"

"Me? I'm a servant, My Prince."

"There is no woman in this room I would rather dance with."

"Is it permissible? I don't want to break any rules."

"It's permissible if I say so," Damon answered, rising and drawing her out to dance.

Again, he drew considerable notice, but in having dainty Madelein with him, he felt human companionship and he felt protective of her.

She was a very good dancer. He kept her on the dance floor for the next dance and the next one also.

They returned to the tables to dine when the music stopped. Beth was seated beside Argon across from Damon. His mother was beside her husband, the king, but she spoke with and paid attention to Argon a great deal.

Sitting beside Damon on the other side was a noble and his wife. Damon ignored them totally. Fortunately, Tabor and Selena were seated on the other side of the king, so Damon didn't have to deal further with them. The king spoke with Beth a great deal, like he was trying to upstage his wife conversing with Argon. Damon was merely an aside to that contest. The king peered crossly at Damon from time to time.

Madelein personally served Damon his meal. He smiled at her and chatted as he was able with her ongoing duties. She was a little abashed at his attention and the notice it drew onto her. Finally the queen turned her head to her son.

"What is this you're doing, Damon? She's a servant in my service. Do you intend another insult?"

"I find Madelein to be a pleasant person. I intend nothing other than civility and friendship, Mother. Should I leave?"

"You're annoying tonight, Son. This isn't acceptable behavior."

"I apologize. I'll keep it in mind if there are future invitations to such events."

"I've tried to be tolerant of your behavior, Damon, but this goes too far."

He looked at Beth and Argon who were listening to his dressing down.

"Yes, ma'am," he said finally. This night had been fraught with potential trouble, but Damon was the author of much of it. His inner distress was starting to evolve with each additional embarrassment. Anger was growing within him and increasingly his responses became defensive and surly. This event was another step down a distressing path.

At one point he sensed Beth's glance and looked to see her expression of disappointment with him. His face flushed with shame and he nearly bolted for the door. They looked at each other intently for only a moment before she looked away at Prince Tabor.

Damon bristled, like she intended to further injure his emotions with her gesture. Tabor was his brother, but he was the bane of his life. He also felt the notice of Argon who was eyeing him intently, like he was on guard if Damon was about to attack everyone in the room.

Damon closed his eyes to concentrate and regain his focus. He worked to shed the disruptive feelings and looked for the battle focus which was so familiar after his training. He blotted out all sound to calm his emotions until he reached his goal. When he opened his eyes with the dark expression of battle readiness and looked up, Argon had a raptor look like Damon was suddenly a clear and present danger. He'd drawn the harsh notice of Beth too. Immediately he made his decision.

"Mother, thank you for the invitation to this gala, but I believe it best if I leave to return to the forest. I hope you understand it has nothing to do with you. I hope you'll explain to the king I meant no offense to him either. I'm not suited for this palace life. It's very plain to me my proper place is elsewhere."

The queen looked sorrowful. "Oh Damon, please don't do this," she said, shaking her head in dismay.

Damon looked at Argon. "Master, I'll see you later. Please don't feel you must cut short your visit to the king's city on my account. I can best make use of my time with further practice of the martial arts back at camp."

Argon said nothing at all.

Damon nodded to Beth. She nodded back stiffly. "Mistress," he whispered and left.

When Damon arose he drew the stern notice of his father and his brother.

He made a brief bow to them before quickly exiting the ball. Again, instead of the main entrance, he went through the nearby kitchen door.

Madelein saw him coming and turned, red faced.

"My Prince," she said with a curtsy.

"I enjoyed our time tonight, Madelein. Thank you. It was a brief bright spot in an otherwise dismal evening. I must leave but I wish you well in your life."

Mathias saw him and ambled over with a confused look.

"How can I be of service, Prince Damon?" He stared at Damon's odd clothing choice.

"Greetings, Master Chef, your food choices tonight were excellent and I thank you, but I must be going away. Goodbye, Mathias." The finality of his remark caught the attention of everyone in the kitchen.

Mathias eyed him with a sad expression. "Goodbye, Prince Damon."

Quickly moving on, gathering his things from his room, he went to the stable for his horse. Damon was gone from the city as rapidly as he could ride racing past the gate guards ignoring their shouted questions at his haste. He never looked back as he headed for the security of his forest home. At that point, he had no desire to ever return to Kragan. As a matter of fact, he toyed with the idea of simply leaving the area altogether for a solitary life on the move.

"It worked for Argon," he muttered pondering a solitary life of travel. "Tabor can have them all. I don't care."

Meanwhile, Argon was in no hurry to leave the gala event in spite of Damon's poor behavior. It was a rare opportunity for him to mingle with other human beings in a pleasant and acceptable setting. He was taken with the queen for many reasons and it amused him to observe her responses to him. It equally amused him to note the king's frequent jealous looks. She was trying mightily to act with proper decorum, but they both knew there was much more emotionally below the surface to contend with between them. He toyed with dangerous ground but he was a man without fear.

After watching his brother's abrupt departure like a dangerous storm front leaving the area, Prince Tabor got up immediately and came over to Beth to exploit the opportunity. It wasn't something she wanted and she tried to turn away from him. Her reaction surprised him as normally women welcomed his attention.

Argon saw her face and stepped in to save her. He spoke quickly.

"I'd like to thank you, Prince Tabor, for including us in your celebration. I hope you understand it isn't our way to stay up late. We're going to bid you farewell, and again you have our profound thanks for a wonderful occasion. Come, Beth, we must be going. Sunrise comes early."

"Prince Tabor," she said with a curtsy.

She took Argon's arm as they left the room.

Neither of them said anything until they got to Damon's palace rooms.

"I don't understand what happened tonight, Master?" asked Beth.

"I think you do," Argon replied. "It isn't difficult to interpret. Damon has fallen madly in love with you, maiden. Your resistance has affected him differently than you imagined. He took your response as a rejection of him as a man. It's an issue he's carried from his earliest childhood. Sibling rivalry in his case was magnified from normal circumstances with his royal heritage and the matter of ascension to the throne of his father at stake between him and his brother. When you showed any attention to Tabor, Damon took that as the ultimate blow that you saw him as unworthy while his brother was a shining example of what you covet. A winner versus a loser in life. Do you see?"

"That's wrong. I didn't intend any of that. I explained to him my reasons and my life goals. I'm not looking for any man at this point. I have nothing against Damon. He's a wonderful and decent person."

"People hear things like they see things, through the filter of their own feelings. He only heard from you that you had no desires for him, and when you acted warmly to his brother, it was a nail in his proverbial coffin. I was worried what he would do tonight. I'm not surprised he left prematurely. It could have been a much worse outcome. He's at a point that he's a dangerous fighter, more than the measure of most and possibly better than his brother at this point."

"Should we go to the forest, Argon? I feel I need to talk to him to straighten out this misunderstanding."

"I'm afraid it's too late for that. Honestly, I'm not sure what to expect from Damon when we get to the camp. We'll sleep in the palace tonight, gather Amal and Berne and be on our way tomorrow morning. Try to put it out of your mind for the time being and get some rest, Beth. There's nothing to be done tonight."

They were surprised by a knock on their door.

Prince Tabor entered along with the king and queen.

Argon and Beth bowed.

"Majesties, how may we serve you?"

"I wish for you to explain to my son my great displeasure for his behavior tonight," said the king. "I realize things between us have ever been strained, but it wasn't my wish. I can endure his slights on a personal level, but when he makes a public display, I must respond as the king because he dishonors the crown. The royal seat must have proper respect from all our subjects, even a son of mine."

"We understand, Majesty. Obviously Damon is grappling with difficult problems. I believe he didn't act out of spite for the crown. He was faced with personal matters which surpassed him unfortunately. He's returned to our forest camp. What we'll find tomorrow when we return there, I honestly don't know. Is there a message you wish for me to give him?"

The king looked distressed.

"It has never been my intention, or that of his family, to cause him strife. I offer him my counsel, though I know he won't avail himself of it. I'm his father, though it always seems he would wish otherwise. I'm not without feelings. I'm proud of what he's done under your guidance. I wish I could make him understand."

"I don't want to sound presumptuous to speak for your son, but his focus is no longer on the city of his birth. He hasn't said his long term plans, but I suspect he wants to move on to other places to seek his fate."

The entire royal family looked very disturbed at that assessment.

"My brother would leave us?" asked Tabor in true astonishment. "Why would he do that?"

"It's not a thing I could explain to you, Prince. I think your father and mother understand. Perhaps they can explain it to you."

Tabor looked shaken. He looked at Beth who was eyeing him sadly.

"He's my brother," he muttered with a sad look.

"Prince Tabor, I understand. I too have been an unwitting cause for his strife. Too late, I realize the consequences of my actions and my choices from his point of view. I agree I think he doesn't wish to return here, but also possibly he no longer wishes to have dealings with us either. I follow my reasons for what I do. I didn't think about how he took it."

"This is not acceptable," the prince replied. "I'll go to speak to him."

"That isn't a good idea, Prince. He's able to elude your search in the forest. You would never find him."

Tabor looked at his mother. She looked disconsolate.

"I'm so sorry, Mother. I know I could have acted better with him. I was so occupied with my success and my plans I didn't pay attention to his pain. I am a cause for all of this happening. He's always put up with it so I wasn't forced to consider the consequences of my actions on others. I'm ashamed I hurt him."

"We can't change the past, Son, and I fear we can't affect the future either. Damon has decided on a lonely path."

Argon looked at them. "Prince, those days of childishness are over. Your brother is a man now. Both of you must make your decisions and live with the present day consequences. I'll deal with Damon to whatever extent I'm allowed, but I can make no promises. From the first day I sensed he was looking for escape from his pain. He just didn't know what he wanted, that's until Beth came into his life. She knew of his strong feelings, but she didn't grasp how he was focused on her. It still remains a decision she must make. That's as much the issue here as any residual sibling rivalries. He spoke truly when he said he didn't want the throne of Kragan. What he does want instead remains to be decided."

"Are you saying our son is lost to us?" asked the queen.

"No, I can't speak for him. I think he wants to forge a new life of his own choosing and it may not involve living here any longer. All of us in this room are issues for him. Do you understand?"

"Regretfully so," she answered.

"Your coming was a great omen," the king related. "I sensed it and didn't have optimistic feelings. I acknowledge you've done a great deal of good, Argon, but I wish you'd never come."

Argon smiled ruefully. "I hear that a great deal in my travels."

"What will you do next?" asked the prince, but he was looking at Beth.

"I would say there isn't much else I could teach them, Prince. We would have made our individual choices of what we'll do and where we'll go. I didn't look for them to become my travel companions. Though I've enjoyed our time together, I could easily return to my solitary life."

"Master, my desire would be to travel with you. I have no home and no family. I thank the queen for her friendship, but I'm not a city dweller. My goals remain to avenge my family. I think that would best be served by staying with you. Prince Tabor, I appreciate your kind attention. I assume Selena is your choice as a mate, but if you had ideas along those lines for me, I tell you what I told your brother. That isn't my path. I may never be a fit wife with my following the way of war. It's no slight to you. Your romantic notice is a great honor for me."

Tabor looked conflicted.

"We'll take no further of your time," said the queen. "Please speak to our son for us. He always has a home here in Kragan. I will miss him terribly."

"Majesties." Argon and Beth bowed.

Beth looked at Argon with concern after they were gone from the room. She spoke her genuine feelings.

"I'm worried about Damon, Argon. I understand now from what you said about how he felt, though I think he was very wrong. Regardless, it's unsettling how he acted, especially in public in front of his family and his people. I made very clear to him it was nothing about him."

"Beth, it serves no purpose to get into that at this point, he's gone. Apparently he's made some decisions. Obviously he didn't see things the way you did. The intrigues of romance can be especially vexing for those who feel slighted. The Damon that's come out the other side of this test is the real issue now. If he had a plan to follow my path, the solitary way, the last thing you can do in his place is display your vulnerabilities for all to see. I don't travel about to places I'm known and therefore I have no friends at hand to aid me. I don't believe he understands what that life is like. His fighting prowess isn't in question, but whether he's capable of good judgment is. He is not me to be able to handle such a lonely life, but I'm not sure he cares at this point."

"I think, Master, people don't understand how they're perceived by others. I'm a simple farm girl, yet these city people treat me with deference like I'm royalty. It makes me uncomfortable. I don't want the attention or notoriety."

"You can see something of where Damon is, child. Though he's a royal prince he wants no part of it. Here, he'll always be seen as a prince. I think this is another reason he looks to depart. He wants to find happiness without knowing where to go or what to look for."

"Do you counsel us to go our own ways, Master?"

"No, I'll leave such choices to each of you. Traveling with me wouldn't be a pleasant life but if you so choose, I won't forbid it."

"I want to say something which I hope you'll understand, Argon. I've made it clear to all the others I'm not looking for a romantic relationship. In your case, for me there is already a bond. Though probably you wouldn't want it, I see you like my father. You're my mentor, but I see you as family. Will that be a problem?"

Argon looked momentarily daunted. "I, eh...Beth, you don't really know me so you don't realize the scope of what you're saying. I'm humbled you feel affection and an attachment to me. I've already told you I feel a father's pride for a daughter with you, but don't ever forget who your real father was. He's your standard, not me. I'm unworthy of it. I'll treasure whatever time we have together, but I have a painful past which will haunt me to the grave. In truth, if you're looking for a role model and a trusted companion, Damon would best fill that role. He would die for you, Beth."

She pondered his words thoughtfully.

"Perhaps you're easier for me to deal with because there are none of those romantic issues to worry about. With Damon, of course I know he feels strongly for me, but he won't take no for an answer. He ignores my wishes. I respect him and possibly to an extent I feel love too, but I'm not going down that road. I'm not at that point in my life. I'm going to avenge my family. That's the only thing which matters to me."

Argon shrugged. "Beth, I understand what you're saying, but simply stating your wishes doesn't wipe away the hopes of others. Damon is an independent entity with goals of his own. If you feel he'll just turn away because you tell him so, I think you're being unrealistic. Your choices are probably all going to be difficult decisions. You can restate your positions to him, you can tell him you wish to part ways, or you could accept his companionship and see where it leads. It may be he's already made his difficult choices and may be on the road on a different path. We can't guarantee he'll even be at the camp any longer."

She sat silently thinking about the possibility.

"I want to add one more point, Beth. About your life goal of revenge, you're young so you don't grasp what that means either. The authors of the slaughter of your family are craven heartless barbarians. If you're talking about the specific individuals responsible for the act, how do you know who they are? Were they the group following you that we already killed? If they're still abroad, how could you ever find and identify them? If you seek to take the fight to the entire Argore nation, you could kill all day every day for the rest of your life and never eliminate significant enough numbers to make a difference. You need to think hard about your own goals. You've become a highly skilled fighter, but still a young woman who has never been tested in battle. Do you understand? I'm not belittling you, I'm saying please be realistic. You would face some enemy fighters who are like giants. They can bash at your best defense and drive you down into the ground from sheer brute strength. They would have no qualms about killing you, and that's after they finished with what they do to women. You already know this. You heard your mother suffer that dire fate."

Beth grimaced at the memory.

“Your feelings I understand very clearly, Beth. We all do, but don’t let them warp you. We can still strike at the Argore but let’s do it in a sane reasoned manner. Let’s approach it with a plan. Don’t shut everybody else out of your life. Amal and Berne love you too. You know they dream of putting a ring on your finger.”

Beth smiled and then chuckled. “Berne and Amal, what a pair they are, Master. They’re good friends to me, but I don’t look at them in those romantic terms.”

“They look at you that way, Beth. That’s the point I’m making, whether Prince Damon, or his friends, you can’t blunt their feelings to suit your mood with a few terse words. You must treat them with dignity like the men they are, respect their hopes and make your decision about what to do.”

“How is it possible I’m in this position? I’m a farmer’s daughter.”

“Beth, you’re so far beyond that point, it’s time to acknowledge you’ve ascended to be a woman of significance. A queen calls you friend. Princes seek your hand.”

She stood up and walked to look out the window. They heard a rap on the door. Amal and Berne came in.

“Where’s Damon?”

“He returned early to our camp,” Argon explained.

“Uh-oh,” said Berne. “That can’t be good. Did he do something stupid again?”

Beth turned to them and chuckled. “Why would you assume that?”

“Mixing Damon with royal balls and pretty women usually leads to a bad outcome.”

Beth didn’t fail to notice the adoring looks in their eyes. She was still adorned in her dress for the party. She thought about what Argon advised her.

“Are you okay, Beth?” asked Amal.

“I’m fine, thank you for asking.”

“Let’s just say he made some poor choices starting with how he dressed,” Argon explained. “He intended it as a rebellious statement against his old life, but it didn’t achieve the effect for what he wanted. It was a mortifying experience stemming from his ill-conceived choice. He left the royal ball early to return to the camp rather than face the consequences of his actions. He was very upset.”

“Should we go tonight, Master?” asked Berne.

“We’ll leave early tomorrow. It will be good to give him time alone to sort out his feelings and gather his composure. I think it best no one bring up the incident. Rather, we’re going to talk about our future plans. Our days of training are over.”

“Yes, Master,” they all said in unison.

They slept the night each with difficult thoughts to contend with and wide ranging opinions to sort out.

* * * *

Meanwhile Damon arose with the sun to hunt and dress the kill. He thought briefly about a trip back to the city to deliver meat to the poor, but dismissed the idea. Taking the chance of running into his family or his friends was the last thing he wanted.

Instead, he sat in the dimness of dawn eating a quick meal of fresh steaks harvested from his kill. The sounds of the forest were all about him, dangerous and sometimes close by. To him it wasn't frightening. This was his world by choice. He steeled his courage to make his difficult decision though again based on his skewed viewpoint.

He still cared about Selena, but she was long since out of his concern. Beth dominated his attention even now with his feeling he'd irreparably lost her through stupid actions. Facing Argon and Beth bothered him. Simply leaving before they came back from the city was an appealing plan in his mind to skirt the contentious issues they would throw at him. As he packed up his things to leave, Damon concluded trying to include Berne and Amal in his flight wouldn't work because they'd wanted to stay with the master. Actually more accurately they wanted to stay with Beth. Damon was disposed to give them their chance to woo her since he felt she had such disdain for him.

He was a young man well acquainted with defeat, pessimism, and outright depression in his prior life experiences. Trying to conceive of a good outcome to the fiasco he created was not a possibility he ever considered. It wasn't just the actions of one foolish evening. It included his whole life of coming up short. Seemingly, he was incapable of escaping the scourge of his own misperceptions chronically painting every event as negative and symptomatic of his personal flaws. He thought about his situation too many times without any happy endings, so it was time to take actions.

Feeling fatalistic like a martyr preparing for his doom, Damon finished eating his food, and gathered his few remaining things he hadn't already packed. Looking in the direction of Kragan, he felt remorse only at leaving his mother. She'd been the one constant he saw with any hope at all. It caused him to pause and he almost reconsidered his ill-conceived plan to leave. In the end, he felt it was too late. He'd closed a door that couldn't be re-opened. Now with his colossal gaff, Beth would never be his. In his mind, he was moving on.

At the time Argon and the others were departing Kragan, Damon strode away leading his horse to go around the vast lake. It was incredibly dangerous, especially at this hour when predators and prey were moving all about in those same areas. Damon kept an arrow notched as he walked still leading his horse and took his time. He was carrying considerable fresh meat which would draw the notice of cats and wolves. He wanted to be able to react quickly if he was attacked.

* * * *

By the time the others arrived at the camp, Damon was gone. He left no note behind not thinking it necessary under the circumstances. His reasons were obvious.

"Oh no," said Beth sorrowfully. "I could have prevented this."

"No, Beth, you couldn't," Argon explained gently. Her distress touched him with sadness.

"We must go after him," said Berne. "He can't go about alone."

Argon looked at them with a troubled expression. He paused before he spoke. "We need to make our decisions. Damon has hastened the need. I had no original plan to stay with you, but you've grown on me, so I'll offer you the opportunity to follow a path together. If you wish to chase down Damon, we must all agree to it."

Everyone looked at Beth.

"What?" She said defensively.

"It's nothing against you, Beth. We see no blame on your part. Damon is who he is. Berne and I are his lifelong friends. There is no other course for us to follow," Amal mentioned gently.

Beth looked at Argon.

"It's your decision, child. I can't make those difficult choices for you. I have no persuasion for or against following Damon, so it comes down to you. If you think to go after him because it's what we want, I advise against that. If you don't want to do this in your heart and only agree to try to please us it will lead to future resentment. You strongly stated your intentions for your life. If you wish to part ways to follow your own path to your destiny, none of us will think less of you."

She looked in the direction of her family farm like she was consulting her dead family.

"Let's go catch up to Damon," she answered finally.

"Good," said Berne. "I don't think I could have parted from you."

Beth smiled at him.

They packed up their belongings in the camp and started moving quickly.

"How do you know which way to go, Master?" asked Amal after a short time riding forward.

"He wants to leave his old life behind and he knows the Argore are on the prowl across the flatlands. Circling the lake to go the other way is logical. It's what I planned to do. Staying in the forest provides cover if he can evade the beasts."

"Do you think he'll try to evade us?" asked Amal.

"Anything is possible, but escaping my search is impossible. We'll find him, that's not the problem. Dealing with him and whatever decisions he's made will be the issue. You must all think about that before we catch up to him."

Beth felt them looking at her but she stared straight ahead.

"Yes, Master," she replied.

They heard a growl nearby. A cat wandered out of the brush and glanced at them before trotting away.

"Beth, beside me," said Argon, looking all about. "Amal, Berne, guard our rear. We need to move quickly." Amal and Berne each led a pack horse carrying their supplies and belongings.

They galloped along the shore after that.

* * * *

Damon was far ahead of them, but he wasn't hurrying. He was equally vigilant to the animal traffic. He witnessed a kill not far ahead of him as a cat surprised a moving herd of deer from close range and downed a straggler. He slowed to let the cat drag it away before he mounted his horse and rode past. The cat eyed him dangerously from just inside the tree line.

Damon kept his eyes on it the whole time until he was past.

Damon didn't look to stop until well after noon, riding off into the trees to find a secure place to have a quick meal of dried meat, and to feed and rest his horse.

His pursuers kept after him, steadily closing the distance. They ate in their saddles without a stop, also eating dried meat and drinking water from their gourds.

His lead evaporated fairly quickly as Argon led them unerringly. Damon had no urgency in his travels and didn't know they were tracking him.

"How you can pick out his tracks from all of these others I don't understand, Master," said Berne.

"It's part intuition, not all tracking. I've taken a chance about his path, but I'm confident I'm right. We'll have him in our net within a few hours at the longest."

"Good," said Amal. "We should never be apart. We're a family."

Chapter Seven

They rode slightly past Damon. Fortuitously, he'd finished his brief meal and was returning to the lake shore to resume his trek. They saw each other at the same time.

Damon scowled, but secretly he wasn't upset to see them. The lure of a solitary life had faded quickly as he rode alone into unfamiliar territory and into the midst of great danger.

He mounted up and rode over to rejoin them. They waited for him to reach them before they turned as a group to look at him.

"Did you have a destination?" asked Argon.

"That way," he answered, pointing along the shoreline.

"Good plan, Damon," said Berne.

Damon tried not to look at Beth, but he failed. She eyed him thoughtfully at his glance. Damon read it as her disapproval, a predictable reaction for him. His defiance rose up like a faulty emotional defense mechanism.

"If you have your own plans, don't let me stand in your way," he retorted frostily.

"Damon, I think we should put the events of the city behind us," Argon related evenly to cool his ire. "It's over and none of us wish to resurrect it. Fall into line with your friends and say no more about it. We're not here to judge you."

Damon's minor rebellion fizzled out. He joined Amal leaving Berne to ride ahead of them beside Beth.

"I'm glad we found you, Damon," said Amal. "None of us was meant to be out in the world alone."

Damon shrugged his shoulders. Beth glanced back at him. He eyed her icily.

Having five in the group was a deterrent against predator attacks. They were in no great hurry but moved at a steady pace nonetheless. When they reached the far side of the lake they struck out into the forest leaving the lake behind. Following a small animal trail, they rode with increased vigilance, subject to the threat of sudden attacks with the heavy foliage so close to them on the narrow pathway.

Riding in a single file Damon was the last in line. He watched behind them for any sign of pursuit. This was territory beyond the farthest point they'd ever come in this direction. Whether from the usual animal risks or the scrutiny of the local inhabitants, they couldn't afford to be caught off guard.

Traveling through the forest here proved to be a much longer trek than anyone anticipated.

Beth was the first of them to smell cook fires.

"I think it's coming from ahead of us," she whispered.

Argon stopped to consider their next move. An instant later they heard sounds all around them of movement. They spurred their horses to a gallop and rode into the ambush.

Thuggish men emerged from the cover of the undergrowth to confront them. Damon noted their numbers and where they positioned themselves. He also concluded they were mere criminals. They shouted and brandished their weapons with a great show of bravado, but when Argon attacked, their courage failed and they fell back.

Argon led the group on a charge through the enemy skirmish line without casualties on either side. Bursting through the attempt to contain and capture the friends, Argon raced ahead quickly distancing them from pursuit and soon the threat was over.

He slowed to a cantor. Beth came up to his side and smiled.

"Not much of a fight," she commented.

"Beth, we were lucky. Every danger we face won't be so easily dispatched. You did well though in keeping your head."

"Thank you, Master."

Damon continued to lag back ostensibly to protect the rear but everyone in the group knew his motives.

"The criminals gave up their prey awfully easily," Berne commented to no one in particular.

"I think they saw we were a deadly test even though they outnumbered us. If they were brave and skilled fighters, they'd be in an army somewhere. These were mere low life miscreants," Argon opined.

"I hope so. We'll see what awaits us ahead."

When they made camp for the night, they were still in the forest with no idea how much farther it went on.

Beth went away to bathe in a stream and take care of herself. She came back refreshed.

"It's good to get clean," she mentioned to Argon.

"Yes, child, hygiene is one of the challenges of a life on the road. It makes us vulnerable during that time taken to cleanse our bodies, but it's necessary. I'd say in the future we stay close even for those moments. If trouble happens when you're indisposed you need your friends to act for you."

"Yes, Master, I don't worry about modesty in the field."

The men took their turn. Damon waited until last. At one point he was alone with Beth while the others took their turns at the stream.

She didn't initiate a conversation, so he remained quiet, overtly on guard over the camp. He never looked at her and moved away to a point separate from her facing away in the other direction. His unspoken message was clear to her and left her feeling sad.

When the others returned, Damon went alone for quite a distance and quickly performed his ablutions, ignoring Argon's warning they all stay close. He heard movement in the brush across the stream so he quickly dried and dressed to return to the safety of camp. To sleep, Damon no longer worried about moving close to Beth with his bedding. He left it to Amal and Berne to flank her while he stayed across the campfire from them all.

The next day they finally reached the edge of the forest, but it was late in the day, so they stopped early and camped within the tree line and watched the open ground ahead. It looked to be farmlands for as far as they could see.

"This reminds me of my home," said Beth.

"It doesn't seem the Argore have come here, yet," Argon replied.

"Perhaps this territory is not in their path. It would be good if these folk were left in peace. This doesn't look to be an area accustomed to war."

Argon didn't look hopeful.

"We'll see, child."

"I'll take first watch, Master," said Damon.

"As you wish, Damon." Argon glanced at him and then the others. No one said anything.

His companions settled into their bedding at dark. Damon climbed a tree to get a better view ahead and behind their campsite.

He looked down at Beth. As always, Amal moved close on one side and Berne on the other. Beth no longer objected to their nearness where they sometimes pressed against her on the pretext of sharing warmth on cool nights. Argon was apart from the three. He stayed awake for a time glancing up once at Damon before he lay down and fell asleep.

Damon mostly paid attention to the forest expecting trouble from there, but late in the night as he was about to climb down to awaken his replacement, he noticed movement in the distance in the flatlands. He peered intently and saw distinct shapes in the dark slinking toward the nearest farm. It was a clear sky so moonlight lent a level of illumination.

He quickly climbed down to alert the others.

Argon watched the raiders closely as they began to deploy for an attack.

"We must go now," said Beth insistently.

"Beth, we can't intervene in every dire situation we encounter."

"If you won't go, I'll go alone. I would have prayed for saviors that terrible night when my family was slaughtered. That farm has no chance."

She started for the horses. Damon, Berne, and Amal took only a moment before following her. Argon hurried over.

"Our strike must be quick and lethal," he advised. "Protect each other. Move as a unit."

They rode away toward the impending attack.

The raiders had surrounded the house and were already moving forward.

Damon rode close enough to Beth to hear her cry out in anguish when the raiders broke in the door and they heard screams from within. She was reliving her nightmare.

Argon charged at full speed and the others followed him. They surprised the attackers striking at their rear and felling numerous of the ambushers before they realized their peril. The pandemonium in the farm house masked their attack and the five were able to shatter the surrounding noose of enemy fighters with deadly efficiency. They were evoked by Beth's strong reactions and it provoked them to deadly and efficient action. Beth's hatred was palpable and it came out in her fighting. She was as pitiless as her opponents.

There were more of them than Damon anticipated, but he charged ahead ferociously nonetheless. This was a real battle for the first time. It was confusing and frightening leaving him no time to think, only to react.

They fought their way up to the house and cleared away the enemies at the door.

The inside of the house was already aflame.

The farmer was courageously defending his wife and little daughters with his two sons, but the outcome wouldn't have been good if not for Argon bursting into the room to attack the enemy leader. The raiders looked around in confusion as Damon leaped to Argon's side along with Beth. Amal and Berne took positions to cover their backs.

It was a vicious fight where both Damon and Beth transformed. They shed their fear totally and fought with abandon, heedless of risk.

Beth was incensed, realizing these were Argore raiders. It was her first chance to strike a blow against her sworn enemies. As she took risks in her fighting, Damon reacted to protect her back.

The fight was in question for a time as the farmer and sons tried to help, but it was Argon's skill that turned the tide. Once their captain fell, the other raiders fell too, though they fought to the last man. The Argore never surrendered.

When it was over they looked around for more enemies.

"Thank you, strangers," said the farmer tentatively, unsure if his family was still in peril from people they didn't know. His wife and daughters were terrified hugging him and sobbing. Both of the sons had been gashed in the battle. Beth grabbed the farm wife pulling her into action cleaning and dressing their wounds. Both sons stared at Beth, agog with her beauty in spite of the circumstances.

"We weren't far away at the edge of the forest," Argon explained. "Our sentry saw them approaching you."

"Who are they? We don't have raiders in this country."

"They're advance scouts of the Argore barbarians from the mountains in the north. I'm sorry to say they're moving into many peaceful lands. I'm afraid you and your neighbors must band together for mutual defense. By killing this team, it may be we've forestall larger numbers of raiders for the time being, but that's only my speculation."

Beth came back with the youngest son. He was afraid, but kept a brave face. He glanced at Beth frequently. The mother came with the other son. She spoke to Argon.

"We would have been killed, or worse. We owe you a life debt, sir."

"We didn't intervene to oblige you, madam."

"My family was slaughtered by these heathens," Beth added. "I couldn't stand by to watch it happen to other innocent citizens. Defending you is striking a blow on behalf of my own dead family."

The farmer and his wife looked at each other. "We have no army here in our land. If more of these demons come, there will be death and war. What can we do? Our feelings of safety in our own home are gone."

"Where is the closest settlement?"

"There's a village ahead, but it has no defenses. Raiders could merely sweep through it like a storm."

"If that's your central point, the people should all gather there and we'll speak to them about what you must do."

"Thank you, sir."

The wife shyly embraced Argon in gratefulness before taking her husband's arm again.

"Will you stay with us here? I'm afraid," asked the smallest daughter. Her brown eyes were wide with her fear.

Argon looked at her with a pained expression. She brought back some memory that punished him.

"Yes, we'll stay," said Beth kneeling down to the child.

She smiled and looked at her mother who nodded reassuringly.

"You're safe now," Beth added.

She followed the girls into the daughter's bedroom to rest there with them.

"Go to your beds," Argon advised. "We'll maintain a watch."

The boys went to their room and the farmer and wife retired.

I'll walk around outside," Damon offered.

"No, you haven't slept. I'll stay up, it was my turn to take over the watch," said Amal.

Damon shrugged. He, Berne, and Argon rested in the living room as best they could on the sofa and chairs. It led to some residual aches and muscle soreness later.

* * * *

In the morning, they gathered the bodies of the dead and took them to the forest for the scavengers to dispose of.

Beth stayed at the farmhouse with the wife and daughters. The farmer and his sons helped the men with the odious task.

"Is this our future?" asked the farmer.

"I'm sorry," Argon responded. "If there is one probe from a raiding party it usually foreshadows the approach of more of the Argore. As I said, killing off this pack we may have delayed their coming for a short time. Are you agreeable to my idea to gather your neighbors and go to the village?"

"I'd be a fool to say no, Argon."

"Then it's best we get to it. Time will never be our friend."

"I warn you there will be those who are stubborn and won't want to leave their homes, even for a short time."

"It can't be helped. We'll help them understand the gravity of the situation here, those who will listen. I think Beth is an effective testament to the dangers the Argore pose. If any are so foolish as to ignore the threat, there will be a terrible price to pay for them and their families."

The farm family gathered some things to make the trip to the nearest village. The two sons rode off to start spreading the word of the danger to their neighbors.

The two daughters stayed close to Beth as they rode away for the half day trek.

The farmer rode beside Argon asking him considerable questions. His wife fell in beside Damon. They rode in silence for a short time before she turned her head.

"There's something different about you."

"He's a prince," said Berne.

"Berne, shut up," Damon groused.

"Truly, you're a prince? I've never met a prince before."

"I'm not much of a prince," Damon replied.

"What does that mean? It doesn't make sense, My Lord."

"If you knew me, it would make sense."

"How is it you lead your comrades here, away from your home?"

"It's a long story, ma'am. I should say a long and boring story."

"I'm sure that's not true. Is Beth your companion?"

"Not in a romantic sense," he answered. "She rides with us, or maybe we ride with her, but she doesn't see me in favorable terms. It's totally my fault."

"This is strange to hear coming from a royal person, not at all what I would expect."

"That's because I'm the least of royal persons."

"He's not explaining it rightly," Berne interjected. "He's much beloved by the people of Kragan."

"We've heard stories about Kragan. It's said the city is a marvel. We've talked about visiting there someday to experience the thrills. Now I know you're toying with me if you're a prince of that great city."

Damon looked at her in surprise.

"Kragan is a great city," Amal added. "We're on a great quest to tame the world."

Amal and Berne laughed heartily, and so did Beth. Damon shook his head in dismay.

"As you can see, madam, I'm traveling with idiots and I'm the most idiotic of them all."

The wife laughed.

"You're a merry band. I wish I could get to know you as friends. Life on a farm has few memorable events. My family is the sum of my adventures."

"That's not a bad thing," Damon reflected. "What we've seen of the cruelty of men is something I'd never wish for you to face. I'm glad we could stand with you against the Argore raiders."

"Why do you say Beth has a bad impression of you?"

Damon paused. "I, eh…I've made a fool of myself too many times before her to expect anything good."

"So you have feelings for her after all. It's not surprising. She's an impressive woman, greater than any I've ever met by far, and she's incredibly beautiful."

She glanced back at Beth who'd been listening to the conversation. Beth smiled at her.

"Beth was a farmer's daughter," said Berne.

"Truly?"

"I was," Beth answered. "My life was simple but happy like yours, but when the Argore marauders came to our farm, there were no benefactors nearby to save us. I've made a promise to my dead family to seek revenge, but also I wish to spare others the horror of such atrocities. I'm no different than you, and I'm no more beautiful than you."

The wife chuckled and fluffed her hair. "Few women could match you, Beth, but thank you for the kind words. If my husband is happy with me, I'm content. I understand who I am."

They rode into the village to find people were already arriving from the surrounding farms.

"I worried they would ignore our warning," said Argon to no one in particular. "I'm surprised. Perhaps there are possibilities here amongst these folk."

They waited until nearly dark before gathering to speak to the assemblage to give more people time to arrive. When Argon stood up to speak there were still families arriving from more distant farms.

"My name is Argon. I've come to share ill tidings I regret to say. We happened upon a raid at the farm of one of your neighbors. Thankfully, we came in time to spare them from the wrath of the Argore. We don't know why they've started coming down from the mountains to raid and pillage in peaceful lands like yours. Nevertheless, it isn't a danger to be ignored. One of our companions, Beth, lost her family to just such an attack. They're pitiless and they work ill on the weak without conscience. They aren't people who can be reasoned with. There is no tribute you could pay to spare their depredations. They aren't interested in your money. They take their due in flesh. Do you understand what I'm saying? You've all dealt with criminals such us thieves and reprobates, but you've never met the likes of the Argore. They are relentless and they never stop attacking. The only answer to the Argore is to wipe them out totally. It's a hard thing to hear, but it's better to know up front what you're dealing with. I believe the raiders we met were scouts probing far away from their main bodies. Because we killed them all, we may have gained a little time. I propose to train you along with my comrades so you can make a defense of your homes and your families. If you don't agree to our help, say so now and we'll move on to leave you to your fate."

There wasn't a sound in the village. The people were shocked by the news, and they were frightened.

"Our little village can't house and feed such numbers," said the leader. "We have no fortifications to repel soldiers."

"We'll work on that very thing. We'll arrange for roving units to travel amongst the farms both to gather supplies and to monitor for Argore incursions. No one will ever go anywhere alone. We'll transform this village into a defensible position and build up our supplies for any length of battle we face. The biggest obstacle is within each of you. You've lived good lives in peace, but now in order to earn the right to keep living you'll need to go to the dark places inside you to stoke the rage to fight back. You must become equal to the challenge of the Argore which means being able to kill. That's not just the men, the women will also train. Beth is an example of what you can do. We'll have too few fighters with both men and women combined. It's an end to your old ways. I regret it, but there is no other choice other than to flee. The Argore would eventually catch you and your ends would be horrible beyond your imaginings."

The faces of the villagers were uniformly grim.

"I see determination as I look at you and that gives me hope. It tells me this fight isn't lost before it even starts. We'll send riders to advise those people farther away to make their own preparations. Don't assume we can't win. Although the Argore are savage, it may be they'll only send raiding parties we can cope with. If their army came, there would be no hope no matter what we did. It's pure chance based on their plans. If their ultimate aim is elsewhere we can survive."

Again there was silence.

"Does anyone have any questions, or observations?"

"What do we do?"

"Tomorrow we'll start the work. The first priority is building our defenses. At the same time, we'll send forces to gather necessities and to begin monitoring the area. Each of us will begin to train you in groups. If there are any of you with training and military experience, please speak out. We need as many trainers as possible."

Five men stepped forward. "We moved here from cities. All of us were soldiers."

"Good, we welcome your help. We need to get better weapons. Some of you have swords and bows but others have nothing. Is there an armorer here?"

"Yes, I provide weapons though there hasn't been a great demand," said a stout man with a full gray beard. "I too have roots in a city."

"We need for you to get busy. We can't be sure how much time we have. Do the best you can. If there are any others able to help you, seek them out."

"Yes, My Lord."

"Next. I'm going to assign you to trainers."

The people started to move before Argon could control them. The preponderance of them tried to line up for Beth. She looked at Argon and chuckled.

"How things have changed, eh Master?"

Argon scowled and then smiled.

"You've come a long way, Beth. There's no denying it. I admit I was skeptical in the beginning, but you've proved your merit. I'm very proud of you."

"I apologize for rejoicing at your compliment. I know I shouldn't savor this accolade, but I do. I guess that makes me a small person." She laughed and hugged Argon.

Damon watched their connection and felt the lesser, again unable to purge his personal demons. Beth seemed to sense his distress and looked at him directly. Her eyes were wide studying him. What she was thinking he could only speculate and he never saw these things in a favorable light.

Damon turned away to see the farmer's two sons had lined up for him. He nodded to acknowledge them. It was a rare gesture of respect he greatly appreciated at a trying moment. They stared at him and at Beth, like they'd figured out the dynamics of the troubled situation and Damon's issues.

Berne and Amal were seemingly impervious to such concerns. They rolled with every punch and showed little outward concern for anything.

* * * *

The enhanced village quickly built fortifications according to Argon's specifications and they were surprisingly formidable. Large wood sharply spiked structures were erected on top of rapidly excavated dirt breastworks circling the village, anchored into the dirt so they couldn't be easily dislodged. They built huge storage bins for grain and other supplies as well as digging additional wells for an adequate water source for the additional people.

Meanwhile the armorer worked long hours to fashion new swords and other weapons. The training sessions began soon afterwards when everyone was armed. All the men and all the women participated, though at different times to allow time to watch over the children. The size of the village was expanded four times over to provide new dwellings for the arriving farm families.

Patrols regularly traveled the area to safeguard farmers working their fields and harvesting crops. No one spent the nights outside of the village. They only went out during the day to labor.

Argon became a *de facto* leader of the village. The headman deferred to him though he never asked for it.

Each day was busy with preparations and training so time went by rapidly. A village wide regimen developed, laboring in the fields, rigorous martial training sessions all day, and utter exhaustion at night.

Soon, Argon started sending patrols farther abroad to watch for Argore incursions. To date there had been no further sightings. The other farmlands farther away attempted to follow Argon's instructions though they were far behind in constructing defenses and they had few men with experience to train them. The fact they were doing something to protect themselves was a positive nonetheless.

"We've been very lucky, Master," said Beth in a meeting with the officials of the village and local farmers. "I feared the Argore would come before we could ready ourselves to face them. At this point I feel good about our state of preparedness."

"I'm making an assumption the reason for our good fortune is the Argore thrust is going elsewhere and other poor villages and cities are suffering the invasion," Argon replied.

"We've done what we could," Damon piped in. "Is there something else we should consider?"

"Did you have something in mind, Damon?"

"I'd like to be sure this whole region is adequately prepared. Rather than sit here and wait, I'd be willing to travel around to spend time helping the other villages get to a competent state."

"Are you proposing we split up?" asked Beth with a skeptical look.

"I'm proposing we share our resources. You should stay here with the master and continue training the troops. This village is already seen as the headquarters for this land. As I travel, I'll send messengers to apprise you of our progress and our needs. That way, Argon can make a realistic plan for all the villages. If the Argore hordes come, we'll need a unified ready response to meet them."

"We'll go with you, Damon," said Berne.

"That's right, we're a team," Amal echoed.

"That's not necessary. I think you should stay with Beth, and the master. There's still a great deal of work to do here."

They all looked at Argon.

"I think perhaps we'll let Damon try his plan and see what develops. We can send others later if it seems a viable solution."

"Good," said Damon. "I'll leave now."

He was gone in a flourish without looking back.

* * * *

The farmer sons approached Argon and Beth. They faced Beth.

"What is this stressful feeling between you? We didn't wish to pry, but it permeates all of us who follow the prince. We respect him greatly and sorrow at his obvious distress."

"It's a private matter and it isn't something I discuss with others," said

Beth with a frown.

Neither son was satisfied with her explanation, or lack thereof.

They walked away muttering to each other glancing back at her reproachfully.

“Perhaps I should follow after Prince Damon to put this matter to rest, once and for all, Master.” She grimaced at the annoying issue.

“That wouldn’t work, Beth. He’s wallowing in his self-pity. Taking contrary steps feeds his pain and strangely that’s what he seeks. I’ve seen this behavior before. Actually I’ve lived it in the past. It isn’t a situation another person can rectify. He needs to come to terms on his own. Until he does, there’s nothing anyone else can do for him.”

“Will he come to terms?”

“I did, but I guess each individual faces their own dragons as best they can. It’s true we can’t predict the outcome of his choices. Keep faith, Beth, and don’t take ownership for what he’s doing.”

“That’s easy to say, Master. His actions affect me, they bother me greatly. I’m struggling to react correctly. I want the problem between us to resolve, but at the same time, my feelings are the same. I don’t want to encourage him to think I’ve reconsidered allowing any romantic interests. I still seek a relationship of that sort with no one.”

“That position will always be a problem for you, Beth. You will draw the notice of men and along with it, their hopes and desires. Great beauty isn’t something you can simply shed like a dress.”

She grimaced, but said nothing further.

“Men are oafs,” she muttered and then looked at Argon. “I didn’t mean you, Master.”

He laughed. “I’m as much an oaf as any other man, child. I understand your frustration.”

* * * *

Damon stopped at the nearest village. He had a hastily drawn map of the region to know where to go. They initially eyed him with suspicion as he explained his mission and their jeopardy. It was a sobering talk and their scowls changed to worried looks as he spoke. It was easy for them to understand Damon was genuine and not looking to take advantage in some way. They sensed no guile in his manner and he had no demands for them.

“I’m just a friend come to try to help,” he explained in conclusion. “My name is Damon.”

“I’m making a guess based on first impressions, I think you’re a decent man, Damon. We’ll offer you our trust and see where it goes,” said the head man. “As you’ve pointed out, we need help quickly and need to look in unconventional ways at our problems. The worrisome rumors we hear about invaders leaves us no other choice but to act to defend our families. Our trust is precious so think hard on what you do around us. We’re not mindless sheep nor are we fools.”

“Thank you, sir, your trust is precious to me. I’ll stand on my actions to prove myself to you.”

The village chief made a further decision and took Damon into his personal home to live with his family. For Damon, this time he spent in the village was idyllic. No one knew him, nor did they know he was a prince. He was just a man with considerable fighting skills. It put him at ease working from an area of strength, especially without Beth nearby to pique his worries. He relaxed and began his work. Fortunately, there were several former soldiers living in the village to help with the training. They acceded to his authority without question and after a short time, their respect and their esteem grew to the point they were his faithful men. It was a level of satisfaction Damon had dreamed of, but had never experienced. He was finally judged exclusively on his deeds. Also, living around children was a new delight for him he didn’t anticipate. They quickly adopted him like a visiting uncle.

The villagers made good progress once the work was started and when he eventually left Damon felt gratified at the rapid success. The village was as ready as he could make it to face possible war. How promptly they fortified their homes and the village and learned fighting skills were remarkable. It gave Damon high hopes going forward about his plans. Parting from the head man’s children later when it was time to move on was difficult which also surprised Damon he could become attached in such relationships.

Damon moved on to the next village to enact the same formula, but some of the men refused to let him travel alone. That happened again when he left the next village after rendering his help as he was beset with determined men and even some women who were in essence creating his personal corps, unsolicited. Damon chose not to argue with them as they wouldn’t have accepted it anyway. Their minds were made up and for Damon it was gratifying to have earned such respect.

Argon led them as a group into the farmlands, but with this choice of Damon to go his own way, it was his fame which started to spread. Without Damon knowing how it happened, they found out he was a prince and treated him accordingly. He didn’t want deference but it became the new and unavoidable reality in his evolving world.

Again totally unsolicited, one day his growing force was carrying a new royal standard at the head of the column, and next like magic they donned uniforms. Suddenly Damon was a political entity in the region, although one without a seat and constantly on the move. The villagers had come up with the ideas and set about creating the uniforms. They'd also sent word and found out the royal insignia of Kragan for the great flag they carried. Damon tried to scowl about it but he was secretly gratified. He felt to actually be a prince for the first time in his life.

After half a year of his travels, he had a formidable royal guard at his back. Since they trained nightly, their competence grew to where Damon didn't fear to face any enemy, including the Argore with his highly skilled armed force.

The entire land had been transformed into fortified hamlets and mini-cities by that time. They performed their agricultural duties each day and built up more than adequate supplies. The initial matter of solitary farm family units evolving to live in social situations with others nearby resolved easily. The people gave the credit to Damon, though he tried to deny it was his works and his words.

The absence of further Argore raids worried Damon. When he finally completed his circuitous route to return to the original village to meet with his old friends, it was eye opening to them. This incarnation of Damon was unrecognizable. All of his uncertainty was gone replaced by a confident easy going leader. The respect they saw in his personal guards was impressive. They were a bold and lethal force and any hint of disrespect from anybody for Damon would bring painful consequences.

As he walked over to her, Damon actually smiled at Beth, which was imminently compelling to her. No longer averting his eyes, he was now more impressive for her to see than Prince Tabor had been. Self confidence in a man is a compelling trait to women.

"Hello, Beth, it's nice to see you again."

Before she could respond his other friends arrived. He accepted hugs and back slaps from his old friends, Amal and Berne.

"You look good, Damon," said Berne. "That idea of yours was a good one. This is the man you should have been all along."

"Thank you. It's good to see all of you also."

He turned back to Beth. She was ecstatic that he took her in his arms.

"You're as breathtaking as ever, Beth. I've missed seeing you."

"I've missed you too, Prince Damon. I'm so happy to see you as you are now. I've regretted any part I played in your prior distress. I hope all of that is behind us now."

"I've grown up in some ways," he replied. "It was a risk going off on this mission, but I'm happy it paid off."

"You're personal protectors are an impressive lot."

"They're a seriously misguided collection of miscreants," Damon joked.

His male corps commander and female second in command laughed.

“We can’t really disagree with you,” she said. She eyed Beth often.

“These are my dear friends Amal and Berne, and this is Beth, whom I’m sure you’ve heard of. This is commander of my corps Gideon and the second in command Layla.”

“Beth, you’re an inspiration to every woman. I would have never tried this path without your example of what we could accomplish,” said Layla. “You’re just like us, a farmer’s daughter. I hope you’ll allow me to be your friend.”

“Of course, Layla, I’m pleased to make your acquaintance. I think if you spend any time around me any myths will disappear quickly. I have plenty of flaws.”

“I think not,” said Layla avidly. “We aspire to emulate you. Perhaps later we can spend some time to have a talk? I have many questions and if you’ll allow it, perhaps we could spar?”

“Certainly, I’ll look forward to it.”

“I can’t believe I’m actually in your presence, Beth. You’re a legend.”

“You are in my presence, Layla. I look forward to shattering your false illusions about me.”

Layla chuckled, along with the men.

Chapter Eight

Damon watched the exchange refusing to allow old feelings to arise to plague him. Beth was a woman who would always draw notice and would always evoke strong feelings in Damon. Allowing himself to finally realize that fact didn't reflect badly on anyone else, it was a quantum leap forward to view Beth in a rational light for the first time. Part of how he could get to that place was the deference which he received from his new corps that propped up his ego and rendered toothless his prior concerns, at least for the short term. Being in her presence, if he could maintain impartiality remained to be determined though.

Beth glanced at him, almost like a reflex reaction. He nodded and smiled benignly at her before turning to Argon.

"Master, I trust my efforts meet with your approval."

"Prince, you've exceeded any realistic expectations I could have. I feel much better about our future prospects here as I see your personal guards. I would imagine you've brought them to the point of full preparedness."

"I have, Master. I think they're the match of any force we meet. They could face any unit from Kragan's army without concern."

"Do you have room for two more?" asked Berne.

"Berne, you and Amal are forces now in your own right. You needn't feel subservient to me or any other man."

"We're not looking to serve you, Damon, merely to resume our friendship and companionship."

"Oh, I should have spoken differently. I'm still thoughtless as you can see. Of course you're welcome at my side if that's your choice. I'm afraid I may have come across as pompous. You know me better than that."

Berne and Amal smiled, but passed on the opportunity to badger him.

"What about Beth?" asked Berne.

"I would imagine she'll follow Master Argon. He has responsibility for the overall defense of the region. She's been his key associate. I very much doubt having the five of us traipsing about like the old days would work well at this point. Things have changed, as have we all."

Beth looked unhappy with his pronouncement.

"To an extent, you have a point," Argon responded. "I will say don't dismiss our rejoining our forces. I never planned to stay in a single place for this length of time. Whether this land prevails or falls won't pivot on the five of us. We've done what we could for them. I may decide it best to move on to other lands. There could be urgent needs elsewhere, do you agree?"

"Of course, Master. If we're spared from attacks here, that must mean they're attacking elsewhere. I agree with your prior opinion regarding the Argore."

"There you have it. In the meantime, I would say if you wish to continue your patrols, don't travel too far away. I tend to make decisions quickly and once I do I want to get moving rapidly."

"As you wish, Master. My thought is to travel next to the border to see if Argore forces are nearby and coming this way."

"If you find them, fight only as you must. Don't get bogged down in a fight where they can pin you down and overwhelm you with their numbers."

"Have you thought about going back to check on home?" asked Amal. "What if the Argore have gone that way? Our families could be in danger."

Damon paused and glanced at Argon.

"It's a legitimate point, Prince. The rumors we heard was the horde was driving ahead into the lands of the city states."

"Is that our best choice, Master?"

"Life is choices. No one can say one choice is better than another. It's a matter of choosing a path and then living with the consequences, whether good or bad. A person never knows what would have happened by choosing the other fork in the road."

"I admit, I've thought about home, but our work here required my presence. I couldn't abandon my friends with a job here unfinished."

"My Prince, if it's your wish to return to your home, we will accompany you," said Layla. It surprised him.

"Thank you Layla, but your family is here. I wouldn't rob them of the security of your protection."

"My Lord, if there is no enemy here, but they're accosting your home city how could we ignore that? We'll aid in their defense. You gave to us freely. How can we not repay your generosity? Our land is readied to the extent it can be while yours may be in peril."

"Layla, I'm awed by your generosity. Going to fight in a major battle against an army of savages is no small thing. I don't wish to lose any of you."

"We knew the risk when we joined your forces, My Prince. Wherever you lead, we will follow."

"I'm at a loss, Master. If I go back to Kragan, am I being selfish? Taking away elite troops from this land at a time where they may be sorely needed, it's a difficult choice."

"Damon, we've completed our work here. If you wish to lead us back to Kragan, we'll follow. I never wanted to lead this group of friends. Now at last I think you will take your rightful place of leadership. See how you've become beloved by people who were strangers to you. I've had faith in you all along. You're more than a prince in name. You're a true prince with your character and your deeds."

Damon glanced at Beth who smiled wryly. He also noticed out of the corner of his eye how Layla bristled. It was an interesting development Damon hadn't anticipated. Layla might have developed romantic thoughts and feelings for him. He didn't think about her in those terms.

"The decision is yours, Damon."

"Beth, when we last talked about our future course, you had strong feelings and considered going your own way," said Damon pointedly.

"I would say some of that is still true, but our efforts and our progress here have matured my thinking. I think part of what I said came from my loss and personal pain. It was never about any of my comrades. I've been pleased to dwell with all of you in the interim. You're my close friends. Does that answer your doubts, Prince Damon?"

Now it was Damon who smiled wryly.

"If you wish to put the decision in my hands, I say we make a sweep along the border again to check for Argore scouts and if the area is clear, and then we make the journey back to Kragan. It wouldn't be a permanent relocation, merely a visit."

No one objected. Damon shrugged acquiescing to the mantle of leadership Argon put on him.

"We'll leave early tomorrow morning."

"Beth, I'd still like the opportunity to speak with you and to spar," said Layla.

"Come along then," Beth replied with a confident air.

"Will you join us, Damon?" asked Layla. She eyed him hopefully.

"If you wish, ladies, we have a little time before we must prepare to leave."

The event took on epic proportions as Damon's guards saw it as a challenge to their relative competence. Beth was respected to the point of people being awed, but nonetheless, Layla was intent on scoring a win against Beth on many levels, not the least of which was in impressing the prince.

Beth understood fully the challenge from Layla and was very confident regardless. She looked at Argon rather than Damon, like it was he she wanted to impress. She was his protégé and didn't want to besmirch his reputation by losing a match.

Damon settled back with Amal and Berne to watch the female battle.

"Can this Layla of yours win, Damon?" asked Berne. "Beth can beat men."

"I wouldn't make a prediction, but I will say Layla is equally driven though her reasons are much different than Beth's. I think Beth will need to be at her best because Layla doesn't take defeat well at all."

"It's stimulating watching women fight," said Berne.

"You're such a reprobate, Berne," said Amal, laughing.

"I didn't mean it that way," Berne objected.

"Sure you didn't, we just need some quality mud for them to wrestle in," Amal replied derisively. "You're not alone. Look how ramped up everybody is."

"Have some decorum," Damon chided.

"You're the worst of them, Damon," Amal joked. "You love this too."

The friends laughed.

The women squared off just after dinner. The first attacks were tentative, feeling out each other for strengths and weaknesses, and for differences of fighting style.

It was like a switch was flipped because they went to full fighting in an instant. It was initially even and Layla started to press Beth with savage attacks battering at her defense. Beth reacted and dodged harm numerous times.

Damon watched the fight clinically gauging how he'd trained Layla against Beth's skill and strategy. He could see Beth was letting Layla exert her energy to tire her. Layla was strong and kept after Beth beyond what Beth anticipated. Beth changed her tactics and began to challenge Layla forcing her to the defensive, but still Layla persevered doggedly. The match continued relatively evenly and both women began to breathe heavily under the strain of continuous fighting. They could see the women were talking to each other though speaking too low for anyone else to hear what they said. Layla spoke and Beth chuckled frequently, like taunts were amusing to her.

Damon was conflicted as he didn't want either woman to lose. He sensed Beth was starting to gain an edge. Layla sensed it too and took action to turn the tide, but she was tiring. Her aggressive strikes drove Beth back, but Damon could see in her eyes she knew she would win. Layla yelled and attacked with all of her remaining energy. Beth parried each blow and waited.

Layla made a critical mistake at the end of a flourish and left an opening which Beth quickly exploited stepping under a swing to close on Layla. She grabbed Layla's sword hand with one hand and held her sword point to Layla's unprotected chest with her other hand.

Layla shrieked in frustration and turned to Damon like she deserved capital punishment for losing.

"Layla," said Argon stepping forward quickly. "That was a magnificent battle. There is no shame here. If you fought again, you could win the next contest. We're all proud of both of you. For women to reach such expertise in this world is remarkable. I'm blessed to have lived to see it. I would be proud to have either of you protecting my back."

Damon walked over.

"Congratulations, Beth. That was a fight for the ages. We all salute your prowess."

"Thank you, Prince Damon."

Damon reached a hand for Layla. She took it hesitantly.

"Did you hear Master Argon? His words are the highest of compliments. Your fight here exceeded any training I could have given you. It was more than skill. You fought with your heart and proved why I picked you as a leader of my guards. You're both rare women without peer."

The guards all cheered loudly along with the rest of the spectators.

"I should have won," she replied softly. She looked at Beth. "I'm forced to bow to your superiority, though it shames me to do so."

"Layla, I respect you greatly and worried if I could win the fight. You shouldn't despair. I feel fortunate to have won. I think as we spend time together you'll learn some things which will aid you in future fights. You're already a formidable fighter."

"You would be a friend, Beth?" she asked in true astonishment.

"Of course, it would be my honor, Layla. A person can't have too many friends."

The women smiled and then chuckled. Beth embraced Layla with a firm hug.

"We can pack our things for the early departure tomorrow," Damon added.

The women headed off to bathe after their lengthy contest.

* * * *

It felt good to Damon to be moving in the direction of home. Being gone for over a year healed Damon's inner bruises and he missed seeing his mother. Having a smart looking personal corps at his back bolstered his confidence and he no longer worried about dwelling in the shadow of his brother. The additional incentive to intervene if the Argore had come to their walls was a spur which hastened their pace.

They entered the great forest but with a force of this size they didn't worry about predators attacking them and continued to move rapidly along the shoreline once they reached the lake.

Passing their old hunting blind brought back memories for the friends and again when they passed their training camp.

Once they broke out of the forest and saw Kragan in the distance Damon's excitement rose. They were all happy to see no sign of battle. At this point in time the city was free of attack from the Argore horde. The King's standard still flapped in the breeze.

Damon felt proud to ride up to the gates, in force.

The guards scurried to readiness at the approach of an armed force.

"Prince Damon?" asked the guard captain when he got close enough.

"Greetings, my friends, it's good to be back. Please send word to the palace we've come to visit."

A little later they dismounted and entered the palace. It was an auspicious occasion to have the eldest prince of the realm returned, especially with an elite force of his personal guards numbering over a thousand.

They entered the throne room which was packed with his family, counselors, military leaders, courtesans, and various high ranking officials of the city.

They marched up to the throne and halted with a martial shout. When Damon went to a knee his people followed his example.

"Rise," said the king. "Welcome home, Son. It appears you've prospered in your time away on the road."

"Thank you, Father," he answered, turning his head slightly and smiling. "Hello, Mother."

She had tears in her eyes and suddenly rushed down to embrace him. They hugged tightly whispering to each other.

"I missed you, Damon."

"Mother, it's so good to see you again. I was worried the Argore might attack while I was gone."

"We're safe, at least so far, son."

He turned his head toward Tabor.

"Hello Brother, you look good. Hello, Selena."

Tabor smiled. "I hope our dark times are behind us, Brother. It was never my wish to have strife between us."

"They are as far as I'm concerned. My time away gave me a chance to grow up and put away childish feelings and mistakes. It's good to be home. Father, I must tell you it's a marvel to see Kragan. Your rule is a blessing for the people. I can appreciate it so much more now having been to other places. You have my respect and always did though I did poorly in telling you so."

"Thank you, Damon. I can't tell you how much that means to me. I do what I can though ruling is not so easy a job as other people might think."

"I understand, Father. I've been blessed to have some exposure to leading others. It's a heavy burden worrying about them. I know what you're saying."

"My Son, we're glad you're home. Argon, I'm sorry we so misjudged you in the beginning. What you've accomplished is nothing short of remarkable. What you promised you've fulfilled. Damon, Amal, and Berne are now men of great stature, worthy of renown. We thank you deeply."

"I started them on a path, but it's they that provided the heart and soul to reach for their destiny. I feel fortunate to have been able to accompany them, and I'm thankful they forced me to end my solitary and pointless life. I feel gratified to have done something to be proud of. My life hasn't always been such."

"Beth, I must say, your radiance lights up any room," the king added. "You're breathtaking even though you're incredibly dangerous."

Everybody laughed, including Beth.

"Thank you, Your Majesty. I appreciate your kind words, but I'll never see myself in those terms. I'm still a farmer's daughter. I just happen to carry a sword."

Everybody laughed again.

"Father, with your permission, I'll get my command settled into rooms. I look forward to spending time with my family later, if you can accommodate us."

"Of course, Damon, we'll have a banquet to celebrate your return. Your mother and I would be happy if you visit the royal suite for some private time."

"Perhaps I could come in several hours?"

The king looked at his wife.

"We'll see you then, Son," she replied.

"Tabor, I assume you'll be there too," Damon added.

"I, eh…I will," he stammered in pleased surprise.

"Good, it's been too long since our family was gathered together."

He marched his guards out to the barracks where they were given rooms. The royal troops eyed them curiously.

"You're free to tour the city," he told them. "Captain Gideon and Lieutenant Layla will accompany me to the royal festivities this evening. I'm sure I don't need to tell any of you not to make fools of yourselves in the city. Your behavior is a reflection on me and the entire corps, so use your heads."

The guardsmen chuckled.

Damon dressed appropriately for a Kragan social event to reflect his maturation. It was compelling to see Beth dressed up in feminine clothes. She'd even managed to convince Layla to discard her uniform for the evening. Layla was attractive in her own right. She eyed Damon closely to see what impression she made wearing an attractive and expensive dress. He smiled and nodded to her.

"You look lovely, Layla."

She smiled warmly.

"I hope this means I can dance with you at the party, My Prince."

"As long as you have protection on your feet from my clumsy dance steps," he replied jokingly.

Layla looked confused and looked at Beth.

"He's joking, Layla. The prince is a fine dancer."

Layla smiled at her and then at Damon.

"I'll look forward to our dancing, My Prince."

Damon looked at rugged Gideon who was stoic. He wasn't a person to seek social occasions. His focus was elsewhere. Socializing held no interest for him.

"Gideon, you'll be dancing also tonight." Damon smiled playfully.

Gideon grimaced. He shrugged but glared at both women who chuckled at his discomfort.

"Gideon, it's not so odious a task dancing with a woman," Beth commented.

"Indeed," he replied without mirth.

"This promises to be a great time," said Damon. Gideon looked like he was going to slug Damon for forcing him to participate in the event.

"Honestly, Gideon, I understand how you feel. I disdained these events most of my life and have only recently come to terms with the niceties of expected conduct in civilized society. You'll do fine. Just smile a lot."

"Smile while you dance with me, Gideon," Beth added with a mirthful look. He genuinely smiled at that comment.

They were about to leave to go to the ball room when there was a knock at the door. The guards ushered in Selena. She was dressed to kill and eyed both Beth and Layla.

"Prince Damon," she said in greeting with a bow. "I see you've developed a knack for attracting beautiful women. Hello, Beth, it's good to see you again."

"Hello, Selena, how is your betrothed, Prince Tabor?"

"He's well, thank you. We're not yet technically engaged. Most see it as a foregone conclusion, but the onus is on Prince Tabor to finalize such an arrangement. Does that mean I can hope for a dance with you, My Prince?"

"I find I'm deluged by requests to dance suddenly. I would say to you all, beware what you wish for because you might just get it. Dancing with me is something to avoid for your own protection. I can cause great injury with my ineptitude."

Gideon laughed which was a radical departure from his usual stern countenance.

"Thank you, Gideon," Damon responded ruefully. "I'm so glad my flaws provide you with such entertainment."

Gideon continued to laugh. The women joined with him in chuckling.

The women continued to eye each other, as if there would be another battle that evening, but this one of a different sort than Beth's epic fight with Layla. This one would be a fight to establish feminine dominance in front of a room full of admirers. It was a contest Selena was well suited to fight. Selena's "visit" put her competitors on notice she was throwing down the gauntlet, so to speak, in her area of strength.

Selena well remembered Beth's triumph previously with her incredible dress. This time Selena was determined to be ready for the challenge. Her dress on this night was incredible, perfectly complimenting her excellent physique. Beth and Layla's female forms were never in question with the demanding physical lives they lived. All three women were breathtaking physical specimens.

Gideon looked at the female standoff and then looked at Damon who shrugged and smiled wryly.

"Would you allow me to accompany you, Prince Damon?" Selena continued.

"That's fine, but I would have thought my brother would be coming for you."

"I'll see him there. He had another matter to look into I was told."

Prince Damon looked at her in curiosity but let the matter drop. Selena took his arm and they walked off. Layla took Gideon's arm and Beth joined arms with Argon when they saw him waiting at the door to the ballroom.

"Beth, you look incredible," he remarked. "You'll give an old man a heart attack."

"Quiet, Master Argon. Your attempts at being charming aren't necessary with me." She smiled warmly at him nonetheless.

Again, entering the room was dazzling with the sounds of music, the rainbow colors, the mass of swirling bodies, and the scents of the sumptuous feast.

Tabor was standing beside the king talking to him seriously. He didn't even look at Selena until Damon brought her close to them. The queen magically appeared making her way straight to her son.

"This is so much better, Damon. Thank you. I feel my days of worrying about you are over."

"I'm sorry I was such a pain in your life, Mother. I want you to know I'm on my best behavior tonight, though I've never really had any best behavior, but at least I realize it and I'm not looking to thwart your party."

She laughed heartily and looked at the young women.

"Ladies, you look magnificent."

"Your Majesty, you're still the fairest of us all," said Selena.

"It's a new time, your time to shine. I appreciate your kind words, but my best days are behind me and I'm fine with that. I don't envy the travails of romantic pursuit. I'm content to step back and concede the spotlight to youth."

Selena bowed to the queen and glanced at Damon. Tabor was still intent on his conversation. It piqued Damon's curiosity.

"Excuse me ladies, I wish to greet the king and the crown prince."

When he walked to their sides they looked at him lost in their thoughts.

"Is there a problem? You both look to be distressed."

"We've gotten word that Argore raiding elements have pressed forward in our direction. Although for some reason, they don't have the mass of the horde with them, they're still in numbers to threaten each of our cities. They're not at our gates, but it's a change in tactics. They hadn't been moving in our direction before," Tabor explained.

"I'll let Argon know. He's probably the best of us to interpret Argore motives and goals. Should I seek him out? He's dancing with Beth."

"No, don't spoil the mood, Son," the king replied. "This is meant to celebrate your return. Let's enjoy our evening, all of us. We'll leave our deliberations for the morning."

"As you wish, Your Majesty. Brother, I've brought Selena for you."

Tabor nodded to Damon before he looked at her, surrounded by her friends basking in the attention and worship of the mass of courtesans. Then he looked at Beth dancing with Argon. Beth noticed and looked back at him with a smile and a nod which Damon noticed. Before Damon could take a step down his old punishing path, they were interrupted as suddenly Layla walked boldly up to them.

"You're the other prince, Damon's brother?"

"I am," he replied in amused surprise. "You're Layla. I'm told your fight with Beth was epic. With her abilities, I'm awed at both of your great fighting prowess."

Layla laughed heartily and looked at Damon who smiled.

"Crown Prince Tabor, do you dance with strangers who are farmer's daughters, and peasants?"

"Yes, ma'am, I do," he replied. "It would be my honor and my great pleasure."

Layla took Tabor's arm but eyed Damon the whole way as she led his brother out to the dance floor, once again, to try to gauge the effect she was having. Tabor looked at her looking at Damon, realized it and was amused his brother was on new ground with female folk. Damon was equally amused. It was an arena where the women ruled and made their moves.

Not to be outdone, Selena requested Damon for the next dance, not allowing him to stand on the sidelines. He never left the dance floor after that until the meal was served as there were an endless number of ladies waiting for their turn with him. Tabor was smooth with his transition in reclaiming Selena after she parted from Damon. She was gratified like she'd won a contest with the crown prince bending him to her will. She eyed the other women smugly.

For her part, Layla paid little attention to the doings of the other women, except Beth. She zoomed in on Damon as often as she could, sometimes elbowing other women out of her way. It entertained Damon seeing the silliness of female competition in this format. It was a night off from the rigors of his military life.

For Damon, to be seen on a par with his dazzling brother was a quantum shift in his universe. It was gratifying and daunting at the same time.

At last, Damon's dance partner was Beth. She was in as high demand as Damon. She smiled coyly like it was a step in a game they were playing.

"You look much better this evening than the last time I was here for a ball," she chided.

"Thank you for reminding me, Beth," he replied. "I love remembering my many failures."

She chuckled. "I think it isn't so much a trauma now, Prince Damon. Those days are long past. You're a prize here for all the women to fight over."

Damon smiled. "I don't see you fighting anybody."

"I'm of a different temperament."

"Yes, I saw that when you fought Layla."

"Are you judging me?"

"I'm not in a position to judge anyone. I'm simply making an observation."

"I don't like to lose."

"Nor do I. You realize Layla is in your thrall. You're a standard she covets both in martial skill and also in personal composure and comportment. Whatever you truly seek as your goals, you allow no one else to know. Outwardly you mask your truth in this impervious façade of universal disdain for all other living beings. It has a predictable effect."

"I don't disdain anyone, Damon. It's a matter of my attention being focused elsewhere. The intrigues of others hold no interest for me."

"In that way, you remind me of Gideon. He's a grizzled man that seeks battle and little else."

"You would be surprised what else he values. I see similar attributes with me so perhaps I perceive what others miss in him. We're both peasants so royal concerns were never part of our upbringing."

"I find it hard to believe your only desire in life is to kill Argore. You can tell me that story again and again and I still won't believe it. Down deep somewhere in you is the truth. There is something you want. I'm determined to discover what it is. I see hints from time to time, like your forbearance and your appreciation of my brother. It bothered me because you know I want you. I could only cope by accepting your feelings aren't the same as mine. You can be moved by other men in the way I want to move you. It was a galling defeat for me, but it set me free. I still desire you and always will, but your part of it is in your hands."

Beth was staring at him, clearly affected.

"This isn't the place for this conversation," she said finally. "I think we will talk again, Prince Damon."

"I'm always available at any time you wish. I can say without hesitation that I love you down to my core, Beth. That won't change regardless of what you choose."

Again, if she was affected she refused to answer the lure of his powerful pronouncement.

When the dance ended, she bowed to him. He noticed her reluctance and her immediately parting from him. Speaking his feelings to her was always a risk and thus far it had never achieved the happy ending he craved. She was always elusive about romantic attachments.

"Thank you for the dance, My Prince."

She went to the refreshment table for a beverage of berry wine. Layla nabbed her there for an intense conversation. Beth smiled a great deal to Layla's avid questions and said little. He realized watching them it was clearly a matter of Layla acting territorial about Damon.

Damon was immensely curious, but forced himself to turn away. He went to his mother who was catching her breath.

"Are you enjoying the ball, Mother?"

"This is possibly the best of these things and it's because you're happy, Son."

"Will you dance with me? I need a break from the onslaught of women strangers. They're persistent tonight unlike anything I've ever faced before. They're like an insect attack you can't escape. You can swat at the gnats but they continue to swirl around your head."

The queen laughed. "I think this isn't the worst problem you could face. For most of your life you would have given anything to be in this position."

"That's probably true, Mother."

The king danced with Beth, again, while Damon danced with his mother.

She was an incredible dancer.

Layla approached them boldly at the end of the dance.

"My Prince, I'm free for the next dance."

It wasn't a question, it was a statement. The queen smiled at her son's discomfort.

"All right, Layla, but after this my feet need a rest."

Layla smiled broadly in triumph.

Tabor managed another dance with Beth. She always looked to be taken with him and he didn't fail to notice, nor did Damon. It tweaked that buried anxiety Damon worked so diligently to erase, without success. He could never ignore what occurred with Beth.

It was the latest Damon ever stayed at a royal ball when they finally gathered their things to leave. He was amused to see Gideon actually looked exhausted from the numerous dances, many of which were with Beth.

Beth took Gideon's arm possessively when they left. Layla quickly enmeshed Damon like her trophy to walk back to the sleeping quarters.

"Would you like a foot rub, My Prince?"

"Thank you, but no, Layla. I just want to sleep."

"It's your loss, Sire," she retorted, with a sassy smirk.

"I'll have to live with the loss, Layla, but thank you anyway."

It was a relief when he was finally alone just to relax and let his guard down. He fell asleep in an instant in the soft royal bed, like a ball was far more exhausting than having a battle.

He dreamed vivid dreams that night in which he was chasing after Beth who was in the company of his brother, both eyeing Damon scornfully. His brother smirked at Damon's failure to catch them. They were always beyond his grasp and laughing at him.

He didn't lapse into deep sleep until very late.

He was poorly rested when he went to the royal breakfast in the morning somewhat disheveled.

Chef Mathias eyed him reproachfully like he was a drunk embarrassing the realm. "Prince Damon, there is a price to pay for poor living habits and sloth."

It struck Damon as hilarious and he laughed heartily drawing in everyone else to laughter also. Chef Mathias was the last person to point to poor habits in others with his own considerable issues in that area. Beth looked at Damon, smiling pleasantly, that he wasn't acting boorish socially which eased his anxiety.

"It's good to see you laugh," she said as he walked past.

"It's good to have a reason to laugh," he replied.

Chapter Nine

While the city of Kragan began a bright sunny day in peace, hostile eyes watched them from the nearby forest. The Argore invasion was still a remote peril in the thoughts of the city residents, but the reality of lesser numbers of enemies coming to the area wasn't remote. These units were fast moving and feral, serving both as scouts for their brethren and opportunists if they found vulnerable victims to exploit.

The king had previously instituted regular patrols into the countryside, but they were easily avoided by the stealthy raiders. Their leader was a thick necked soulless brute but he was also shrewd. He avoided some pillaging opportunities so as not to tip off the city of their presence. He chose instead to spend a little time studying the city, their relative competence, and their habits and patterns.

When Damon rode into the woods along with friends and his guards, the Argore took notice. With over a thousand crack troops so near to them, the Argore faded back to use the utmost caution. Their leader had seen enough city forces in their lengthy travels to recognize good troops from bad. This city looked to be the greatest challenge they'd seen, by far. Their fortifications were better, their readiness was unquestioned, and it seemed this was a focal point for the lesser cities which were their neighbors. It would be a great gem to conquer and to plunder.

Rather than stay any longer, the Argore pulled out that evening under the cover of darkness to head back to their main camp and their leaders. This city was the logical place to concentrate their might, like the magnet drawing them to a great triumph.

Damon had no idea of their passing. He was momentarily inattentive distracted with the entertaining contest of the women in his life. Actually, more accurately it was Layla trying to contest with Beth, who shrugged off the silliness. Beth was amused by Layla and had rapidly developed great affection for her. Having lived most of her life apart from societies, it was gratifying to Beth to have a woman friend. Layla didn't yet qualify as a best friend, but she was speedily moving in that direction.

On the other hand, if Beth was growing fond of Damon, from his viewpoint she hid it well. Seemingly from his perceptions of her reactions, he was just another annoying man in her life for her to deter from his romantic goals.

Therefore for his part, he maintained his new found persona and outwardly acted is if Beth had no effect on him any longer. It wasn't true, of course, but he was determined she wouldn't know it. It did lead to an easier symbiosis between them. He made no moves she could interpret as romantic but it was an effort. He squelched his true feelings on a daily basis. She was tantalizing beyond description being so close at hand and yet always unattainable through any actions he could take.

Upon arriving in the forest they hunted to bring meat, vegetables, and fruits back to Kragan. Damon never forgot his cares for the poor. It made a favorable impression on Beth, but a huge impression on Layla, who was already taken with Damon. Seeing his fine inner qualities only strengthened her feelings about him. Gradually though, she competed less with Beth about the prince because Beth competed not at all. Rather, Beth showed her interest instead in Layla.

Damon sought out the widow and found she'd flourished in the interim, starting up a new business making clothing.

"Thank you for the food, My Prince. We've missed you here in Kragan. It's good to have you home."

"I'm not sure I can stay," he explained. "I fear my destiny is on the road rather than staying in one place."

"That would be our great loss," she reflected. "We hear rumors and many of them are frightening. It's nice to feel the safety of you and your little army of great fighters here to protect us."

"I'll be here as long as I can. I must say your children have grown a great deal from when I saw them last."

"They're good boys and girls. They help me fill the emptiness in my life with having no husband. It's not the same, but it's a help."

"I wish I could do something about that to help you, madam."

"It's my fate, Sire. Don't dwell on it. I'm doing fine."

"You're a remarkable woman. Don't close your mind to finding another mate."

"That's not an easy choice. Trusting strangers is difficult for the poor. We're so often abused and taken advantage of."

"If anyone tries any mischief with you, I want you to come to me personally and I'll deal with the matter."

The widow smiled. "I will, thank you, My Prince."

"I must go, but I bid you a good day, madam."

As Damon got back on his horse, he noticed Beth watching him. He looked and she smiled.

"What?"

"This side of you is so gratifying, Prince Damon. You truly are this person who genuinely cares about others. That's a rare and wonderful trait."

He shrugged. Trying to say something self-effacing and humble didn't seem a good idea, like she'd see it as shallow. He merely turned and moved on back to the palace.

The dynamics in the palace remained different for Damon. Selena paid much more attention to him and Tabor paid a great deal of attention to Beth. Layla chose to insert herself into those moments with Tabor, like she was the personal protector for Beth's virtue.

Tabor quickly grew annoyed with never having Beth to himself. Equally, Selena was provoked when her advances failed to click with Damon. He remained aloof and overtly polite.

Tabor wasn't accustomed to not getting his way when it came to women. Usually, there was little effort necessary on his part because they were in his thrall and often the aggressors. Having to deal with Layla's protective instincts left him bewildered. Beth never gave him any hope that he impressed her. For the first time in his life, he felt inadequate to the task, a glimpse into Damon's world.

Layla was either glued to Beth's side or making overt advances to Damon.

Meanwhile, Argon used his time back in the city very skillfully. He never made any questionable moves toward the queen, but it just seemed he was in her company a great deal. It was a serious dilemma for the king who needed Argon's alliance, yet it was clear to everyone the queen held a special place for him. Argon smiled blithely and the queen acted courteous but if a person watched them, there were occasional glances, a subtle touch, and a few whispered words exchanged on the sly.

Beth and Layla noted the connection and spoke in private about it.

"Can it be Master Argon has dubious designs regarding the queen?" asked Layla. "I never expected such a thing could be within him. I never thought of him as a regular man with flaws."

"We can't make assumptions, Layla. My thought is he's a lonely man who has no relationship with a woman to cherish and to feed his soul. At the same time, he's no fool. If the queen is vulnerable about him, and I'm not saying she is, he knows the price of crossing that line. I think that both harbor secret yearnings but they control them. I can't say what problems she might have in her marriage to the king. It may be there is more to this we don't know. The queen is an incredible woman in so many ways. Argon isn't the only person drawn by her beauty and her charm."

"Do you think Argon may have known her before she married the king, Beth?"

"That's possible, I suppose. They're of a similar age and he's traveled widely. Regardless, the realities of the current situation is I don't think he'd put anyone in jeopardy with poor choices."

"He's the master to us. As I said, I never thought of him in those terms of being a man with a man's needs. He teaches us the war arts."

"Why not, Layla? He's a man like any other. What man, or woman for that matter, doesn't have needs? I find him to be a compelling and attractive person. Why not the queen too? Because people marry doesn't mean they no longer have eyes. They see other people and finding another person attractive isn't inconceivable, it's nature. The wrong is in acting on those impulses."

"I think when you're young, you don't imagine older people having intimacies."

"Layla, think about what you just said. Is there an age you would want to say no more loving allowed because other people think I'm too old?"

They both chuckled.

"You have an excellent point there, Beth. Let me ask you something else. Do you think married people who've been together a long time, well, become discontent or unfulfilled with the same partner? I've never been married to know. Does the luster fade with time until they feel the need to look elsewhere?"

"I have no basis to judge that either, Layla. If the king and queen have an issue about that, I couldn't guess it. My opinion is various people react differently and in some cases radically different. There probably are women who marry and find it isn't what they expected and possibly they do look about at others to quench unfulfilled needs. Actually, I think secret activities in that area may be far more prevalent than you would think."

"I wonder what that means for us, Beth. Will we be put in that situation in our futures?"

Beth shrugged.

"What if I was weak and stumbled," Layla continued.

"If you did, you wouldn't be alone, far from it."

"I suppose we can't speak to the queen. Perhaps she needs strong friends close at hand to help her do the right thing."

"Right, Layla. You already know the answer. Bringing up such a question would probably anger the queen and it wouldn't be good for us. It's a situation between Argon and the queen. We must keep our distance about that difficult possibility."

"I can't help but worry about the problems of others, Beth. It's in my nature."

"I know that, Layla. I'm well aware of your scrutiny of me and so is Prince Tabor. I hope you know I don't need a chaperone for matters of my personal life."

"I'm sorry, Beth, but I perceived he had ill designs for you. I didn't want you to be taken advantage of."

"That needs to be my decision. If I do or don't want to be taken advantage of isn't a matter for your intervention. By the way, I won't be scrutinizing your actions either."

"Oh, I, eh…I never considered you might be agreeable to, well, being with Prince Tabor. As far as my actions, there's nothing to scrutinize."

"That's not what I said. I'm only talking about making my own choices. My situation is no different than the queen. I must consider the consequences of my actions. Prince Tabor is alluring, obviously, but for me he's no more intriguing than Prince Damon."

"Yet you spurn Damon time after time while you seem receptive to Tabor's advances."

"That's not exactly the case, but the reasons are mine. It has nothing to do with Damon. There may be a time when I look to begin a relationship and Prince Damon would be at the head of the line of my considerations."

"In the meantime, I hope you understand I'll continue to pursue him too. If I catch him at a weak moment, I'll become his wife so fast…"

They both laughed.

"You're a shameless hussy, Layla."

"For Damon I would be whatever it takes."

"I accept you putting me on notice, Layla. I'm not conceding him to you."

"In a fair fight, I have no chance if you decide to claim him, but in the interim I'm going to live my fantasy and pretend I could have a happy ending in the royal bed."

"That's fine, Layla. Perhaps you'll suit Damon's fancy and he'll choose you. I think you'd be a fine wife for him, or any other man."

"Beth, that's the kindest thing anyone has ever said to me. I'm humbled by your magnanimous spirit. Self-interest is one of my many flaws, I strive to be better about it and I fail on a daily basis. It's no secret I covet the prince, but I know I have no chance with him. It's fun for me to dream."

Beth looked solemnly at Layla. "You know I have unfinished business on behalf of my family, but I have other issues I'm coping with. I don't really want to explain right now, but I may tell you at a later time. I have questions I need to answer to my own satisfaction. Layla, you're dear to me. I never had a sister, or a best girlfriend. Maybe my neediness will become odious for you."

"You've got to be kidding, Beth. You're a treasure to all who know you. I love that you allow me to be a part of your world. I feel unworthy, but thankful."

She embraced Beth who hugged her tightly.

"Beth, do you truly not see that other women would die to trade places with you, to be acknowledged by you, to be included in your circle, and to be cherished by you?"

"If that's true, they're very misguided."

"I think not. You've piqued my curiosity. It's hard to imagine you would have any problems or issues to trouble you. I'm happy to listen to hear your woes and to help you."

"I'm not ready, Layla."

"As you wish, Beth, but if you carry a burden it gets heavier and starts to affect you increasingly. I say lance the boil now and be done with it. You know you can trust me with anything to keep your secrets."

"Lance the boil, that's quite an analogy, Layla."

"I tell it like it is, Beth." She smiled impishly.

"I trust you, Layla, I really do, but it's me. I have some things to figure out on my own. When I'm ready, you'll be the first to know."

"I'll hold you to that, Beth. I won't wait forever."

"Fair enough, Layla."

* * * *

An Argore raiding party rode into the main camp which sprawled across a flat area just below their mountain home. The vast array of tents looked like an endless mushroom field with their shape and uniform grayish coloring. The high chieftain's massive tent dwarfed any other tent and there was continuous traffic into and out of it. The raiders headed straight there.

Their leader dismounted and walked boldly inside.

The council was in conference with the chieftain who spotted him immediately. He nodded for the raider to approach.

"You have news?"

"I do. We found a city that looks to be what we want. They're the most formidable by far and the most prosperous. Their forces looked to be a worthy challenge and I suspect once we breech their defenses what waits inside will be a treasure in loot and in new slaves. We saw some of their women and they were very appealing. I made no move to save us our options. There were no other destinations anywhere near the quality of this city."

"Good work. I've grown restless sitting here. We'll mobilize the camp and be moving within the week. Return to that city but take sufficient force to strike at them if needed. We have too many Argore idled and thirsting for war without meaningful battles to fight."

"As you command, My Chief."

The following day a significant force of Argore rode away back in the direction of Kragan. They raided along the way striking at easy targets, but concentrated on covering the distance as quickly as possible.

* * * *

Damon's father had been listening to Argon's warnings and had sent word to the other cities about the need for cooperation for mutual defense. Those cities closest to the Argore threat sent patrols, but more than that, they established secret watching stations. They spotted the large force leaving the main Argore camp and sent word via fast riding teams to the other cities.

Kragan received notice of the Argore thrust in advance to be able to prepare for an attack.

"Part of your plans should include failure contingencies," Argon explained to the king and his council. "It's fine to believe you can defeat any foe and I admit your outer defenses are formidable, but my experience in war is things don't always go as you expect. Losing in war to the Argore means annihilation. You must have plans to save your women and children. The forest is an obvious escape route, but the Argore will know that too. It's what you do next and where you go that matters. We've been beyond the forest and prepared those farm settlements, but their fortified hamlets can't withstand major Argore attacks. Where else you can go, I can't really suggest."

"You believe we have no chance to withstand the invasion?" asked the king.

"They have time to wait while you consume your stores of supplies. Eventually they'll starve you out to meet them in open ground. Until then, yes you can bleed them as they try to scale your walls. Unfortunately they never give up and would never just go away."

Argon looked at the sober faces staring at him.

"I'm sorry to be the bearer of such dire news, but that's how I see it. If anyone has another idea, it's your choice to consider it."

The king looked around, already knowing there were no other options. His counselors stared at him in helplessness. He looked at his beautiful wife, the queen. She watched him solemnly.

"Argon, you have no stake here in Kragan. Can I ask you to organize and plan the contingency, the failure scenario? I would trust you to take our loved ones to safety if it can be done at all. It would fall on you to decide where to go afterwards to flee from the Argore."

Argon looked at the queen. "Of course, Your Majesty, if that's your will. I'll do what I can. I would say we must move stores and supplies into the forest as a first stop if we flee. It would also give you another option to have separate forces not tied down trapped in the city. They could strike at the enemy to relieve the pressure on Kragan and evade their counterattacks with fast moving tactics, avoiding pitched battles. I don't know if it would change the ultimate outcome of the war, but it could extend your survival time."

"I agree."

"A second thing you must consider is that as the Argore approach there will be floods of refugees from the other cities that have fallen. They will be added fighters but additional mouths to feed at a time when your stores of food are finite."

"We've spoken about that," the king replied. "It's a terrible choice. We've chosen to be compassionate people in Kragan. When it comes to our survival versus that of those others…"

"It's a decision forced on you that no one wants," Argon mentioned. "I know what that's like."

"I suspect there's little else to say," said the king in sorrow. "We're left with the difficult truth that our ending could be coming to our gates. We'll fight while we still stand, but I tend to think Argon is correct, we need to make provision for our families."

"Father, what would you have me say to the army?" asked Tabor.

"Tell them war is coming. They need to give their utmost in defense of Kragan. We're fighting for the right to continue existing."

"We'll have sufficient water, sire," said one of his main advisors. "They can't affect our deep wells. It's the food that will be our problem. I estimate we could subsist for up to a year if we wisely apportion meals to the populace. That's not including any refugees we take in."

The king looked at his eldest son. "Damon, I assume you'll be with Argon's command. I trust you to safeguard your mother."

"No one will be allowed to harm her," Damon replied grimly.

"Good, Son, it's reassuring to hear."

"Father, I for one don't intend to abandon Kragan. My guards are highly skilled and we will be lethal if the Argore attack. We can cause major problems for them. I'm not willing to concede defeat to the Argore. They can be killed like any other enemy. We've wiped them out every time we've met in battle."

The people in the room muttered ascent. Damon inspired their fighting spirits.

The king smiled. "This is true, Son."

"Don't get overly optimistic," Argon cautioned. "Those fights were with small numbers of them. This war will be different."

"My question is when should we consider evacuating the women and children? If we wait until we're surrounded and cut off from escape, it's too late."

"Sire, that's the obvious dilemma for all Kragans. If you send them away before the Argore arrive you give them the chance to escape, you greatly extend your time before you use up your supplies, and the men can concentrate on the battle without worrying enemy raiders have found a way to infiltrate the city and accost the innocent."

"We know that, Argon, but it's not an easy thing to part from your family."

"In that decision I can offer you no advice. I have no family and have been a traveler most of my life. Being tied down to one place hasn't been my fate as it is yours. You must seek your answers among your own families. They won't want to leave you either."

"We still have some time. I've sent patrols farther afield to watch for the Argore. I hope to gain an advantage knowing where they are and when they'll arrive here."

The queen stood up. "I don't want to speak for the other women, but I want to say, if Kragan falls, I have no wish to live as a widow. I would rather die here with my husband. We appreciate what you want to do to safeguard us, but living out there in the open ground running ahead of Argore pursuit isn't a life I choose. I suspect they would eventually run us down and we'd suffer our same fate but just a little later in time. I'm not naïve. I know what they do to women. I still have the power to end my life before they could take me. Do you understand?"

"Mother, have some faith in me. I'm not willing to lose you, or Father."

"I don't doubt your bravery, or war skills, Damon. As Argon has said, battle is a risk. A lucky enemy sword stroke or a stray arrow can claim the lives of even the greatest of warriors. Going outside on the run takes away our feelings of security and lessens our options as women."

"We'll talk about this further," said the king.

When Damon went out of the room after the conference ended, Beth was waiting along with Layla and Gideon.

"There's no final decision," he told them.

"Do you have any orders?" asked Beth.

Damon smiled. "You're pretending you take orders from me now, Beth?"

They all chuckled.

"I've always noted your requests, Damon. Argon wishes for you to be our leader so I honor his wishes."

"I take that to mean I didn't earn your loyalty on my own."

"You always look for ulterior meanings, Damon. You've always had my esteem."

Beth shook her head in frustration and looked at Layla. "Do you see what I say? Men are impossible to understand, or to deal with."

"I do, Beth." She smiled mischievously at Damon.

He looked at Gideon who was listening to the exchange clinically, as if human interactions could never affect him personally.

"To answer your question, Beth, I have no orders, per se. I thought I'd lead a patrol to check the frontier on my own. It may be we'll spot something the others might miss."

"We'll go change clothes and meet you shortly," Beth replied.

Damon watched Layla and Beth walking away, chuckling and joking together. They acted like sisters. He looked again at impassive Gideon.

"Let's go gather the guards, my friend."

As Damon walked along with Gideon, Tabor approached along with Selena.

"What are you going to do, brother?" he asked.

"We're going out on patrol. My command gets restless very easily. They're not city bred folk."

Selena smiled in amusement. Tabor got a bemused look too.

"I've come to understand what you've said all these years, Damon. The lure of breaking the bonds of the city and traveling about freely is becoming far more appealing. I didn't understand when you said you didn't want the throne. Now I understand. I'm envious of your life of freedom. I wish I had your options."

Damon shrugged and glanced at Selena holding his brother's arm. No longer being a lure with Beth occupying that place in his mind, he could deal with her without emotional torment.

"Selena, you look lovely today."

"Thank you, Prince Damon." She smiled warmly.

Tabor showed no sign of jealousy at his brother's statement. It truly was a new dynamic between them. He'd matured and saw his brother with different eyes, no longer the perpetual rival. In truth, the lure of Beth was a major factor for both men. Her never ending intransigence about romance added to her irresistible appeal. It wasn't difficult for Tabor to imagine Beth on his arm rather than Selena. He didn't act on the impulse as he knew it would do no good anyway, but it was alive in his mind.

Damon, for his part, chose to avoid such entanglements after having such a punishing past. He'd spent much of his life commiserating over relationship issues to his great chagrin. Currently, it had proven much easier to block them out of his mind and follow Beth's lead to act aloof. It was the only way he'd found where he could function.

"Have a good day," he said and left with Gideon.

* * * *

An hour later they rode at the head of his guards toward the city's main gate. Argon joined Beth for the mission. They were riding immediately behind Gideon and Layla. On this day, Damon chose to ride alone at the head of the column.

He pondered a number of things as they turned toward the frontier. It felt unusual rather than taking their normal route to the forest.

They passed a returning Kragan patrol on the road.

"What word from ahead?" asked Damon.

"There's talk of raids across the whole front, but we saw nothing, My Prince."

"Thank you, captain, and safe journey home."

Damon led them riding rapidly and passed their nearest neighboring city without stopping there. One of that city's patrols approached and normally it could have led to an incident, but under these circumstances of a unified threat to all cities the petty squabbles had been put aside. The captain merely nodded to Damon.

Damon saluted him which put a smile on his face. "You're Prince Damon. No one else would be so magnanimous showing respect with strangers."

"We're both just soldiers, captain. Good hunting to you. Show no mercy when you meet the Argore. They're vicious, heartless and deadly."

"We will, sire. Good hunting to you also."

They rode until dark before making camp. Beth bunked beside Argon, as she always did. Berne and Amal bunked near her, as they always did. They were no less the friends of Damon, but the boyhood bonds had changed. As men, Beth was a blazing flame that drew any man. Damon had Layla bunked near to him, although it was becoming more frequent she would bunk by Beth too, splitting time between the two.

Argon existed in a new world of companionship he didn't choose, but one he didn't reject. It was difficult for others to read what he was thinking. Having beautiful Beth in his thrall was gratifying even for him. He felt contentment that he'd lacked for much of his life. His hidden demons he kept private.

Damon had no limit to how far they'd travel. Mostly he was looking for something out of the ordinary. They passed other cities and other patrols until one day they saw smoke on the horizon. Beth saw it first and grew grim with a feral look. She rode toward the scene without waiting for Damon's decision. The command followed her at the gallop as she rode at full speed.

By the time they got to the battle, it was lost by a collection of farmers gathered to fight together to save a farm.

There were screams from the house as the Argore raiders broke in the front door. The barn was on fire. Several farmers were fighting to survive surrounded by fierce raiders.

Beth was the first to arrive, hacking down surprised Argore in her rage. Damon and the guards were right behind her as the impending disaster at the farmhouse was quickly changed into a rout the other way.

The Argore fought savagely, but these weren't farmers they were fighting. Damon and his superb command mowed them down with no remorse. He hurried to catch Beth who raced alone into the farmhouse. Argon was right behind him entering through the door.

Beth was beset by five Argore but she was holding her own. Layla quickly leaped to her side along with Argon and numerous guardsmen. Argon and Damon went into the other rooms to deal with the depredations of the Argore on the helpless wives.

It was grisly work slaughtering these killers, but one which they didn't back away from.

After it was over, the farm survivors sat hollow eyed and traumatized. They'd lost dear friends and it hadn't hit them yet. Some wives were now widows, some children fatherless.

Beth was greatly affected, going about personally consoling them, tears streaming down her cheeks. The pain in their eyes resonated with her memories and feelings about her own tragic night on her father's farm.

Layla was equally moved and accompanied Beth everywhere in helping the survivors.

"Beth's reliving her own tragedy with this," Gideon muttered, stating the obvious. He looked sad at the development.

Damon nodded his head in agreement. "Maybe this will help her get past it by helping others. It's been the main driver in her life since I've known her. I hope she does because I believe this fixation with revenge won't have a happy ending."

"Very true," said Argon who walked up to them. "In the meantime we must continue to be patient with her. I know you get frustrated, Damon. Letting her heal and evolve can't be rushed. It will be worth the wait when she moves past these emotional troubles. She has strong feelings for you, Prince."

"I hope so, Argon. I have yet to see it. She has stronger feelings for you."

"I'm the father figure. It plays into her pain of loss of her own father. Don't mistake it for a romance of some sort. I'm not a competitor for her hand. I wouldn't saddle any woman with tying them to me. I'm not a candidate to marry any woman and especially not Beth."

"Argon, I think you're wrong. It's glaringly obvious to the world how I feel about Beth, but until I'm satisfied she shares those feelings for me, I'm not ruling out any other possibility. It may be she doesn't see you as off limits in spite of your opinion. If it's a direction she picks, I must be able to cope with it. Maybe it's an impossible scenario in your mind, but you can't speak for what's in her mind, or her heart. Differences of age aren't so key a factor for some people. I've given her every opportunity to express feelings for me, but consistently, she warms to every other man but me. Essentially, it's her decision, not mine. I've only recently come to a viable accommodation in my own mind dealing with her and that accommodation is basically not dealing with her. If she comes to me I'm cordial, but it works best for me to let her follow a separate path with those other people she chooses. Does that make sense to you? It's just a survival mechanism for my emotions. You don't have to agree, but there it is."

Argon looked concerned. He glanced at Gideon.

"I have no thoughts about this," Gideon advised. "Relationships and bonding aren't an area I know about. What Damon says makes sense to me. I think a young woman can be impulsive and sometimes she makes decisions that seem to defy male logic. She may have plans in her mind involving you, Master Argon. I wouldn't discount it."

Argon looked away in the direction of Beth and Layla, like he was suddenly in mortal peril.

* * * *

They stayed at the farm that night. In the morning, the farm families decided to head for the closest settlement for protection.

Damon didn't discuss the obvious fact the Argore invasion would sweep away the small communities like a tidal wave passing through. Whether fleeing in front of the invaders was a better choice, he honestly didn't know.

He led his command toward the advance of the Argore invaders. It wasn't long before they saw battles ahead in numerous places across the front as patrols from various cities clashed with the approaching scouts of the Argore advance.

Ironically, they just missed the passing of the large force heading toward Kragan. It was the original scouts who'd re-directed the focus of the entire horde. They were greatly increased in size and a potent threat to anyone they came upon.

As Damon traveled further they also encountered a radical increase in refugees fleeing the fall of the initial cities the Argore attacked. Their stories of the carnage were graphic and disturbing.

"They're monsters," Damon heard from numerous people. "They have no humanity and they delight in the most horrible of actions. Sire, you need to wipe them off the planet. They should all burn in hell."

It evoked Damon's anger. Too many of the refugees were helpless women and children. Their husband's and son's had fought to the death to spare them, but in battles that could end only one way. Those fights had been mismatches between the opposing sides before the battles ever began.

Chapter Ten

Damon sat at the campfire that evening talking with his close friends highly evoked by the actions of the invaders.

"I'm enraged by what we see," he uttered in terse tones. "It moves me to seek them out and strike a savage blow. War is ugly, but they take it beyond the realm of conquest for gain of money or goods. They delight in the worst of behaviors. We can't allow it here and certainly not for the people in Kragan."

"Damon, you can't let your emotions rule, you must use good sense," Argon replied. "You have a formidable force, but going against the horde is like emptying a vast lake a bucket at a time. It would be easy enough for them to surround us, pin us down, and pick us off. They have near to endless bodies to throw into such a fight. Do you see? We're all outraged at their callous acts and their vile excesses, but this isn't the answer. Meeting them in the open to battle their patrols and advance groups, that's the best plan of action at this point. The great battle will come, but not out there where they have the advantage."

Damon looked at Beth who was simmering with rage. She said nothing, but it was obvious how she felt and what she wanted to do. Argon turned to her.

"Beth, I understand this has awakened your memories, and your nightmares. You look at those victims, those innocent families and you want to protect them all. It's impossible. There are too many and we are too few. We need to make our best choices and take action that will have an effect. If we take impulsive action and we're slaughtered, how does that help the victims? We're a powerful force for good, but only if we stay alive. Our own emotions can be among the greatest challenges we face in life and that's true for more than just war."

Layla put her arm sympathetically around Beth's shoulders. Some of the hardness softened in Beth's eyes. She relaxed visibly.

"Do you want to go closer to them, Damon?" asked Berne.

"I guess it doesn't serve a purpose at this point. If we're not going to do battle there's no reason to stay here. As Argon says, the helpless must be left to flee and fend for themselves as best they can. I don't like it, but I admit there's no better way I can think of. I feel what Beth feels, an abiding hatred that isn't easily assuaged. When the time comes, our time, I plan to exercise every fiber of my being to punish the Argore. They deserve worse than anything I could do to them."

Beth looked at him like he'd finally found a shared wavelength. She patted Layla on the knee and stood up.

"I'm going to stretch my legs," she muttered. "I need a break from this depressing conversation."

"I'll walk with you," Layla added quickly. They walked away into the darkening night talking softly.

Damon felt his old anxiety, like he'd been dismissed again, rendered irrelevant. His recent coping strategy of trying to ignore her didn't always work. He could never eliminate the fact he cared deeply for Beth and her actions would always impact him, but in her times of need she always looked elsewhere to other people and he still couldn't cope with that.

Looking up self-consciously, Damon saw all the men staring at him, Berne, Amal, Argon, and Gideon. He felt defensive even though he wasn't being attacked. These were his friends. Though they were on his side, Damon still felt their judgment of his weaknesses.

"What?" he asked, with too much ire. They all shrugged and glanced at each other, like an 'I told you so' moment had unmasked the truth buried inside him in spite of his outer pretense. His ruse was a failure and Beth was still his undoing.

"I'm going to take a turn at guard duty tonight," Damon added with a grimace. "I can't sleep now anyway."

"As you wish," Argon replied with a pensive look.

Although he had concerns about the two women potentially wandering out of camp and into trouble in the night, Damon took up a position to keep watch over the camp rather than seeking them out. When they finally returned to camp much later they did so stealthily in the darkness so he had no idea if they'd been gone for a short walk, or not, his personally having never seen them re-enter the sentry line to the safety of the camp. Whatever they'd needed to talk about was their matter, or so he told himself.

Damon awoke his replacement in the deep of night at the proper time and went to his bedroll to salvage some sleep. All the people around him were shadows in the darkness. The camp fire was nearly out so there was virtually no illumination. Just before he lay back to close his eyes, he heard soft sounds to his right. He squinted to see what it was but it was too dark. It appeared there was movement some ways away in the blankets, but he could discern nothing.

If it was someone in his command restless in their sleep, it relieved his mind about Argore sneaking in, but he couldn't be certain.

The movements and the faint sounds continued. He was curious, but not enough to go over to investigate. Damon lay back and fell asleep nearly instantly.

The following morning, Damon awoke late. Most of the camp had already eaten breakfast.

"You should have awoken me, Gideon?"

"You needed the sleep. I'll get you some breakfast while you wash up."

Damon glanced around. Beth was happy, smiling talking with Layla, Berne, and Amal.

Damon couldn't stop his feet from walking over to them.

"I'm glad to see you two."

Beth looked at him thoughtfully. Layla always paid close attention when Damon came near.

"I was a little worried when you wandered off in the dark. Argore could be shadowing us. Two stragglers would have been easy prey."

The women chuckled. "The day an Argore attacks us as easy prey will be his last day to draw breath," Beth retorted.

"I didn't see you come back?"

"It was late. We wanted to talk about some things. Time got away from us. We don't need…"

"I know, Beth," he snapped, cutting her off. "So I was worried, I'm sorry. Go back to whatever you're doing."

"Damon?" asked Layla. "We're skilled warriors that have seen much fighting. We can be trusted to make safe choices. I don't understand why you're upset?"

"Forget I said anything," he groused.

"You need more sleep," Beth added. "You're cranky this morning."

He felt like a petulant child being chastised by adults, not a leader of the camp. Damon took a long drink of coffee as Gideon approached with his breakfast.

"Thank you, Gideon."

He sat down but with his back to the others to gobble down the food for his breakfast. He drank the coffee in large gulps.

Berne came to sit on one side and Amal on the other.

"Damon, what was that?" asked Berne.

"Berne," he replied in exasperation, "we're not always at our best. Can I get a pass for one day? The women already got me. Isn't that enough punishment?"

Berne glanced at Amal. They got up and left him.

"If you need us…" said Amal as they walked away to rejoin the two women.

It was a poor start to his day and the start of a depressed mood that stayed around long afterwards.

Their trek toward the horde ended, they turned to arc back toward Kragan. The flood of fleeing refugees all around them escalated as they traveled.

"It appears the Argore main body is moving from the reports we get and the increased refugee traffic," Gideon mentioned to Argon.

"It seems they were searching for something, like a hunter seeking prey. Apparently, they found it and are moving to close the trap, Gideon."

"Indeed, that's my thought also. I guess it doesn't really change anything for us as far as our plans."

Damon listened to their conversation without comment. His mind was occupied pondering his usual conundrum, Beth. On this day he was content to merely follow wherever they led the column.

At that point in time when Damon stopped each night it was becoming routine that they drew refugees seeking out food and safety in unfamiliar ground.

"Please, my lord, we ask for mercy," Damon heard time and time again.

He didn't deny anybody sanctuary for the night. These citizens could just as easily be Kragans. In reality, he was disappointed he couldn't do more for them.

The stories the survivors told were eerily similar about their encounters with the Argore. Their battle tactics were merely to overwhelm inferior foes. Once they prevailed, their warriors were turned loose on the hapless civilians and what they did was appalling.

It wasn't conquest to accumulate more lands and to enslave people. It was decimation, humiliation, and utter destruction. What remained behind when they left an area was a living nightmare. People survived those dire scenes by mere chance, hiding during the attack, moving to a place the Argore didn't happen to visit, it could have been anything that spared them over less fortunate neighbors. Survival by random chance didn't occur to people more or less worthy. Virtuous people were captured as often as people of low character.

"It doesn't make sense to me, Argon. Killing for no other reason than they can, it accomplishes nothing. Can living beings be so deranged as to do such things merely for enjoyment? Is there a secret reason we're missing? Do they have some ancient grievance against the lowland cities? How can an entire society be so craven?"

"Prince Damon, I've been in their mountains and I can give you no explanation to their behavior. Every minute I was there I was on the run in mortal peril. An outsider is only seen as an enemy. They hunt you until either you or they are dead. As I told you, I had to kill all of my pursuers to be able to survive. I know they have internal conflict and the weak among them have short lives, but as far as their society, no one knows about it. They selectively send some captives back to their mountains. I don't know what standard they use to make their selections. They can be any sex, any age, there's no particular targeted physical appearance, like they're random choices. The only consistency about the Argore is they're always unpredictable, and they're deadly opponents."

"It sounds like anybody who isn't Argore needs to adopt the Argore method and kill every one of them that they meet."

"Unfortunately, that may be the case, Damon."

"Then we have a big job ahead of us, Argon. We have a horde to wipe out."

The camp that evening was particularly congested as multiple parties of refugees converged drawn by the camp fires and the smell of food.

The picket line of sentries had to triple the area they guarded which meant more troops had to be on duty for each shift. Damon took another turn on guard duty. On this night there were so many bodies trying to sleep Damon never spotted Beth, Layla, Berne, Amal, or even Gideon, for that matter.

He stayed alert because he sensed something was amiss. Danger was nearby. When it was nearly time to change the shift, they attacked. There were no shouts, war whoops, or other signals to alert the camp. It happened Damon noticed something in the shadows and shouted to warn his comrades.

This late, it took a few moments for the sleepers in camp to arouse and realize there was an attack under way.

The sentries began to fire arrows and they heard yelps of Argore being struck. The Argore started to shout and sprint forward, but there was just enough distance for them to cover even on the dead run that reinforcements from camp arrived to bolster the skirmish line. The two forces met in a clash of swords, shouts, and screams as fighters on both sides met their end.

Damon fought fiercely. Here was his chance to vent his hatred, but his mind wouldn't allow him to succumb totally to berserker frenzy. He started to gauge the fight, and look for problems. When guardsmen pressed close to his position and forced themselves in front to protect Damon he ran along the line. If there were Argore breakthroughs, Damon personally led the assault of reserves to drive them back and preserve the defensive line.

He found the people he cared about on the complete opposite side fighting shoulder to shoulder. Amal and Berne flanked Beth and Layla, Argon and Gideon were nearby like two angels of death scything down enemies.

Damon was tempted to step in to join them, but they had matters well in hand, so he continued his circuit.

This was a sizeable attack and the numbers appeared to be even on each side, at least in the beginning of the battle.

The civilians huddled in terror in the center of the fighting.

The Argore fought like demons, insane and relentless, but they could be killed. They were fighting a different breed of soldier here. Damon's crack troops didn't back down, didn't lose faith they could win, and they weren't intimidated fighting the legendary invincible Argore. They were trained to a superior state and their battle tactics were flawless. The Argore fighters weren't accustomed to meeting such skill and it showed in the fighting.

Both sides incurred losses, but as the battle raged, Damon's side turned the tide and felled Argore fighters to a point the Argore commander realized he would lose this fight. He tried to withdraw his survivors to come back another time with much greater numbers. Damon knew this, so they pursued the retreating Argore leaving none they could catch alive. The commander was captured though some of his men got away. Most of his force lay on the ground dead or dying.

Damon had him dragged into the camp and they kindled the fire.

People among the civilians recognized him and rose up to take revenge. Damon had to restrain them.

"Wait, I don't keep him alive to show mercy. I need to learn what I can about them. He'll pay the price for his sins, believe me."

For this, Beth sought him out and stood at Damon's side glaring at the beaten but unrepentant Argore leader.

"My lord, he killed my family before my eyes," said a young woman.

"I understand, will you be patient for a short time?"

She nodded, but her hatred moved them all.

The Argore captive stared at the ground.

"Argon, can you talk to him?"

Argon walked up solemnly. He spoke in their language. The Argore sneered and spat at Argon.

Suddenly Beth stepped up to him, grabbed the hair on the top of his head and pulled it back to turn his face to her. She started to talk to him in his language, a phrase over and over again.

The Argore looked shocked and confused.

"Beth, no," said Argon rushing up to grab her.

"What was that?" asked Damon.

"When they caught my mother, they made her repeat it all the way to the end. It was the last thing she said when they killed her." Beth was shaking with rage.

"Argon, what did she say?"

"It was…terrible. They forced her to beg for their…"

The entire camp murmured and gripped their weapons.

"Beth, please come away," Argon pleaded.

Damon walked over and touched her shoulder. "You know why I want to question him. He's not long for this world."

"I'll make him talk," she hissed.

The Argore eyed her warily. She had a knife in her hand.

"Having a few less body parts will loosen his tongue. They gave no mercy to my mother."

"Beth, let us deal with this."

He looked over to Layla who hurried to them putting a hand to Beth's shoulder.

"Come, Beth, please," she asked.

Beth grudgingly allowed Layla to drag her back, murder in her eyes staring back at the captive.

"Tell him what to expect, Argon."

Argon spoke to him, but he merely turned his head away with a contemptuous look.

"They don't fear torture, Damon. I suspect it's a part of their daily lives."

"Do you have another way?"

"I don't know enough about them. If there is something he fears, we have no way to discover it."

"Take him away," said Damon reluctantly. It was a step he didn't want to take in spite of the sins of the man.

His screams went on for hours as survivors joined the 'interrogation' which ultimately was just his slow death. He never revealed anything of the Argore plans or goals. Damon was in the same position as he was prior to the capture. The only difference was their spirits were darker and Damon felt some remorse at what they'd done. Killing an enemy in battle wasn't the same to him as torturing one to death. It had nothing to do with if he deserved it.

Watching Beth go to join the punishment and then seeing her face afterwards was a chilling experience. It was Gideon who came over to him seeing his distress.

"I'm worried about her, Gideon."

"My Prince, she carries a heavy burden on her heart. She felt she needed to strike at her foe. Not every choice we make in life is a good one."

"Did you see her face? This wasn't an act of closure. I think she opened a worse wound. I'd try to talk to her, but I'd be wasting my time."

"Don't discount your influence with her, sire. She's in emotional pain, but she still sees you as an important figure in her life. I think perhaps she feels unworthy of you."

"That's ridiculous, Gideon."

"That doesn't make it untrue, My Lord. Individuals can have different interpretations of a same event, and sometimes radically different."

Turning their heads, they watched Argon follow the young women going off to have a talk.

"See, my lord, he will intercede. He watches over her."

Damon shrugged.

"I'll see about the refugees. I'm sure that was a terrible shock for the women and children after what they'd already been through with the battles."

"I'll help you, sire."

Berne and Amal were already there talking to little ones reassuring and comforting them. Uniformly, the children quaked and had fear in their eyes.

His childhood friends nodded to Damon as he came to sit down with them.

"Hello," said Damon to a tiny girl who stared at him with terror in her eyes. Damon took her on his lap where she put her arms around him and buried her face against his chest.

Damon looked around for her family.

"Some of them are orphans," said Berne sadly.

"My god, she's little more than a baby," Damon lamented.

Finally a young woman came over.

"I'm sorry, My Prince. She wandered away in the confusion. Her family was killed so we took her with us. They were neighbors in our city."

The child didn't want to release her hold on him. It struck him deeply but he relinquished her to the woman, having no other choice. The child moaned softly.

"Thank you for saving us, sire," said the woman in parting. The little girl kept her eyes on Damon as she was led away. Her feelings of security had been stolen from her. Damon wondered if he could ever return safety to her life.

Continuing a slow circuit amongst the refugees speaking to numerous strangers saying what they could to give them comfort, Damon led his friends feeling overwhelmed by the daunting losses. There were just too few men amongst the survivors. As bad as the current circumstances of these poor wretches, what worried Damon was their future prospects were bleak with the coming of the Argore horde. Initially escaping the carnage was no guarantee they wouldn't face future horrors.

As they walked along, Damon saw Argon speaking solemnly to Beth with Layla close beside her with her arm around her back with a worried look on her face. Beth was staring at the ground.

Damon continued past them with barely a glance. Layla noticed at him, but the other two continued their serious talk, oblivious to his passing by. Damon increased his pace.

At long last the camp settled back down to salvage some sleep after the turmoil. They got a late start the following morning. The Argore dead were left in the open for scavengers. Beth had bedded beside Argon and Layla stayed with her. Damon ate his breakfast quickly and busied with mundane camp planning along with Gideon, refusing to be sidetracked worrying about Beth.

It was slow going that day because they allowed the refugees to accompany them. Damon didn't have the heart to abandon them after the camp fight.

Behind them there seemed to be no end to the columns of smoke on the horizon. The Argore were attacking across the entire horizon in force driving relentlessly forward.

"Each of these cities, they're sitting ducks for the Argore horde," Berne mentioned as they rode along. "There is no defense they can mount to save their cities and their peoples.

"If there was a way for all the city militia's to gather together, perhaps we'd have a chance," Amal added.

"I don't think Kragan will fare any better," Berne replied.

They looked to Damon. He didn't reply because he had no solution, and he didn't disagree.

Beth was behind them riding beside Argon. It looked to be a continuation of their prior discussion as Argon spoke in low tones. Beth mostly listened.

Layla rode up to take her place beside Gideon.

"Is everything okay back there, Layla?" asked Damon.

"She has…issues. Her brutality with that captive Argore shocked her. Argon is telling her about his life and his mistakes. I think it's helping her to cope."

"She never told us the details about what happened with her mother."

"Damon, I can't say I would react any differently after hearing it. She told us she thinks you got them all when they followed her into the forest and you ambushed them. That helps. People who could do such things shouldn't be allowed to live."

"Do whatever you need to with her, Layla."

"Thank you, My Prince. If you have need of me just call me forth. I won't be far away."

"I should be fine. We're all together in the same camp. As you say, you wouldn't be far away if a problem arose. I don't need you at my elbow every moment."

She eyed him closely. "I get the feeling you're unhappy in some way. Is there something I'm doing to cause this, My Prince? Do you not want me to aid Beth?"

"Of course I want you to help her, Layla. Don't assume you're the reason for everything I do, or feel. I'm facing serious problems with the plight of the refugees, the threat of the Argore, and the lack of options to win in the end against them."

"I'll ask that if I do cause a problem, please tell me."

"Layla, I'm a worrier. I don't want to turn you into a worrier also."

"Yes, My Lord."

She went to rejoin Argon and Beth who continued their talk.

The problem of the refugees didn't diminish. In fact, Damon's camp seemed to be a magnet drawing them from all across the frontier. They came in groups, some small and some not so small. It quickly put a strain on their limited supplies.

"We can send out teams to hunt and to gather food," said Gideon. "I think we need to increase our pace going back to Kragan. I don't want to seem insensitive to these poor wretches who've lost their homes, but if we don't make this change, we'll be bogged down and vulnerable. The survivors will need to move to cities they come upon for temporary relief, at least until the Argore horde arrives. We can't afford to be trapped here in the open if an attack comes from superior numbers."

Damon glanced at the others in the circle. Argon, Amal, Berne, and Layla eyed him keenly. Beth always looked at the ground these days, lost in her private misery.

"I don't disagree, Gideon. If anyone has a better idea, say so now. I've tried to think of a way to detach the command, yet still safeguard the civilians. I don't know if we can assign some men to lead them to the nearest city and then ride to rejoin us."

Beth looked up. "I'll volunteer to be in that force."

The others looked at Damon to see what he'd say.

"I'll lead a detachment," Layla offered. "Gideon is your first subordinate, so he'd still be here if you encounter major battle. I imagine there must be a city in the vicinity hereabouts."

Damon was conflicted, not wanting to relinquish Beth in spite of the confused situation between them.

"Argon, do you foresee a problem with their idea?"

"I'll accompany them, Damon."

"So be it," he said finally. "The command will depart at first light. We'll head straight toward Kragan. Once you're finished leading the refugees to safety, come after us with all haste."

On this night, Layla brought her bedding over to sleep near Damon.

"Layla?" he asked.

"It isn't impossible we could be ambushed," she answered. "I want to spend this night with you in case it's my last."

It was a chilling thought. Damon rose up.

"I'll be right back. I want to speak with Beth and Argon a moment."

Beth had just lain down and pulled her cover over her body. She saw him coming and stared.

"Argon, Beth, Layla just said something that bothered me, about if your mission met with a bad ending. Argon, you're my mentor, but to me, you're family. I know you'll be cautious, but please don't let yourselves be taken or killed out there. Beth, I've told you my feelings. Because you had reservations about me, I've tried to keep my distance, but I love you no less than I ever did. It's the most difficult test I've faced letting you leave. I don't like it. In spite of whatever issues you're fighting, I remain hopeful about us for the future. Obviously the choice is yours as to a life with me, or with another. Perhaps you didn't want to hear this from me, but I had to say it for myself."

He got up to walk away.

"Damon," she said. "Thank you. I care about you too. I'll be careful."

He smiled and was warmed when she smiled back.

When he returned from his brief visit, Layla noticed the smile when he crawled into his bedding.

"Good, Damon," she whispered. "I told you not to give up on her."

"You did, Layla."

They parted company in the morning splitting off and going in different directions.

After grim goodbyes, Damon set a brisk pace for the command. It made it difficult for refugees to catch up to them and gradually they were going into lands where refugees hadn't gotten to yet. It was the regrettable step Damon had to take.

He thought about his love, riding apart from him. It was stressful so he tried to concentrate on what to do when they got to Kragan. He still had no viable solutions to that future problem.

As with every other day, behind them were the signs of war. New cities were coming under assault and inevitably falling to the Argore juggernaut. The Argore horde could have smothered the new refugees at the battle sites but they seemed content to let them run just ahead of the assault wave. If they came upon their makeshift camps, they were as ruthless as when they attacked the cities, but if the refugees could remain free of their attention, they didn't try particularly hard to chase them down.

The hour glass was running out on Kragan's days of freedom. Damon ran into the first of his home city's long patrols.

"Prince Damon?" asked the patrol captain. "What news from the war?"

"It's as bad as we expected. There will be huge waves of terrified people racing ahead of the Argore to seek safety behind our walls. The attack will soon follow. We need to go back to Kragan immediately. You should come with us.

There's nothing to gain for you out here. We already know what's coming."

As they traveled, Damon worried more each day when their friends didn't appear to rejoin them. The signs of fighting behind them were getting closer.

Damon decided to send five of his men to ride back to their own homes beyond the forest to warn the hamlets the Argore were at hand.

"If you wish to stay there to defend your families and homes, I'll understand," Damon explained.

"My lord, we're pledged to you. Five of us remaining behind will make no difference back there. Our hamlets won't stand up under attack if these cities couldn't. We need to stop the Argore here if our people are to survive. We'll return to Kragan as quickly as we can."

"Be very careful when you return in case the Argore have moved into the forest."

"Yes, my lord."

Again he was conflicted watching part of his men ride away. They were important to him and he took personal responsibility for each and every one of them.

The sight of Kragan ahead was comforting as they rode along, but there was still no sign of Argon, Layla, and Beth and the men they'd taken on their mission. Stopping to make a final camp in the field, Damon had trouble sleeping that night with his worries.

He awoke in the morning, groggy again. That sorry condition seemed to be happening with too much frequency. Considerable coffee wasn't solving the problem.

Increasingly, Amal and Berne sat apart from him talking in low tones rather than endure his depressing moods. They felt his same worries but wanted to be optimistic for a good outcome. Gideon was businesslike, as always. He went about the camp talking with the men to focus them on their tasks at hand. Nothing seemed to faze Gideon.

Damon's force rode through the city gates at noon. Kragan had tried to strengthen their defenses in the interim, but Damon doubted it would make a difference as he examined the superficial changes.

They went directly to the palace.

Prince Tabor met him at the stairs to the palace.

"Brother, judging by your expression, I suspect you have dire news from the field."

"Tabor, there are no miracles waiting to save us. We have the same harsh truth as always except now we've run out of time until we face our fate."

Tabor shrugged, but his face mirrored Damon's worry. In that way, he was like his brother stewing over each new problem they faced.

The king was in conference with the general staff when his sons were ushered into the room.

He looked up in surprise.

"Damon, where are your other friends? Where is Beth?"

"They split off on a mission of mercy, Father. Argon, Beth, and Layla led a mass of refugees to the nearest city. They were…I don't want to say a burden, but we couldn't feed them all and we could make no progress getting back here."

"They've sent no word on their fate, I take it."

"We don't know what happened to them. If they got caught up in a battle…"

He grimaced at the thought his friends might no longer be alive, or worse as captives of the Argore.

"I regret that dire news, son. I'm sorry. I know you care deeply for Beth, and those others. Argon was a great aid to us in our deliberations. I hope they have found a way to avoid the snare and are coming to us at this very moment."

"I saw your additional defense measures, Father. I wish I could say I'm optimistic, but every city has been swept away by the horde. They're relentless and they pay no heed to their losses. They care only for victory at any cost."

"What are they trying to gain, Damon? We've heard they leave behind nothing but destruction. They don't look to conquer, only to destroy and decimate. How does this help them? It's barbaric but more than that, it's insane."

"I wish I knew, Father. We've talked often about that very thing. We caught one of their commanders, but he refused to tell us anything, even the simplest of things. He died an agonized death, but he had no fear to die. It makes them a frightening foe. It forces us to be as brutal as they."

"Tabor?" asked the king.

"I've heard back from the couriers we sent to the other cities, those that are still standing. They have no better plans. The idea of pulling all of our forces out of the cities to make a unified stand in pitched battle, didn't appeal to any of them. They prefer to fight on their own grounds. I think each secretly believes they can prevail where all others have failed. They're idiots, Father."

"I expected this. Damon, what about these refugees? What should we do?"

"Take them in, Father. I think their potential drain on our supplies is a moot point. Making a lengthy defense isn't the probability based on what happened to the other cities. Somehow the Argore have a way to breech the best of our defenses. I'm sorry to say it, but it's better to be realistic. Have you thought further about the plan to save the women and children?"

"They are adamant, son. They will live or die with us. I could command them to leave, but they would ignore the edict."

"Honestly, I expected that, Father. I understand how they feel, but I think we must make that difficult choice for them. Dying in that way at the hands of the Argore isn't acceptable."

"Are you going to stay in the city to join with us for the final battle?"

"I'm not sure yet. As I said before, we could be a great factor striking from the forest against them. Our thousand aren't sufficient to overcome such an ocean of troops as they will bring, but we can inflict grievous injury to them at critical times and use the forest to evade their forays. I wish Argon was here to give us his opinion. As the battle draws nearer, it's not so easy to be overconfident. There's been nothing good that's happened against them with the other cities so far to give us hope."

The king turned his head to Damon's second in command.

"You're Gideon," said the king rhetorically.

"I'm at your service, Sire."

"What thoughts do you have about this? You come from the farm communities beyond the forest."

"I'm not a tactician, Sire. Your generals are better for that task. My perspective is I've ridden with your son long enough to feel hopeful in spite of these dire views. He tends to find a way where others would fall. We've beaten the Argore in every fight we've had with them so we don't see them as invincible. They have many fighters so we just need to eat a little extra food to have the energy to kill them all."

The men in the room laughed. It helped lift the depressive mood. The king nodded in appreciation. Suddenly the room was filled with a new spirit. Hope wasn't dead after all.

Chapter Eleven

The attack came as a total surprise. Argon, Beth, and Layla had just finished their latest difficult and lengthy argument with city officials to agree to accept the refugees. It took a week of protracted negotiations to overcome their complaints.

They had ten of Damon's guards with them and they'd started for the main gate to leave the city when deep horns from the city palace sounded the alarm across the countryside. The city militia was shocked out of their lethargy to race to man the gates and the walls as dark waves of the Argore hordes appeared and surrounded the city. The barbarians shouted and banged their shields in a terrifying cacophony of noise that sent citizens screaming and racing into their homes. They pounded deep drums that added to the fright and to a feeling of impending doom.

Argon expertly eyed the defenses. They'd done what they could with the limited time they had to prepare, but against this onslaught, Argon had no optimism this city could prevail. The militiamen gripped their weapons in terror. They were soldiers who understood what the bureaucrats did not. They realized they had no chance to win this fight. They were beaten before the first sword was crossed with the enemy.

"What should we do?" asked Layla worriedly.

"We have no choice but to fight for our lives."

Beth said nothing. Her face was avid with battle lust. It worried both Argon and Layla seeing her dangerous mood.

He gathered the troops.

"We need to stay together at all costs. Fight your enemies, but defend each other so there are no openings for them to exploit. We fight together, move together, and we attack together, understood? Be alert because my decisions will be swift. We can't save this doomed city. We must survive and flee when the chance comes. Have courage and we'll find a way to escape."

The men replied with a martial shout. That made Beth smile at Argon like he was the measure of any test. He noticed her glance.

"Beth, be very careful about this," Argon whispered to her.

"Argon, there's a time and a place for everything. Today I begin to repay those savages for what they do. This is more than my personal losses. It's for all of these wretches who've been driven out of their homes and their lands. Have some faith in us. We won't fail you."

"Beth, this isn't going to be like those other fights we've had. In their horde formations, they fight with utter frenzy, overwhelm with their numbers and slaughter without conscience. If we can survive this through some miracle, we must escape. I repeat, we can't save this city so we can only try to save ourselves. You need to hear me. Your dreams of revenge may not be what reality will be for us today."

She looked at him. "Of course, Master." He wasn't reassured by her comment. It didn't seem to be sincere, but rather she looked to be lost in her personal hatreds.

The Argore serenaded the city for a day and a night to heighten the fear before they attacked. Argon picked a place near the main gate to position the squad.

The battle was one sided from the start as soon Argore fighters were pouring over the walls and engaging the city troops inside the city walls.

Argon made a decision quickly.

"We'll fight to keep them from opening the gates. We've got to embolden these city troops to stand their ground and protect with our example of courage in the battle."

Argore invaders swarmed at them quickly as Argon backed away toward the best defensible position he could find. To that point the Argore drove back the defenders without much resistance and thought Argon's little group would be easy meat. They were greatly mistaken.

"Hold!" Argon shouted as the militiamen started to disperse and flee. "Your families will die if you give up the gate."

The retreating militia stopped and quickly formed up behind Argon to form a solid skirmish line shoulder to shoulder. The Argore attacked immediately, but this time with Argon as a spear point they met stiff resistance and started to incur losses. The skill of Argon and his small troop inspired the city militiamen to their best efforts too.

Beth scythed her way into the middle of the fighting heedless of the risk. She was a whirling dervish of flying sword strokes leaving a bloody swath in her wake. The rabid Argore were drawn to her and she was quickly surrounded, yet she managed to survive and she continued to mete out death to any who got too close.

Argon saw her peril and drove forward to break the circle of death surrounding her. Layla fought frantically at his side. The ten guards were an invincible bubble in the midst of the mayhem. Argore invaders were falling all around them to the point the bodies made it difficult for the barbarians to drive forward, a buffer for the defenders composed of dead flesh.

The Argore commander recognized they were the key to the battle as his forces raced throughout the city against light opposition. Argon would not budge and reinforced assaults from the Argore failed to dislodge the stubborn knot of defenders fighting the invaders to a draw in the center of the fight for the main gate.

As always, the Argore had nearly unlimited bodies to throw into the battle and they were scaling the walls nearly unimpeded. With time, Argon's force was greatly outnumbered, but they were also in a position to withstand the Argore assault waves who couldn't bring their numbers to bear. Only so many could confront Argon's array of deadly swords at a time.

As the hours passed, he worried about fatigue, but his troops were fighting for their lives so they tapped inner reserves of courage to keep up the fight.

Suddenly the Argore pulled back a short distance and ceased fighting. The commander came forward alone.

He walked right up to Argon.

"You've fought bravely, but you know how this battle will end. We respect your courage and your prowess, so I'm offering you a chance to surrender peacefully. That isn't the Argore way."

"Would you surrender if the roles were reversed, Commander?" Argon asked him. "If we put down our arms, I think our fate would be dark. The Argore don't let enemies exist in their midst."

"I think we can find new lives for you. This maiden who fights like one of us, red with the blood of her victims, she would make a fine wife, this other female also. We allow some men to do our work as slaves. If you prefer, we'll give you a quick clean death rather than being tortured for a week before you die."

"Thank you for your offer. I know you think you're being generous. Ladies, would you like to become wives to the Argore?"

"I prefer to die," Beth hissed at the enemy commander. "Come for me if you think you can take my life. I'll be waiting."

The commander laughed.

"See this, men," he shouted. "This is how a woman should be, bold and brash. Her spirit calls to me. Our children would be invincible. I'll fight to prove my worth before her eyes. I'll be the one to personally knock the sword out of her hand, and I'll be the one to tame her as my wife. This is a blessed day for me."

The Argore roared in delight.

Beth eyed him with malice, her blood stained hand locked on the hilt of her sword, though her tired muscles quivered from the strain of the lengthy fight.

Instead of attacking, he returned to his forces where they took their time and ate a meal while the defenders stood by helpless, unable to feed themselves cut off and surrounded.

A little later, as the sky darkened with the approach of night the Argore attacked again.

"Courage men," Argon shouted. None of them had any hope of success. There were no fewer Argore confronting them and there were no reinforcements coming to save the defenders.

Still, the battle was surprisingly equal as the dynamics hadn't changed. The Argore could only bring so many men into the fight and the defenders maintained a solid front defending each other. Again it was a fight of attrition where the attackers gained with each defender they felled.

At that point, the enemy commander entered the fray making a beeline straight toward Beth. She fought flawlessly creating a wide circle of dead victims all around her. They came at her with deadly intent but she prevailed in every case. By the time the commander was close, bodies blocked his way. The men all around stopped attacking her for a moment. She panted heavily with her extreme effort but with her sword held at the ready. She locked eyes again with her enemy, the commander of Argore forces.

"Come here," she taunted. "You want to embrace me, now is your chance, just you and me."

He climbed over the pile of bodies into the impromptu arena. Beth attacked immediately. It was an epic fight as the commander was a superb champion. Beth gave him everything he could handle though. She forced him to fight in a way that could kill her, or vice versa.

Their fight slowed the fighting around them, like the outcome of the contest would decide the winner for the entire battle for the city.

Argon was very worried, but there was nothing he could do. Beth had her fate in her own hands now. Layla grabbed his arm in worry as the sword strokes came close to killing blows both ways.

Beth refused to back down. She pressed at him forcing him to defend and back away from her wrath. In spite of a long day of fighting, she showed no sign of giving up. The commander fought evenly, but Argon could see he was shocked he couldn't gain an edge over a woman.

Beth was no average woman. He had no idea the ferocity of her motivation. She didn't fear to die and that made her a deadly opponent even for elite fighters.

She whispered the Argore phrase over and over again, just like her mother had been forced to do. The commander heard her soft words and it puzzled him. They made no sense at all to him. She was begging for his touch while trying her utmost to take his life. It was disconcerting. The Argore didn't teach their language to outsiders, only slaves.

The commander tried to think of a way to end the fight without killing her. He made a feint and then a lightning move to gain the advantage, but Beth was ready. Argon had prepared her for virtually any tactic. She blunted his attack and made her own lightning move bashing him in the face with an elbow and then a kick to his stomach. It buckled him and he went to his knees. She tried to make the final swing to take off his head, but his nearby troops intervened to block her stroke, grab her bodily and take her down to the ground.

Argon's heart dropped as the Argore attacked before he could try to save Beth and forced back the defenders into a tight knot pressed against one another. They saw Beth disarmed and dragged away from sight but they were helpless to do anything for her. The battle was lost but the Argore paused momentarily, celebrating Beth's capture, so Argon ordered the main gate open and they rushed out to escape the trap. Outside the city the Argore host was widely dispersed so they were able to fight their way forward quickly. They could hear the screams coming from the city. It was mortifying they couldn't help those hapless and doomed people but at this point they had to concentrate on escape and surviving.

Where Beth was taken to they never saw so they could only try to personally survive moment to moment. Argon directed them in an arc around the city and headed toward the nearest forest. All of Damon's ten guards had survived and a significant number of city militia. They raced away ahead of the Argore who were content at that point to concentrate on the spoils in the city. People fled away trying to escape, but most were trapped behind exposed to Argore horrors.

Argon's path to the forest was surprisingly clear, like they weren't seen as a threat by the Argore. Losing Beth was galling for them all, but trying to rescue her was impossible. They had no chance to try to find Beth who could be anywhere at that point in time.

Once they fled into the trees, Argon set some guards and they stopped to rest and to try to make a plan. The city troops were badly shaken. They knew their families were doomed and probably already dead. Racing back into the city was suicide and it wouldn't save them. None of them joined in speaking with Argon about future plans. Their lives were shattered.

"I believe we should try to get in front of the Argore advance and return to Kragan."

"Argon, do you propose to leave Beth to the Argore?" Layla was incensed.

"Do you think that's what I wish," he retorted angrily? "No one wishes that fate on her, but what would you have us do, Layla?"

She simmered with misplaced anger eyeing Argon like it was his fault.

"We all feel the same rage, but would making a suicidal ride into the Argore horde help Beth? We would never see her and we'd die needlessly. At least if we rejoin our friends we can strike at them again. Look around, we're not the only ones suffering from terrible loss."

"How could this happen?" she questioned in misery.

"I'm afraid Beth will need to find courage within herself to face this tragedy. It's a terrible turn but one which we must cope with. She was intent on killing Argore and it led her to this."

"I feel ashamed, Argon. I should never have allowed her to be separated from me."

"This isn't your fault, Layla, any more than the rest of us. In battle each person tries to survive."

"How can I face Prince Damon with this failure?"

Argon grimaced. "We'll tell him the truth. There's no other way."

They sat in silence for a short time.

"We need to hunt for food and gather water so we can move rapidly," Argon continued. "This isn't a place we can spend any time at all. The Argore won't be idle long before resuming their push ahead."

* * * *

Beth stopped struggling against the restraining hands once they left the city. There was no longer any point in resisting. They were stronger than her and without her weapons she could do nothing against them.

They hustled her along leaving the city behind returning to their base camp at the gallop.

The sheer numbers of Argore warriors she saw were staggering. In camp, Beth also saw Argore women for the first time. They were as wild as the men screaming taunts and derision at her. She didn't understand their words, but their gestures were graphic enough she understood the abusive meanings.

Beth was frightened but determined to make a brave end. Memories of what happened to her mother evoked great fear though she labored to show no emotions to her captors. The commander walked close to her when they hauled her off the horse in their camp. It wasn't reassuring as his intentions were clear. He'd told her he would make her his wife and now she had no weapons to take action about it.

She felt a failure in her quest to avenge her family. All of Argon's warnings returned to her mind, but too late. An image of Prince Damon crossed her mind, how he would react to the news. It bothered her as much as her fears about what the Argore would do to her.

The huge camp coalesced into an impromptu gathering with Beth as the prized spectacle.

The commander stepped to the center dragging Beth by her hair and tossing her to the ground at his feet. He shouted in their language inciting the mob to raucous shouts and frenzy. They thirsted for the worst humiliations to be done before their eyes. Beth closed her eyes to focus her concentration for a final stand. If she injured this posturing braggart, perhaps they would be enraged and would quickly kill her and end this nightmare. That was her hope.

He continued his oration with ample shouts and responses from the crowd. They were agitated and looking for thrills, which in their case often involved bleeding victims.

Beth blocked out the pandemonium to regain control of her breathing, readying her body for the moment she'd spring into action with fists and feet. Since they were completely encircled, there was no place for her to flee. This would be suicide by mob attack.

As he ceased his diatribe and turned to her, she coiled like a snake ready to strike, but he anticipated her move. Guards had crept close and grabbed her as she made her move. The crowd laughed as she was overwhelmed, subdued, and humiliated in their immodest hands. The commander raised his fist to the applause and shouts of the mob before he had her dragged away into his tent where she was bound and gagged. They tossed her onto a bed and stationed guards to watch her. The commander left but she had no doubts he would be back.

She lay in misery, helpless even to take her own life at this point. All of her hard work learning the war arts had come to naught in the end. She was just a vulnerable woman tied on a bed, just like her mother, helpless in the hands of the Argore barbarians. Beth was terrified.

* * * *

Kragan bulged with the inbound mass of humanity streaming away from the war. There were enough displaced soldiers arriving from other cities they tripled the number of soldiers Kragan had available under arms.

The day Argon led his survivors into Kragan, Damon shrieked in torment learning about losing Beth to the Argore. He made a quick decision to move his people to the forest to establish a second defense front there. With so many unattached soldiers milling about, they gravitated to him there and soon his old forest camp became a teeming hub of military might. Kragan could accommodate no additional troops and Damon was a growing battle legend.

His personal guards, and Argon, ruggedly tested and trained those foreign soldiers to assess their skills and generally they were somewhat competent. Those soldiers learned quickly under unforgiving tutors and joined Damon's rapidly growing forces. Their losses of home cities and of relatives living there fueled the hatred Damon sought in his new troops. Old rivalries long forgotten they melded into a single minded army driven to exact revenge, just like their new leader. They quickly felt loyalty to Damon unlike they'd ever felt back in their home cities.

Damon was feral in his mood with the loss of Beth. He had little patience for anybody. Only Gideon, Argon, Layla, and a few key captains ventured near him. Training and incorporating the soldiers from the other cities into his corps, he left to others. His single order to his underlings was full competence without delay for his growing army.

The approach of the war wasn't far behind as each day columns of smoke were closer, and toward the end they heard the battle at the city closest to them. It was over in a single day.

Again floods of fleeing civilians and dislocated troops raced toward them.

There was no room for further stragglers in Kragan, so Damon took them all into the forest sending the women and children toward the hamlets on the other side of the woods to the refugee camps. The additional troops meant he had men enough to station throughout the entire forest for his strategy of traps, ambushes, and quick death for the enemy.

The Argore's main body appeared after noon and sauntered toward the city shouting and banging their drums and shields in derision.

"When they surround the city and begin their attack, we'll strike at their rear and open a path to the city main gates. When they come after us, we'll draw them after us and wipe them out here in the trees," Damon growled.

No one disagreed with him. It would have done no good. They had no other choice anyway. They weren't motivated by confidence, only by their hatred at that point.

Damon brought forward a huge battery of archers to the edge of the tree line and formed up cavalry behind them to wait for the right moment.

The Argore made camp instead.

"Do you think Beth is there, Argon?" asked the prince.

"If she is how could we find her? Damon, don't make her mistake and rush headlong into hopeless situations. Your death serves no purpose. Too many people depend on you to lead them, so lead. Put aside those troublesome thoughts. You can do nothing about her current state. You can only win this war."

Argon looked to see the response of the prince. Damon said nothing but simply stared darkly at the enemy troops covering the countryside for as far as they could see.

They stayed deployed all night at the forest edge. When Argore scouts tried to filter into the forest they were summarily butchered. None of them returned to report to their camp about Damon's hidden army.

At sunup the Argore horde sent forces to surround and cut off Kragan. They attacked quickly surging toward the city walls. This was followed immediately by a sky filled with arrows shot from the forest. They pelted the invaders continuously dropping numerous enemy dead, but they were replaced by Argore reinforcements streaming in from their camp.

Damon signaled the attack once the Argore were fully engaged and concentrating on Kragan. His army roared in hatred and defiance and attacked the rear, surprising the Argore forces focused on the city walls.

The fighting was vicious with neither side giving quarter. Damon was a beast at the front of the assault killing any he could reach. The ferocity of the Argore couldn't protect them from his rage. Beth was theirs, he would avenge her in the only way he could, taking away their lives.

His guards were like a single entity giving no opening to the enemy and mirroring Damon's hatred. Argore waves tried to overwhelm them but died for their efforts. Damon drove relentlessly toward the main gate which was the focal point of the Argore strategy. He could see considerable fighting on the walls so it was difficult to know how many of them were inside the city. The gates remained closed.

The Argore commander was shocked when Damon drove straight into the heart of his best unit and fought them evenly. The unanticipated counterattack stalled the invasion attempt and allowed the city defenders to take the initiative. Argore fighters were starting to be dropped over the walls and those trying to scale it were being rebuffed.

"Forward men, push forward," Damon shouted. His mounted men were more than Argore foot soldiers could contain regardless of their numbers. The initial Argore's clear path to the gate dissipated and then disappeared as Damon formed a skirmish line of deadly sword strokes rebuffing the barbarian assault in a pitched battle.

The casualties were huge as the Argore expended lives extravagantly for the merest of gains. The defenders knew this was the moment of their life or death. This was their last chance to stem the tide, if it could be done. No city prevailed before against the invincible barbarians. The test of whether any defenders could prevail was at hand.

The Argore formula for quick victories didn't work at Kragan. The stubborn resistance defied all of their best strategies in the day long battle. The defenders would not buckle under the extreme enemy pressure.

When it got dark, they pulled back to their camp in consternation.

Damon remained in position with his men. With the attack ended, the city gate opened and the king rode out with Prince Tabor. Both of them bloodied and nicked up.

"My son, you've saved us, at least for a day. Thank you for your courage. I want to clear the city of the civilians while we have the chance. Your mother is livid, but I won't have her in the hands of these savages. As I see what's coming against us, my hope for victory is dim. You know what I'm saying. Save those who you can. We'll occupy the Argore for as long as we can. I'm afraid you may be forced to create a new life for the survivors elsewhere. Tabor has chosen to stand with me here to the end. It may fall on you to carry on the family name, son."

Damon looked at them solemnly. "It isn't acceptable to me for you to sacrifice your lives. Don't get killed."

He didn't mean it as a joke but it caused them to smile.

"We'll do our best, son."

* * * *

The commander returned to his tent livid. It was the first time they'd been thwarted in any battle and it irked him a great deal. It made him think of another recent fight, a personal one, where for the first time he hadn't technically prevailed having to be rescued by his men. That city military force attacking their rear from the forest had been a surprise, but shouldn't have made a difference in the outcome of the battle. There was something in that leader who refused to lose. It was just like her.

He looked at her beautiful face, eyeing him with hatred. Even now, she refused to accept defeat or a new life with him. Each day she was as dangerous as the prior day watching for an opening to strike at him. She was like no other female he'd ever encountered and it evoked him greatly.

The commander suspected there was something different for her with this particular city, selected as the object of the entire Argore offensive.

As he pondered it, he realized this could be her home. Her family could be before them.

"I'm speaking in your language so you understand me. This is not the Argore way. You don't understand how I honor you. I think these are your people. I see your spirit in how they fight. If you will accede to me, act as a proper wife, perhaps we'll consider sparing those in that city you hold dear. What do you say to that? Is it better to maintain your defiance and see them die horribly? We could drag you forth to their walls to personally watch what we do to those who defy us."

She blinked but said nothing, refusing to speak. It was another way she chose to annoy him. Threats of violence from him made no impression on her. She attacked any time she had a chance. From the very first it was easy for her to understand he was romantically taken with her and therefore had that vulnerability.

"Do you have false hope because they survived the first day? There is no victory against the Argore. There is only our iron will, and our triumph. If you wish for me to salute their valor, I can mount their heads on higher poles to be seen farther away. This entire land is rubble under our feet. Do you not have eyes to see the truth?"

She stared at him balefully and remained silent.

He stood up and walked over to her in frustration. "You're the most confounding female ever born. I don't know why I keep you alive here in my tent. Your transgressions are too numerous to count. Even the Argore women scream that I throw you into their hands to give you the punishment you so richly deserve."

"So do it," she snapped. "I ask for nothing from you or your people. Give me my weapons and we can end this here and now."

He dragged her to her feet by the hair in rage out of her chair and tossed her onto his bunk. They'd had this battle of wills many times always with the same result, his defeat.

* * * *

In the forest Damon was restless. He listened to the objections of the women, including his mother, recently forced to leave Kragan.

"You know my will, Damon. I won't abandon Kragan, or my husband. You can't drag us away to be widows."

"The king has decreed it, I'm sorry. He's right though. We've seen what they do afterwards. Your thought to bravely end your life with dignity and spare the…it wouldn't play out that way. Having a queen as a symbol and an object for their misuse would be unimaginable degradation. They aren't like city dwellers, Mother. Here at least we can protect you and move away from danger. You have no idea. They don't see us as worthy of respect or compassion. They'd do their worst and they may keep a queen as their plaything for years."

She shuddered at the image he presented, but steeled her facial expression.

"Damon, Selena has asked to speak with you, Son. Will you speak to her?"

"Mother, I care nothing for palace games. That was a long time ago."

"I'm not sure that's what she wants. These are different times."

He shrugged.

* * * *

A significant Argore unit tried to force their way into the forest. Damon's people mowed them down systematically striking from ambush.

Argon commanded the defenders across the forest edge. Their array was perfect with no weaknesses. The Argore raiders never had a chance.

Gideon came to Damon with a report about the skirmishes, along with Layla.

"If they want to fight us here in our woods, I think we can win every time, My Prince."

"That's good to hear."

Damon looked at Layla who was a changed person since they'd lost Beth. She was honest about her feelings in that she felt responsible. That Damon understood, but he saw some of Beth's unreasoning rage manifesting in Layla. She was also showing alarming indifference for danger in battle with too many risky actions, another of Beth's bad habits.

She eyed him with a hollow expression, grim, silent and deadly, like the turmoil within her could never be abated.

Out of the corner of his eyes he noticed Selena edging close. She looked at Layla who ignored her. Damon turned his head to Selena.

"What is it, Selena?"

"I want to extend my sympathy about Beth. I haven't seen you to be able to say so. If there's anything I can do for you, please tell me, Prince Damon."

"I'll do what I can to beat the Argore and spare my brother from being a casualty, your fiancé," he replied pointedly.

"Thank you," she said after a moment. "Layla, I would be your friend if you'll allow it."

"I'm afraid my time is completely occupied in battle." The dark look on Layla's face was disconcerting. "I'm sure you understand."

Damon had never seen Selena out of her element acting unsure of herself. Her normal doting companions were huddled in fright with the other women from the city, so Selena was by herself for possibly the first time. Her world was changing for the worse and she was realizing it with fear. Coping seemed to be beyond her at that point. Layla wasn't going to be reassuring.

He wasn't unsympathetic and he still felt warmly toward her, but his adolescent days were long past. Beth occupied his thoughts along with the danger to Kragan from the Argore invasion. Compared to Beth, Selena seemed weak and inconsequential. Beth was a force of nature that awed her enemies as much as her friends. Selena would never be like Beth in any way meaningful to Damon.

The queen stood by firmly staring at her son. "Don't do this to us,

Damon."

"Mother, there are no better options. You can't be here in the battle zone. I'm going to move all of the civilians past the lake and out the other side of the forest into the protection of the hamlets. I'll send sufficient troops to supplement the forces we've created there to protect you. The best way I can save my father and brother is to concentrate here on finding ways to win this war. The Argore horde has vast numbers and that gives them a great advantage. I need to find advantages for our side that can tip the scales in our favor. I'm sorry Mother, but people die in wars. It can't be avoided. We've got to earn our right to survive and it will take more than just courage."

She wasn't happy, but she nodded in acquiescence after a moment.

"Will you help me, Mother? If you accept my plan, the other women will follow. I don't need chaos and discord here in my camp. They can't turn to whining."

"I will, Son. You know my feelings, but I accept the truth in what you're saying."

They talked briefly about preparations to move the mass of huddling civilians. His mother walked off and called her aides to give them instructions. Once she made the decision she was decisive in her actions which helped Damon immensely. Equally, it helped with her staff giving them the feeling of important duties to perform to help shake off the dread. They went about those duties with determination organizing the retreat.

Hours later the camp cleared of the civilians as the procession moved to the lake shore to travel to their new home beyond the forest. As he'd promised, Damon sent a sizeable force to protect them.

With that worry resolved Damon turned his attention back to the Argore threat.

Each day of fighting followed the same script and met with the same end. The Argore tried their strategy to overwhelm Kragan and every day Damon's incursion thwarted them. Kragan was still standing free weeks into the fight.

Meanwhile, Damon sent patrols in the other direction along the lake shore to assess what was happening along that front. What they found was huge numbers of refugees were making a wide arc around the Argore horde seeking safety and entered the vast forest from another direction. Included in those displaced people were considerable soldiers from the many cities that had fallen. They were happy to join Damon's command in order to strike back at the Argore. Damon's forces there grew radically, unbeknownst to him. Like their predecessors, they willingly dropped any former petty squabbles with troops from rival cities to become a unified command, and there was a continuous flood of more survivors streaming into the area. This force would just keep growing.

Damon decided on a forging a personal imprint and rode over to meet them. His impromptu speech inspired and motivated his new companions as he gave them back their hope with his message they could prevail.

"Men, we won't accept defeat and destruction from these barbarians. We will find a way to weather this storm and then we'll push them back to their mountains and beat them so badly in the process they'll never come back."

The response from the men was deafening. It ran chills down Damon's spine.

They deployed those forces in that camp according to the same plan Damon used from his camp. It was an endless interlocking series of snares and traps designed to bleed the Argore from the safety of hidden lairs. They were created in numerous layers behind the front line so there was no opportunity for the enemy to break through the net. They were immersed into a maze of convoluted turns filled with arrows and deadly sword strokes. Here their numeric advantage meant nothing, just more barbarians to die. The civilians he directed to move out the other end of the forest to the hamlets to join the other refugees in camps being established to house them temporarily.

For the first time, Damon started to feel a little optimism. That former rival soldiers would so quickly accept him and join his army, it was very heartening. For Damon it was also surprising to hear from strangers how his fame had spread. It wasn't Kragan, the king, or his brother they sought, it was Prince Damon who was renowned amongst the refugees.

It was a strange feeling as he rode back to his command center to feel his burden lightened, but as he neared the camp, his thoughts about Beth returned along with his anxiety. She was still out there as a captive, assuming she was still alive. He couldn't be sure what the Argore would do to her. Thinking about it was so disturbing he had to forcibly block those thoughts.

Berne and Amal met him when he rode into camp.

"I heard you found good things, Damon," said Berne.

"It was a fortuitous trip. I think the Argore have bitten off more than they can chew. Those people are incensed at what happened to their cities and they're willing to die if necessary to beat those bastards."

Damon went with his friends to talk to Argon and Layla, Gideon was away on a mission.

"Argon, why do you think they don't change their strategy? I know their plan worked on every other city, and worked well, but here in Kragan we've proven the measure of that type of assault."

"Damon, I'm sure they're talking about this very thing. We need to anticipate what they could do differently and have an answer. We can afford no surprises."

"We can bleed them nearly endlessly, Argon. They had huge advantages with each individual city they struck, but here all the remnants from those cities are gathering in the same place. Each day we grow noticeably stronger and they lose fighters. I start to think we have a chance to win this war. I don't see them dislodging us from the forest where we have every advantage. Throwing numbers at us here serves no purpose. Now I can strike at them along a wider area when they attack Kragan with far greater force at my disposal. The city has toughened to their tactics and I think they can stand as long as we continue to weaken the Argore assault from the outside."

"It goes back to the first question I ever gave to you. What's the reason they came and what's their ultimate goals? That answer would probably explain a great deal for us."

"Hopefully those answers won't matter if we continue to have success, Argon. As more stragglers join us, the numeric edge will become much less a factor. Already, our fighters have risen to match their frenzy. What was the most frightening aspect of the Argore invasion is gone. Also, I see a difference in the enemy soldiers now. They've lost huge numbers and that can't go unnoticed amongst the common troops. The heedless abandon is tempered. They value their own lives and are less willing to die needlessly."

"I think we need to make an attempt for Beth," said Layla suddenly.

Nobody replied.

"Who knows what she's forced to endure. I can't continue this way not knowing her fate. If it were me there in captivity, my hope would rest in the knowledge someone is coming to rescue me. Do you hear what I'm saying?"

Argon eyed her sadly.

"Layla, we feel as you feel. The problem with a rescue hasn't changed. None of us lack the courage for the attempt, or the willingness to risk our lives, but we don't know where she might be, or if she's still alive."

"They wouldn't kill her," Layla replied fretfully. "She's too great a person. No one would kill her. You know why they'd keep her alive, the vile bastards. It's intolerable and I won't stand for it any longer."

Chapter Twelve

At that moment, Beth was unexpectedly taken from the tent of the field commander of the Argore horde and dragged up a hill to a gathering of elderly men sitting in a circle. The commander was standing beside a grizzled vicious looking man seated in a prominent place. He leered at her and she scowled in response, but what caught her attention was another ancient stick man, spindly and wild looking. He wore garish colored clothes, a headdress of feather and bones a with bone necklace and barbed wrist bracelets. It chilled her because those bones didn't appear to be from animals. There appeared to be some worse and more frightening trophies hanging from his leather jerkin. She looked away in fear.

The savage man had an insane, though distant, look in his eyes. He held a great staff which had rattles that sounded when he shook it. Beth wondered if he was drugged up on something.

The guards forced her close to him. He had an overpowering unpleasant smell, like he'd lathered himself in rancid animal fat or some other noisome substance. Beth tried not to breathe in the reek.

The repulsive man spoke in their language in a high squeaky voice. He eyed Beth closely and pointed his staff at her. His lengthy discourse gave her no clue what he was saying. The massed throng was completely silent during his speech. Beth averted her eyes the whole time. This close she could see what those trophies were and it made her feel ill.

When he finished speaking the commander walked to her side. The strange man spoke again, at length, ending by rattling his staff loudly at her.

The guards stepped up to drag her away from the meeting. The commander came away soon afterward. The mass of people stared at her in complete silence. They no longer taunted her with words and gestures.

Later back in the tent she sat in turmoil, unable to quell her curiosity. The commander recognized it and smiled.

"Well, what's this, my contentious lovely, have the Argore piqued your interest at last?"

"Who were they?"

"I'm sure you realized it was the high council of all the Argore, and the high chief himself."

"No, I know who they were. That smelly skeleton, I'm asking who was that? He was disgusting."

The commander chuckled. "He's the shaman, our spiritual guide. It's his vision we follow. He sees the future and advises us about it."

"This seer, did he see you failing at the gates of Kragan?"

"So that's the name of the city. You do know it."

She simply stared at him, but a plan was forming in her mind. At last, she saw something that she could do to affect the war.

"I've been with you long enough to understand you, Beth. We've interrogated enough captives to learn you're the favored of the city king and his sons. You could have been a future queen, but you chose to take up arms in an impossible battle spurning a comfortable life, but why? You uttered words to me in my language, but the phrase made no sense. I didn't have the reason or the context of it. Unarmed, do you honestly think you can take action here in the middle of our might. Use your head, woman. Did you think to strike down the high chief or the shaman? The high chief won his seat through his fighting prowess. Any may challenge him, but no one does. He savors taking life in the most brutal ways. He would show no mercy to you just because you're a beautiful woman. He would lust to see the life fade out of your eyes from his fatal strike as your blood spills onto the ground. Do you understand, or are you so unrealistic you can't use good sense. If you hope to die here, know that I won't allow it. I've been kind to you and daily I question why. You know I could take you at any time, but I've allowed you to remain pure. That's no guarantee for the future. I've given you the chance to become my wife and retain your dignity. You don't understand the honor I bestow. I'm the highest ranking soldier among all Argore. Only the council elders are higher than me."

"What did the skeleton say?"

He chuckled again shaking his head in disbelief. She knew how to marginalize him with her words and it always worked in annoying him. Even though he knew it was coming, it happened nonetheless stirring his emotions.

"He said it's fortuitous we have you among us. You're the important player in this scene. You'll be the catalyst for what comes about. I spoke truly when I said you and me are unique, above others. Our children would be champions fit to lead the world. Can you not fathom the chance you have here? Do you think you had a great destiny tied to those city people? They have no capacity to see your true worth and greatness. They would dress you up as their pretty toy and take advantage of you eventually. You'd be mother to some squalling brat of a useless noble. The Argore can conquer the world if called forth. You can be my wife and their treasure. Your babies would be given the best life possible and molded into the greatest warriors the world has ever seen."

She eyed him darkly and said nothing.

"I was told the prince pursued you, but you gave him no favor. This Damon, the first born of the king, who couldn't even beat his younger brother to be crown prince, you recognized down deep he was unworthy of you. Your mate could only be someone comparable, someone like me."

She smirked, and it irked him greatly. "You say Damon is unworthy? What does that make you? I hear your empty boasting about who rules on the battlefield but Kragan still stands after all this time. Ride into the forest if you're so confidant and face Damon. We'll see if you ride out or if you're just another dead body to toss on the fire."

He simmered with anger and moved close. She continued to smirk.

"Do it," she taunted. "Show me this love of yours. I think what you really offer me is the back of your hand. The Argore are mere savages and there's no great destiny at work for you. Your shaman is a lunatic and you're idiots to follow him."

He took her face in his hands and instead of violence, he kissed her deeply. She tried to pull back but he held her in his grip.

"You will be my wife," he muttered firmly.

"You can try," she retorted. "I'll never stop fighting you. I would find a way sooner or later to take your life. I'll never give you my love. If you want a life of mortal peril, feel free."

He pondered her very real threat for a moment. He had no doubts about the sincerity of what she said or her undying desire to kill him. He sat back and looked at her curiously.

"I think at this point you have no reason not to be honest. You whispered a phrase in the Argore language. How did you learn it and what meaning does it have in your life. Begging for my touch? How would you know about a man's touch? Our women assure me you're still pure."

She considered a moment before she replied. "Okay, I'll tell you. As you say, it makes no difference at this point. I was a daughter of a farmer on the frontier near your mountains. One night your raiders came for us. My father hid me under the floor, but my mother refused. My father and older brother died killing Argore scum but they were slaughtered eventually, two brave souls against an army of villains. Your foul brethren took my mother and tormented her for hours before they took her life. They made her beg for their touch all the way to the end. I'll never forget those words, and I'll never end my vendetta to wipe out every living Argore, or die. I don't care which."

It was sobering for the commander to hear her hatred explained in all its ugliness. He had no response to her tragic story. He understood her motives very clearly at last. It was not reassuring for his romantic aspirations.

"You see, even you understand the wrongness you do to the world. Perhaps you have no feelings for family or about rightness even with strangers. I don't care. The evil you do in life will come back on you. There's no escaping the punishment you've earned for your sins."

He turned and left her. The affront had affected him. She was right that the Argore paid no heed to the plight of their victims. It was part of their current religion, or at least as interpreted by the shaman.

Beth had ample fodder for thought now. The Argore had vulnerabilities. There had to be a way to get the news to Damon and Argon. She thought about her friends briefly, but it was too painful so she blotted it out, again. In this camp she could only afford to concentrate on surviving day to day.

It was at these times when she was briefly alone that she bathed. Letting them see her undress was too much of a risk. She quickly exposed various places to wash and rapidly recovered them under her clothes. Thus far, it had worked well enough keeping her free from their touches.

Another decision she'd made was to abandon the idea to fast trying to starve to death. Keeping up her strength was the better choice by far, so she exercised in secret to keep fit and ready for any opportunities that came her way.

The commander kept her weapons close enough to tempt her, but the guards were always vigilant. It was part of his response to her campaign of insults and rebukes. She could only bide her time.

* * * *

Layla was intent on saving Beth. Although she could persuade none of the leaders to create a plan, she secretly pondered and plotted. Layla couldn't accept the thought of Beth being dead so she planned with the idea she was alive and in need of intervention.

Surprisingly, she found sympathetic and eager ears with Berne and Amal. The three of them talked frequently trying to hatch a plot that had even a remote chance of success.

"Layla, we're willing to risk our lives and we certainly don't want Beth in captivity any longer than necessary, but we must have something other than our courage," Berne explained. "We love Beth also."

"I'm sorry, Berne. I don't question your courage. I'm frustrated from talking to Argon and Damon. They're too willing to let her suffer under those vile hands. Damon proclaims his love to the world, but then he sits in the woods on his hands."

"Don't blame him, Layla. He truly loves Beth, more than you know, but he's responsible for the war. The king sits penned up in the city, so it's what Damon does outside that matters. Tabor mans the walls of Kragan. It's Damon that risks his life and rides forth into the maelstrom daily. We've blunted the Argore invasion. No city could do it and that would have included Kragan without us here to turn the tide in our favor from the woods."

"Meanwhile, Beth is left to her fate. If they can do nothing it leaves us to fill the void."

Amal and Berne squirmed in discomfort at Layla's assertion.

"Do you have an idea, Layla?" asked Amal.

"I wonder if we could dress as Argore and slip into their camp. They never face attack there so perhaps their guards are complacent."

"If we got in, what then, Layla?" asked Berne. "That camp is the size of five Kragans. Do you suppose we could walk about freely and draw no notice? Do we look like Argore? Even if that impossibility happened, Beth would be heavily guarded. She's probably bloodied enough noses that they take great care around her."

"That's my Beth," said Layla with a smile. "I say we give it a try. If we think of a better plan in the meantime…"

"Layla, there is no better plan," Amal replied with a solemn look. "We need to get our affairs in order with this suicide scheme of yours."

* * * *

The high chief of the Argore didn't question the shaman's vision and their invasion of the lowlands, but he was starting to question their tactics. It was over a month since they'd first struck Kragan and the impasse remained unchanged. Continuing to throw troops at the walls only to be sniped from the forest was insane. After all, the shaman prophesied about war with this city being their destiny, not what tactics to use.

He sent word for his horde commander.

It was the second time Beth saw the Argore leadership when they brought her along with the commander to meet with the high chief and the elders of the high council.

Again, he eyed her frankly, disrespectfully, and whispered to the others who chuckled at his crude remark.

Beth bristled a moment, but decided not to give them any satisfaction in knowing they'd gotten to her.

She stood impassive and oblivious.

"Beth, this is not the time or place for your rebellion," the commander whispered. "The high chief doesn't have the regard or the patience which I show you."

"Has he never seen a woman before?" she growled.

"Beth, I warn you. Please don't do something rash. You're here to answer some questions, nothing more."

"What questions?"

"Be silent, please."

The high chief watched the exchange with amusement. He spoke to the commander in their tongue.

"Is he telling you to control me?" she asked.

"No."

"What did he say?"

"Nothing you want to hear."

They brought the shaman into the meeting. He sat down carefully with his spindly body and then looked at Beth. He began a narrative immediately that went on for some time.

When he stopped talking all eyes focused on Beth. Elders began asking questions.

"Beth, I'll tell you the questions. You must answer honestly. If you attempt to deceive there will be consequences. I can't protect you from that. Simply tell the truth and we can leave shortly."

Beth shrugged.

"They asked about the city defense, and about this maverick in the forest."

"What am I supposed to say? That wasn't a question. It's obvious Prince Damon maintains a separate position and the reason is also obvious. It's changed the battlefield dynamics in the favor of Kragan. That was a stupid remark."

The commander uttered a quick sentence and received a flood of questions.

"What's your position in the city? Do you have great esteem?"

"I told you I'm a farmer's daughter from the frontier. I only recently came to Kragan, chased there by the Argore raiders who killed my family. There'll all dead now by the way. We killed them."

The commander paused before answering. It evoked another flood of questions.

"They wonder if threatening you would alter the war or if sending your head to them in the city would cause a rash response and make them vulnerable."

"Of course not, who am I to the king of a distant city? I've made their acquaintance, but I'm not significant. Do you think a significant person would be far from the city fighting in combat?"

They mulled her answer, talking to each other. Beth waited.

"What are their weaknesses? What would provoke them?"

"This invasion provoked them, but they're no fools. You should know that since they're still standing after over a month. Whatever you did to try to evoke an ill-considered response would come to naught. They won't do anything to give you advantage and if that means sacrificing people like me, they'll do what they must."

"The high chief doubts your explanation about you. What we've learned from prisoners tells a much different story. Prince Damon would do anything to save you. I'm surprised he hasn't tried a rescue attempt already."

"He's a man, like any other. My focus isn't on him any more than it is on you. Your entreaties for my hand strike me as foolish, childish, and show me the weakness in you, Commander. The same thing is true for Prince Damon. Neither of you should have become vulnerable to a pretty face."

He fought to keep from responding to the barb in front of the keen eyes of the council.

"Beth, I told you this isn't the place for such words. You're in severe danger. You think you're brave because of your prowess in battle, but weaponless, naked and tied at a torture rack you'll beg for death. You've never felt the kind of pain our experts inflict. They can keep you alive as long as they wish. Hear me now if you've heard nothing else I've said. Let this threat pass. Play the game for once and live. If you truly have hopes of rescue from your prince, dying horribly on the rack dismembered is not the answer. They would send your head and the other pieces of your body to your Kragan friends in stages."

This time she listened. Fear swamped her at the thought of what he said. She looked at the faces staring at her. They were killers and watching her slaughtered would have been entertainment to them, not horror.

"What do you need for me to say, Commander?"

"Do they have weaknesses?"

"If they do, I don't know what they are. As you've seen, all of the rival cities have joined together to oppose you. That's never happened before."

He made a lengthy reply and the council pondered the answer.

The shaman began to talk again. The commander got a worried look on his face.

"What is it?" she whispered.

"He wants to personally question you. He'll report what he finds back to them."

"Is that a danger to me?"

"I'll be there to translate, but I can't interfere. Whatever he chooses to do…"

Guards came to claim her. They dragged her away to the shaman's tent. The commander came in behind them.

They tied her hands and feet to the four corner posts of a table propped on a slant.

The shaman edged close and looked into her eyes.

"You will tell me what I want to know, one way or another," he muttered in her language. His stench was overpowering. It made her gag and close her eyes. The insane look on his face terrified Beth. This was a man without normal human feelings of compassion. She had no doubts he was capable of horrific actions.

Beth was frightened like never before. She felt the same helplessness of being hidden under the floor by her father only here she was in severe danger and possibly mortal peril.

She pulled on the restraints but she was held tight and going nowhere. Beth was in his control, this evil looking man. He smiled wickedly brandishing a sharp knife.

"Test me if you dare," he taunted. "I can teach you real pain."

She looked over at the commander. He looked on the verge of becoming ill. This appalling wild man threatening her wasn't bluffing.

"I'll tell you whatever you want. No one wants to be tortured."

"Good."

He put the sharp point of the blade against her neck. He nicked her slightly and drew a tiny drop of her blood.

"Just so you understand, woman."

Her heart thumped wildly in fear. He was a lunatic and might not show restraint with his innate blood lust.

"Do the city dwellers have a weakness?"

"I told you the truth. I don't know. I didn't live in that city and only briefly met them. Most of my time was spent in the field in training."

He eyed her skeptically.

"I know this to be true," said the commander.

The shaman looked at him angrily. "Perhaps you should return to your tent."

"I'm sorry, I'll say no more."

The shaman looked back at Beth.

"You're the loveliest of females. How do think your suitors would see you if you're scarred?"

He cut open her top with his razor sharp blade. She felt horrified, frightened and vulnerable as he pulled open the ripped clothing.

"A woman's breasts are her pride. You can survive without them, but what kind of life would you have? What man would want you?"

Beth tried to be brave, but the threat and the danger he would act was making her ill. Tears began to roll down her cheeks.

"Please don't," she moaned.

He glided the knife lightly over her chest.

"It would be the simplest thing. This soft skin is easy to slice. What compels men to lust for you can be rendered into mere lumps of useless discarded flesh lying on the floor with the merest of cuts."

She saw the insanity in his eyes and his hunger at the diseased idea. She groaned in terror as he grasped one of her full breasts and brought the razor sharp blade under it.

"Shaman, please," said the commander suddenly. "What purpose does it serve to disfigure her? She's terrified. Look at her and ask your questions. She'll tell you honestly."

It broke his rabid moment and his terrible intent. The shaman turned in rage at being thwarted, a monster denied his prey. The commander refused to back down and took a step forward.

"I follow your visions as do all Argore, shaman, but this woman is special. You've said it yourself. I know you feel strong needs and wish to punish her defiance, but there are others to vent your wrath upon. I pray you leave her to me, unharmed. She can be a great boon for the Argore. The children she will give me would be unmatched, the finest in body and mind. They would be great Argore leaders and savage fighters, but they need their mother to be able to feed them her milk."

The Shaman looked back at her, his face thankfully transformed to calculation rather than savage lust. He gave her breast one last gentle squeeze before releasing it.

"She would be a lovely adornment for an Argore bed, Commander, but hear me woman, don't think you're beyond my power, or my touch. The commander may not always be here to spare you the fate you've earned with your contemptible actions. I won't ever be far away. I might decide to finish this punishment at any time. Think about that the next time you choose to flaunt us with scorn."

He leered at her before allowing the guards to remove the restrains.

She sat up, covered her body defensively folding her arms over her chest and meekly followed the commander back to his tent.

"I warned you," he huffed at her. "This isn't your weak world. There is danger for you every minute of every day. You thought you were clever to defy me. Now perhaps you understand I was never your enemy. The high chief and the shaman can render your life a horror with no release into death. You have no power here. I keep telling you your prowess with weapons is lost as a captive but you don't listen to me. You need to think about the rest of your life. Your dreams of escape are just dreams, false hopes. As my wife, I will offer you the best life you can have. What was here before in this land with those petty cities, they're all destroyed, their people scattered. That life is gone too. Think hard tonight about my offer. You'll get no better one. Do you want to be on the shaman's table again? He would do the worst to you. Cutting you would be just the beginning of the horror he can enact. He's done terrible things to women before. Listen to what I tell you. I fear him and you should too."

"Thank you for saving me," she answered softly. "I thought he was going to hurt me."

"Beth, he was going to hurt you. I spoke to save you without a belief he would heed me."

She lay back in the fetal position staring at the opposite wall of the tent.

"I must see to some things. I'll leave extra guards to ward you. Do not leave this tent. I'll be back when I can."

Her bravado, her defiance, her fatalistic approach, they were all gone. She couldn't get the memory of her near miss out of her mind. That demented creature was the spiritual guide of the horde and now she was centered in his awareness.

Beth dozed off eventually. She was asleep when the commander returned, unaware he looked at her lovingly, as she lay resting peacefully.

They slept in the same bed every night though she would never allow him to touch her, even the most innocent of touches.

After the incident, Beth was subdued. She didn't challenge the commander in any way. The threat of the shaman had been that frightening for her.

The commander let her be for the time being having another battle to fight that day.

Beth's taunt about confronting Damon in the forest had made an impression on him.

Instead of their usual tactics for the assault on the city, the commander launched a direct attack at the forest and at Damon's position. By this time, Damon had built a near impregnable defensive array and his manpower continuously grew on a daily basis.

The ensuing battle of the forest was titanic, but again Damon's strategy offset Argore numbers luring them into killing fields with no hope of victory. The commander personally rode into the fight. He never saw Damon but he did see the genius of the defense. A concerted push into the forest would have gained nothing but more casualties with no chance to break through. The commander drew back out of the woods to join the ongoing assault on the city walls. He waited to fight Damon's forces when they came out of the woods to strike at the Argore.

Motivated by the forest battle, Damon unleashed an attack that rivaled the ferocity of the fabled Argore frenzy. Both sides fought evenly for a time, but incredible to the commander, he saw his forces battered and driven back. Damon's guards were the spear point of the attack and they seemed invincible. None of these men were intimidated fighting against Argore warriors. The commander was forced to draw back time after time. The flood of reinforcements coming out of the woods to join the battle seemed endless.

At last, in the distance, the commander saw what he was waiting for, Damon streaking forward at the gallop on his great war horse. He was an inspiring sight even though he was the enemy. His appearance tipped the battle and started a rout sending the Argore racing back to join their brethren fleeing the attack on the walls. Damon didn't stop battling all the way to the gates.

The commander fought diligently trying to approach Damon who was surrounded by crack troops and what had to be his inner circle. Layla stood out in that she fought like Beth did.

The commander reached a point to be in Damon's line of sight. Damon looked up and recognized he was seeing the enemy leader, but he stopped when he realized the commander was merely staring at him. Damon was puzzled. At his side, Layla noticed too and she looked at the commander in puzzlement.

He shouted to them. "I'll tell Beth I've seen you. I concede this day, Prince Damon, but this war is not over. It can only end one way."

Damon and Layla were shocked and charged at him instantly but the glut of fighting troops blocked the way.

The commander rode back to the camp and straight to his tent. He walked in purposefully. It caught Beth's notice as he smiled smugly at her.

"I've seen your prince, and your woman friend."

"Damon, Layla," she cried standing up.

It was exactly what he wanted to get a reaction from her, and her full attention.

"They live so put your fears to rest, Beth. I didn't slay them. Your prince has a great strategy, a formidable lair, and competent troops. This is a war worthy of the Argore. Both sides fought magnificently today. I told your friends I would speak to you."

Her expression changed to anger. "You let them know I'm alive and I'm here. You did it so they would try to come for me."

"Actually, it was by chance I saw them. It was a sudden impulse to greet them. If they act on it and make an attempt here, it's their choice and their doom. I hope you'll acknowledge I thought about your feelings rather than having my archers fill them full of holes with arrows."

He saw some of the old fight back in her eyes.

"That's better, you look yourself again."

She looked at him.

"I'm eternally your enemy. None of us chose this for our land. You Argore came upon us. I appreciate the protection you've given me and for saving me from your insane shaman. I don't know if you understand that your wishes for me to comply, to bear your children, that's never going to happen. I've never decided if I want to bring children into this world much less who would be the father. You can't simply make decisions for me as if I have no choice in my life. For an Argore, I've seen some few redeeming qualities in you. That surprises me, but it doesn't change the facts. You should look elsewhere for a wife. You need some simpering ninny that will bow to you and act the mindless vassal. That's not me."

He laughed. "A simpering ninny? Thank you, but no. I desire a strong woman with spirit. I want a special woman, and that's you, Beth. You have no peer."

She looked at him.

"If I promise not to harm you, can I have my weapons? I fear the shaman could come for me at any time. I need to be able to defend myself."

"Put weapons back in your hands? How could I find any problem with that? Beth, I love you, but I still have my mind. I'm sorry but you're going to have to depend on my men to protect you."

"How can they protect me from your shaman? He would just order them out of his way, or have them killed."

"I stay as near as I can."

"You heard him at his tent. That matter between us isn't over. It's just a matter of time and when he comes again, he's going to have serious intent. I'm going to be in real trouble."

The commander got a troubled look.

"Beth, I've thought about that very thing."

"Thank you for thinking about it, but I need answers. I saw him slinking through camp when you were in the battle. He kept looking at this tent. I think he's already plotting to make a move. It could come at any time. I'm not safe regardless of how many guards you post."

"Beth, you're a bad influence on me. I've started thinking in forbidden ways."

"What does that mean?"

"I…eh, I've thought about taking you away, just you and me to make a life far from here. I would be a good husband. I wouldn't expect you to act as an Argore woman. You could act like one of your people. Is that something you'd consider? I think if you're honest, you have feelings for me."

She looked at him in astonishment. "Did you not hear what I told you? I'm not looking for a husband, a marriage, babies, or anything like that. You men get so caught up in your desires you never consider the wishes of the woman. Why is that?"

"What is it you want for your life?" he asked in true curiosity. "Can you not see all men want you Beth? You're perfect."

"I have some thoughts," she answered after a moment. "I have feelings I need to understand. Perhaps without that day of death at my family farm I would see things differently. I may not go in a conventional way with my life. I may wish to try new things, different things."

"Now, I must ask, what does that mean?"

"I'm not going to talk with you about my private thoughts. I will say to your statement I'm perfect, no, I'm not. I have plenty of weaknesses which are my business. I have no ambitions to lead, or be led. I don't seek fame, or even fortune. Right now, I've been content to dwell with my friends and enjoy life in their companionship. The Argore have taken that life away, so I don't know what I would do next. Right now I just avoid that sick bastard shaman of yours and try to survive for another day. Someday maybe I'll be free again."

"Beth, my offer will always stand. I hope you'll reconsider at some point."

She shrugged. "Go find a wife elsewhere. By the way, you've never told me your name?"

"We don't give our names to any but Argore. To learn my name you must marry me."

"I don't need your name. I was just curious."

"Come, let's get some food, Beth." He smiled though his ploy failed miserably.

Beth was no fool. She followed him out of the tent. The sky was darkening as daylight dimmed and a storm front was moving in.

"Those storms can do some damage," she told him conversationally.

He nodded his head, like for a rare moment they had rapport.

The Argore always watched her when she walked around the camp. It was a mixture of awe at her beauty and distrust for an important enemy captive moving about amongst them. She only watched for the shaman. There were always watchers not far away, so she felt he had eyes on her at all times. It would make an escape so much the more difficult.

They carried the food back to the tent to be away from prying eyes.

"Your prince was a dashing figure, Beth. I was inspired watching him fight and he's my enemy. He's obviously the inspiration for his troops."

"He's not my prince, but did you say you saw Layla?"

"When I saw her fight I thought of you. She has the same fire within her and many of the same moves. She also stirs a man's blood."

He looked at her as she stared away pensively.

"She's your close friend?"

"I never had a sister. I think she's closer to me than a sister would be. She I can understand and I can trust. Men are…well, men. They can't be understood by a rational mind. They're clumsy, they're clods, and they annoy a woman to no end. How any woman can pair up with one of them I don't understand?"

"Your viewpoint may change with time, Beth. Men have their good points."

"I have yet to see any."

"You'll just have to trust me about it."

"Trust you?"

"Yes, trust me, Beth. This war will end and it will be easier to sort things out in peacetime. I think I'm no longer a monster in your eyes. All Argore are not the same."

"Yes, Commander, just keep killing my people. It makes a great statement to me about your worthless words and who you really are."

"You know I have no choice about that, Beth. Did you not kill my people?"

"Yes I did, after they killed my family, including the rape murder of my mother. Would you have done otherwise? You have no concept of civilized society. There are consequences in this life, even for your people."

"That's not true, you're saying we have no concept of civilized society."

She turned her back to him.

"I've had enough of talk. Leave me in peace."

He was frustrated but he dropped the matter for the moment, angry she could evoke him so easily. Much of his anger was realization of the truth that he had fallen hopelessly in love with her, and it didn't matter to her.

Chapter Thirteen

The shocking taunt from the Argore commander about Beth in the middle of a pitched battle affected Damon and all the other friends profoundly.

"She's alive," Layla shouted at them like an accusation when they got back to camp. "We've done nothing for her and she's been in their hands all this time. Who knows what they've done to her. I will not let this crime go on any longer. If I must ride alone into their camp to save her, I will."

She was fuming, red faced, and hyperventilating.

"Layla," said Argon gently.

"Stop! I've heard it from you enough. Save your meaningless words for the sheep."

The men all around them bristled listening to the exchange and looked at Argon grimly.

Seldom was Argon at a loss with a situation and he looked helplessly at Damon before speaking. He scowled a moment and then looked around at the angry faces.

"Don't you think we all feel the same way, but stop to think a moment. If that commander said those things to rile you into precipitous action and lured you into an ambush does that save Beth, if she's actually still alive? They can say anything. I love Beth like a daughter. It haunts me that she was taken when we were but feet away and blocked from saving her. I wanted to die on that day, but I fight on for all these other people. They need us or else all is lost. I'm not counseling inaction."

Damon stood in consternation listening to Argon struggle searching for an elusive answer. Difficult choices had become the bane of his life as well as for Argon.

Argon looked at him squarely after turning away from Layla's angry face.

"If you decide to attack their camp, Damon, you must consider the obvious. They're waiting for you, and your chances of success decrease if you fail and must try again. They may kill Beth if she's alive and you get near to her, not even considering the fact you have no idea where she is. The problems with doing this have not changed, my friends. I appreciate your fire, Layla, but think about reality. If you rushed into their camp, do you see the end would logically be your death or your capture? You'd be just another pretty thing for their use. This isn't the time for bravado."

"So you want to stand here and do nothing!"

"No, I don't."

"Layla, brought up the idea of us dressing like Argore to infiltrate their camp," said Berne suddenly. "Perhaps some of us could do that and go in the dark. Once we find where they're holding her we can give a signal so you can attack a specific place."

"That would probably be a suicide mission, Berne," Damon replied.

"Obviously, you wouldn't be one of the volunteers to sneak into that camp," Argon said to Damon.

He grimaced. "Layla, make your preparations. We'll wait a little time so they think we've thought better about a rescue attempt. We may be better able to surprise them later on. I don't like her being captive either but Argon is right. This could be an elaborate ploy to lure us into a death trap."

"Thank you, Damon. Amal, Berne, come with me. We need to talk." Layla walked away without waiting to see if Amal and Berne were following her.

Damon started to follow.

"You can't join them, Damon," Argon insisted. "I want to be in that rescue group too, but if we fall, what happens to the defense of the city, and the people? We have heavy responsibilities whether we want them or not."

"Argon, I already know that. It isn't necessary to keep repeating it. I realize my place," he snapped in anger.

"Damon, you've had many impulsive moments. If you acted on a poor idea and I found out after the fact, it might be too late to react if the attempt failed. Do you understand? I don't mean to annoy you, but I can only plan based on your past behaviors."

"I've made mistakes, I admit that, but I will say that I think battlefield dynamics have changed. Our continuing personnel gains give us new options because we're not so badly outnumbered any longer. We can afford to take the initiative and go after them."

"That's true, but within reason, Damon. Fighting on their ground in the open isn't the same as here in our forest where we're near to invincible. Our soldiers can be killed too, don't forget."

"Something must be done to break the stalemate, Argon. My father can do nothing pinned down in the city. There are only us to turn the tide. I worry that you're too cautious."

"I worry that you're not cautious enough, My Prince. Our past triumphs here are no guarantee of victory in attacking their camp."

"I feel Layla's pain and frustration."

"As do I, Damon."

"You're confounding to reason with, Argon."

He smiled. "It isn't an easy problem. I must be the voice of good sense."

"Do you think she's still alive?"

"In my gut, I'd say yes. Beth is one of those rare women who dazzle. Even barbarians couldn't fail to notice. Merely killing her would have served no purpose. Keeping her alive, well, you can see they have our full attention because of it. They can manipulate the situation to their advantage against us. They'll prepare for any plan we could hatch. If we sneak into their camp in small numbers, they'll be watching. It will be pure luck for us to have success in finding her much less stealing her back. You already know this, Damon."

"Layla won't take no for an answer."

"Therefore, we must take whatever plan they come up with and make it better."

They were correct in that Layla proposed to go that very night when she returned later to talk to them.

"No, Layla," Damon answered. "We'll wait, as I told you, until they think we've abandoned the rescue idea."

Layla looked to be on the verge of pulling her sword on Damon. The look in her eyes was daunting for Damon to see from a person he cared about.

"If anything bad happens to her because of this delay…"

"I'll do myself in, Layla."

She wasn't mollified. She was a different person completely to Damon at this point. Her endless worship of him was gone, like he was now a merely a barrier to overcome and therefore an adversary. Like Damon, Layla wasn't always rational about Beth.

They parted company upset, both motivated in different though negative ways.

Amal and Berne looked to be conflicted by the standoff. They looked at Damon sadly, but went after Layla.

"The burden of leadership is a heavy mantle," Argon commented. "You may have saved all of their lives with your decision. It was the only one you could make with that difficult choice. I'm sorry you must bear the burden of Layla's wrathful feelings. You're not at fault here."

* * * *

In the Argore camp, Beth waited anxiously. She was worried her friends would stumble into the ambush. She tried to hide her concern, but the commander stared at her intently noting her mood.

"You think they will make an attempt. I can see it in your eyes."

"If any of them come to harm, I promise you I'll find a way to repay your sins. Holding me captive is my problem, but if you extend your crimes to my friends, there will be a heavy price for you to pay, no matter how long it takes. No one is perfect. There will be a time when you will make a mistake and that will be the last day you draw breath in this world."

"I keep telling you, Beth, I'm not your enemy here. The shaman has plans for you. I can sense it. That is your real worry. If your friends choose to make an ill-fated rescue attempt, how am I to blame?"

"You started this situation by taunting my friends. You can't talk away your part in whatever happens. I will hold you personally responsible. As far as your council, they can be killed. As I said, it doesn't matter to me how long it takes."

"Beth, I know you won't take this in the right spirit, but there are other things in play here I can't tell you. If you can exercise patience, it may be that things will change. I still want you to know I love you and want you to be my wife and I'm willing to wait. No Argore has ever given such an honor to a woman, especially a foreign woman. The Argore take whomever they wish. Do you understand how important this is what I'm telling you?"

"I don't care, Commander. I don't care. That matters to you, not to me. Saying this over and over again won't change me. I only care about my friends and my people."

"It seems to be a moot point, Beth. Nothing has happened. Either your friends feared to take the risk, or didn't believe you're still alive. You're bashing me for no reason. I let it pass as I always do with you. I know I shouldn't. The council thinks me weak because of how tolerant I am about you. They say I should have marked you as mine the first night and taught you the proper place of a woman. You should have been compelled to cooperate and be an obedient wife. You should already swell with our first child in your belly."

"It's your choice to try, Commander. I won't cooperate and I won't go quietly."

He smiled ruefully. "I have no doubts about that, Beth. You're safe in my tent regardless of your mouth. My tolerant actions should speak to you even though you choose not to listen."

She smiled. "Give me back my weapons and my actions can speak to you very clearly."

He smiled wryly.

"No, Beth, I don't need your actions to explain anything to me. We already had that fight, remember?"

"I'm going to sleep now, Commander." She crawled under the covers and turned away from him. Her dismissive acts always strongly evoked his emotions. Argore men and especially ones of great consequence were never treated with disdain and disrespect, yet he endured it from Beth without any punishment to her. In his mind he dreamed of clever retorts and pithy acts to dazzle her and bring her to heel. He was hopelessly agog about a woman beyond has grasp.

* * * *

In a departure from their routine, the Argore held off on attacking Kragan the next day and also on the next. Spending lives endlessly without progress was causing dissension in the ranks. No one would openly challenge the council and in particular the shaman, but the background resentment simmered nonetheless.

For Damon it was a significant sign, the unexpected day of respite. He voiced his views to his staff.

"I think the Argore have a problem. A city they can't conquer, it never occurred to them. After all this time, I think they can see our defense can be nearly endless so they can't starve out the city. During the lull, we funneled supplies into Kragan continuously and they did nothing to halt us."

"I'm happy too, Damon." Argon agreed, but his face reflected his reservations about being optimistic.

"But..."

"Though I'm a cautious person by nature, I accept this favorable turn of circumstances."

Damon eyed him skeptically and chuckled. "I think it hurts you to concede anything. Your dour way is too comfortable for you."

"I'll be optimistic when Beth stands amongst us again, Damon."

"*Touché*, Argon."

Layla walked over to them. "Gentlemen, is this a good time to make our attempt? The Argore are taking a holiday it seems."

"I doubt that their vigilance is decreased, Layla," Argon replied.

"Of course, Master," she groused. "How could we ever consider taking action where there's any hint of risk? If I choose to put my life out there because it's the right thing to do for Beth, where is the wrong of it? If I was killed, then I would have died in a noble purpose. Our darling has survived long enough over there at the mercy of those barbarians. Berne and Amal are of the same opinion. They offer their support and will stand with me through the attempt. You said you wanted us to wait for a time, Damon. We've waited."

He could think of no response. He shrugged his shoulders, conceding to her wishes.

"We'll ready an attack on the Argore camp. If through some miracle you survive long enough to find her, give us a signal so we know where to concentrate the assault."

Layla smiled. "I know you think this a mistake, but I always believed it would come down to this. Unless Beth could find a way to free herself, this was the only option."

"Layla, please be careful. This is deadly dangerous business. There is no room for error. There's no mercy in that camp."

"I know, Damon." She looked at him soberly before she left to find his two childhood friends. The three boyhood friends were all men now and their youthful days were long past. Amal and Berne could make adult decisions which Damon could no longer thwart.

Reluctantly, Damon went to find Gideon to explain what was about to happen. It was dusk with the sun low on the horizon with light dimming rapidly so they had little time to make final preparations, give instructions, and deploy the forest army.

Instead of what Damon described as a significant force, they ended up preparing his entire army to attack. Damon felt uneasy at his dearest friends taking such risk. He sought them out.

He saw Layla, Amal, and Berne put on captured Argore garb. It was painfully obvious Layla was a woman. Her superb feminine physique couldn't be masked and this would stand out because there were no women fighters amongst the barbarians.

"Okay," she responded, thinking quickly at Damon's skeptical look. "Amal and Berne will be my captors and will drag me through that camp. I'll wear my clothes and they will carry my weapons as if they disarmed me."

She didn't wait for a reply but simply discarded the Argore clothes and put back on her own battle gear.

They left quickly before Damon could say anything to stop them. Damon grimaced but held his tongue.

Damon, Argon, Gideon and the entire rest of his command watched anxiously from the edge of the forest as the three hopeful rescuers slipped away toward the unknown. The reality was few people were optimistic about their chances. Layla occupied a place of esteem that rivaled that of Beth. It was torture to allow her to leave their protective ranks at risk of her life.

In the dim light they couldn't see when Amal and Berne dragged Layla up to the nearest sentries around the Argore camp. They had their hoods up to obscure their features.

The sentries eyed them and said something in Argore. Amal and Berne merely nodded and kept walking holding their breath they could perpetrate the ruse.

Getting past them was the first big test. Wandering freely in the camp was another. They moved purposefully as if they had a destination. Layla drew plenty of notice for her beauty. Whenever any Argore tried to approach them she snarled and kicked to keep them away. It kept the stares on her rather than the fact her “captors” weren’t Argore warriors.

The sheer number of the enemies in the massive camp was staggering. Walking along, it seemed there was no end to the array of tents.

“Move toward the center,” she whispered. “The leaders will logically be found there, and that’s where they’ll have Beth.”

It was a very long walk in the dark and took hours. The huge tents were easy to spot in the distance on a small rise in the ground silhouetted from the light of large campfires. There were considerable guards moving about in clear view protecting the site.

“That’s a problem,” Berne muttered. “We can’t speak their language so we can’t talk our way in there.”

“I’ve got an idea,” she replied. “I can’t just walk up and surrender. If you two create a diversion to draw them off, I can slip in and find Beth.”

“What?” Amal huffed. “Find Beth how? Which tent is she in? You don’t have time to check them all, there are too many.”

“This whole plan is a risk, Amal. We have to do something edgy. I’m sorry. If Beth knows we’re here, she’ll find a way to show us where to go.”

“So, this diversion, it will be the two of us against the whole Argore horde?” asked Berne. “I don’t really like our chances.”

“Do something to draw their notice and get out away from it in a hurry. Set something afire. You won’t stand out running around amongst all the others.”

“If we’re running the wrong way, you don’t think someone will notice?”

“It’s a risk, I admit it, Berne. Get going, we’re here so let’s get busy and do this thing.”

Berne and Amal looked into her eyes. They all stood a moment as if it was their last and clasped hands.

“This will work,” she ventured. “You’re both incredibly brave. It’s been my honor to know you and to be your friend. If this goes badly, we’ll be together on the other side of life.”

They turned and hurried away skirting the phalanx of troops guarding the Argore leadership.

Layla was in the most jeopardy now with them gone, a stranger in the middle of the camp unescorted. Casually wandering along, she donned her weapons again.

She didn’t have to wait for long before guards noticed her and started in her direction, but the distraction occurred before they got close. They heard shouts as a large fire burned a big tent. Guards hurried away in the confusion. Layla waded in to strike down the guards who noticed her. It was a very difficult fight as these were skilled fighters, among the best of the Argore horde.

When the fire and the shouting started, Beth jumped out of bed. She knew what it meant, and so did the commander. He smiled at her.

"Ah, their misguided attempt at last. I worried they were too cowardly to come for you."

Beth glanced at the weapons hanging nearby, and the guards standing between them and her. They stared intently, daring her to make a move.

"You know I won't allow you to rearm, my darling."

"I'm not your darling," she hissed.

The burning tent was very near. Guards burst into the commander's tent.

"How many of them are there?"

"We don't know. There have been casualties from arrows. It's said they're dressed in our clothes. They haven't been located and pinned down yet."

"Guard her with your lives," he ordered and followed them out. He went to the nearest wounded man.

"This is one of our arrows," he said.

"Perhaps they took weapons off our dead, Commander."

"Or we're shooting at our own men in the confusion," he grumbled.

Beth was aggravated. This was her chance, yet there were too many guards to overpower without weapons. They eyed her still but some of them stood at the entrance to the tent watching what was happening in the camp.

In the meantime, Layla hurried along, the only clear enemy target, so she had continuous fights, but in the dark the confusion was spreading and often Argore warriors clashed with each other seeking enemies dressed like them.

It was a miracle not only that Amal and Berne were able to stay alive but to then to find her. At that moment she was beset by four Argore fighters completely surrounding her and stopping her forward progress. Amal and Berne interceded and soon the four enemy soldiers were lying on the ground, slain.

"I think I saw something," said Berne in a gasp. "Where we set the fire, I think there was a tent nearby of some significant person. There were many more guards than anywhere else."

"Lead the way, Berne," she replied.

It was amazing to them how many fights they passed as Argore sought the 'infiltrators'.

The commander looked about at the pandemonium as the three approached. He barked commands and sent units of men in all directions. A huge force gathered around some other huge tents. The high chief and the shaman appeared to survey the scene. Layla paid close attention.

"That's a bad one," she said eyeing the shaman who looked like an apparition from hell.

The commander suddenly went to his tent. When the guards opened the entrance, the three rescuers got a glimpse of Beth inside held at bay.

"She's there," said Layla excitedly.

She raced impulsively toward the tent before the men could stop her. Amal and Berne hurried to try to protect her when she lashed into the guards at the tent entrance. Beth saw her coming. Her eyes went wide and it caused the commander to look back.

Layla struck with rage and hatred and quickly the startled guards started to drop around her from killing wounds, recipients of her fury.

"This is your friend," he said, smiling at Beth. Beth had a desperate look in her eyes and looked again at her weapons so tantalizingly close.

"Beth," Layla shouted as she was forced on the defensive, suddenly greatly outnumbered.

Amal and Berne tore into the guards behind her and evened the fight for just a moment.

Layla fought ferociously and burst her way into the tent.

The commander simply stood by passively watching her. Layla tried to attack him, but there were too many guards blocking her way.

Amal and Berne entered the tent. With only three of them, they were still able to wreak havoc against the best fighters in the Argore horde. It wasn't a matter of skill, but sheer numbers that thwarted their courageous attempt. In the end, all three were kneeling wounded and bloodied, and disarmed.

Beth cried out in anguish and rushed over to embrace Layla.

"You shouldn't have come, darling," she moaned.

"How could I not, Beth," she answered in a voice choked with emotion.

The commander stepped close. "I've seen you many times fighting beside your prince. You fight like an Argore. You've inspire me. Your name is Layla? I think this must be Amal and Berne. I'm not surprised at your courage, my friends. I'm surprised you picked such a plan to have no chance of success. Now you've robbed your side of key inspirational leaders. I don't think it's a good day for your side."

"What are you going to do with us? We're not afraid to die."

"I know that, Layla. Beth thought she would die on the torture rack and yet here she is unscathed. Your deaths wouldn't accomplish anything. Having you as captives will strengthen the lure for your side to act. I think your prince might finally make his move. Of course we'll be waiting for him."

"You can't kill us all," Beth retorted.

"That's not our goal," the commander replied evenly.

Beth pulled Layla up to her feet, her arms wrapped around her protectively. “If you try to harm her in any way, you’ll need to kill me first.”

“I won’t harm her, Beth. She’ll even be allowed to join us here in our home.”

“Has he…?” asked Layla.

“No, she’s still pure,” he replied.

Layla looked at Beth.

“It’s true. He hasn’t touched me in that way, Layla.”

The commander turned his head to look at Amal and Berne.

“I’m sorry for your deaths, my friends. You showed great courage. Take them away,” said the commander nodding to Amal and Berne but before they could leave they heard commotion in the camp. Both men had stoic looks on their faces. They looked sadly at the two women, their attempt at a rescue a failure.

* * * *

When they heard noise and then saw a distant fire in the Argore camp, Damon signaled the charge immediately. A vast wave of irate troops rushed out of their forest cover waving their weapons and screaming hatred as they attacked the Argore camp. They blew past the sentries like they were tissue paper and surged into the startled horde warriors as they came out of the tents into deadly sword strokes and flying arrows.

There was no place in the camp for them to make a stand so Damon drove ahead relentlessly aiming toward the site of the fire.

The sheer mass of Argore fighters began to slow the charge but they never succeeded in stopping the progress forward completely.

As they gradually drew closer to the commander’s tent the sound of fighting was unmistakable. The four captives felt hope.

“I think you might be right about Prince Damon, Commander,” Beth taunted. “I think he decided to come for me. It seems your boast about the invincible Argore army has a hollow ring.”

The commander scowled and shouted orders to his men.

Outside, the shaman was screeching loudly and shaking his staff toward the approaching allied surge.

Even in the midst of heavy fighting, Damon noticed the elevated place and realized the enemy leaders were close at hand. He had no idea if his friends were still alive, but charged ahead anyway.

“Push forward, men,” he yelled. They shouted in response and drove purposefully into the Argore deployment blocking the way. Again, it worked against the Argore there was no place they could make a stand. The allies paid no attention to what was happening behind them, or if the Argore could cut them off. They scythed their way toward the goal heedless of the danger.

The commander went outside to personally lead his forces. He saw Prince Damon and the two locked eyes. Seeing him Damon knew Beth was near. He roared in rage and they charged ahead with serious intent that rivaled Argore frenzy. Impossibly as it would have seemed before the attack, now it was the Commander trying to stand his ground, but the Prince would not be denied. The sudden battle in the darkness drew notice from the city of Kragan.

Significantly, the guards in Kragan had awakened the king once Damon's attack began. The king sent Tabor out with a large force from the royal army to support Damon's army in his rescue attempt. The King cautioned his youngest son.

"I have no idea what's happening, but he wouldn't go into their camp without a good reason. Be careful, son."

"I'll save them, Father."

Their sudden intervention was critical because they followed Damon's path of destruction so when the Argore army tried to close in behind Damon's massive force they were met by the new attack from the city soldiers. The enemy was caught with battle ahead of and behind them.

In the dark, and in the confusion, the Argore couldn't get orders to their entire army throughout the sprawling camp. They remained in confusion striking as individuals rather than as an army. It played into Damon's hands. Even though they were outnumbered, he could be the aggressor and dictate battle tactics. The Commander could only try to react and he was in an unfavorable place trying to defend the council, and Beth.

Damon fought his way up to the commander who eyed him contemplatively. He saw the tent behind him and knew this was his focus of defense for the commander.

The commander was ready for a final fight with Damon, but instead, Damon quickly swerved around him and literally rode into the tent on his horse. His men were feral striking at the knot of determined guards surrounding Beth, Layla, Amal, and Berne.

"Damon," Beth shouted. It spurred him to personally dismount and personally erase the expert Argore fighters standing in his way. He grabbed Beth and hugged her tightly, overwhelmed with his feelings of relief to have her in his arms again, but that could only be for a moment as the commander broke into the tent seething with fury.

"Beth?" he cried out in anguish.

He attacked Damon immediately and it was a fight for the ages as both men refused to lose her. Beth hurried over to retrieve her own weapons, at last.

She came over to join Damon. The commander backed off staring at her like he'd been betrayed.

She looked momentarily daunted.

"I told you, I appreciate everything you did for me with your protection, but I also told you I commit nothing about your wishes. It was your choices that brought you to this point. It could only have ended like this. I was never going to be your wife."

Damon stood in confusion at the strange conversation, but it wasn't the time to sort it out here in the middle of a serious fight.

He started to attack, but Beth restrained him. "No, Damon, leave him be."

He stopped in astonishment and turned his head back to the commander.

"If you've shown kindness to Beth, I give you your life for this night. Tomorrow on the battlefield nothing is changed between us. If you take your people back home to your mountains, there can be peace between us."

"Know this, Prince. I won't ever give up on Beth. She's my soul mate."

"I could say the same thing, Commander."

The men eyed each other a moment before Damon quickly exited the tent with his friends. Damon drove back with the forest army toward the city soldiers, battling to get out of the amorphous Argore noose. The Argore warriors were still disorganized and confused without the direction of their leaders, fighting whoever came close, sometimes their own soldiers.

Beth was shouting something to him, but they were beset with terrible fighting so he couldn't stop to listen.

When they had traveled far enough to break through Argore resistance they saw leading the surge of city troops was Prince Tabor. The two brothers met.

"Again I must save you, Damon."

Damon smiled. "You're a happy sight, Tabor."

Tabor turned to Beth and smiled.

"It's a blessing to see you safe again, Beth."

"Thank you, Crown Prince."

Even in the midst of terrible battle, it evoked Damon as he watched the moment when they, Beth and Tabor, locked eyes for an unspoken connection. He could never escape those adverse feelings and worries when it came to her.

When they left the boundary of the Argore camp and rode to the point where the two forces split, Tabor hugged Beth and she returned his embrace. He whispered something to her and she smiled in return.

Layla was riding close to Beth, like she would never let her out of her sight, ever again.

"Goodbye Brother," said Tabor glancing back at Damon.

"Goodbye."

Damon turned, steeled his turbulent feelings, and rode ahead at the gallop, alone. His momentary thrill when Beth called his name in the tent had passed. It appeared everything between them was back to the usual. From his skewed viewpoint, she remained elusive, focused on anyone else but Damon.

Also as he rode, Damon was curious about the mystifying exchange between Beth and the Argore commander. He'd made an assumption about her helpless state in barbarian hands. This was a confusing twist. What it meant worried him adding to his numerous other concerns, the last thing he needed. There were no answers for him to find within the confines of his personal thoughts.

When they arrived at camp, there was considerable work to do tending to the wounded and redeploying the army in case the Argore made a quick response to the rescue.

Damon made a point of busying himself to avoid the chance of any snubs from Beth. It surprised him when she sought him out.

"Come, Prince Damon, I need a moment of your time," she asked. "We must speak with Argon."

He nodded and they hurried to find their master. Amal, Berne, Layla, and Gideon joined them for Beth's explanation.

"When I was held in their camp I learned nothing about their society, but I did find what may be the key in this war. Argon, you ventured in the beginning that we needed to learn their reasons for coming here and their goal. I may have some idea. They have a high chief who presides over the horde as their political leader, but their guidance comes from the shaman. He's a vile demented man, but they follow his visions nonetheless. I believe it's he that's the reason they've come and I think taking him out would end the threat. I think many in their camp don't like this war where they spend their lives on the walls of Kragan only because of the dreams of a madman. The commander didn't explain it, but he implied there's unrest afoot in that camp, and that soon there might be a change. He was unexpectedly kind and solicitous to me. I can come up with no other explanation."

"Really, Beth?" asked Damon skeptically. "The man is obviously lost in his feelings for you. It's hard to imagine you can't recognize that. We could all see he was besotted and not thinking rationally. It's affected his battle readiness in our favor. It shouldn't have been so easy for us to waltz into the heart of their camp. Whatever you did there definitely conquered him."

The group stood awkwardly at the uncomfortable moment at Damon's ill-conceived outburst. Damon instantly regretted he'd erred again about Beth, this time seriously. He hadn't planned to lash out against her but in this case the impulse overcame him. The words couldn't be taken back though. It was too late.

She eyed him grimly. "What are you saying, Prince Damon, that I somehow cherished my time in their hands, that I secretly longed for fulfillment in his bed. Do you imagine we wiled away the hours in love's sweet embrace? Perhaps I should leave now to return to the man I truly love?"

"Beth, he didn't mean it that way," Layla whispered.

"Is that right, Layla? I have no trouble gleaning his meaning from his cruel words. You've heard what I had to say about the Argore motivation and what needs to be done. I'll leave you gentlemen to your own deliberations."

She turned abruptly and stormed away, Layla at her side looking back angrily at Damon.

"Damon, I think you could have handled that better," said Berne.

"Really, Berne?" he retorted sharply. He stomped away in his personal funk to seek a secluded area to brood. He was back to familiar ground from the bad ole days.

"Damon, how can you be such an idiot? I think this time you've ruined it for good," he muttered in frustration.

In the morning when he finally resurfaced Argon sought him out.

"Damon, I thought your jealousy was no longer an issue; that you'd managed to gain control over it. I was wrong. This isn't something we can continue to ignore. You've seriously wounded Beth at a time when she needed the opposite. I understand what drives you, but you're making serious errors in judgment. In so many words, you blamed Beth because the Argore commander romantically pursues her. If you can't see the wrong of it, I'm very worried about the future for all of us. You're our leader. You can't do these things because we all pay the price of it."

"Argon, I was wrong. I already know it. My emotions have been pent up for so long they just exploded. I didn't plan for any of that to happen. I can find her to apologize, but I suspect the damage is too great to repair this time."

"If that's true, Damon, you especially need to find inner courage. As I said, you're still our leader and we're still in the middle of a war where the outcome is in question. I think that enemy commander is coming for you now, just like you went after him after his taunt."

"I'd welcome it. That kind of challenge I can handle. If it's he and I with swords, I can accept the outcome. The better man wins in the end."

Chapter Fourteen

The commander was highly agitated after the attack and especially with losing Beth right out of his personal tent. He began to gather his trusted forces to go after her, but before he could leave he was called for by the high chief and the shaman. He knew it meant trouble.

"Now we see the end result of your weakness," the shaman hissed scornfully. "She lay on my rack for her own shameful doings and you spared her the punishment she'd so richly earned. You said she would bear your children. Did you mark her that night?"

"No."

The shaman turned to the high chief. "I warned you about this. He was a great warrior of the Argore, but he allowed this heathen woman to snare him with her wiles. He mooned after her like an adolescent boy. Even now he cares only to bring her back. The holy war is gone from his mind and his heart. You know you have no choice but to act. He can no longer lead the horde. He's unworthy and he deserves death. He was the greatest champion in our camp for the enemy. He shamed his place of high regard in Argore lore. He no longer has honor."

The commander simmered on the brink of impulsive action at the shaman's attack. The high chief was torn by the situation. The commander had always been one of his favorites and had never done anything foolish that wouldn't merit the high esteem. Now it was a matter which couldn't be ignored after the allied success attacking the heart of the Argore camp.

"What is your judgment?" the shaman insisted.

"I'll take action," the high chief muttered in a near whisper.

"What action?" the shaman snapped with an insolent look, a clear challenge to the authority of the high chief.

The affront by the shaman was a mistake as the high chief turned toward him with a deadly look. "Do you challenge me now, priest? Do you dream of taking my place? If so, draw down on me now. We'll see who still rules the

Argore horde."

The shaman realized immediately he'd gone too far, that death for him was very near. He had no chance in a fight with the savage high chief. Testing him was a foolish ploy.

"Of course, High Chief, your word is law. I didn't mean to imply…"

"Silence, I've heard enough from you. We've followed your course and we see what it's brought us, countless dead with no end in sight. Many counseled me against this campaign but I gave you your wish against my better judgment. Don't think this brave warrior is the only person in question here. You have no authority to punish him. I decide what is to be done in my camp, if anything. Leave my sight. I will to see you no longer today."

The shaman glowered at the commander before he left. He rattled his ceremonial staff like he was putting a curse on the commander.

"Thank you, high chief," said the commander once the shaman was gone.

"Don't think you're free from consequence, commander. What the shaman said had much truth in it. I saw this woman as you did and I admit she is special, but you went too far and you were too lenient. She needed to be controlled. If she tested you there should have been consequences which taught her the error of such ways. She was very lovely so it was easy to imagine her as your mate, but you should have just taken her. She was in your power. Thinking she would eventually succumb to love and come to cherish you; that idea was beyond foolishness. They see us as sub-human and unworthy of them. This woman scorned you from the start and never changed that perception yet you still gave her leniency. We show none of this weakness to our own women. Why would you do so for a heathen woman, an unbeliever?"

"I accept whatever punishment you wish, High Chief. You've been like a father to me. I'm sorry I failed you. I was wrong and I deserve your wrath."

The high chief eyed him thoughtfully, pondering what he should do to his greatest warrior. He made a decision and spoke to the commander.

"It's good you acknowledge your errors. It shows me there is hope you can still return to being the instrument of Argore vengeance. If you're going after her, this must be a well-considered attack, just like what they did to us. They will expect you to do so. Instead, you must do what they don't expect."

The commander looked up in surprise.

"Yes, High Chief. I've thought that very thing. What about the shaman and the war?"

"I've been thinking about this for a time now. While the victories were easy he could tout his vision as the true way but he would have the Argore peoples in perpetual war. We're not cowards, but this plan serves us poorly. We destroy and make enemies for life who will seek revenge for their slain families. Did you not say this is the fire in Beth's heart, Argore raiders slew her loved ones? Hearing her utter that phrase in Argore was chilling. That raiding party didn't help our cause and they paid for it with their lives."

"High Chief, none of us question our way of life, but at the same time I'm of the opinion we need to learn from the other people in the world. We've been universally avoided as anathema and deemed worthless as a people. Can we honestly say those arguments have no merit? Are we not capable of better?"

"Be careful, Commander. Beth's lure was more than just lust for her superb body. She acts in a way to evoke a man, to belittle, and to mislead. The life of any man as her husband would be a constant challenge. She would be contrary, argumentative, manipulative, and she would take control as if she were the greater. It's a situation no Argore man could tolerate."

"I know I showed poor judgment in dealing with her, High Chief. I will do better."

"Be very careful because that forest prince is also in her thrall. He will be a deadly opponent and a crafty adversary. You've seen the devious traps he's created in his forest. He continues to find ingenious ways to prevail. The dynamics of the war have changed solely due to his brilliance."

"He could have been a great Argore."

"Commander, you're a great Argore. Go out and prove it to the people."

"Yes, High Chief, I won't fail you."

* * * *

Damon decided to ride into Kragan rather than face the indignity of Beth's scorn the next day as well as the justified disapproval of everyone else in his camp. Word of his monumental misstep spread quickly. The Argore had yet to resume full scale attacks, though they struck in small groups probing as always for weaknesses.

It was a different city being on a war footing and with the women and children gone. Damon rode straight to the palace.

The king and the crown prince were in council with their advisors.

"Damon, my son, welcome," said his father. "Come and join us. Have a little wine."

"Thank you, Sire. I will have some wine. I need it right about now."

"With Beth recovered, I imagine you've had your first misunderstanding with her," said Tabor. "A man must always be on guard around her as she is a rare creature, always tantalizing, but one with sharp claws."

"So true, Brother, if you don't use great caution every time you're around her there's a terrible price to pay. It takes a toll over time."

"You can relax here, Damon. There are none of them left in this city to pose the challenges women bring."

"I think you're in distress, my son," the king reflected. "Do you wish to tell us what happened?"

"I'm usually a fool around her, but this time I made a supreme error. I think possibly I've ruined our relationship irreparably."

"If that's true, it would be a great shame, son. Rest here in the meantime. Perhaps in a few days the situation will improve once tempers cool. It seems our Argore friends have decided again to give us a respite. I'm sure continually charging our walls, failing, and dying for their efforts is taxing on their resolve. We have you to thank for our survival."

"Father, Beth brought us knowledge from her time in their camp. She said they have a shaman who is the driving force behind their invasion. He supposedly had visions of conquest of all the city states and persuaded the horde to follow him. She also said he's insane. If we were to manage to kill this charlatan perhaps it might lead to the end of the war. The Argore commander implied to Beth there was unrest in the enemy camp and things could change there."

"Beth was on familiar terms with the Argore commander?" asked Tabor.

"I know, Brother, it struck me badly too. She says he didn't touch her intimately but instead he expressed a desire for her to be his wife. That puzzling issue, it's how I managed to put my foot in my mouth in front of everyone. I handled it badly and now I think she sees me as her enemy."

"Did she accept his proposal?"

The council laughed.

"No Brother, I don't know there's any man who could tame Beth. Strangely when we crossed swords in his tent, I saw the same misery in him that I feel. It was like I was fighting against another me. Beth armed herself and intervened to spare his life. He was emotionally crushed, like she had betrayed him. He just stopped fighting and stood staring at her. She had the same contempt for his feelings I've lived with since I've known her. I felt sorry for him for some reason and just walked away and let him be."

"Incredible," said the king. "If this weren't such a serious matter with the war threatening our lives and our way of life, I would be fascinated by these strange developments. We never see the barbarians as people, yet obviously they are. To imagine they suffer the same feelings and weaknesses as we do is eye opening. It makes me think differently about our precepts and that possibly we should change our strategy."

"I sensed he saw us much differently than I would have imagined. This wasn't some rabid animal baying at the moon. He's a man like me and an accomplished warrior who I can respect on that level. What a thing for me to say about our bitter enemy."

"Damon, you know he'll make an attempt to recover Beth."

"I know, Father. We've prepared a warm welcome in the forest if and when they show up."

"They learned from your attack on their camp. Don't give them a chance to surprise you. Whatever preparations you've made, they've thought about ways around them."

"That being the case, brother, why are you here now instead of overseeing your plans?"

"I guess, mostly I'm ashamed of my emotional failure in front of Beth and my friends. I didn't want to face it. I'll return soon, but I like father's idea of wine. For one day, I can have peace and seek solace at the bottom of a drinking glass."

Again, the council laughed.

The king eyed him and spoke regretfully.

"Damon, I know your mother punished you with her words for her anger at me. How was she when you last saw her?"

"She was…well you already know how she was. What helped me deal with the civilian problem was when she took responsibility for the task of the movement of the civilians through the forest and into the land of the fortified hamlets. Once she'd verbally gotten out her rage, she moved on to tackle the task at hand. I think it helped her to have important business to handle. They've been settled there beyond the forest and are doing well, Father, from what I've been told."

"Good. I've prayed for the day when this war is done and we can go back to normal."

"Do you think there can be normal again after the war, Father? The Argore have utterly destroyed most of the other cities. If they can be rebuilt, I don't know if the people could be fed long enough to have time for the labor needed for such a monumental task. So many lost their lives, the refugees are in turmoil and leaderless. I wonder if there are any families who haven't lost someone."

"I understand, Son. Those few cities that are spared will do what we can, but I suspect a future won't be what we had in the past. Perhaps that's a good thing. Maybe we can work together at last. The survivors have certainly taken to you, Damon."

"I doubt it's me personally. I'd say it's more that we give them safe haven and food when there are no other options. It's easy to be grateful when you're backed against the wall. If the war ended, they would start to see my many flaws and I think their worship would evaporate quickly."

"I don't think so, son. You've done great things and though you can't seem to see it, others can."

Damon shrugged dismissively. "Can you pass the wine, Tabor? My glass is empty."

The council chuckled.

"I'm sorry, Father. I didn't mean to interrupt your meeting. Please continue."

* * * *

The commander gathered his best men.

"You all know what we face so I don't need to say it. They'll have surprises for us so we need to think on our feet and react. We move fast and decisively. We'll strike at their heart because that's where she'll be. If you have doubts about chasing down Beth, that it's just a childish whim of mine, no one will think less if you opt out of this mission. There's much more at stake than just my hurt feelings. It's no secret I covet her, but much more important is while she's in our custody it changes the battlefield landscape. Prince Damon will no longer sit back in his sanctuary and control the battle. He'd be forced to venture out again where we can pick and choose where to have the fight. You know he thinks and fights like one of us, so use your heads. We can still win this war. Without Damon assailing our attacks, that city will fall to us and we can finally think about going home."

He looked around. None of his men left. He smiled in appreciation.

"Thank you. We'll form up shortly. They'll expect a night raid, so we'll change the game and go as a daytime reconnaissance foray and we'll approach the forest far from their stronghold. Once we hit the trees, it will be constant battle so get your minds ready for it. We can't allow them to turn us back because we'll get no other chance."

Later, the fast moving Argore force rode out of their camp and arced gradually away from the approach toward Kragan. Damon's sentries noted the movement but when they didn't approach and rode instead away on an angle leaving the vicinity, it didn't seem a danger so they remained in place and didn't report it. It wasn't unusual to have random Argore troop movements across the front.

The commander led them determinedly along the tree line going much farther than where Damon would have been able to station crack troops. Farther along in this part of the forest would be gathered common soldiers from the lesser cities. They were equally motivated against the Argore enemy, but not of the caliber of men trained by Damon and Argon.

After hours of steady riding, they veered sharply to head into the woods. They were met by arrow volleys, but in a small amount. It did nothing to alter the attack and soon they entered the trees to confront the sentry line. They were there but not in numbers that could stop the commander or even particularly slow him. They broke through the initial defense easily and rode rapidly along the main trail. Various troops tried to intercept them, but again, they were dispersed over a wide area and there was no time to gather and confront the Argore in sufficient numbers. They were going too fast to allow anyone to race in front of them with word of the incursion.

As they rode along, the commander was pleased his risky idea was bearing fruit. Getting through the defense array at the tree line had gone much better than he anticipated. They slammed ahead breaking through light opposition covering considerable ground and closing in on Damon's main camp from the rear which was behind the formidable defenses at the forest edge in that part of the forest. He smiled in anticipation of seeing her again, the woman who owned his heart whether she accepted it or not.

* * * *

While Damon imbibed for a day with his father and brother to drown his sorrows, danger stalked Beth. She spent the day away from the men. Even Argon was out of favor for a day in Beth's anger against men in general after Damon's outburst. Layla was with her and no one else on this occasion. They talked frankly about her time as a captive.

"I know you didn't lie to me when you said that the Argore commander didn't take you intimately, Beth."

"Why is that so difficult for men to grasp?"

"They're ruled by their passions much more so than women. Damon is utterly taken with you and the thought of you with another man punishes his emotions, making his jealousy out of his control. I'm sure he regrets his ill thought outburst. I was told he went to Kragan to hide from his shame. You know that's what he would do having never been able to cope with his strong feelings about you."

"You understand me when I say I'm surprised any woman can live with a man. They seem to be more trouble than they're worth."

"They have their moments, Beth. You know that also. When you learned about Prince Damon's kindnesses to the poor it moved you greatly."

"Yes, but then there is this other side of him that annoys me to death."

"I think it means you care for him, or else he couldn't affect you. How did you feel when he burst into the commander's tent and saved us?"

Beth frowned, pondering for a moment.

"Perhaps you're right, but I'm not going to change my views. I still don't want a mate. I'm not some man's thing to use as he wishes. I'll not let my feelings about the prince sway me into trying to please him. I'm a person with goals of my own."

"It did seem that the Argore commander was agog with you, Beth. I'm sure it was a predicament totally of his own making, but you don't realize your normal way is like a flame that draws them like moths. When you're so very resistance and seemingly contemptuous, it irks them and hurts their feelings of manhood. They're so much the more motivated to conquer you, romantically speaking. They question themselves and men don't like that."

"I can't win about this. Men just won't leave me alone. That's all I've asked of any of them. About the commander, I was surprised he could gain my respect and I guess to an extent I do have some feelings, but not love or desire. I have strong feelings for Argon who is my mentor, like my father."

"Would you be shocked if Argon had secret desires for you, Beth?"

"Impossible, he's not the sort of man to…"

"Have urges? What are you basing that on, Beth. You talk how you want things to be, not how they really are. Argon is a bastion for you, and deservedly so, but in his heart you don't know his secrets. What secrets do you harbor, Beth. Men are no different than you. We're human and were flawed, both men and women."

She further pondered the assertion a moment and then scowled. It wasn't a point she wanted to concede. She wanted to focus only on her warlike life goals of revenge.

"Let's go spar, Layla. I need to get back my fighting edge."

"Yes ma'am."

Several hours later when the women took a break from a rigorous routine, they heard the alarm sounded in camp.

Hurrying to return to join the defense they ran directly into the Argore commander's assault against a startled and unprepared rear guard that were being driven backwards and out of position. The commander spotted the women and charged instantly. He was mounted and they were on foot so they were quickly surrounded. His men threw heavy nets over the women, took them to the ground and disarmed them. They bound them helpless, mounted them onto spare horses, reversed direction and headed back the way they came at the gallop.

It was ridiculously easy. It didn't dawn on anyone in the camp for some time that Beth and Layla were missing. The raid had been so fast and ended so quickly, most people were confused about the purpose of the attack.

Once Argon got word it appeared Beth and Layla were captured again, he sent word to Kragan to the prince.

Damon's day of carousing with wine ended badly.

"No," he shouted in frustration. "How could this happen?"

He rode at the gallop back to his camp. Argon, Gideon, Amal, and Berne were waiting with solemn expressions.

Damon didn't rage at them, which was a surprise. Instead he tried to craft another rescue plan.

"Damon," said Argon finally. "You know it won't work."

He glared at his friends who stood by with stoic expressions as Argon continued.

"If you wish to blame us for this setback, that's your choice, My Prince. They have you where they want you now, on the verge of a foolish attempt. If they can kill you in battle, this war could quickly be lost."

"Argon, sometimes I could knock you senseless. Now I'm speaking Layla's words. Do you feel we should abandon them to the Argore? Did you not hear what Beth told you about this shaman and what he was going to do to her? Do you think he'll be thwarted now that they have her again?"

"They are too many, Damon. We could muster every soldier here in the forest and those in the city and attack with no guarantee we could prevail. I'm sure that's exactly what they want us to do. They'll never win the war under current battlefield conditions. It would change things in their favor and put an end to us."

Damon turned his face rather than look at the faces of his friends, all in agreement with Argon.

"Beth," he muttered softly.

* * * *

They rode down any opposition in their way and raced back to their Argore camp at the full gallop.

Beth and Layla were shocked they could have been taken again. Neither of them had any hopes. There would be no miracle rescue this time. Beth could only think of an inevitable trip to the shaman's torture rack.

The commander rode through camp in triumph to the shouts of the Argore masses, like he'd just conquered the world. When he got to his tent he purposefully ignored the shaman who wasn't far away eyeing Beth avidly as she was dragged past him.

The shaman came down to visit them, but so did the high chief.

With their weapons gone, guards nearby, and their hands tied the captive women were on their knees and vulnerable. The commander knew the effect of humbling the women before the public. It added to his aura with the masses accomplishing the seemingly impossible after so many defeats against the allies.

"Well, well," said the shaman deviously stepping before Beth. "Here you are in our control again, woman. Did you think you could escape us and see me no more? We're fated to be here, both of us. It's our destiny and your fate is tied to the Argore. Your prince is a fool and he'll make the mistake of a second attempt for you. It will lead to ending this war. I saw it happen before we ever left our mountains. You have only a few choices. You can bear the children of the commander, or you can return to me for a different fate."

Beth shuddered and averted her eyes. The look in his eyes was too frightening to see. His stench was no less offensive.

"This other woman, I think I can take her now. She has no value for the Argore. She'll pay the price for your crimes, Beth."

"No," Beth shouted. "Please don't hurt Layla. If you allow her to stay here, unharmed, I'll…"

They waited.

"What will you do?" asked the shaman with a sneer.

"I'll consider your wishes, Commander."

"Beth," he started, but then turned to the shaman. "I think there is no need for you to disfigure either of these women."

"That remains to be seen," the shaman replied, like he'd won a contest. "My vision has proven true again. Woman, the fruit of your womb will start a line that will rule the Argore in splendor for a thousand years. All of the peoples of this world will kneel down before you, but as an obedient wife. Your legend will live forever. I've foreseen this in my vision and it will come to pass. It's your unavoidable destiny."

He grabbed her to pull her up and it wasn't in a proper way. The commander glowered, but he couldn't interfere. The high chief stared directly at him to see if he would act foolishly about this infidel woman who owned him. The shaman grasped Beth shamefully, sneered, and then looked at the commander also, daring him to say anything.

She stood in shock. The moment was surreal, like she needed to awaken from a dream, or a nightmare. She stared at the self-satisfied shaman, pleased at groping her to shame her before the public.

"You thought this day could never come, yet here you are. See what I can do to you. Think on that the next time you try to scorn the Argore. We've beaten you and you have no hope."

Reflexively her hand went to where her sword would have been. The shaman noticed and cackled like a loon, galling her with further public indignity.

"You no longer have your teeth, little she-cat."

The assembled throng cheered loudly trying to incite worse actions.

Layla leaned against her. It was a comfort in the midst of the emotional maelstrom.

"This isn't over, Beth," she whispered. She fearlessly glared at the shaman. It caused the shaman to cease.

"Come," said the commander quickly, stepping in to retrieve the women.

His personal guards surrounded them and escorted the women away. He took them inside his tent and closed the entrance, to the disappointed cries of the people. Their rabid lusts for further publicly shaming the captive women remained unfulfilled. He stepped in front of them once in the safety of his tent.

"I'm sorry it came to this, Beth. I know it isn't the outcome you wanted."

"Then why did you do it? Why couldn't you leave me alone? It's all I've ever asked. If you think I'll cooperate with spawning your brood, you're greatly mistaken."

"I can't speak for the shaman," he replied. "Those were his words, not mine."

"I'm going to say something so I hope you're listening. I developed some respect for you when I was here before. I think you know that, but I tell you the truth when I speak. I'm never going to be your wife. If you choose to take me by force, I will kill you, no matter how long it takes me. You Argore need to do something about that raving lunatic. How many of you have died? Wiping out the other cities, what good did that do? It created enemies for life."

"I told you Beth, things may change. I don't lie either. When I said I love you, there is nothing truer than that. I've endured so much that you don't know. I don't say you're responsible because it was my choice, but don't dismiss what I say as meaningless or irrelevant. Your life is still very much in question. That 'lunatic' as you call him, has a considerable following. He's not simply dismissed. His priests are avid beyond your imagining. They do terrible things at his behest because they think they're blessed and have no guilt if they follow the way. If he told them to cut you into pieces, they wouldn't bat an eye. Do you understand? They care nothing for your beauty and your spirit. It would make them all the more avid to do the worst."

"I understand that, Commander." Beth answered softly, her face showed her worry at the image.

"I've come to realize your prince and I are traveling the same tormented path. Perhaps it's a path of doom for both of us, but neither of us is willing to abandon our hopes for you."

"That's your problem, Commander. I've warned you."

"Here, it's your problem too, Beth. Without me there's no one else between you and the shaman. You'll scheme together and try to escape, I know that, but if you do something that puts you in the hands of the shaman and his followers, it would be a horrible ending and it would not be quick. Courage in battle isn't the same as helplessness tied to the rack."

"What about his vision of my mothering your royal line?"

"I think his visions can vary to meet current situations and his changing moods. He can claim things have changed and you've become a dire threat. His wishes to see your belly swell with an Argore baby are equally matched by his lust to torture you to see you suffer and bleed. He's a dark and evil man. If he gets you on his rack again…well we can't let it happen."

"On that, we can agree, Commander. Will you safe guard Layla? Without that, I won't cooperate with anything in spite of the shaman."

"I will."

Beth looked at Layla.

"Must we still be bound?" asked Layla.

The commander walked behind them to cut their bindings. His guards circled the women, twice as many as she faced before. She looked at him.

"There are two of you now. I need twice the protection."

The women sat down on the bed.

"I'll have our food brought here, ladies."

They turned away from him dismissively. He grimaced before leaving the tent, gripped with frustration, again. This time the situation was far more dangerous and uncertain.

"If we don't do something quickly, I'm afraid our chances will slip away, Layla."

"What did you have in mind? We can't get past these guards to our weapons."

"I know, I think we may need to take a risk."

"Uh-oh, that doesn't sound good. I've got to tell you I'm afraid of that shaman. What he almost did to you tells me he has none of the restraint of a sane person. I remember a sick man in a nearby village when I was back at home. What he did was shocking, unbelievable really. His victims were just in the wrong place at the wrong time. He was so lost in his insanity there was nothing we could do so we had to put him down. I think this shaman is like him, but he has power here so he pays no price for indulging his horrible lusts. The commander doesn't approve but it doesn't matter. The shaman can work his will regardless. If his acolytes are like him, they frighten me to death. I can fight in battles, but helpless strapped to a torture rack I'd be a quivering wreck."

"No one is brave at a time like that, Layla. It was the worst experience I've ever had. He was moments away from cutting me. I have no doubts about that. He would have reveled in disfiguring me and causing such pain. I've never met such a person before who could do such vile things to a fellow human being, woman or otherwise."

"My point, Beth, is I'm not the best partner for you with hazardous plans. I can't put the consequences of failing out of my mind. I don't want to die for an entire week in excruciating pain while they cut me up while I'm still alive. I'm sorry."

"I don't want that either, Layla. We'll think about it. In the end, if we find no escape, I'll marry him to spare you."

"Beth, I don't want that for you. Can we trust them to honor their word? I wonder about that."

"We'll cross that bridge if we're forced to, Layla."

* * * *

Prince Damon stewed and paced about angry at his predicament. The last thing he'd said to Beth he couldn't take back and now she was gone again and in terrible danger.

"I know what you're thinking, Damon," said Argon. "It would be suicide this time. They'll kill anybody approaching their lines."

"Perhaps it's time to break this stalemate, once and for all. We've hidden here in our lair and feared to face them in open ground. What are we waiting for? Nothing is going to change on this battlefield, Argon. Are you so certain they'd win that fight? We've fought them evenly for three months. Granted we were dug in here in superior position, but out there when they attacked the walls of Kragan, they didn't drive us away. They died just like any other soldiers. We cut them down in their own camp."

"You're leader here, Damon. If that's your decision, of course we'll follow you. I've told you I'm a cautious person. It's much of the reason I'm still alive. I never said I have all the answers. I suffer just like you do about Beth and Layla."

Argon looked at determination in Damon's eyes. It was obvious he was intent to take action.

"We should send word to your father about what you plan to do, Damon."

He grimaced, but nodded in agreement.

"Gideon, prepare the army for battle."

"Yes, My Prince."

"Send word along the whole forest. Everyone joins this attack."

He then looked at Argon expecting a rebuff. Argon just looked back at him.

"I know this is dangerous, but the time for decisive action has come, Argon. If I die, so be it. If we fail there would be nothing more we could do for them at that point anyway. The commander would have won. The world they would create would be hell and I couldn't live in it."

Argon put aside his great reservations, turned away and went to help with the preparations.

A messenger was dispatched and galloped toward Kragan at full speed to apprise the king of what they were going to do.

Damon was firm in his choice and didn't wait for a reply from his father. He joined Argon in readying his men for the attack.

He stood to address them grim faced.

"We've fought in this rut long enough. I'm not of a mind to live my life in perpetual war, so we're going to end this war here and now. I know the danger of going out of the forest to face them, but I see no other way. Sooner or later it was going to come down to this. They're deadly and dangerous, but so are we. You've fought them enough to know they're not our superiors. They won in those other battles because they greatly outmanned their opponents and the cities weren't prepared properly. Today you fight so your families can live free. You know what would happen to them in Argore hands. You must prevail, we must prevail. There is no other option."

The massed men roared their defiance at the Argore invaders which ran chills down Damon's spine. He raised a fist and added his yell to the massage sound. After a time he turned to Argon.

"We're going to leave in an hour. They'll expect attacks to come at sun-up. We're not going to wait."

His troops gathered quickly, heading for their assigned positions for the attack.

Damon then went to the edge of the forest to survey the Argore camp. They were deployed to reinforce their usual sentry line, but not in battlefield formations.

"When we strike, it must be with such fury as to daunt our enemy. They believe only they can terrify on the battlefield. They're wrong about that. I want the drums and trumpets to signal our charge. We need to make the noise of ten armies, Argon."

"I'm not much of a trumpeter," Argon replied with a smile.

Damon chuckled. "Argon, I know you think this is a big mistake."

"Actually, Damon, I'm with you on this one. I agree we needed to make this attempt. We had to take the fight to them. This is as good a time as any."

"Good, my friend. If this is our day to die, I want to say I'm honored to have known you and to have fought at your side. You've made me into a better man."

"You've done more for me, Damon, than I ever did for you. I was lost and wandering about through my life without purpose. At least I have a chance here to do something meaningful and something noble."

"Let's go save Beth and Layla."

The army formed up just inside the tree line. When they rode out of the concealment they saw the city gates open as the entire royal army came to join the attack.

Enemy sentries spotted the vast deployments and raced away to spread the warning.

The commander had just finished eating with the women in the tent when they heard the commotion.

"I'm surprised, ladies. Your prince is impulsive. I'm truly sorry, but I'm afraid it will cost him dearly. He may not see another day. I would regret that as he's a decent man. Such things happen in battles."

They stared at him murderously.

"It isn't by my choice. I'm commander of the Argore horde. I must do my duty."

He saw them glance at their weapons.

"I keep telling you, that won't happen. They won't allow it."

He nodded to his burly guards.

"They're among the finest warriors I have. Don't be foolish, Beth. They're here to guard you, but they're also deterrents to the followers of the shaman."

Chapter Fifteen

Damon was surprisingly calm on the eve of what could be the deciding battle of the war. The thought he could die that day usually frightened him enough to be careful, it was missing on this day. Instead, all of his experiences with Beth replayed in his mind, painful as they were to remember, causing fatalistic feelings and some suicidal impulses. He kept back from the others until the last possible moment honing his anger like an additional weapon, righteous indignation.

They heard the alarms go up in the Argore camp and saw them hurrying to take up positions as the combined allied armies approached in battle formations from the city and the forest like an unstoppable tidal wave.

The Kragans rode boldly toward Damon, the standard of the king flapping in the breeze before them. Their bright armor gleamed reflecting the rays of the sun in the early morning.

Damon looked in the other direction and saw troops emerging from the forest for as far as he could see. There were more men in the allied army now than he realized. They were no longer greatly outnumbered by their enemy, if they were even outnumbered at all with the displaced populations of the city states gathered in the same place.

"They have erected no barriers behind which to make their defense," Gideon noted clinically.

"They're always on the offensive. This is new to them having to defend. Hopefully it will give us the edge we need," Argon replied.

Damon rose up in his saddle, roared his order with his sword held high in his hand and was answered by the screams of his massive army. They charged to the blast of trumpets and drums and with banging their shields.

The Argore roared their defiance, but they stayed in place rather than charge. It was a strange reversal of roles for both sides. Damon's cavalry were at the front of the attack going against Argore foot soldiers forming the skirmish line.

Damon looked ahead in the camp to where their leaders were located. It was centered deep in the vast field of tents protected by wave after wave of Argore fighters in tight formations.

Equally evoked inside the commander's tent, Beth and Layla were frantic as they heard the deafening sounds. It stirred them to a feeling of frenzy.

"Damon's bringing an all-out attack," said Layla excitedly.

"We were fools to be taken, Layla, and put him in this position. We've got to do something."

The guards were as motivated as the women to watch the unfolding spectacle, but they were no less vigilant.

The initial sound of the two armies meeting was distinct as metal struck metal in countless individual battles. The women could only imagine what was happening, captive as they were in the tent and unable to see for themselves.

Personally heading the charge and disdaining the risk, Damon rode at the front of the charge leading the men and was one of the first to cross swords with the enemy. He fought like Beth, heedless of the danger, intent on his dubious goal of victory or death.

The Argore army's hastily assembled front skirmish line buckled under the attack of the mounted allied army. Both sides showered their opponents with wave after wave of arrows from the rows of archers in forward positions. Already the ground was littered with dead and dying in the intense battle.

Trying to react to fast developing events, the Argore commander surveyed the scene and sent reinforcements to block the numerous incursions into the defensive line. The high chief came down to stand with him.

"This is a serious fight, Commander. I believe the entire war hinges on this outcome."

"Yes, High Chief. Their numbers have swelled because the stragglers were allowed to join them in the woods. We no longer have the advantage of greater numbers."

"Commander, if this battle doesn't go well, and if I fall, you must take charge to lead the people away to safety before all is lost. The shaman will try to seize control and he will sacrifice us to the last man. Do what you must even if you must kill him to save the people."

"I understand, high chief."

"I know you want this heathen woman, but don't let it destroy the people. You can't be vulnerable because of her any longer."

"I won't, I'll do what must be done."

"It may be she must die for us to prevail. Can you do that? Watching her killed in front of them will tear the heart out of our enemies."

He looked directly at the high chief.

"I'm Argore. Nothing is above that."

"I knew I could trust you, Commander. Now let's go answer this enemy challenge. We'll show them what it means to war against the holy Argore horde."

The battle raged as the aggrieved allies looked to exact revenge for their personal losses but also to save their families. The Argore fury wasn't diminished. It was just that their opponents rose up to that level with matching hatred.

For a considerable time the lines swayed back and forth, neither side could claim an advantage, but as time went on the open Argore positions started to crumble and allied troops broke behind their lines with more frequency.

The Argore commander had too many holes to fill too quickly to completely stem the tide and reach a stalemate.

At one point he saw Damon driving toward him, determined and unstoppable.

"I would do the same for her, my friend," he muttered. His best men were already engaged elsewhere so it became apparent this particular thrust wouldn't be stopped. The entire battle pivoted on this flash point and Damon was winning the fight leading his men by fearless example.

The commander recognized Amal and Berne flanking Damon. These were Beth's dear ones, those whom she cared about. They were immersed in the close quarter fighting leaving the commander unable to have archers pick them off.

Suddenly Damon looked up and saw the commander staring at him. The commander gave him a salute and turned away.

Damon spurred his horse forward trampling Argore foot soldiers in the process. Where the commander was, there the women would be.

The commander hurried back to his tent to find the flap open and his men killed. There was only one explanation. He looked around and saw the shaman mounted and riding away with his followers. Beth and Layla were tied and helpless, captive in their control mounted on horses being led by acolytes.

He thought about the words of the high chief about his duties. Here was the acid test. Could he allow Beth to die hideously at the hands of the shaman along with Layla?

Behind him the fight was breaking down as the allies gained control in the battle and pressed their advantage. The Argore warriors were struggling without firm leadership.

It was a supreme trauma turning away from her. He ran back toward the war only to find men carrying the high chief toward him, mortally wounded by an arrow to the chest.

"Take us out of here," he rasped before he expired.

The commander didn't hesitate and ordered the retreat but it was a precarious situation. All of his fighters were being pressed by deadly allied attacks.

"Sound the great horn," he ordered.

The blast echoed across the battlefield. For a moment everything stopped. The Argore had never retreated before so they paused before realizing the fight was over. When the first Argore ran away it started a flood.

Damon's army roared in triumph and looked to him. Oblivious, Damon was racing up the hill personally getting to the commander at his tent before he could flee.

Damon jumped off his horse and ran into the tent. He re-emerged with a feral look.

"Where are they?"

"The shaman, his followers killed my guards and took the women away. They're escaping as we stand here."

"How could you?" Damon hissed, preparing to strike at the commander. To his surprise the commander made no attempt to defend himself.

"They're fleeing and the women are in mortal peril, Prince. Will you join me to chase them down before it's too late? You know what awaits them in the shaman's hands."

Argon, and Damon's other friends arrived. Simultaneously, some of the commander's elite fighters arrived and moved into position to protect him. The two opposing forces eyed each other prepared to resume the fighting.

"We're going after the women," said Damon. "The shaman has them. We have no time to lose."

"With them?" Gideon questioned in astonishment, like Damon had lost his mind.

"Yes, they'll help us track down the shaman. They know what he'll do and where he'll go. This battle is over so shedding more Argore blood serves no good purpose."

Both sides stared at the commander and Damon in disbelief as they shook hands to agree to combine forces for the pursuit, the last development anybody could have expected to happen on the battlefield where so much blood had been spilled.

Incredibly, a mixed force of Damon's personal guards and the commander's elite warriors rode away together chasing after evil, the battle seemingly forgotten for the moment as the Argore masses fled away from the battle site routed and looking only to survive.

The commander rode beside Damon as they raced through countless fleeing Argore warriors but their quarry wasn't in sight.

"Where will he go?" Damon shouted.

"He'll ride toward our mountains but when it gets dark, he'll find a place, perhaps an abandoned farm house. He won't wait to…well, do his will."

"Then we find him now."

It worried Damon as they continued to ride, the fleeing Argore troops around them became sparser and still there was no sign of the shaman. The sun was already low on the horizon.

"Commander," he shouted.

"I'm worried also," he replied.

"How much longer can you track them? Are you sure it's them we're following?"

"To answer your question, perhaps for an hour longer can we follow the trail, at the most, Prince. I worry we've already passed them, though I do still see the tracks. You must trust me that it's them we follow."

"We're all she has, Layla too," Damon replied frantically.

An hour later, they slowed and looked all around. There were no farm houses visible and there was no sign of the enemy.

"We've got to do something. We can't leave them to him."

The commander was equally distressed. He looked at Damon who was staring at him for answers.

"Is the shaman the reason all of you came after us?" asked the Prince.

"Yes, it was his vision."

"You didn't know he was insane? All of these needless deaths on both sides you could have prevented."

"You don't understand our society, but this isn't the time for a philosophic discussion. If we spread out and send a signal if we find them it's the only option we have left."

Argon rode over. "It's difficult for us to trust you, Commander. If you found the women without us, you could simply ride away with her and we'd be none the wiser."

"That can be said both ways. We have no time to debate. They could be in mortal peril at this very moment. There's no more time."

"We'll intersperse our forces so we're never apart. I'll ride with you, Commander."

The search began as they covered ground as quickly as possible under the darkening sky. It wasn't quick for fear of the horses breaking a leg stumbling into a hole in the dark.

They rode along trying to see ahead but it was increasingly difficult.

It wasn't a building or other object that tipped them off. One of the teams of Argore and allies searchers heard the cry of a woman and fired up a burning arrow into the sky as a signal.

The rescue forces quickly converged toward the signal and closed in on the sound of women weeping.

Behind a small hillock Beth and Layla were bared and staked out spread eagle. They were surrounded by twenty of the shaman's acolytes. The shaman was sitting on Layla's belly holding his knife against her delicate flesh whispering to her. She was blubbering in terror.

"Oh no, pleased don't hurt me," she repeated over and over.

Several of the acolytes knelt around Beth taunting and groping her and sliding sharp blades over her skin to heighten her terror. Damon heard one of them speak to Beth.

"When the shaman finishes off your friend, it will be your turn, heathen unbeliever. You'll know true pain at last. You've avoided your punishment too long. We will rejoice in your screams of agony at the spilling of your blood and rending your delicate flesh."

Those Acolytes were dropped in death quickly between the sudden barrage of arrows and then the flying swords of the rescuers racing in out of the dark.

It took the shaman time to realize he was in peril he was so lost in his hunger to savage the women. Taking extra time to try to heighten Layla's terror before he harmed her, it cost him by giving Damon and the Argore commander just enough time to act to save her.

Damon grabbed the back of his hair and yanked him bodily off of Layla tossing him onto the ground. Damon raised his sword for a fatal strike.

The shaman surprised him by rolling away and coming to his feet in an attack pose. He struck at Damon immediately and he was a dangerous fighter.

"Damon, beware those animal talons he wears. They're tipped with fast acting poison," the commander shouted.

Damon backed away as the shaman took a swipe that barely missed landing a deadly wound.

The commander knelt down to release Beth. She was shaking with fear. He would leave it to Damon to deal with the shaman. The object of his concern lay before him in a fetal position.

"I wasn't going to let him hurt you, Beth," he whispered.

She blinked her eyes, turned her head and focused, like she was coming out of a mental fog. She got a curious expression on her face. "What are you doing riding with the prince?"

"It's a long story. All that matters is you're safe now."

The shaman shrieked and threw dirt in Damon's eyes. He fled into the darkness and escaped along with some of his people, those who hadn't been killed.

Allies and Argore alike looked at Damon if they should pursue the fleeing shaman.

"It's too dark," he muttered. "We'll worry about him another day."

Damon walked over to Layla. She was badly shaken sitting up folding her arms defensively over her chest.

"Is Beth hurt?" she asked.

"She's fine, Layla. Are you hurt?"

"I don't think so. He nicked me with his knife when you pulled him off, but it's not a deep cut. I'm so glad to see you, Damon. I thought it was over for me. I've never been so terrified in my life."

He embraced her and she hugged him tightly. It was a weird moment for him. Holding a nude woman couldn't help but evoke a response.

Damon turned his head and looked over. Naked Beth was surrounded by all of his friends. In the arms of the Argore commander she wasn't resisting his embrace. It was a difficult emotional dilemma. Then he realized the unclothed women needed to get dressed.

"Find their clothes, quickly."

Layla looked into his eyes with gratefulness, but also with love. Damon blinked. Wisely he didn't say anything. Trying he restate he loved Beth wasn't what Layla needed to hear after her terrible experience.

The women promptly donned their garments while the troops respectfully averted their eyes.

Re-clad and rearmed, Beth walked over to Damon accompanied by the commander. Damon steeled his emotions, unsure what to expect. Again, wisely, he didn't speak.

"I don't know what happened, how you two are working together, but I thank you both for saving us. I thought this time he would do his will, hurt us, and then end our lives."

"We feared losing you in the dark, Beth. We can't leave now to go home so late in the night and there's plenty of retreating Argore soldiers coming this way. Will you continue to safeguard us, Commander? You have the advantage here with plenty of Argore warriors moving about around us you could call upon."

"I will protect you, Prince Damon. The war is over. The high chief was slain in the battle so it falls on me to collect our people. We'll return to our mountains. Beth, you're welcome to come with me."

Damon felt a surge of nausea as she looked at the Argore commander and smiled.

"Thank you, Commander. You know my answer, but understand I really appreciate your offer. I've come to know you as a good man, a fellow soldier doing his duty. I would have never thought that possible about an Argore male."

Beth's answer surprised Damon as he always anticipated the worst. He spoke quickly.

"Commander, I hope there will be peace between our peoples. We have so much damage and so many dead. We'll have our hands full for years trying to recover and rebuild. You could attack us again in our weakened state."

"No, Prince, we have vast casualties too. There will be too many empty homes and grieving widows in our mountains. I'll spend my time there. Beth, will you allow me to keep in contact? I doubt I'll ever lose my wish to make you my wife."

She chuckled. "You're a hard headed man, Commander. I am still curious about your name."

"Marry me and I'll tell you."

She smiled warmly but shaking her head no, but she did hug him and kiss his cheek. Damon stood by awkwardly.

Beth went over to join Layla and the women sat down together completely surrounded by troops of both sides. They began a close and intense conversation about the near miss with the evil shaman.

In the darkness a little later they heard an eerie sound.

"The shaman has put a curse on us. He informs us we're his enemies for life. He will never rest until he's cut out our living beating hearts from our bodies to eat before our eyes as we die. Don't scoff at the danger, Prince. He's a dangerous man and he might surprise you what he can do. Look at what he's done already nearly wiping out your society." The commander had a very solemn look.

The guards kept the fire low but burning nonetheless. Damon lay as close to Beth to sleep as he'd been since their days in training under Argon in the forest. She lay next to Layla. He heard them whispering before they went to sleep.

In the morning, Damon looked at the commander.

"We're returning to Kragan."

"I'll travel across the frontier gathering my people."

"Are you in danger from the shaman? How many followers does he have?"

"There could very well be soldiers who will still turn to him. I have adequate defense here but when I go home there will be hazards there. He's resourceful and he's driven. Until the people accept me as new high chief, he can do great harm."

"Be careful, Commander," said Beth. She hugged him one more time. "Thank you again for all you did for me. I'm sorry I couldn't give you what you want."

"That matter is still open from my point of view, Beth."

She chuckled. "Have a safe journey home, and don't bring your army back here ever again."

He smiled and the Argore forces rode away. Beth stared at the departing

Argore commander, now a significant person in her life.

Damon looked at Beth and her pensive expression. It was a moment before she looked back. Damon assumed she was moved by the commander's marriage offer. He pondered what to say. He began a tentative tendril to try to clarify her state of mind.

"Do you still hold my stupid words against me? I was jealous and I'm sorry. My senseless actions prove the wisdom of your decision to reject me. I admit it. I hope we can still be friends."

She got a strange smile on her face and shook her head. Damon wasn't sure what it meant. It was easy to see it as scorn for him, his usual assumption.

"I forgive you. I knew why you said those things, Prince, but you need to listen to what I say. I'm not looking for a mate. You and the commander compliment me with your persistence, but it's best if you truly treat me as just your friend. That's where I am in my life at the moment."

"I guess I'll echo what the commander said. I hope you'll change your mind, Beth. I'd like for you to be my wife, but I'm no longer going to beat a dead horse. You're free of me if that pleases you. I suspect you've wanted to hear that from me all along."

She got an enigmatic smile, shook her head, and returned to join Layla for the ride back to the king's city.

They rode steadily on the long ride back toward Kragan. When they went through the remnants of the Argore camp there were many people collecting the dead bodies for disposal to be burned 'en masse' in funeral pyres. The field was littered with bodies and the detritus of discarded Argore camp refuse. The allied army milled about waiting for Damon's return, and his instructions. The vast number of survivors from the other cities had no leaders to turn to. They gravitated to Damon also.

The king rode out of the city along with Prince Tabor to meet Damon when he appeared from the frontier leading Beth and Layla back into safe hands.

"Incredible, my son, I feared we couldn't win this war and were doomed. What you've accomplished boggles the mind. I have no adequate words to express how I feel, or how all Kragans feel. I'm very proud of you, Damon."

Damon looked at the consternation on his brother's face as he listened to his father's compliment.

"Tabor, I still don't want the throne of Kragan. Nothing has changed for me. That's all yours. Please hear what I'm saying because it will never change. I will never be a political rival or a threat to you."

Tabor looked at him sadly.

"Damon, you've always been the better man. I salute your indomitable spirit and your genuine forbearance. It pains me what a selfish person I've been all of my life. You're a shining example of decency for me to try to emulate for the rest of my life. You've brilliantly proven who the better leader between us is."

Damon glanced at Beth before continuing.

"You should pick and choose what you mimic of my attributes, Brother. My skill at driving women away is undiminished. I repeat, I don't want the throne of Kragan, it's all yours."

Tabor peered at Damon pensively.

Beth got annoyed at Damon's statement and rode away talking with Layla and paying no further attention to the princely brothers.

"Damon, I wouldn't take it so personally. Beth disdains every man from what I've seen. I understand her lure. Being around her evokes you. Perhaps it's time to look at the army of other women who wouldn't act so badly toward you. It seems neither of us was destined to tame Beth. If there is a living man somewhere you can do that daunting task, my hat is off to him."

Damon shrugged. "Feelings are what they are, Brother. Possibly I'm too much a glutton for punishment. I doubt I'm capable of changing my feelings about Beth. Apparently her abuse is too comfortable for me to eliminate from my life. I would know no other way to live if I'm not in emotional distress."

The men chuckled. They turned as the king rejoined them.

"Damon, I'm sending your brother through the forest to bring back our women. I'm sure I'm in for a blistering tirade from your mother. She wasn't happy when I forced her to leave."

"In her case, Father, you know you're loved. I've come to understand how priceless that is and I'm jealous."

Tabor nodded and rode off at the head of a great column of royal Kragan soldiers. The king eyed Damon sympathetically seeing the consternation on Damon's face as he looked at Beth from afar.

"Put aside your thoughts about Beth, Son. We have far too much work to do to heal the land and the peoples. More than just Kragan has suffered from the war. There are too many desperate people in misery in need of a champion."

"Yes, sir, you're right, but one more thing, Father. The shaman escaped so he's still out there and he will always be a serious danger. He has a following amongst the Argore and it's not impossible he could bring back another invasion in the future."

"We'll watch for him and his followers, Damon. What he does isn't in our control."

* * * *

Damon returned back to the assembled masses that waited patiently for him to speak. With Argon, Gideon, Amal, and Berne, they walked about talking to them in smaller groups. It would have been impossible with so many people to try to talk to them all at one time.

"What should we do, Prince Damon?" It was their resounding question for him.

"I would say we travel back to your homes to see what can be salvaged. It may be that cities can be rebuilt and farms reclaimed."

"There have been so many losses, Prince. All of our royalty from our cities was wiped out. We have no leaders."

"I'll offer what guidance I can in the interim. I'm not the best choice for the job, but I realize it's a critical void and an imperative to start the rebuilding work right away."

He had the same conversation numerous times. Universally, there was no resistance to following him. In reality, he was the only man they would follow.

"Argon, will you help me? I can't do this alone. You'd be the better choice to lead these lost souls. If you have plans with Beth, I'll understand."

"Damon, don't speak foolishly. My days as your mentor are long past. That's true with all my other apprentices. Beth and Layla aren't under my direction. Whatever they plan is of their own choosing."

"Layla has told me she desires to remain in your corps, Damon," Gideon advised. "She didn't say what Beth plans to do. With the Argore threat gone for the moment, I think Beth's a little confused about what to do next. It was her only goal to seek revenge in killing them. I suspect she didn't have a backup plan for after the war."

"My idea is to accumulate supplies to travel back with the refugees to their homes. I think in the interim we'd need to create a continuous supply line of food to keep them alive until they can rebuild their lives and support themselves again. At the same time, I think we need to keep our eyes on the mountains. The commander didn't say he was the new high chief. If there is some process amongst the Argore where another could achieve power, the dynamics could change quickly and war could return. I think the shaman is a deadly threat even with our driving him away in defeat."

Damon stayed centered around his forest camp long enough to see the large procession of the women and children returning from the hamlets. He grinned when he saw his mother and rushed to hug her tightly.

"Damon, you're going to crush the air out of my lungs," she wheezed.

"I'm sorry, Mother, but it's so good to see you."

"You know I was very angry about being forced to leave and I said some harsh things, son."

"Mother, I don't care."

"I admit, you were right, though I won't hold off on my retribution against your father."

"He expects it, Mother. He's missed you desperately, like all of us."

"Did he say it?"

"Yes, ma'am, but you already know that."

She smiled smugly. "This is good to hear, son. It will give me better leverage to twist the knife with the king, so to speak."

They both laughed.

Tabor rode up and dismounted.

"Here she is, Damon, safe and sound, thanks to your planning and good sense creating a safe haven for our vulnerable loved ones."

"What are you going to do next, Son?"

"Argon and the others have agreed to go with me to take the refugees home. We'll do what we can to help rebuild out there across the land."

"That's a vast undertaking, Damon. I can think of no man better able to do it than you."

"Thank you, Mother, but I'd put your hopes in Argon. He's experienced and resourceful. I'm just brash."

"No, Damon, you've got a good heart. I knew it right away when you fed the poor even as a young boy. I'm not ignoring Argon because it's true he's a remarkable man."

They saw Layla approaching along with Beth.

"Your Majesty, it's so good to see you," Layla said with a warm smile.

"Greetings, Your Majesty," Beth added.

The queen smiled in return. "I can't wait to sleep in my own bed again, ladies. We made do in the field, but I wouldn't mind a few indulgences for a change. Will you come with me into the city? Do your duties here allow it?"

"Sure," Damon replied before they could answer the queen. "It will be some time before we can amass enough food for the trip. They're free anyway to choose whatever they want to do from this point forward. Their war duties are over. I release them into your custody, Mother."

"I'll continue to follow you and do my duty, Prince Damon," Layla replied with a look of consternation. "Was there ever a question about that in your mind?"

"I guess not."

Damon glanced at Beth but didn't wait for her to explain her plans.

"I have pressing matters to see about. Good day to you, ladies. Enjoy your visit to the palace."

Argon came up to them and smiled warmly at the queen. He bowed.

"Your Majesty, it's good to see you returned in safety to your home and family."

"Master Argon. Thank you, it's good to be back."

"I trust your time away from the palace wasn't too distressing for your royal personage."

"I'm not fragile, Argon." She laughed and again, Damon saw reactions in her he saw with no other person she met, almost like adolescent infatuation behavior.

"Of course you're not, Your Majesty."

The queen blushed when Argon winked at her.

"I must be going, the king is waiting. I think it's time at last for our frank discussion about his forcing the women out of the city."

"I don't envy him," Argon retorted with a smirk. "I'm glad to have seen you again, Your Majesty."

"Likewise, Master Argon. Good fortune to you."

"Beth, and Layla, I hope to see you in Kragan at the palace shortly," the queen added.

"Yes, Your Majesty, as our duties allow. We'll be there."

Beth glanced at Damon who turned away, got on his horse and rode off.

The queen's party departed at the same time, branching off on the road toward the city. Damon watched them go and saw Tabor guiding them with a full royal detachment with the king's standard flapping prominently at the head of the column. Tabor rode beside his mother as they talked continuously.

Damon headed toward the front of the amassing refugees. They'd started to differentiate by the cities they came from. It was a vast assemblage and the daunting task hit Damon as he surveyed the tumultuous scene. There were so many widowed families struggling without their men.

"Are you ready for this?" asked Amal.

"Who would have thought we could be at the head of anything with how lame we were as youths," Berne added.

"We're still lame, but they can't seem to recognize it," Damon retorted. The childhood friends smiled at his attempt at levity, but the daunting task took away their mirth.

Riding away toward the frontier gave Damon a feeling of usefulness, and the side benefit of leaving the issue of Beth behind remedied his feelings of stress in the short term. Concentrating his thoughts on the myriad of problems of the refugees left him no time to brood over his lost love object and his bruised ego. He glanced one last time at Kragan before turning to lead the peoples away. Emotionally he intended to close the door on the past.

Argon was riding separately as they'd decided to initially go to two separate sites to begin their rebuilding. Splitting the survivors allowed camps to be smaller, although they weren't small there were so many displaced people.

When they stopped for a meal a delegation of survivors from multiple cities came to talk to Damon.

"Prince Damon, we'd like to discuss an idea with you."

"What is it, my friends?"

"We've talked about how things were before and what it led to. The former cities were small minded in their petty rivalries. As you know, few of us prospered because of it. The nobles sought to line their pockets and leave their citizens to suffer privation while they sat in opulence squandering the city treasure. None of us wish to repeat that mistake. What we propose is a different political hierarchy."

They eyed him intently as he waited in silence for their proposal. They waited for him to respond. It took a moment for him to realize they were waiting for a reply.

"I'm not sure what you're saying, my friends. Don't assume I have the mind of a great scholar. You need to explain things clearly for me to grasp your ideas."

"We think it best as we saw the life in Kragan, and we watched you conduct the war that…"

They paused again.

"Say whatever is on your mind because I'm in the dark about your meaning."

"We think it best to have a single realm…with a single leadership. We should be an empire with one army to protect all, and one emperor."

Damon waited for them to say more. He realized they were waiting again for his reply and it started to sink in what they were asking of him.

"Me? You want me to be your emperor?" he asked in true astonishment. The concept struck him as ludicrous.

"Who else would all of the people follow? There is no one else."

"Why not, Damon?" asked Berne interjecting his question.

"I, eh…"

"He accepts," said Amal.

"Good," said the envoys, smiling and pressing forward to shake his hand.

"I think this is a big mistake," Damon replied, but he was ignored.

"We will build a great imperial city to be your home, Prince Damon. Kragan has shown us the way."

"What are you doing to me," Damon groused after they left. Gideon arrived and joined with Amal and Berne chuckling happily.

"You never want to take the bull by the horns, Damon," Berne accused him.

"We just did what needed to be done," Amal added. "When you think about it, they're right. You can build a great nation and you'll govern fairly, like your father."

"I never wanted power in Kragan, and I certainly don't want it here, especially on this scale."

"Sorry, Damon, you can't say no. The decision is already made."

"Don't think I won't find a way to pay you back for this. You're supposed to be my friends. What have you gotten me into? I think I'll appoint each one of you to the worst positions I can find in your new empire. You guys are fools dragging me into this. It's going to be a disaster."

His friends laughed and produced alcohol to celebrate the moment, ignoring his mood.

They traveled for a week before they arrived at the site the refugees picked to start building the newly proposed imperial city. It was in a perfect location. As much as Damon wanted to complain, there was nothing to find fault with. The nearby former city had been reduced to rubble burned to the ground.

Rather than disperse to go back to their former cities and farms, the vast bulk of the people stayed there and began working. It shocked Damon at how quickly they made progress and how many people were there working on the project. Among the survivors were numerous master builders from other cities who took charge of the construction, the design and layout of the city, and organized work teams. There was no lack of manpower to accomplish the task.

The center of the city would house the palace and it would be on a scale never attempted before. It wasn't by Damon's wish. It was the desire of the grateful people to give a gift to Damon in return for his saving their lives.

Food and supplies flowed from Kragan and the forest to feed the masses, but at the same time people gradually repopulated farms and looked to resurrect the economy producing food crops.

It was a tenuous existence in the beginning but with each passing day their situation improved.

With so many people working constantly on building the city, they made rapid progress.

With a month of work they could see the layout of the city though not many buildings were finished yet. A few shops were occupied and open, though they still needed to gather supplies and wares. The streets and boulevards were busy avenues full of construction traffic and arriving supply caravans.

The master builders concentrated on the palace first. It dwarfed the Kragan royal palace in size and opulence promising to be a wonder for the land.

In addition, the people had started calling Damon, Emperor.

At first it made him want to laugh, but the realization of what a responsibility it would be sobered him quickly.

It was at that one month point that Layla rode in from Kragan to join them.

"I heard about your ascension to Emperor, Damon. Congratulations. Your father told me to pass on his pride at the honor. He certainly supports you and even is willing to swear allegiance to the new empire."

"What? He's my father, and my king. I can't be over him."

"You are over him, Damon. You're the emperor. You're no longer a prince. The whole land applauds this change. He said you'll do a remarkable job."

"This is getting very weird," Damon replied and shook his head.

He looked pointedly at Layla. She smiled at him in satisfaction. Though he didn't ask her, she explained further.

"She's staying in Kragan for a time helping the poor. She's never forgotten what you did for them. I think she wants to feel good inside, if that makes sense to you. The killing and hating in the war warped her and I think she feels it's an open wound inside she needs to heal before she can move on. Damon, it's a part of why she couldn't look at you, or any other man. Helping the victims is cleansing for her spirit. She can't simply dismiss her dark deeds from the war."

"You two were very close, Layla. I'm surprised you choose to be apart from her."

A troubled look crossed Layla's face. She paused a moment before she replied.

"Yes, Damon, we are close. After much soul searching, I couldn't follow her lead and live with her back there, although what she's doing to help others is very noble. We've talked a great deal and agree with many things. There are other matters in which we don't agree. Do you understand?"

"I'm not sure. I think I have an idea what you're alluding to, Layla."

"I think some of the discord you felt for Beth showered onto me. It was a great distress to me, Damon. I hope you remember the things I've told you before. My feelings haven't changed. Beth has issues she wants to sort out that aren't my issues. I've helped her but it was time I consider where I want to go and what I want to do. I'm not Beth."

Damon nodded thoughtfully.

"Am I welcome here, Emperor?" she asked with a smirk.

They both laughed. Damon shook his head in resignation. She embraced him warmly.

"I'm going to regret this emperor thing, I can tell."

"No one else will regret the emperor thing, Emperor." Layla laughed hilariously at her play on words. Damon didn't share her amusement.

"I told Amal and Berne I'd find the worst possible jobs for them. Perhaps I should add you to that list."

"I serve at your pleasure, my liege," she retorted playfully, snickering.

Chapter Sixteen

Gradually, people migrated back to their original homes as time passed by. The network of farms redeveloped rapidly, but rather than feed dispersed small cities with limited resources, a process grew where product flowed to the new imperial city which was being built at an incredible rate. Farmers could sell their harvests and prosper along with the businesses in the growing economy.

Once those foodstuffs were received and processed, newly affluent business owners sold supplies locally and also started to build secondary stores across the frontier. Some of the former cities, the ones least damaged, were being rebuilt too. The caravans transporting foodstuffs as well as clothing and other products for sale were a priority for the imperial commanders for protecting. It was the main mission in the field overseeing commerce lanes.

There was a great deal to do to restore the land to vitality, but with the Argore threat seemingly gone, brave people traveled out to conquer the challenge. Damon instituted wide ranging patrols of imperial soldiers to protect the people from those criminal types looking to take advantage of vulnerabilities. Those roving gangs, solely composed of miscreant people who didn't listen to reason from the authorities, nor had any thought about the good of the whole, posed a manageable threat to tranquility in the empire. They only looked for ill-gotten gains at the expense of the weak. With them, Damon ordered his forces to be ruthless.

The first main building to open in the imperial city was the palace. The new citizens of the city, a diverse mix from across the former city states, pressed Damon to name the new city. He was at a loss to select an adequate name with sufficient majesty.

"No, Damon, you can't name the city Beth," Berne joked.

"What do you think about the name, Dysteria?"

"It sounds like a disease," Amal observed with a sneer.

"Did you ask Layla? Maybe a woman's perspective would be a good idea," Berne added.

"I did ask her."

"Well?" asked Amal and Berne, simultaneously.

"She suggested calling it Glory, the City of Glory."

"I like it," both friends agreed.

"You didn't want to use a woman's choice, did you Damon," said Berne.

"I just didn't think it was appropriate. It had nothing to do with Layla being a woman."

Amal challenged him, "Layla is connected to Beth, and therefore she gets the punishment you intend for Beth."

"No, no, no," Damon objected. "Glory struck me as a little presumptuous, like we're too proud of ourselves. I don't like bragging."

"That's you, Damon. None of the rest of us has those issues. I vote for Glory."

"Me too."

"Well, I can see where the lame vote rests," Damon groused.

Argon, Layla, and Gideon came over to them at that moment.

"Layla, that's a great name for the city, Glory," Berne expressed smugly.

"Thank you, Berne." She looked at Damon. His glum look expressed his opinion in glowing terms.

Argon and Gideon simply looked at him, bemused.

"You too?" asked Damon.

"It's a nice statement about your city, Damon," Argon replied.

"Do I even have a choice?"

"I think naming the city that disease name you thought takes away your choice," Berne joked.

"Fine, you win, Glory it is. They say pride cometh before a fall. I'll be watching for all of you to fall."

Everyone laughed except Damon.

"Let it go, Damon," Layla chided finally.

* * * *

Moving into his new home at the palace was mind bending for Emperor Damon. The scale of the architecture dwarfed anything he'd ever seen, and the opulence frankly embarrassed him. Because they had so many of the craftsmen from all the other former cities concentrated in one place they created their masterpiece in a short time. It satisfied the demands of the public for a structure worthy of an emperor and as their reward for Damon for what he'd accomplished.

Damon's huge soft bed could have accommodated five people without any of them touching. Damon complained about it and virtually everything else, as well. People learned to ignore his sour moods since he had no valid points to make.

His 'ascension' to power was unwanted but unavoidable from Damon's perspective. His father, mother and brother came to Glory to attend the formal installation ceremony of an emperor for the realm. Having his family swear allegiance from their knees made Damon feel very uncomfortable. The only person who followed the ritual that pleased him was when Beth went to a knee before him sitting on his throne. He couldn't suppress a smile. She didn't fail to notice eyeing him with a smile of her own.

It was the first time he'd seen her since his leaving Kragan. She looked to be much more at peace than he'd ever seen her. Content, she was a different person.

After the ceremony, he sought her out immediately.

"I've heard about your noble efforts with the orphans of Kragan, Beth. I'm happy you're doing something you like. It's a wonderful thing that speaks well about who you really are as a person."

"I can never match your lifelong record of kindnesses to the poor, Your Majesty, but I do what I can in my modest way."

"You know I don't like that title. You called me Damon before. Can't you just keep doing so?"

"I think not. You're an emperor now, whether you like it or not. The people have installed you by acclamation. You belong to them now and I applaud their choice."

"I didn't want it, and I don't want it."

"What a tragic life, Your Majesty, ruler of all you can survey, beloved by your subjects, the unifier of the land, fearsome conqueror of the invincible Argore, what a horrible turn of events for you, forced to endure the adoration of your subjects," she chided with a smirk.

"I would trade it all for…"

Beth eyed him a moment. "Be careful, Damon. Your wishes can come back to haunt you."

"I'm willing to take the risk, Beth. Do you think living alone is a pleasure for me?"

"No, I don't."

"Well?"

"I'm not ready to think about that yet. It's a comfort to hear from you, Damon, that you think well of me and I think I'm moving in a good direction now, at last. I feel wholesome when I'm with the children. I haven't felt that in a very long time. Still I advise you to look elsewhere for a wife, but that choice is yours if you want to wait. It isn't just my personal issues I must deal with, and it's still the fact there are better women out there for you."

Damon looked at her, annoyed again. "Must we say the same things over and over again?"

Beth got an amused look.

"You delight in this, Beth. You know I'm your slave. You're a cruel woman and I'm a sap for being helplessly in love with you."

"I think there was a compliment in there somewhere amongst the ire, Damon. Thank you, I think."

Damon muttered. He saw Beth glance to the side and her face lit up. He turned to see Layla.

"Hi," said Beth, gently.

"Hello," Layla replied, staring in Beth's eyes.

"I wanted to see you while I was here, Layla. I hope you're fine with that."

"To talk about…"

"No, we had that talk. We've put that matter to rest."

"Good," Layla replied with a smile, visibly relaxing. "I'm glad to be back where I belong in the army. This is my place and this is what I do. I serve at the pleasure of the emperor."

"I can say I might be where I belong too, Layla. Working with the children has helped me so much. It was exactly what I needed. As you know, I was in rough shape inside. I think I'm a better person than I've ever been before. Does that make sense to you?"

"It makes perfect sense, Beth. I'm very glad to hear it. Things were getting confusing for me, as you know. I think it was good we both stepped back for a while to clarify a number of things."

"Are we friends again?"

"We never stopped being friends, Beth."

"I was worried when you left. I regretted some things I said."

"I know, I think we both could have handled it better."

Damon felt like a lamp post as the women ignored him, standing right there. Whatever they were talking about, he had no idea, nor did they seem disposed to explain it to him.

"Are you going to be at the imperial table for dinner?"

"Yes, Damon has the staff in attendance for all his meals."

They looked at him.

"That's true, Beth. If you two have things to talk about, you can certainly sit together."

"No, we're done with our talks, Damon." Beth smiled and so did Layla, but it looked like a Cheshire cat smile on both their faces.

* * * *

Beth stayed in the new city of Glory after the festivities for a time as Damon's guest in the palace. Despite their pronouncements before him, she spent time talking with Layla frequently.

Meanwhile, the citizens of the new empire weren't the only ones watching the new city being built. The commander had Argore spies lurking about to monitor allied activities and also to watch for Beth. Seeing her come to Glory generated a fast rider heading back to the mountains to tell the commander.

He wasn't the only one watching. The shaman had gone back to the mountains too. He wasn't immune to possible retribution there, but at the same time he had significant numbers of followers and sympathizers even after the failure of the war. Consolidating his position quickly, he created something of an alternative Argore society only this one didn't have any of the constraints of civilized folk. Their impulses, and base natures were given free reign and the result was reprehensible, more monsters created in the image of the shaman.

The shaman also sent forces to spy on the allies but his motivation and his goals were far different. He simmered with undying rage at being thwarted and that Beth was still out there untouched, free of his ill intentions for her. The shaman was solely fixated on her at that point in time.

The commander wasn't able to react to the reemergence of the shaman as a force because the succession to high chief was a cloudy matter. The shaman sent a candidate for the post who further muddied the waters and stymied a backlash against the shaman.

Agents of the shaman crept close to Glory under the cover of darkness but were unable to gain entrance into the city. Damon was no fool and took no chances with such things. Once the gates were closed at night, nobody gained admittance and in spite of the seeming peace in the land, Damon posted ample and redundant guards as if attack was still imminent.

Those agents did see Beth, however, when she went out for a ride with Layla and a detachment of Damon's personal guards accompanying them.

* * * *

Meanwhile, Damon put Argon in charge of the creation and training of the new imperial army. Dressed in red uniforms with gold piping, epaulets, stripes, and helmets, they were an inspiring sight. Since the men had plenty of battle experience from the recent war, they formed into competent units rapidly. Damon appointed Argon as field marshal and his staff as generals.

The new army patrolled farther out into the countryside to provide continued protection from criminals for the farms and now also for all of the new cities. No city sought to resume a status as a city state. They declared allegiance to Damon and provided bases to deploy and house the imperial troops abroad. Having imperial troops available saved the cities the expense of raising their own militias. They were happy to transfer responsibility for their safety onto Damon, and the cost of it.

A new standard flew over Glory and all the other new cities. It was Damon's imperial crest in gold in the center of a red banner. The crest was placed on the imperial uniforms and was displayed proudly by all of the citizenry of the land.

Kragan retained the king's flag, but it flew below the imperial flag. A large detachment of imperial troops were housed in the city along with the city forces. They both answered to Argon and the high command in Glory.

On the surface, things could not have gone better for the allies.

* * * *

Beth concluded her conversations with Layla and departed Glory to return to Kragan. Damon regretted seeing her go and he insisted she ride with a relief column of imperial soldiers heading to Kragan as replacements.

The shaman's spies measured their limited numbers against the sizeable imperial column and decided against an attempt to take Beth on the road.

When word of it got back to the shaman, he was irate. Immediately he sent larger forces into the empire and they made their way toward Kragan following Beth.

She had no idea she was being stalked and that danger was so close at hand.

She resumed her work in Kragan with the orphaned children happy to be back at her chosen task. Unlike Glory, it wasn't as difficult to gain entrance through the Kragan gate. The fact the shaman's spies were obvious Argore would have made them stand out and would have drawn notice from the city guards so they couldn't simply waltz in the main gate. They bided their time watching traffic into and out of Kragan on the chance Beth might wander into their trap unawares.

That nearly happened as she decided to ride back to the forest to their old camp near the lake for a little quiet time, although the forest was no longer vacant. The camps built from the war were still manned and patrols traveled the forest near the road to Kragan. They'd mostly driven the dangerous animals around to the other sides of the lake to decrease some of the perils. Predators weren't totally gone though. They remained dangerous and posed a threat to the careless even in the occupied portion of the great forest.

As she was about to get on her horse, Selena appeared.

"I'd like to know if you'd come to the palace to help me with my planning for my wedding to Prince Tabor. We decided there was no reason to wait any longer. Am I interrupting some mission of yours?"

"No, I was just going to ride to the forest for the day. I can come with you back to the palace, Selena."

Unknowingly, it spared her facing vicious enemies and mortal danger, at least for that day.

Going back into the palace, where Beth spent little time, was always enjoyable because the queen was there.

The queen joined the ladies for the event. Beth looked at Selena's friends, the same ones who'd been so cruel when she'd first come. Now they treated Beth like royalty. Though they never said it, the widespread assumption was she'd be the new empress as bride to Damon. Therefore she was an obvious choice for them to curry favor.

"Your Majesty," said Beth warmly. "It's so good to see you again."

"Beth you can come here anytime, you know that. I'd hoped you'd avail yourself of the opportunity. Perhaps I'm too selfish to covet your time."

Beth smiled warmly. "I find I'm very busy with my work. I didn't think it would be so consuming a task, but I can't be around those children without feeling for their pain. They've lost parents and have no one else. They need the love of caring adults and there are too few willing to take on the task. I'm only one person. I end each day exhausted."

"Did you get a chance to speak to my son very much in Glory?"

"We chatted, but he's very busy as you know. I appreciate what little time he could spare."

Every woman in the room stared at her in disbelief at her spin on the topic. Damon would have devoted every moment to her if she'd allowed it and they all knew it, and the queen's purpose was clear.

"Indeed," said the queen eyeing her intently. "Perhaps he will find more time later."

"Perhaps, Your Majesty, I wouldn't want to be a bother to him. He's building a nation and that takes precedence over all other considerations."

"I don't think he sees you as a bother, Beth," said Selena skeptically.

"We each have our interpretations," Beth replied smoothly. She smiled placidly.

"Has Layla settled back in with her military duties?" Selena asked.

"Yes, she has," Beth replied with a broad smile. "We were able to spend time together at length. It was food for my soul. If she was born from my mother, I couldn't be closer to her. She matters a great deal to me."

"Yes," Selena answered, eyeing her thoughtfully. "We realize that, Beth." She glanced at her friends. "Too bad she must live apart from you. Your very close friendship is well known in Kragan."

Beth looked away lost in some thought or memory of her own and didn't pay attention to Selena's comment.

"Perhaps we should get to the business at hand," the queen interrupted pointedly, scowling at Selena.

"Of course, Your Majesty," Selena replied without contrition.

The ladies began their tasks. Beth nodded and smiled blithely. This wasn't a matter she had any interest in. Watching the other women exclaim over fabric colors and talk about wedding decisions as if they were significant in the world, it struck Beth as inane, childish, and boring. Most of her time there she talked with the queen.

Outside the city walls, the shaman's spies lurked in the forest easily eluding allied patrols and camps each day. They were in a position there to stay for a nearly unlimited period waiting for their chance to snag Beth. There was readily available food and water and the enemy weren't looking for them. They had no idea Beth's luck saved her, but it was a never ending threat. Failure wasn't an option knowing the wrath of the shaman if they returned to the mountains empty handed.

Beth returned to her place in Kragan after she left the palace that evening. She'd opted again to forgo the queen's ongoing invitation to live in the palace in favor of a simple life in modest surroundings.

Her 'family', the large mass of orphaned children, surrounded her giving her the warm feelings she craved. They lived in her house, an abandoned huge building Beth resettled as the former owner had been killed in the war.

Feeding so many little mouths didn't prove to be a problem as her fame and the love of the people for Damon's kindnesses motivated the people to donate food and also to rotate volunteers helping Beth with caring for the children.

For her, it was a good life and she was content.

Although she didn't ask, the queen made clear to Beth the resources of the palace was available to her also. Beth opted to work outside of royal influence unless she got into a bind. Palace entanglements were the last thing she wanted. Selena's competitions never seemed to end in spite of the fact Beth wouldn't cooperate in such silliness. She avoided Selena and her retinue as much as possible but they still sought her out frequently. Beth, like Damon, couldn't escape the curse of her fame.

As far as her work with the children, Beth drew the line at her bedroom door. She didn't let any children sleep in her room. It was her only private place to have time for herself. They were little sponges that soaked up all the love she could shower on them and more. Beth needed to recuperate each night for her long and exhausting days. She allocated certain rooms in the house for volunteers to have them there in the mornings.

It was at those private moments she thought about her future, what it was she wanted. She knew what everyone else wanted for her but that only evoked her stubbornness. The thought of marrying Damon to share a life wasn't unpleasant. It was just the idea of accepting the notoriety, the adulation, and the crush of selfish manipulative people surrounding her if she became the empress that was daunting. All the things she'd hated about Selena and her friends in the beginning would become Beth's life if she moved to Glory and married Damon.

It wasn't her only consideration. Some issues were beyond her control.

Beth decided to resume an old practice. In the morning she got up early before the children awakened to go outside and practice her fighting skills. She wanted the exercise and to stay sharp. The practice also helped her with relieving stress from ongoing worries about her orphan's welfare and their futures. Any time any one of them got sick, Beth took it personally, like she was somehow at fault for the disease.

Her sword in her hand again was like an old friend, very familiar and comforting. Her old life and her new life merged together in a way during her workout sessions. It was another step in her 'self-healing' from her early traumas and her war experiences. She couldn't forget all the evil that happened to her family or the lives she'd taken as a result, but at last she was finding a measure of peace with it. She was no worse a person than any other soldier doing their duty. In war, people die. It was kill, or be killed after all but that realization didn't assuage her feelings of guilt. So many worthy people died and yet she survived. It seemed patently unfair.

On this day, Beth decided to take her ride out to the forest to all the old haunts where she'd trained with her mentor and her friends, the beginning of her life after losing her family.

After the children finished breakfast, Beth arranged for neighbor women to watch over them while she was gone.

She rode out of the city gates in the bright warm sunshine of mid-morning. It was an absolutely beautiful day and Beth felt invigorated. She trotted her horse along steadily but in no hurry. She'd donned her old uniform for the day instead of the dresses she wore around the children.

The Argorc spies spotted her with glee at their very good luck. She was riding on a trail which would take her to the nearest guard camp, so they had little time to react.

Beth was in a pleasant mood riding along, but her wartime wariness remained within her. She heard sound to her side as riders burst out from cover to confront her. She was shocked but responded quickly. Seeing acolytes of the shaman here was concerning, and she knew they aimed to capture her for him.

They charged her quickly and silently. She was greatly outnumbered, but she'd fought in such mismatches before. The nearest attacker went down with one savage sweep of her sword. She spurred her horse ahead at full speed so they couldn't surround her.

It was very dangerous because they tried to fire darts at her tipped with immobilizing toxins.

She managed to evade those shots and gallop away toward the safety of the armed forest camp garrison.

Her horse was superb and more than the measure of the Argore horses. She started to gain separation from the pursuit when a lucky shot hit her back. The toxin was fast acting and it frightened Beth.

She screamed while she still could although she became wobbly in the saddle quickly.

As her consciousness waned, she fought to stay awake, but it was a losing effort. She fell out of the saddle and was unaware when the Argore surrounding her were attacked by an allied patrol that were nearby and heard her screams.

It was a savage fight as the two sides were about the same size in numbers.

The Argore fought insanely, with their legendary fury, but these were experienced war veterans who would not concede Beth to them. They'd fought successfully against Argore rage before and weren't intimidated.

Had the stalemate continued, the fight could have gone either way, but the sounds of fighting drew a quick response from allied reinforcements who ended the ambush wiping out all but the leader of the acolytes. He slipped away into the woods and escaped.

They carried Beth to the outpost but they didn't have an antidote for the toxin. They could only leave her to sleep until it worked out of her system.

When she awoke one full day later, she was subdued, rattled by her near miss with the shaman.

"My god," she muttered, sitting up dizzy and weak. "I'm going to have to do something about that bastard."

She looked at the camp captain.

"We got nearly all of them," he explained. "I think the leader escaped."

"Who knows how long they've been here," she reflected.

"We've started a sweep of the whole woods, ma'am. We'll catch him if he's still here."

"I'm sure he's gone by now to go back to report his failure to the shaman, but thank you, Captain. I'm in your debt."

Beth tried to stand but had to sit back down.

"That's nasty stuff," she muttered.

"Rest here until you feel better. You're safe, Ma'am."

"I think I will. Thank you again for saving my life."

The king, the crown prince, the queen, the city, and all the military forces of Kragan and the imperial forces housed there were incensed to hear about

Beth's near miss. They shook off their lethargy about the ongoing threat from the mountains. The king doubled the patrols immediately, reinforced the camps in the forest and a fast rider was sent to Glory to advise Emperor Damon of the incident.

When he was told, Damon was so angry he pondered invading the mountains to seek out the shaman to end his schemes once and for all, even if it meant a new war with the Argore horde.

"That stinking charlatan has caused too much strife in the world. If the Argore commander can't do something about him, maybe we need to do it for him. The Argore people's leadership vacuum gives the shaman opportunities."

"Damon, we can't be sure where he is. For all we know he could be holed up anywhere in the empire."

Damon looked at Argon crossly.

"I'm sorry, but we've got to be realistic. Beth survived the attack. The Kragans have doubled their patrols. There's nothing more we can do right now. If the shaman keeps making these attempts, sooner or later we'll find him."

"Wait again, is that the plan, Argon."

"I know it isn't what you want to hear. If anyone has a better plan, we'll certainly look at it."

"I've been here before so many times, Field Marshall. I should be accustomed to being helpless after as many times as I've been down this road."

"Did you have a message you wish to send to your family and to Beth?"

"Not really. Beth doesn't pay attention to what I have to say anyway."

Argon eyed Damon critically. Damon glared back and spoke impulsively.

"Why don't you send her a message, Argon?"

"Perhaps I will. I think she appreciates the concerns of others for her welfare. That would include hearing from you, Your Majesty."

"I think I'm going to lead a patrol out into the field today. I'm getting annoyed sitting here as a target for all the vultures that hang around thrones trying to weasel an agenda."

"Don't get any ideas about staying in the field, your highness. I will come after you."

Damon laughed. "I have no doubts about that, Field Marshall."

Damon's small foray into the fresh air grew rapidly as others joined the 'mission' unsolicited. By the time he rode out the city gates his entire two thousand man personal guard corps was at his back in addition to relief columns headed to frontier posts as replacements. Initially there were over ten thousand in Damon's force. With so many troops leaving, rumors spread quickly the Argore had returned and war was imminent.

It didn't faze Damon who was simply glad to be free and away from the imperial city on the road for a time.

Gideon and Layla rode directly behind him, acting as if they had a destination of significance ahead instead of just a ride through the country.

Damon's departure from Glory included sending two riders back toward the mountains, one going to the commander and the other going in search of the hiding place of the shaman.

* * * *

Meanwhile hiding in his lair, the shaman had just gotten word about Beth's miraculous escape so he was in a foul mood ranting and raving to anybody who came near. Threatening his own people, he vowed savage reprisals for any further failures. The failed leader returned with the message quaked in fear of his life.

"We will get her back to face her punishment she's earned. I swear it on my life. No heathen can be allowed to dishonor the people. She is not beyond my grasp."

His followers stared at him.

Suddenly, he changed abruptly dropping his insane facial expression for a look of cunning. He turned to his men after thinking for a time.

"You think me mad for focusing on her rather than what you think should be important. You don't understand. She is the critical piece. My visions are true. She's destined to bear the children of the Argore and birth our future. Once she's fulfilled that role, believe me she will face an ending of horror such as no other person has ever faced. It will be a living death of such agony none will ever challenge my truth ever again. In the end, I will personally cut her living beating heart out of her body to devour as she fades. It will be the last sight she'll ever see with her dying eyes. Her children will never know her. It is our purpose. You can never fail again about Beth. Who becomes the new high chief doesn't matter. This is the only goal we must achieve."

No one uttered a word.

"We're going to break camp and return to the lowlands. We'll disperse to travel in small groups and meet at the designated rendezvous point near Kragan. You must not draw undue attention to our movements so be very careful. The enemy is on their guard now because of your failures."

They left the mountains that very night. There were a considerable number of his acolytes and devotees following the shaman's call. His influence continued to grow and draw new followers. Religious zealots weren't the only people to come. There were also considerable warriors from the army. They fanned out dispersing according to the Shaman's plan and traveled toward their distant destination.

The commander received belated word about their departure after they were gone. His men watching the Shaman weren't in a position to stop them. He was still tied up with the high chief selection matter and unable to react as he wished to do. He did decide to send word to Damon since there was no doubt what the shaman was trying to do. Beth would be in terrible danger and only Damon was in a position to protect her.

Weeks later when the commander's messenger arrived at Glory with the warning, Damon was still in the field on his excursion. Argon met the man and received the commander's warning. He sent a rider speeding toward Kragan realizing the shaman had an advantage of time. The rider he sent after Damon only had a generalized idea where to find him so Damon wouldn't be getting prompt notice of the development.

* * * *

Meanwhile back in Kragan, Beth labored in her duties within the city walls trying to put the fright of her near miss behind her. She was shaken, but determined to forge ahead with her life. Having the care of the children to handle each day helped by keeping her busy. Inside the city it was easier for her to feel safe surrounded by people and city patrols. Regardless, she kept her weapons close by. She was unsure what the Shaman could or would do next.

The shaman and his forces arrived near to Kragan well ahead of the messenger from Glory. He sent men to infiltrate the city disguised as merchants. Although the gate guards were vigilant, the spies managed to get inside Kragan anyway.

They rode toward the palace since they had no idea Beth lived separately. It was ironic they rode on the same road past her large house without seeing her as she was inside feeding the children a meal at the time.

Beth heard the sound of many hooves and wagons rumbling past and glanced out her window in curiosity as danger passed by her door.

"Selena must be planning another event. That's a large supply train."

Continuing on unaware of her being nearby, the Argore moved in close to the palace and deployed at dusk. They sent a team to a side entrance and overpowered the guards. Slipping inside in the dark they hurried down the halls searching for Beth. When they reached royal chambers they faced more guards.

Rather than go into the central abode and the obvious location of the king and queen, they went to side rooms and entered Selena's bedroom after taking down her door guards.

They captured her easily and dragged her away hurrying out of the palace and escaping.

Traveling most of the way toward the main gate before their crime was discovered and the alarm sounded at the palace, the Argore readied for a fight to escape Kragan with their prize.

The Argore charged the gate surprising the gate guards and fleeing before they could be blocked and apprehended.

Beth awoke startled and frightened and jumped out of bed when she heard the alarm. All she could think was the Argore army had returned.

She donned her uniform, armed herself and raced out to meet royal authorities.

She rode to and intersected Prince Tabor riding out from the palace with a highly motivated and enraged corps.

"What's happened?" she shouted as she rode to his side.

"Someone broke into the palace and abducted Selena."

"What? Who? Why?"

"There was a fight at the main gate when they broke out of the city. I don't know the answers, Beth."

They rode rapidly and as they left the city at the head of the royal guard, considerable imperial troops joined them for the chase.

* * * *

The shaman watched his men return with anticipation, but when he looked and saw they'd captured Selena instead of Beth he simmered with rage.

"You fools, this isn't Beth."

Selena shivered in terror.

"What do you want from me?"

"Who are you, woman?"

"My name is Selena."

"Where is Beth?"

"You want Beth? Why?"

The shaman slapped her face.

"Answer my question."

Selena sobbed. The shaman grabbed her by the hair and put a knife to her throat.

"Where is Beth?"

"She doesn't live at the palace. She has her own house in the city."

"Why would she do that?"

"She takes care of orphaned children."

The shaman tossed her aside thinking on a new plan.

He looked at Selena. "Either they will trade Beth for you, or you'll face a horrible death."

"Oh no," Selena wailed. "Please don't hurt me."

"That's in the hands of your countrymen."

“They won’t deal with you. I know you. You’re the shaman of the Argore.”

“If that’s the case, perhaps I should send them one of your fingers.”

Selena started to cry in fear.

“Their soldiers are riding out of the city, Shaman,” said the leader of the kidnappers. “Also their camps in the forest are rousing up. We have little time before we face a major battle.”

“If they attack, we’ll use this woman. I think they won’t want to see her cut up into pieces before their eyes.”

“Yes, Shaman.”

They yanked Selena to her feet and dragged her to the front of their defensive position and waited.

It wasn’t long before allied troops started to arrive. They raced toward the Argore, but stopped when they saw Selena in the grasp of the shaman. He showed no fear of being killed glaring at them in defiance.

Chapter Seventeen

Beth rode right beside Tabor when they came upon the desperate scene. When she saw the shaman himself, it sent a chill of fear down her spine. He stared back at Beth hungrily. It was unnerving to her to be near him again.

He brazenly ripped open Selena's top with his razor sharp blade placed against her flesh. She shuddered in abject terror whimpering for mercy.

"You see, Beth," he taunted. "You're fated to the Argore. There's no place you can go where we can't touch you. I have the life of this woman in my hands. I can carve her into pieces before your eyes if you don't cooperate. She would not die quickly."

Selena whimpered loudly and nearly collapsed.

"Accept your destiny, Beth, or she will die. You'll ride away willingly with us, or she won't die alone. You'll birth the future of the Argore people. That's always been your destiny."

Tabor was terribly conflicted. There was nothing he could do for his fiancée but letting Beth go to such a horrible fate with a madman was inconceivable. He had no answer to the dilemma.

Beth paused only a moment.

"I accept, let her go."

"No, we will all ride away out of the grasp of your army. Once we're free we'll release this female."

"No Beth," the prince whispered. "You can't do this. He can't be trusted."

"There's no other way. I won't let Selena die in my place. The shaman will kill her horribly, Tabor. I can't allow that."

Ignoring the Tabor's protests, she rode forward and got off her horse. The shaman's men quickly tied her, took her weapons, and put her back on her horse. The Argore war party rode away at the gallop into the darkness.

An agonized Tabor sent men to follow them at a discreet distance, and then sent orders for the entire army in the city to mobilize into action. He sent a fast riding messenger to alert Damon in Glory of the adverse turn of events. He felt a total failure he couldn't stop the Shaman.

* * * *

Beth felt terrible foreboding as she rode along, like her miracles had finally run out. The impossible happened. The shaman had her again. Dodging his insane lusts two prior times, expecting another miracle seemed unrealistic. She thought about her orphaned children and what would become of them without her. It nearly brought her to tears.

Selena sobbed continuously riding beside her. "Beth, I'm so sorry."

"It's not your fault, Selena."

They rode through most of the night before they stopped.

The Shaman sauntered over to Beth looking smug.

"You've escaped my people. Let Selena go free," Beth urged.

"She's additional leverage against the heathens," he replied. "Her life is in my hands too. I can think of many uses for her and as a great lesson to the enemy."

"Do you really think you can do this and face no consequences?"

"I don't fear my death. Can you say the same? I saw the terror in your eyes when you were under my knife."

"If this is my end, so be it, Shaman. What do you accomplish by hurting Selena? She's nothing to you, and not in one of your demented visions."

"You have no power to negotiate, Beth. I can do as I wish to her, and to you."

"If you let her go free, I'll agree to birth the children you want."

The shaman sneered. "You say that lie thinking it's a way to control me like I'm weak. I'm not the commander agog in your thrall. You'll be put with child regardless. You have no say over that. I have no need of your pretend acquiescence. Perhaps this other one should join you in going to the marriage bed."

"Oh no," Selena gasped covering her face with her hands.

The shaman laughed at her. "You're weak. No Argore woman would show such fear in facing her fate. If you die it would be no loss for this world. Both of you put too much store in your beauty as a way to manipulate men. I'm above such petty schemes. Your wiles will not save you here."

"Leave her alone," Beth hissed. "You came here for me so leave her be."

"I don't think so," he retorted scornfully. "Now, both of you lie down and sleep. Rest briefly as we leave shortly."

Selena lay against Beth trembling in fear.

"Beth, how could this happen?"

"It's my fault, Selena. I had unfinished business with the Shaman. I should have gone after him to end this when I had the chance."

"I'm afraid. I think he really would do all those terrible things."

"Don't think about it."

"I wish I had your courage, Beth."

"I'm scared too, Selena. I don't want to die either, but none of us can choose how we go out of this world. For the moment, we have each other."

Selena started to cry again and buried her face in Beth's shoulder hugging her tightly. Beth felt equally disconsolate. She thought about her orphan children again, left alone now and this time it brought tears to her eyes.

It seemed like only moments before they were shaken awake and were back on the horses heading toward the distant mountains.

They traveled evasively to avoid settlements and the notice of the locals, but a sizeable warlike force couldn't pass through the area completely unseen.

The inevitable happened. A farm wife spotted them crossing a field in the dim light of sunrise and called her husband.

"Who are they?"

"I heard rumors about trouble from the Argore again. They have the look of trouble. We'll ride to tell the imperial soldiers at the fort. I'm not leaving you alone here with them out there moving about."

At the fort, it wasn't fully the immediate notice from the farmer of an enemy force passing through which elicited a response, but with word of Damon's recent alert, the post commander sent a large detachment to chase after the Argore column.

It happened Damon's huge circuit in the hinterland brought him close enough that he got word of the enemy being in the area before he heard Beth and Selena had been taken.

He had no reason to rush back to Glory, so he set out to join the chase. His secret hope was for combat again, not realizing at that point he was chasing after the women.

The Shaman rode for another day before they spotted the pursuit on their trail. It gave Beth and Selena hope to know friendly forces were trying to save them.

Prince Tabor was also in hot pursuit, but his force was too far behind to catch the shaman before he got to the mountains.

Damon rode at the head of the column leading his large force angling toward where he plotted his quarry would be going. It cut off considerable distance and gave them a chance to arrive in time to make a difference.

The race continued with the imperial patrol matching the brisk Argore pace, but with Damon closing in rapidly from the side. The Argore saw them too late to change their course to evade a confrontation. It was close as to whether they got to the mountains before they were caught. It didn't matter to

Damon. He would keep after them no matter how long it took or where they went. The Argore border was no factor for him with an Argore raiding party in imperial lands. He would have his fight no matter where it occurred.

As they approached the foothills the sun hung low on the horizon so the light was starting to get dim.

When Damon saw who was there, and then he saw female captives, he screamed the charge. His forces responded with a roar. The other approaching column of imperial troops responded seeing his reaction and raced to join with their emperor.

The Shaman led his force across the border. A group of his followers were waiting there to provide cover and reinforcements, but Damon had an army of the fiercest of his fighters at his back closing the distance rapidly.

They struck the Argore skirmish line like scythes harvesting wheat. The Shaman was unable to create separation in escaping as Damon refused to be turned away.

The second imperial column arrived and struck which broke the inadequate Argore resistance line.

The joint force raced after the shaman ignoring his acolytes who ran away fleeing in numerous different directions.

The shaman rode quickly behind a huge boulder and changed direction to try to elude pursuit. One of Damon's leading scouts caught on to the maneuver and followed them unerringly.

The shaman led them on a convoluted path but he couldn't lose them. Meanwhile Damon closed the gap in reaching his forward scouts.

Finally they surrounded the fleeing kidnappers. Damon was shocked to see Beth and Selena.

The shaman jumped off his horse. His men pulled down the women and held them while he pulled out his deadly blade.

"We meet again, heathen. Do you see I have your woman, again? I can take her life before you can move to interfere. If you don't leave right now, both of these women will die before your eyes."

Damon stared at him trying to think of a solution. There was none.

"I'm willing to die right here, Damon. Are you willing to let your woman die too?"

Layla touched Damon's arm to break his impasse.

"You're a dead man walking, Shaman," Damon hissed.

"It was her fate to be mother to our new future leaders. It can't be changed. Leave us now and make no attempt to come for her. If I see your face ever again it will be the last day Beth draws breath."

"You will see me again, Shaman, and it will be the last day you draw breath. Now give us Selena."

The shaman pondered the situation and then nodded to his men. They released Selena who rushed over to safety.

"Oh Beth," she cried in anguish. "I just couldn't let them hurt me. I'm so sorry."

"Don't worry, Selena. I understand. Go back to your prince and live a good life. I'll deal with this."

The shaman gave Selena a contemptuous sneer. She cowered and hid her face.

"You're worthless," he spat at her.

Selena started to cry in response.

Layla looked to be on the verge of attacking the shaman. He turned his glance and eyed her viciously.

"If you wish to be the cause of her death instead of him, she is still dead. Leave me now or I'll lose my patience and cut off her head."

Damon looked at Beth in consternation. She looked defeated with her head down staring at the ground.

"GO," the shaman shouted. "I will wait no longer."

Damon whirled and led his men away.

"You can't abandon her, Damon," Layla cried.

"There was nothing we could do in that situation. I'm not giving her up."

He sent a rider to the nearest outpost to relay a message to Argon back in Glory.

Damon also sent special men to track the Shaman. They were his best trackers and the ones most able to avoid detection.

Meanwhile he made a show of riding back over the mountain border of the Argore into the empire.

They made a camp not far away.

Layla glared at Selena who shuddered in shame and kept her head down. Layla also glared at Damon.

"If she is harmed, Damon, I will never forgive you. I'll do my duties in your service but our bond between us will be broken forever."

Damon sat stoically. Her threat hurt him deeply, and he was equally worried about Beth.

The men in the camp were subdued sitting in their own frustration at the terrible turn of events. They were willing to attack the Argore, but they also understood the difficult situation Damon was placed in with Beth's life hanging in the balance. The men understood Damon's dilemma and incredibly difficult decision but Layla wasn't sympathetic. She was feral moving about in camp in a rage. Wisely, no one attempted to speak to her.

Damon stood up and walked away from his subdued staffers looking for a particular man. He spotted him sitting at the edge of the camp.

Damon went to a knee to speak with him.

"You're the best archer I've ever seen. I want to ask if you'd consider a mission once we find the Shaman's camp, if you'll go to join my scouts in chasing him down. If there is ever a shot where you can take him down I want you in position to do so. It would be very hazardous for Beth, but there's no option without risk for us to save her. I need options and backup plans. Is it something you can do realistically? It might be it's an impossible shot."

"Of course, Your Majesty, thank you for your faith in me. I do what I can in my craft. I would say there is no shot which is impossible for me."

"We'll watch for a signal from you to attack. Send a flaming arrow up to point us where to go. Her life depends on you. I put my faith in your unique abilities. I have no other options."

"I will do as you ask, Your Majesty."

"There is one other thing. He's said he wants her to birth their babies, but if you see he's changed his mind to succumb to his lusts for torture. Don't let Beth suffer. Do you understand? If you see she's being savaged and defaced, or dismembered end her pain."

The man looked at him solemnly. "I will kill this monster, sire. That other horrible situation will never happen. I promise you."

"Remember, the shaman is insane. He can change quickly and his decisions may not be rational. You must be on your guard constantly. You're all she has now and time is running out for us to save her."

Damon looked at the rage in the man's eyes and he was pleased. This is what he needed to see to know he had the right man for the job.

"I'm going to send you out with two scouts. You know to exercise the utmost care in approaching that camp. Any mistake will mean instant death for Beth. Our hope is the shaman thinks he's won and will let down his guard on his home ground. Remember, he's no fool so exercise utmost care in what you do."

"Yes, Sire."

"My other scouts ahead of you will be watching for you to come join them. Good luck."

Damon went back to join his staff. He wasn't fully convinced this attempt would work, but at least he was doing something. He was hopeful and at a time like that, he needed it, regardless of how remote were the chances of success.

Layla still had a sour look on her face which shook his confidence when he sat down beside her.

"I've sent a man, an archer, to try for a killing shot on the shaman."

"I don't agree with us sitting here, Your Highness," she replied with terse words. "You saw what he was going to do to us when we were under his knife."

"I know I'm gambling on his words to use her for birthing babies. They wouldn't cut her in that circumstance."

"You hope," Layla snarled. "You have no guarantee he wasn't lying. She might already be under his knife. You should let me go with your archer."

"If you took precipitous action, Layla, it could cause Beth to be killed before we could intercede. The archer has already gone."

"I think it's worth the risk with the danger she faces. You weren't lying on the ground with him sitting on your chest like I was. He was just seconds away from cutting me for his pleasure. You didn't see the insane look in his eyes, like an animal. He reveled in my fear and in the pain he would inflict. I've had men approach me in my life looking for love who didn't look that avid. He's a disease that must be wiped out."

"I understand, Layla," he replied gently. "I was there and I saw it too. I was as horrified as you and I agree he's got to be taken out. Nobody is saying we shouldn't take action, but I think this is the best course for us have a real chance at success."

"I'm not happy with this, Damon," she groused. "This falls on you."

* * * *

Beth had a feeling of defeat when Damon was forced to leave. Her brave words to Selena didn't reflect her inner terror. Whatever could happen in the control of the shaman would not be good, one way or another.

The good life she had in Kragan with her orphaned children seemed to be over.

They dragged her away. She glanced back at Damon's forces disappearing from her view and her heart sank. Feelings of depression weren't far behind for her.

"They'll try to follow us," said the shaman. "Let them think they've succeeded. We'll send a large body of followers to another of our camps and we'll have a woman there to look like Beth. I'm taking her to our secret camp."

He looked at Beth. "There will be no further miracles for you. Now you will face your fate."

He grabbed her by the hair and laughed like the lunatic he was. "You're mine and there is nothing you can do about it."

They traveled in the darkest of night to the secret camp which was actually located in a large cave in the nearest mountain. Going in the entrance Beth felt like her last hope for rescue was over. She felt on the verge of being sick with the fear of what would happen to her in that hole in the ground.

There were easily a hundred of his acolytes residing in the massive cave. The roaring fire caused a stinging in her eyes from the acrid smoke. She blinked at the tears that formed and rolled down her cheeks.

"I think we'll have a feast in your honor, Beth," the Shaman exclaimed expansively. The acolytes laughed with him.

The shaman started a chant that evoked a unison response from his people, their version of a prayer. Whom they were praying to, she had no idea. She simply waited helplessly for the worst to happen.

The 'ceremony' took a little time after which the acolytes fell upon her. They led her to female servants who took her away. They bathed her in a large tub and then dressed her in an immodest flimsy dress. It highlighted her body more than it covered it. It was tight and it was short, a clothing piece she would never have chosen to wear in public.

The acolytes hauled her back to the shaman who leered at her. They held her in their grasp so she could do nothing to protect herself.

"Yes, this is pleasing. You're readied for your duty to inflame a man, and then to start bearing Argore babies."

He stepped close. His reek was overpowering and nauseating. She turned her head away fighting against nausea.

"Yes, Beth, this will happen and your fighting prowess can't save you here."

She said nothing, staring straight ahead. She tried to ignore the Shaman as he savored verbally inflicting her indignities. Instead she thought about better days and other people. She also thought about her little ones and that brought a lump to her throat. She even imagined Damon miraculously bursting into the cave to save her.

* * * *

The archer and his guides joined the other of Damon's scouts in the chase but as he watched he grew suspicious as he watched the camp.

"There's something wrong here," he whispered. "I think we've been duped. That woman isn't Beth. They've taken her somewhere else."

The scouts looked at him in shock.

"There was another small group," said one of the scouts. "They veered off. I followed them so I know where they went."

"We need to go there immediately," said the archer. "We need to send word to Damon."

"They went into a cave."

"That's all the more reason to hurry."

It took several hours for the messenger to creep stealthily out of the mountains to go to back to Damon's camp across the border.

"Assemble, quickly," Damon commanded after he heard the message. "We go now."

They formed up and rushed away into the mountain realm of the Argore to pursue the Shaman into his secret lair.

This time, they used no caution and often ran into the shaman's patrols, but those were mismatches as the allies mowed down their enemy and moved on quickly. They moved fast enough that the shaman got no pre-warning Damon was coming. The few survivors who tried to race ahead to warn him ran into Damon's scouts outside the cave mouth and were taken out in ambushes.

When Damon stood at last near the cave mouth he gathered his troops. Fire light flickered from the cave interior but not enough to fully expose the sentry positions.

"We outnumber them and they have nowhere to go to escape. The shaman will turn to desperate measures when we attack and that will be harming or killing Beth. We have to make a lightning strike and the focus has got to be quickly killing the Shaman before he can act. Do you have any questions?"

No one said anything.

"We'll let our archers take out the sentries and then we'll charge immediately. Be silent, relentless and merciless. These bastards deserve what we're going to give them."

It was difficult shots because the sentries weren't at the mouth of the cave. They were recessed and barely visible.

The archers notched their arrows, checked the wind and carefully took aim. It felt like time stood still for Damon as he waited breathlessly. There was so much that could go wrong and the price of failure was more than he could endure. If they missed any sentry, that was all that the shaman needed, a warning to take deadly action against Beth.

When they released their arrows the action happened rapidly. One of the sentries dropped with an arrow through his throat and the other was struck in the chest above the heart. He went down, but they saw he was alive and moving. They rushed the cave but the sentry continued crawling along trying to warn his comrades.

Damon was at the head of the column but it was Layla who struck the wounded sentry to end his threat.

They sprinted farther down the tunnel into the main cavern which at that point was brightly lit from the raging fire. The acolytes were in the midst of a ceremony chanting wildly watching the Shaman and unprepared for Damon's sudden attack.

Beth was tied to the four posts of a bed by her hands and feet unable to move.

With the cacophony of noise and the single minded lust of the Shaman, they didn't immediately realize they were under attack and that was all Damon needed.

The allies swept into their ranks slaughtering the enemy before they could mount a defense of any kind.

Still the shaman didn't notice the battle as he crawled unto the bed leering at Beth.

Damon raced up and landed a bone crushing blow to his head knocking him onto the floor of the cave.

He readied his sword for the killing blow.

"No, Damon," Beth cried. "Free me so I can deal with him."

Damon hesitated.

"Do it!" Beth roared in rage.

He cut the bindings and she walked naked to claim her sword. She turned to the Shaman who jumped up bleeding from the face but snarling with rage.

For her, the Shaman was the personification and the embodiment of evil, the reason her family was dead. He was the object of her hatred. Here she would exercise vengeance at last, or die in the attempt, she didn't care which. Knowing that even if she was killed, Damon would slaughter the Shaman, it was enough for Beth. This was her choice to fight, even with the hazard of his poisoned claws with her bared skin. She needed catharsis even if it was a trauma in itself. All else around her in the cave blurred as she focused her attention exclusively on her enemy. There was only she and him.

The shaman leered her at perfect body. "Come to me, woman. You will accompany me to the next life as my maiden. I will mark you as mine when we get there. Dying here won't spare you from your fate. I have seen it and I don't fear death. Glory awaits me in the great beyond. I've been pure to the cause and will be rewarded in the afterlife."

He attacked quickly, but Beth had dreamed of this moment. She was mentally prepared for it as well as being physically ready. She was perfection of motion as she parried his quick strike with his blade and countered with a deadly stroke of her own. Her grueling training had hardened her for this fight. She felt no fear being consumed with righteous hatred.

The shaman was a dangerous fighter too so the struggle wasn't easy or quick.

In the background, the allies overwhelmed and killed his force of acolytes until only the Shaman remained. He was oblivious to anything but Beth and the battle.

She was an incredible sight. The most beautiful woman a man could see in her alluring splendor yet engaged in a fight to the death. She fought flawlessly, avoiding numerous near misses from the shaman's weapons, and his poisoned claws.

Damon stood by helplessly watching in agony at Beth's danger. He instantly regretted not killing the shaman himself for fear he might get lucky with a strike against Beth.

Heedless of her peril, she fought fearlessly and even a little recklessly. Knowing he had poisoned claws, she kept him from closing in on her time after time to use that tactic.

The level of the struggle stayed at a high degree though both combatants started to pant from the exertion of the savage fight. The end was sudden and shocking as she used a feint and followed up quickly with a blinding attack in a blur of motion wounding him in the abdomen. He paused to look at his blood seeping from the wound when she screamed and took a savage swing beheading him and ending his life in the world.

Beth stood panting with tears streaming down her cheeks. Layla rushed over to wrap her up in a blanket.

Beth wept resting her head on Layla's shoulder for a moment, but suddenly she looked up at Damon. Beth pulled out of Layla's embrace to walk to the prince.

"Thank you, Damon. I prayed you would find me."

She put her arms around him in a tight hug. He crushed her in his own embrace.

"You're safe now," he muttered. "You got him. It's all over at last."

Damon nodded to Gideon and the soldiers filed out of the cave leaving the dead bodies of the enemy behind untended, food for the scavengers.

Emerging from the cave, they were surprised to see the Argore commander waiting at the entrance with a large force of Argore warriors.

"Is he gone?"

"Yes, Commander, Beth killed him. Are you here to war with us for coming onto your land?"

"No, Damon. This had to be done. The shaman lost his mind and posed a threat to the Argore people as well as to your people. We have no wish for more war. Too many died already for the ravings of a madman. You may go in peace. Beth, I'm glad I could see you again. It warms my heart."

"Thank you, Commander. I'm glad to see you also. It's nice to be alive still."

"My offer still stands, Beth. You look fetching in that blanket."

She chuckled.

"I know and I thank you, but I've decided I want to make a life with Damon, even though there is the severe drawback of his being an emperor now."

Damon smiled in shock at her reversal of position and hugged her tightly.

"May you both have long and happy lives. The Argore are no longer your enemies. Let there be peace between our peoples."

Damon nodded gratefully. They parted ways and headed for their respective camps.

Damon only spent the one night in the makeshift camp before departing to return to Glory. It was a feeling he'd never had before with Beth making her decision, and her commitment to him. He felt optimism and felt spiritual peace finally.

"Beth, can I ask you what changed your mind about me? I'm no better a person than I ever was."

"When I was totally at the mercy of the shaman and it appeared he would take me, I only thought about you. I love the orphans but arrangements can be made about them. My hesitance about the attention focused on me from being your wife wasn't a good excuse. I realized it at last."

"Thank god," he whispered.

She smiled at him.

"Beth, will that be a problem for your friendship with Layla? She has strong feelings for you."

"As do I have strong feelings for her, Damon. You must understand, I never had a sister, and I never had any female close in my life other than my mother. I think we both got a little confused for a time, but we came to the same conclusions about what we wanted. I'm afraid though I rained on her hopes you'd consider her for your mate."

"She'll make a wonderful wife for somebody, but for me it was always you, Beth. I never thought about anyone else. I just worried I really was unworthy of a great lady like you, and don't tell me you're just a farmer's daughter. The world worships you."

"I am just a farmer's daughter, but I'll stop fighting the misperceptions of the masses."

"I don't know about how you feel, but I don't need a long engagement period. I'd like to have a wedding as soon as it can be arranged."

"As you wish, My Emperor." She smiled warmly. "I must admit, I feel much better, like a weight has been lifted off my shoulders. You know word of this will spread like wildfire."

"My mother will be very happy. She loves you like a daughter already. Now you will be her daughter. I'm not worried about keeping it secret. I'd like to stand on the palace walls and shout the news to the world."

"As you wish, My Lord," she replied with a warm smile. "I'll stand at your side to be sure you don't fall off the palace wall."

They laughed together, betrothed at last.

Later after a pleasant journey home, they rode into Glory in triumph. The enemy was defeated and the threat was gone at last with the death of the evil shaman. The story of Beth's fight killing her deadly antagonist spread quickly and added to her aura. It was debatable at that point as to who was more beloved and higher in the esteem of the people, the emperor or his beautiful wife to be.

Argon waited at the palace entrance to greet them. Berne and Amal flanked him.

"Here we are again, the five of us. What we started so long ago in that forest has brought us to an ending I never anticipated. I knew you were capable of great things, but you've both transformed this world in ways I would not have thought possible. I'm so happy you decided to marry. I think we're on the verge of a golden age in the empire."

"Thank you, Argon. You'll always be our mentor. I assume you're content leading my army."

"I am content, though I envy you for gaining the love of such a remarkable woman. It's been a hole in my life for a very long time in being alone."

"That's a matter that can be remedied, Argon. There are plenty of wonderful women around you if you decide to pick one."

"Damon, women aren't low hanging fruit dangling from a tree," Beth objected.

"I'm not the best with words, darling. Now I'll have you to teach me in that area."

"And none too soon, in my opinion. You've been your own worst enemy for as long as I've known you."

"Ah, the words of love. Aren't they sweet, Argon?" he joked.

Beth eyed him critically then swatted his arm.

"We'll get those things straightened out with time, Your Majesty," she retorted scornfully. "I'll speak with Layla now, gentlemen."

They watched her walk away.

"I think my life has radically changed, Argon."

"Have no doubts about that. Taking a wife is no small thing and they do take custody of you in that new life."

"I can't say it worries me. It seems I've waited all my life for this moment. After the war and all the other turmoil we've been through, I've got to think the worst is over. I'm glad the shaman is no longer alive to threaten the world. I believe the Argore are happy to be rid of him."

"I'll see about negotiations with the Argore once they formalize a new high chief. Perhaps we can create a peace treaty and work together for the well-being of both peoples."

"I like that idea, Argon."

"I assume we have a wedding to plan for and a new empress to celebrate."

Damon smiled broadly. "That will be a day for the ages, marrying Beth."

"Indeed, I'll speak to some people about preliminary plans."

* * * *

Beth told Layla, again, she was marrying Damon. Layla smiled and talked happily about the prospects of such an event though it appeared she was forcing a smile. Beth saw something in her eyes and made an assumption she was inwardly disappointed she wouldn't have Damon. Layla never made it a secret about her feelings but it was still distressing for Beth to see in Layla's eyes. Beth was partially correct about it. From Layla's side, there was more. She'd come to cherish her closeness with Beth. In light of their prior ambivalence Layla had arbitrarily parted from her in lieu of some difficult choices.

After a moment Beth spoke to her. "Layla, I tell you we'll still have our friendship. I'll become a wife but that doesn't mean we no longer keep in touch."

"I hope so, Beth. I…"

Beth put a finger to her lips. "It's not necessary, darling. I understand. Let's look ahead. The past is gone. We can look forward to what the future holds for us."

"You're right. I need to move on too."

"With the war done, perhaps you can put down your sword and look at taking a husband."

"I never really paid attention to any man but Damon," she blurted, and looked at Beth abashedly.

Beth chuckled. "It's okay. I'm not offended. I understand completely. I never thought about other men in that role either. I'm not saying I didn't find some other men interesting. Some were very interesting."

They looked at each other and laughed.

"What a vixen you are, future empress."

"I just looked, Layla. That's harmless enough."

"Perhaps I should tell the emperor he needs a big lock on the royal bed chamber when he's away. Maybe he needs to purchase a chastity belt."

They laughed again.

"Will you help me with the planning, Layla? I'll ask his mother too, but I want you to share this experience with me. In a way, you're my family."

"Of course I will, Beth."

"I'll send for the queen to come to Glory. She's the only mother I have at this point."

"Good, this will be wonderful. I'm looking forward to it, Beth."

They wandered to the door but stopped.

"Are you ready to be empress of the realm, Beth? It will be a challenge living the life you hated so much in Kragan."

"Hopefully, I can be a different person than those shallow…"

"Be nice."

"I can afford to be magnanimous, my dear. Perhaps I'll develop a sudden hearing problem when it comes to courtesans."

* * * *

They sent word to the queen in Kragan and she did, in fact, accept the invitation to help with planning the wedding. Tabor's wedding to Selena was scheduled for the following month so the queen had the happy dilemma of both of her boys taking a mate but near to the same times.

She came for a visit to Glory and talked at length with Beth and Layla until they all returned together to Kragan for Tabor's wedding.

Tabor and his new bride went to Glory after returning from their honeymoon to be a part of Damon's wedding soon afterwards.

It was a massive spectacle as not only did Damon's friends and associates go all out with the festivities, the citizenry across the empire made it a holiday and traveled to Glory for the event. The area surrounding the city was clogged with a sea of tents to accommodate the throng.

Meanwhile, the Argore commander finally achieved the designation as the new high chief besting his rivals for the post. The newly appointed shaman was young, and devout, but he wasn't insane or misguided. He preached to the people about bettering themselves. The days of mayhem were finally over.

That new shaman was included in the commander's delegation in coming to Glory to attend the wedding ceremonies as Damon took a bride, the empress of the realm. It was a bittersweet occasion for the Argore commander watching the love of his life marry his rival.

Postlude

Beth was gracious in meeting the commander. His torment was clear in his eyes watching her join to another man to make her life. Meeting the new shaman was a test for her, but after seeing he was a decent man she handled it well.

"I know what the former shaman did and I want to apologize. It never was the Argore way to do such things," said the new shaman. "My hope is you can get past those horrors. The days of evil are over."

"Thank you, and I accept your words of apology, Shaman. I believe you'll lead your people in a new direction where we can all prosper in peace. Also, I wish you well, Commander. Congratulations on being named the new High Chief of the Argore peoples. I'll always see you as a close friend. Your kindnesses and your protection through my dark times are a debt I can never repay."

"Beth, I'm content just to be in your presence. Obviously things didn't work out as I would have wished, but your husband to be is a great man. He's right to be your husband. I hope we can still see each other in friendship in the future."

"Of course, Commander, I look forward to it. I mean High Chief."

* * * *

The ceremony was magnificent, the splendor was dazzling, and the aftermath went on for a week.

Damon had his bride at last. The 'farmer's daughter' was now an empress. She turned her full attention to her husband and Damon knew true contentment at last. It was better than he'd imagined life could be. Beth complemented him, his soul mate and perfect companion. What was even better for Damon was she seemed to be as happy as he was, satisfied with her choice to marry him and equally agog at the fulfilling new life they had together.

Layla surprised everyone later when she became engaged to the stoic Gideon. Even Amal and Berne left the ranks of the single to marry. Incredibly, it was with Selena's two friends, Katherine and Elle. The prevailing rumor was the women pursued the men rather than the other way around, although neither Amal nor Berne were unhappy to be 'captured' in the bonds of romance.

Argon had friendships with a number of women, but he remained unattached. He did continue his close friendship with the queen.

Beth birthed a daughter followed by three sons and finally a second daughter. The young one, Abby, was a firebrand from the start. She was strong willed, self-reliant, headstrong, and determined. Trying to curb her moods and her sometimes impulsive behavior proved to be the most difficult parenting challenge Damon and Beth faced. Abby picked up a sword early and fought against her brothers in mock battles.

As she grew, her father was usually exasperated but adored her as his favorite in spite of his attempts to be equal with all his children.

"Beth, she's just like you." Damon said often.

"Is that a compliment, Damon?" She would always ask him the same question.

"It's a good thing, Darling. I couldn't be happier with our life together. Thank you, My Darling for giving me our precious children."

"I'm happy too, Damon. For too long I didn't let you know how much you meant to me. I just struggled with the wreckage in my life."

"We had a happy outcome, that's what's important."

* * * *

The realm prospered with the passage of time and the aura of Damon and Beth grew along with it to epic proportions. They became larger than life figures in the minds of the people beloved and revered. They both accepted who they were and embraced their roles and responsibilities.

Sometime later, Damon's father, the king, contracted a deadly disease and passed away prematurely. Tabor ascended to the throne, but he was a broken hearted new king.

The queen was crushed by the loss sudden loss of her mate. She decided to travel to Glory to spend time away from familiar places that reminded her of her dead husband.

Damon did his best to console his mother, but spending time with her grandchildren did much more as a balm for her wounded spirit.

Argon became a frequent visitor for the queen and they were often seen together dining, or seeing the sights of the imperial city.

That friendship led to their marriage, although some thought it scandalously too short a grieving period.

Damon was initially conflicted by the development, but he came to peace with it quickly.

"Should your mother sit alone needlessly," Beth argued. "I'm glad for them both. They always had a connection. Now they can be happy together. She doesn't mean any slight to your father. He's dead, she's a free woman to choose who she wishes."

"You're right. It's just a shock."

"Get over it."

"Yes, Ma'am."

* * * *

The most unexpected twist was as the imperial children grew into adulthood and married, the last single child was Abby. She was like a new version of her mother, a stunning beauty coveted universally and constantly beset by armies of suitors. Just like her mother, she concentrated on honing her fighting skills and maintaining an independent life.

With the frequent visits of the commander and his family, Abby met one of his son's and they started a relationship that on the surface seemed more a competition and a symbiosis. In spite of their insults, boasts, and martial sparring, he managed what no other man could do. He got her attention and her interest.

When Abby decided to take a visit to the Argore's mountains Damon started to realize something momentous was afoot for his beloved baby daughter.

When she didn't promptly return and instead they received notice she was now betrothed, he was in turmoil. They went at the head of a great delegation to the home city of the commander in time for a hastily arranged wedding.

He tried to reason with his daughter, but that was impossible.

"Why should I not marry the man of my choice, Father, what's wrong with him? He's a good person, one of the few men I can say I respect and I want him."

"You're my baby girl, Abby. It's hard for me to lose you."

"Father, I appreciate that, but I'm not a little girl any longer, I'm a woman, and I'm ready to take a mate of my own. He's my choice. You're not losing me, you're gaining him."

"Abby, you're a delight in my life. I love all of my children, but you know you own a special place in my heart."

"I know I remind you of Mom, but you've got to let me go. It's time. I want to start my own life with the man I've chosen. I'll be fine, Father. I really will be okay."

Damon saw tears of emotion forming in her eyes. It evoked his tender feelings for his child.

"This is a scary step for me too, Father, but it's one I want to take."

"I'm sorry, Abby, I still have a lot of trouble letting you go, but you're right. It's my problem. If he's your choice, I'll support you, my little darling, but tell him if he messes up in any way I will come after him personally with an army at my back."

She laughed and hugged her father. "Dad, I'm really good with a sword. I could take care of him on my own."

"Honestly, he's a good young man. I have nothing against him, Darling. Actually I like him better than your sister's husband. To corral you, he had to be something special."

"Thank you, Daddy," she purred happily. She kissed his cheek and hugged him warmly.

They walked back arm in arm to join the group.

Beth was in her own private conversation with the commander whose wife had stepped away to join her son, the impending groom. The old Damon would have been crushed with jealousy at their closeness and the implications she was looking elsewhere for illicit romance. This incarnation of Damon had come to peace with such issues. That was possible because he fully trusted his wife's love after many wonderful years. She didn't look or act guilty as she turned her face.

They looked up at Damon and Abby and smiled. Beth's eyes sparkled as she glanced at her husband and daughter.

"Mama," said Abby, embracing her. "I'm so happy."

"What a strange development," said the commander. "In a way, the vision of the old shaman has come true. Although it isn't Beth who mothers the line of our future leaders, it's her daughter."

Damon looked at Abby. Seeing her as a future mother with her own children seemed weird to him. He could only see her as that tiny little bundle he'd held in his arms so lovingly on the day she was born. On that day, she hadn't cried, but looked him straight in the eyes like she was a tiny adult destined for great things, and like she was about to speak on her first day on the planet.

Damon hugged his daughter, one last time before she became a wife.

It wasn't long before the wedding occurred. Emperor Damon walked her down the aisle way before the gathered throng from across the empire and the Argore mountains, putting her hand into that of her new husband. It returned memories of his own wedding day with Beth. Abby, like her mother, was a force of nature and soon after returning from their honeymoon the Argore quickly realized their universe had changed irreparably.

Argore customs, beliefs and practices meant nothing to Abby going forward. She had no problem challenging anything and everything, starting with the subservient place of women in Argore society. Her husband found out family dynamics from his home upbringing wouldn't be the same in his life married to Abby. She would never be a docile obedient Argore wife. His only choice was to accept her terms or risk losing her.

Abby's rebellion didn't stop at her marriage, refusing to accept a lesser place for Argore women and she was vocal about it. Over the protest of men, she instituted female schooling, created positions for women in high places, and went toe to toe with the men stuck in the past. Abby didn't lose those arguments no matter how serious were the issues. Her husband tried initially to temper her ferocity and quickly learned it couldn't be done. His consequences of clashing with her were too costly, such as being banned from the marriage bed. It worked in that Abby didn't ever lose arguments with her husband. He wasn't allowed to merely stand on the sideline in her fights against the male establishment. He was forced to actively fight with and support her radical positions.

Particularly, crimes men could commit against women with impunity in the past were no longer tolerated, like beating wives, and so forth. Abby demanded strong punishment to deter reprehensible behaviors and women loved her for it. Where in the past any women whether married or single, could be accosted by a male and then blamed for it; that foul practice was stopped completely. Women were allowed to train in the war arts, like Abby. Being able to defend themselves was imminently empowering. In spite of considerable grumbling from men, Abby persevered fearlessly. Had those men done something foolish, their own women would have risen up to defend Abby and forcefully so.

Another right Abby championed was giving women choice in who they marry. Men could no longer simply pluck pretty young women from their families for a whim. Older men who tired of their wives and looked for fresh naïve young replacements were prime targets for Abby's wrath. She had no patience for men who didn't fulfill their obligations of faithfulness in a marriage.

As a side issue, with the terrible losses from the war, there was a shortage of men in the mountains as well as in the empire. As a temporary measure until the numbers evened out, men were allowed to have multiple wives. It was a situation that proved to be dicey and somewhat tenuous as some wives adjusted to having another woman sharing affections with their husband, and some wives didn't handle it well. Women traveled out of their homelands frequently going both ways. Some Argore women married in the empire, and some lowlands women married in the mountains. The birth rate sky rocketed.

Abby rapidly developed a strong female following and a groundswell of support became an unstoppable tide.

As the supposed spiritual guide in society and interpreter of the law, the new shaman was constantly pressed to rein in the explosive Abby without any modicum of success. When he cautiously came to her with a disagreement she railed at him and when he left he was never the victor. Her liberal version of Argore religion, dogma, and proper behavior was unique to her. She left him no other choice but to get on board with her views. If she got a delegation of 'concerned' males she rebuffed them in no uncertain terms and then she sought out the shaman as if he deserved punishment too. It was unnerving to them that she attended those meetings wearing her sword. Her daunting fighting prowess was reminiscent of that of her mother, Beth.

Surprisingly, the havoc she wreaked didn't alienate her amongst the total Argore populace. Just the opposite, she became much beloved as a true protector of the weak and champion of the common people. Her 'common sense' mantra always benefitted the people in the end. The Argore peoples evolved and were no longer seen as barbarians and anathema by the rest of the world. The other societies became less resistant to the Argore peoples and what followed were frequent intermarriage, trade, and prosperity. The world Abby's children would know didn't remotely resemble the troubled world her mother had lived through.

One other thing she accomplished was as the wife of the high chief's favored son, who would become the future high chief, she became an Argore and entitled to all the rights and benefits of membership in the peoples.

Abby rode home one day for a visit to the imperial capital of Glory to see her family with her husband and her recently newborn first child, a daughter she named Mystica, a compromise name between her and the Argore.

She carried with her an unexpected gift for her mother. After they'd arrived at the imperial palace and settled into their rooms, Abby went to see in mother in private. Beth was curious about the mystery and the secret gift her daughter had promised.

"Mother, you can't speak this to anybody else, even Father."

"Speak what, Abby?"

"The Argore commander, he who became high chief, the man who loved and protected you in the war, and the man who is my father-in-law, it's no secret to you that he loves you still. It took a long time for him to control his feelings for you, though they will always be there. His wife knows this and has come to terms but only after considerable time and a great number of serious arguments. What I'm going to tell you now, it's not a slight to his wife or an advance to you as a married woman, but against their laws he allows me to tell you his name is Zhakur."

Beth chuckled and hugged her daughter. "Thank you, my darling daughter. I always wondered about the answer to that question and now I have it, and it didn't involve my marrying the wrong man."

"Mother, no matter how long it takes, I always get what I want. I'm not too popular in certain circles back home."

"Abby, I've got to tell you, I'm just like your father in telling you that you're my favorite child too. I love all of my kids, but watching your magical life is my main distraction from the stress of being an empress. There is so much good you do in this world. When I was your age, the Argore back then were a horror. You changed all that for the better. Frankly, I'm amazed. I wouldn't have thought it could be done."

Abby got a bemused look on her face.

"I must tell you, my husband is a beast in private who has plans for me and it involves more children, I think many more children. Men are single minded about some things. I think if I allowed it, we would never leave our bedroom."

"That's true, Darling, we evoke them. We have to just accept it. It's not really a bad thing if you're honest about it. I think having a spouse who adores you is much better than the alternative. They are demanding beasts about that, but we're in control of them."

"I can't disagree, Mother. I admit, I like his gentle attentions a great deal."

"In that area, you're just like me, Abby.

They laughed and hugged again.

The End

About the Author

Dennis Hausker is retired from a career as a medical insurance specialist for an insurance company. Post retirement he works part time as a financial consultant and he is the finance chair person at his church. He has been married since 1968. He and his wife met at Michigan State University from which they graduated in 1969. She is a retired teacher who volunteers helping adults with learning impairments. Dennis is a veteran of the Vietnam War. He served at Long Binh as a finance clerk paying field combat units. He loves to write with his preferred genre being Epic Fantasy, although he has the goal to also write books in other genres. He is very grateful for the business partnership he has established with Melange Books in terms of their professional support services and encouraging friendly atmosphere. His hope is his stories will be captivating, unique, and compelling for the reader.

www.denniskhausker.com

Other works by the Author with Melange Books, LLC

Mortus, Book 1 of the Faenum Quest Series
The Gathering Storm, Book 2 of the Faenum Quest Series
The Faenum War, Book 3 of the Faenum Quest Series
Stirring Sagas, an author anthology
Tales of the Heart, an author anthology
Twisting Fate in R.U.S.H. anthology
The Villager, Book 1 of the Shattered World Saga
Rebel, Book 2 of the Shattered World Saga
Savior, Book 3 of the Shattered World Saga

www.ingramcontent.com/pod-product-compliance
Lightning Source LLC
Chambersburg PA
CBHW050505260626
47157CB00004B/1196

* 9 7 8 1 6 1 2 3 5 8 9 0 1 *